© Natalia Fogarty

In the course of her career, Nicole Alexander has worked both in Australia and Singapore in financial services, fashion, corporate publishing and agriculture. A fourth-generation grazier, Nicole returned to her family's property in the early 1990s. She is currently the business manager there and has a hands-on role in the running of the property.

Nicole has a Master of Letters in creative writing and her novels, poetry, travel and genealogy articles have been published in Australia, Germany, America and Singapore. She is also the author of *The Bark Cutters*, *A Changing Land*, *Absolution Creek* and *The Great Plains*.

Also by Nicole Alexander

The Bark Cutters
A Changing Land
Absolution Creek
The Great Plains

Divertissements: Love, War, Society – Selected Poems

NICOLE ALEXANDER

SUNSET RIDGE

BANTAM
SYDNEY AUCKLAND TORONTO NEW YORK LONDON

A Bantam book
Published by Random House Australia Pty Ltd
Level 3, 100 Pacific Highway, North Sydney NSW 2060
www.randomhouse.com.au

First published by Bantam in 2013
This edition published in 2014

Addresses for companies within the Random House Group can be found at
www.randomhouse.com.au/offices

National Library of Australia
Cataloguing-in-Publication Entry

Alexander, Nicole L., author
Sunset ridge/Nicole Alexander

ISBN 978 1 86471 278 0 (paperback)

A823.4

Cover photograph of girl's face © Corbis
Cover design by Luke Causby
Internal design by Midland Typesetters, Australia
Typeset in 12/16 Fairfield LT Light by Midland Typesetters, Australia
Printed in Australia by Griffin Press, an accredited ISO AS/NZS 14001:2004 Environmental
Management System printer

Random House Australia uses papers that are natural, renewable and recyclable products and
made from wood grown in sustainable forests. The logging and manufacturing processes are
expected to conform to the environmental regulations of the country of origin.

Author's Note

I never knew my paternal grandfather. Frederick John Alexander fought on the Western Front during the First World War and was awarded the Military Medal for conspicuous gallantry at Strazeele, northern France in April 1918. He was seriously wounded the following day. His recovery from a gunshot wound to the head was lengthy, however eventually Grandfather returned to our family property to resume its management.

It was his experience in France during the Great War and my own sadness at never having met him (although I see him in my father's eyes) that led me to first consider writing on the topic. This I did as part of my dissertation for a Masters of Letters through Central Queensland University, knowing that at some stage I would try my hand at a longer work of fiction.

Much of the period detail in *Sunset Ridge* comes from the Alexander family archives. These include the diary my grandfather used on Salisbury Plain in England during training as a Lewis Gunner in 1916, and the letters he wrote home. The scene in the novel where Sister Valois peels a deep scab from the forehead of one of the wounded soldiers at the temporary field hospital in France is based on my grandfather's personal experience at the Central Military Hospital in Eastbourne, England. Apparently it was a most painful undertaking done on a regular basis to aid healing.

The temporary field hospital and casualty clearing station at Verdun are based on numerous works from the period, including a number of diaries and personal letters written by both French and

English nurses and voluntary aides. I am also indebted to both the New South Wales State and National Libraries for their assistance in obtaining descriptions of the Saint-Omer region in France, while original photographs in the *Illustrated London News* from the period (from the Alexander archives), among other publications, brought home the decimation of the French landscape from the horrific artillery bombardments.

During the First World War, vast numbers of dogs, and many other animals, were employed in varied roles. Some of these included: sentries, messengers, ammunition, food and cigarette carriers, scouts, draught dogs, guard dogs, ambulance dogs, ratters and Red Cross casualty dogs. The messenger dogs were credited with indirectly saving thousands of lives through the delivery of vital dispatches when phone lines broke down between units at the front and military headquarters behind the lines. Allied Red Cross casualty dogs, much like the German mercy dogs, were also vital components of the war effort. They were trained to find the wounded and return to their handler with a part of the uniform to indicate that they had located someone.

A French Red Cross dog named Prusco is credited with saving the lives of over 100 men in one day, including even pulling some back into the safety of the trenches. In *Sunset Ridge* Roland the war dog is based on Prusco and I marvel at the tenacity of such an animal, who traversed barbed wire, slit trenches, shell holes and chemical gases while under fire to rescue the wounded.

Thank you, as always, to my family and friends who have supported me throughout the writing of this novel. In particular I must thank my parents, Ian and Marita, for their continued guidance and deep interest in my work; my patient partner, David; and my ever-supportive sister, Brooke.

A book's production is very much a team effort. Thank you to Random House and the wonderful team there. Special mention must be made of my long-suffering editors, Claire de Medici and

Catherine Hill, and my publisher, Beverley Cousins. Thank you also to my literary agent, Tara Wynne, for her friendship and advice.

As an Australian rural dweller I would like to shine a light on the north-west New South Wales town of Moree. Should you be seeking rest and relaxation on the famous black soil plains, our artesian waters are waiting for you.

Lastly, to the many booksellers, here and abroad; my friends and readers, old and new – thank you. The dream continues ...

To those men and women
who served during
the
Great War for civilisation

1914–1919

≪ Chapter 1 ≫

Sunset Ridge, south-west Queensland, Australia
February 2000

Madeleine swore under her breath as she swerved and skidded in the red dirt to avoid hitting a sheep. She had forgotten the distances involved when it came to travelling in outback Queensland – the last road trip she had undertaken had been a relatively easy three-hour drive from Sydney to an emerging artist's exhibition in the Hunter Valley. In contrast, seven hours in a car heading south-west, after flying into Brisbane from Sydney the night before, was akin to a marathon. Her eyes felt as if they were receding into her brain, a sensation not helped by a night on the chardonnay with her mother, Jude.

At seventy, Jude Harrow-Boyne was the poster child for most women her age. Athletic and youthful, she was intelligent if somewhat scatty at times. Known equally for her fierce temper and artistic ability, Jude had an almost complete disregard for other people's opinions, a personality flaw that was difficult to take at times. With this knowledge in mind, Madeleine knew that her brief stay with her mother in Brisbane would not go well, which was why she had arrived at the ground-floor apartment the previous day with two bottles of white wine and a bunch of flowers. Neither gift made a dent in Jude's attitude; if anything, the peace offerings were treated with suspicion. Her mother was expecting positive news and Madeleine had none to give.

The rental car charged up each rolling ridge, a hazy mirage of dirt and sky enticing Madeleine onwards. Nondescript trees blurred the edges of the road as a trickle of sweat rolled down her back. She could feel the sun burning her face and arms through the window and her eyes were smeary from the glare. About an hour earlier she had considered pulling up under a tree to try to sleep. However, the temptation to rest had been tempered by the heat. Madeleine scrabbled on the passenger seat for the last water bottle. She shook it for any remaining drops, then tossed it over her shoulder onto the back seat and fiddled with the air-conditioning in an attempt to force air into the vehicle. The more kilometres travelled the less enthusiastic she became. This journey had come at the instigation of her mother some months ago, and in spite of the lecture received last night Madeleine felt instinctively that this visit to the Harrow family property would be a waste of time. By agreeing to undertake the trip, an olive branch had been extended, though a few of the leaves were already bruised.

Eighteen months ago her mother had approached Madeleine with the suggestion of staging a retrospective of her late grand-father's work. An artist of renown, David Harrow had died well before Madeleine and her older brother George were born, and even Jude admitted that between boarding school and art college she had barely known her widowed father. It was with a great degree of reluctance that Madeleine, in her role as personal assis-tant to the director of the Stepworth Gallery, agreed to investigate the feasibility of the project. There were professional reasons for her hesitancy as well as a number of personal ones.

David Harrow had died in the early 1950s, bequeathing to his only daughter a debt-ridden rural property that had been in the family for generations – absurdly named Sunset Ridge – and forty landscape paintings. The paintings were found stored within the Sunset Ridge homestead, and when auctioned at an estate sale they had created quite a buzz in the art world. The hitherto unknown artist had emerged posthumously to acclaim, and his collective works were touted as one of the great finds in Australian art history.

From Madeleine's perspective, however, his legacy had been lost, sold by her parents more than forty-five years ago to restore the Harrow family property to viability. To Madeleine, such an action made Jude's ongoing devotional attitude towards her father almost hypocritical. And Madeleine couldn't help but feel both annoyed by and disinclined to support Jude's idea of a retrospective. If her mother cared so much about her father and his art, why sell it all? The closest Madeleine ever got to her grandfather was through the study of his painting techniques as part of the university syllabus while completing her Fine Arts degree or when Jude paraded the original 1950s art catalogue on each anniversary of his death. Meanwhile Madeleine's brother George lived out here in the back of beyond on the family farm, which she and her mother rarely visited.

After seven hours in the car she was starting to remember why.

Madeleine missed the turn-off to Sunset Ridge by a good two kilometres. On retracing her route she saw that the signpost had been removed from the opposite side of the road and that the battered ramp and the old fridge once used as the mailbox had been replaced with a white boundary gate and matching mailbox upon which 'Sunset Ridge' was painted in black. It was a much-needed improvement, she thought as she accelerated through the open gate. She guessed that the temperature outside had hit forty degrees. What constituted a heatwave across much of Australia was merely another day in this part of the world. The thought of spending two weeks lying awake night after night with the sweat streaming from her body was disheartening. Changing down through the gears to drive over a stock grid, Madeleine relived last night's fractious discussion with her mother.

'You're the assistant to the gallery director, Madeleine, and your grandfather was a brilliant artist – and you're telling me it hasn't even been discussed yet? You said you would table it at the board meeting months ago.' Jude slid a menthol cigarette out of its soft packet, dried paint rimming her fingernails.

'Well, I did say it would be difficult, Mum,' Madeleine argued. 'I have to present a clear and compelling case to show why Grandfather deserves a retrospective, without opening myself up to accusations of bias. Remember, Mum, I'm championing a man I never knew, and I have limited archival material to work with.'

'But we have the forty paintings!' Jude retorted. 'Most of the owners have said they will lend their works, haven't they? And we have a couple of his early sketches.'

'Yes, Mum, but a good retrospective should include details of the artist's life, early drawings, personal correspondence: a timeline of his life and the influences on his work.'

Jude looked away dismissively and tapped ash into a garish pink-and-red ceramic dish. 'Father's work is good enough without having all that extra information.' She returned her gaze to her daughter. 'And if you really think you need all that other material to make the exhibition more interesting, then why haven't you been more proactive? Why haven't you found it?' Jude picked up her wine glass and studied the watercolour of frangipanis sitting on the easel in the middle of the cluttered living room. Her current work-in-progress was a commission of eight paintings for a riverside restaurant.

'The gallery is a business, Mum. It's all about the bottom line. Besides, Australiana isn't the in thing at the moment; everyone is more interested in contemporary and indigenous art.'

'Don't sit there and give me your economic arguments, Madeleine Harrow. I wasn't the one who changed my name by deed poll. Your father, bless him, graced us with the surname of Boyne. You didn't mind using your connection to your grandfather to wangle yourself into a gallery career. The least you can do is honour the name and the man. David Harrow deserves an exhibition, and you know it.'

Madeleine fidgeted with the silk sari covering the armchair. 'But I don't know enough. I didn't know him. Did he paint his lovers like Picasso did? Did he have a muse? Why did he become so reclusive after returning from the First World War?'

Jude took a sip of wine before sitting the glass on the messy coffee table. 'And,' she said defiantly as she flipped open a large sketchpad and removed a sheet of paper, 'why did he not accept his platoon captain's recommendation to be put forward as an official war artist?' She thrust the letter towards Madeleine. 'It's from the Australian War Memorial. Captain Egan thought your grandfather was talented enough to sketch on behalf of us all.'

Madeleine scanned the contents, speechless.

'Well, you said you needed archival material.' Jude passed her daughter a photocopy of a sketch. 'The young man in this portrait is Private Matty Cartwright. Your grandfather sketched this a week before Cartwright was killed by a shell in Belgium in 1917. The original was returned to the Cartwright family with the rest of his personal effects, and it was eventually bequeathed to the War Memorial.'

Madeleine stared at the drawing of the young man.

'There are three more similar sketches,' Jude continued. 'Only one bears my father's initials; however, the art historian attached to the War Memorial seemed convinced that the works could be attributed to your grandfather.' Jude gave a satisfied smile. 'You can close your mouth, dear.'

'This is —'

'Extraordinary? Yes it is. Consider the providence of that drawing, Madeleine: where and when it was sketched, and by whom. Now look closely at the work. It's damn good.'

Jude turned towards the two charcoal sketches hanging on the wall behind her. Both drawings depicted four young men fishing by the Banyan River and displayed all the hallmarks of raw talent. 'It's amazing what you can discover once you start looking,' her mother said pointedly. 'I can only assume that you don't think your grandfather is good enough to warrant a retrospective.'

'I never said that.'

'Then perhaps it would be easier if you stopped thinking like a businesswoman and started behaving like a granddaughter. I am well aware that there are few historical documents available to us, however even you can't dispute the importance of those First World War sketches. In the early stages of his career Father appears to have been ambivalent towards his talent. He doesn't seem to have made notes or kept rough outlines of works-in-progress, and we know he didn't always sign his drawings, which makes your sourcing of them extremely difficult. There isn't even a single sketchbook to be found.' Jude turned back to her daughter. 'What intrigues me is the gap in his work. We have sketches from the war and then nothing until the first landscape dated 1935. Are there more paintings from this lost period or did he simply stop creating, and if so why?' Jude lit another cigarette, inhaling deeply. 'At least we now have something to work with, a starting point.'

Madeleine reluctantly agreed.

'We've had our differences, Maddy. I guess all mothers and daughters do at times, and I am well aware that you believe I did the wrong thing selling your grandfather's paintings all those years ago. And maybe I did. But, Maddy, please don't allow your ill feeling to hinder the chances of staging this retrospective. What if there are more of his drawings?' She pointed at the sketch Madeleine still held. 'More sketches from the war, more works drawn before he enlisted.

'Do you honestly believe he just woke up one morning and decided to paint forty masterpieces in the last twenty-five years of his life?'

'Well, I –'

'Who knows what other pieces could be floating around the world? Who knows how many sketches and paintings sit hidden in attics, hang unheralded on walls, or for that matter were buried in the mud of the Somme? This is your family history too, Maddy, and I'm asking you to use your contacts and your knowledge to make this retrospective happen. I wanted you to be involved not only because you're his granddaughter and understand the art world, but also because we both know that you would benefit professionally if the retrospective goes ahead. But if you keep delaying it I will have no choice but to hand it over to somebody else.' Jude took the sketch from Madeleine and slipped it between the pages of the sketchpad. 'In the end, the retrospective is about honouring a great man, not you and me arguing over our differences.'

Madeleine had never liked ultimatums, and she made a point of telling her mother just that. She had, after all, agreed to visit Sunset Ridge with a view to soaking up the environment that inspired her grandfather, yet still Jude couldn't help but lecture her. Last night's conversation had quickly degenerated, leaving Jude to retreat to her bedroom with a bottle of wine, while Madeleine fell asleep on the couch. The high point of the evening was when Jude handed Madeleine a rusty key and tersely informed her that it belonged to a tin trunk in the Sunset Ridge schoolroom – a trunk containing items that had belonged to Madeleine's father, Ashley, and had not been touched since his death twenty years earlier. George's wife, Rachael, was intent on clearing out the schoolroom and Jude wanted Madeleine to sort through and dispose of the items in the trunk. 'I don't want Rachael touching those things,' Jude had said stiffly. 'It's a family matter.'

The car rattled over the corrugations in the road. The final few kilometres were punctuated by stockless paddocks and desolate cultivations. The drought was biting hard across eastern Australia but apparently George was still managing. The road to the homestead veered through red ridges and uninviting stubby scrub that merged with dry-leafed trees. George's wish of thinning out the dense bushland had not eventuated. Instead, the money was put towards pushing saplings in a far paddock for sheep feed. The result was a narrow track that seemed at constant battle with the scrub lining either side. The rental car bumped over the rough road, wound past a fallen-down crutching shed and hit the straight track and open gateway that led to the homestead. The sixty-acre house block had been systematically cleared a hundred years ago, and the area remained virtually treeless except for three stands of Box trees that sat halfway between the work shed, stables and house dam. Beyond the house paddock to the south-east was a shearing shed and the Banyan River, which had been dry for nearly two years.

Outside the homestead Madeleine stared bleakly at the fan of red dirt extending from the house. The surrounding paddock was devoid of grass. Spirals of dust lifted into the air. A crow cried out soullessly. The sickly stench of something dead floated on the hot breeze. Clutching a suitcase, overnight bag and laptop, she passed through a wrought-iron gate and a sage-green colour-bond fence, gravel crunching underfoot. She did a double-take at these improvements and walked up the back path. The low bougainvillea hedge no longer bordered the front of the house, and the meat-house was gone, replaced with a square slab of cement upon which was arranged a table and four chairs. Madeleine came to a stop at a pale brick wall with two oval windows.

For a moment she thought she was at the wrong house. The brickwork was new, the windows sheltered by fixed green blinds that gave the appearance of sleepy eyelids. For nearly eighty years a bull-nosed veranda had skirted the Harrow family home and the gauze-enclosed porch had remained a welcoming sight with its scattered timber chairs and numerous potted rubber plants. Madeleine recalled sitting on the veranda with her father many years ago, and it seemed to her that with the renovation of the front porch that particular memory, one of her fondest, had been diluted. Where once she could picture old squatter's chairs and her father's dusty boots sitting inside the back door, there was now only a brick wall.

At the new back door, made of shiny inlaid wood, Madeleine dumped her belongings in order to turn the brass doorknob. It refused to budge. She knocked once, twice, three times as the wind picked up and grit whirled about the building, spraying her bare legs in an arching sting. Her beloved father had died in 1980 and his passing made her both angry at the world and scared for the future. Disbelief at her grandfather's legacy being sold to keep the property afloat was not the only reason for her dislike of Sunset Ridge. Her father had given up his own career to work the property after Jude had inherited it, and eventually the land had taken him.

'Hello? Anyone home?'

The steady hum of airconditioning carried through the late-morning air.

'I thought I heard someone. You must be Madeleine. George said you'd be coming. He and the missus are in town for a luncheon.'

The croaky voice belonged to a woman aged somewhere in her sixties. She stood at the corner of the house with an overflowing laundry basket on her hip and a dead chicken in her hand. Her hair was grey and cropped short, and her face was lined. 'I'm Sonia, the housekeeper.'

'Hi.' Madeleine's gaze fell to the bird. Blood dripped from its neck.

'You'll have to lug all that around to the back, I'm afraid. The missus had the front veranda enclosed and now the lock's gone on the door.'

'Gone?' Madeleine repeated as she walked around the house in pursuit of the housekeeper, her belongings burning the muscles in her arms with their combined weight.

'Busted,' Sonia emphasised over her shoulder. 'That's what happens when you get that type of fancy stuff freighted out here. Once it's broke, there ain't no one to fix it.'

The walk along the length of the homestead revealed grass and scraggly clumps of saltbush and flowering plumbago. The house was saved from the worst of the westerly sun by a row of trees outside the garden fence, however part of the ancient bougainvillea hedge had disappeared, leaving the house to suffer the brunt of the weather. The side veranda had been enclosed with cream-painted timber to keep the dust out and although this side of the house was now a bland wall, it held three evenly spaced windows along its length.

At the rear of the house Madeleine noticed a new but empty terraced flower bed at the back of the garden, and a new gazebo with a beige cane table and chairs. The lawn was amazingly green for late February during a roaring drought, yet the garden seemed sparse. She noticed that a number of trees and another hedge were gone from the back of the garden, and with their removal the garden fence had been brought forward twenty metres. For the first time Madeleine could see the house paddock fence glimmer in the midday sun. Beyond lay dense woody timber through which the road wound back to civilisation.

'They've made it smaller,' Sonia explained, as if reading Madeleine's mind. They crossed an expanse of sandstone pavers sheltered by sail-like cloths attached from the house's awning. The sails extended outwards and were secured by three tall aluminium posts. 'They've been carting dam water in one of the thousand-litre fire-fighting units to keep some of the flowers and shrubs going, while the bore water keeps the lawn alive.'

'So, most of those trees at the back of the garden died?'

'Nine in all and a good part of the hedge,' Sonia explained. 'Anything that wasn't a native. George dragged them away with the dozer and then repositioned the fence.'

The Sunset Ridge garden had always been secure and cosy, sheltered and shaded by the thick-girthed trees and hedges. Now the homestead felt exposed and Madeleine realised that she wasn't sure if this was due to the drought-forced changes or her mixed feelings about returning to her childhood home.

Sonia dumped the chicken on the ground. 'Dogs got it,' she explained, nodding towards the mangled bird. 'Follow me.'

Side-stepping the dead chicken, Madeleine followed the older woman onto the gauzed rear veranda, pleased that at least one of the original verandas had been kept intact. In the entrance hallway the tongue-and-groove walls were now a blinding white, and three black wrought-iron chandeliers swung in the breeze from ducted airconditioning. That was an improvement. She could already feel her sweaty shirt drying. At her old bedroom door Madeleine sat the suitcase on the floor.

'Oh no, sorry, girl, but that's the nursery now.'

Madeleine opened the door. Pale blue and white wallpaper had been replaced by mint-green paint. A sense of loss seeped through her as she imagined Rachael clearing out her personal things. 'I didn't know that Rachael was pregnant.'

'She's not,' Sonia answered. 'Here you go. The two other spare rooms are being painted at the moment, so this one is being used as a bit of a –'

'But this is Grandfather's room.'

Sonia stood in the open door. 'Yes, it is. You haven't been home for a while, have you? Well, I only arrived myself about twelve months ago. Anyway, your mother's room is now a guest bathroom.' Sonia adjusted the laundry basket on her hip. 'And although your grandfather's room is being used for storage, it's the only free space we've got. Sorry, love.'

Madeleine raised a smile. 'No problem.' She dumped the suitcase and bag on the timber floor, and laid the laptop on the single bed in the middle of the room. The room smelled musty. Cardboard boxes competed with suitcases, a shoe-filled plastic milk crate, a warped hockey stick and an old blackboard. Madeleine recognised the board immediately: it had hung in the schoolroom. Madeleine and George were the fourth generation to enjoy early marks and mail-delivered lessons courtesy of the Correspondence School – until they were twelve and fourteen. Then their father had died and their world changed. Their mother had leased Sunset Ridge and relocated the family to Brisbane, abandoning the property to others until George was of an age to take over the management of it. For a moment Madeleine found herself reliving those awful days when their world had been turned upside down. She'd forgotten how difficult it was for her to be back in her old home, a feeling made worse by the fact that she no longer had her bedroom to escape to.

Sonia stood at her shoulder. 'I cleared a space in the wardrobe and I dusted down the desk.'

Madeleine thanked her. 'Are you from the Banyan district?'

'I've been back and forth. I lost my last job because of the drought. Machinery dealerships don't need bookkeepers once they go bust.'

'You're a bit over-qualified for this job.'

'Maybe,' she sniffed. 'Anyway, George is a good lad.' The omission of Rachael's name was obvious. 'Personally, I wasn't ever into arty stuff, but your grandfather was a good man. I vaguely recall meeting him.' Sonia squinted in thought.

'You're lucky. I never knew him.'

'Oh, I was a wee thing then, I probably wouldn't have been much older than ten. He had a soft smile and kind eyes.'

'Like George.'

'Well then,' Sonia patted her arm, 'you did know your grandfather; you see him in your brother.'

After Sonia left, Madeleine sat on the lumpy bed. The room was all browns and beige and felt strangely empty. She could not recall it ever being used for guests – and that was exactly how she felt: a guest in her childhood home. Through the window, the old schoolhouse and attached governess quarters were visible within the garden, their white walls glary with sunlight. Madeleine drew the curtains against the heat and slumped back on the bed, breathing deeply as she took in her surroundings. As throughout the house, the walls were the original tongue-and-groove timber, and an old-fashioned manhole was cut into a corner of the ten-foot ceiling. She felt strange: this was the first time she had looked at the homestead through the eyes of David Harrow, the artist. It was hardly a place for inspiration. In winter the land was bitingly cold and lifeless. In summer a string of southerly busters could be relied on to destroy any chance of rain from the north, which is exactly what had happened for a good number of years. Yet as a child Madeleine shared an affinity with the land. She had breathed in its heady scents, raced George on horseback through the tangled scrub along the river and camped happily by its sandy banks. The two of them had grown strong under an endless sky, within the arms of the land that surrounded them. Then their father had committed suicide. He was buried in the Harrow family cemetery on Sunset Ridge. The day they left the property Madeleine didn't look back.

So why had she agreed to Jude's suggestion of a property visit? Perhaps it was simply to placate her mother; perhaps the bitterness Madeleine had held over the years regarding Jude's thoughtless disposal of David Harrow's artworks and legacy was beginning to wane. In truth it was an anger compounded by her father's death and Jude's reaction to it. As a teenager Madeleine learned quickly that suicide was appalling.

Madeleine ran her hand across the chenille bedcover. She was looking forward to catching up with her brother away from the usual Christmas gathering in Brisbane. And having seen the documentation from the Australian War Memorial, her interest in her grandfather and a possible exhibition had been revitalised.

Hanging on the wall above the roll-top desk was a black-and-white photograph of her grandfather and his two older brothers, her great-uncles Thaddeus and Luther, in army uniforms. Despite the typically unsmiling expressions, they looked relaxed and proud of their slouch hats and rising-sun insignias. The great-uncles stood protectively on either side of her grandfather, and Madeleine wondered what Thaddeus and Luther would think of their younger brother's artistic legacy if they were alive today. The boys were similar: wide of eye with broad foreheads, they had defined chins and generous lips. David, only sixteen at the time, appeared slighter than his brothers with a face rounded by remnants of baby fat and a dimpled cheek. Luther, of stockier build, had a slightly cleft chin, an attribute that accentuated his hard-featured handsomeness. Thaddeus, taller by a good few inches, looked distinctly unimpressed. There was something of a haughty demeanour about him, and even if she had not known it, Madeleine would have guessed he was the eldest. The least attractive in her mind, Thaddeus nonetheless would have stood out in a crowd today.

Next to their picture was a faded map of Australia that noted the regimental colours of the Australian Imperial Force from 1914 to 1919, and tucked into the edge of the frame was a postcard depicting a cathedral. The card slipped free easily and Madeleine flipped it over to read the place name, *Cathédrale Notre-Dame de Saint-Omer*. Although the card was blank Madeleine knew that the three Harrow brothers had fought on the Western Front. She had placed an advertisement in one of France's leading art magazines several months ago requesting any information about David Harrow's works that might be housed in French galleries, and it had proved to be a dead end, but an idea now began to take shape in her mind. 'A long shot,' Madeleine mumbled, but as she stared at the photograph again she made a decision: she would advertise in one or two of the local French papers to enquire if anyone had sketches by her grandfather in their homes. Tapping the postcard on her palm, Madeleine thought more about the Harrow boys: she knew that the two youngest were under-age when they enlisted, and she couldn't help but wonder why their parents had let them go. In the meantime, she had a postcard and a place name. If she was serious about fulfilling her mother's wish, Saint-Omer was as good a place as any to start.

≪ Chapter 2 ≫

Chessy farmhouse, ten miles from Saint-Omer, northern France
April 1916

Madame Marie Chessy sidestepped the wooden box housing her best-laying hen. The hen spent much of its life indoors, under Madame's watchful gaze and safe from errant foxes. The woman crossed the flagstone floor and drew the thick bolt closed on the farmhouse door. Pressing an ear against the wood, she concentrated. The sound was muffled, indecipherable. It could be anything, she decided; that was the problem. Still unused to spending so much time alone, she was attuned to the slightest irregularity and her nerves occasionally overtook commonsense. Having expected her twin boys, Francois and Antoine, to be home before this, their delay added to her concern. Lifting the corner of the curtain, she peered out into the fading light. The soft lines of the willow trees that fringed the small stream beyond the farmhouse clearing remained visible, their branches dipping into the water at their feet. Beyond the willows, gently undulating countryside displayed a patchwork of green and yellow fields.

The noise sounded again. Madame Chessy smoothed a dark wave of hair across her forehead. Initially the noise resembled a cough, then a rustling, scratching sound. Perhaps it was the fox. The animal had taken two of her hens during winter, forcing her to board up the fence surrounding their pen so that the poor birds were literally boxed in at night. She glanced at the wooden rolling pin on the table and then at the sturdy chair near the fire. She missed her husband. She would always miss Marcel. 'This is ridiculous,' she murmured. Who or what did she think was outside? A hungry fox or the German army? Two wooden crucifixes flanked the stove's flue. Others hung above her bedroom door and the twins' shared alcove. Madame Chessy crossed herself, noticing not for the first time that the crosses hanging above the oven were cracked from the heat of the fire. Jesus's suffering, it seemed, was ongoing.

A high-pitched whistle broke the silence. The widow sighed with relief at the familiar signal as the hen clucked in annoyance and then resettled in its box against the far wall. Voices could be heard. Her sons. The seventeen-year-old twins were returning from the fields beyond the stream. Throwing a thick woollen shawl about her shoulders, she drew the bolt on the door. The clearing was devoid of movement. The remaining hens and rooster were penned securely for the night, and the pigs and two cows were in the stone barn. A warbler sang in one of the birch trees behind the clutch of buildings, and in an hour or so an owl would take up residence in the branches above the barn. The natural cycle of the world had remained unchanged for eighteen years, since her arrival here. Even her body had settled into the seasons' rhythms. At thirty-five, her bones were adept at warning when a cool change or rain was coming. It was the way it should be for a farm woman, although her beloved mother had once wished for her a better life.

The night air had a bite to it. She rubbed her work-roughened hands together as a smile settled into the care lines etching her mouth. Francois was tall, brown-haired and lean like his father and had inherited the same tendency towards conservatism and learning, while Antoine favoured her family, his stockier build and darker looks complemented by a level of optimism undimmed by the war being waged in their country. Their bobbing heads rose and fell against the paling sky as they jumped the narrow stream. She imagined their feet springing on the soft turf, her daydreams taking her back to another time, seventeen years ago, when she and Marcel had sat in that same spot in the dwindling light, the twins a bulge in her belly. No one else would ever remember her as she was back then: a pretty, high-spirited girl.

The woman could hear Antoine's laughter and the cajoling tone that inevitably meant he was trying to convince his older brother (by two minutes) of some new scheme. His last adventure, before winter, had led them some three miles into the village of Tating-hem. Unbeknown to her, Antoine had tried to barter some of their excess eggs in exchange for a packet of cigarettes. His plan proved unsuccessful and instead he and Francois returned home with the dozen eggs and ten soldiers and a British officer, who quickly informed Madame Chessy that his men were to be billeted on her small holding for a week. Although she was happy to oblige, she made a point of taking several minutes to reflect on the officer's request before answering. Demanding, instead of asking politely, was never an attitude she had taken to.

The Chessy farmhouse had been noted by the Allies as a potential billet for troops in early 1915, however their use of the farm had been limited to date. The ancient town of Saint-Omer, the current Allied headquarters, was ten miles away and the surrounding villages absorbed the majority of troops. Yet a small stream of soldiers on leave from the front found peace and a semblance of rejuvenation at the farm during the bitter winter. And it was through them the widow learned of the true extent of the war. Although firmly situated on French soil, she expected a difficult year ahead. The Germans, with their huge army, were aggressive in their attempts at invasion and a long thin line of defence on a map was all that protected her beloved country. The West Flanders city of Ypres lay to the north and was something of a defining line for the British Empire. Madame knew only too well that Ypres stood in the path of Germany's planned sweep across the rest of Belgium and into France, and would also give the invading army access to the French port cities bordering the Channel.

'Mama.'

She waved in response to the boys' greeting, their features still indistinct.

Ypres. How she wished she had never heard of the place. It was to this battleground that her beloved husband, Marcel, was forced to travel in 1915. When she objected to him leaving, he argued that if the British were prepared to make a stand and join the war in 1914 having guaranteed Belgium neutrality, then he too would proudly accept the call for his beloved France. How she hated conscription.

As the distance closed between her sons and the farmhouse, Madame Chessy noticed a third shape, an animal of some sort, a –

'No, no, no,' she lamented, checking worriedly on her hen before firmly closing the farmhouse door. The dog was large and ungainly looking, a wolf-like mongrel if ever she had seen one.

'Please, Mama.' Antoine's cheek dimpled. 'Can't we keep him?'

Francois did his customary shrug, as if the events of the day were beyond him. He was so like his father.

'He has been with us in the field since noon,' Francois explained as the lumbering animal covered a kneeling Antoine's face with slobber.

The animal was shaggy-haired, its colouring white, black and grey, which spoke of a mismatch of breeds. Madame Chessy could hardly imagine what it would take to feed such a giant of a dog.

'He came from the north, Mama,' Antoine stated, the words causing the three of them to look in that direction. It was the place the boys' father had gone to, and from where he had never returned.

'Ypres?' Madame Chessy murmured, the question hanging in the air. The dog was sitting, his brown eyes fixed on hers.

'He has no home,' Antoine pursued quietly.

'Many have no home, Antoine,' she snapped. She did not want a dog. There were chickens and pigs to mind, and cows and fields to tend, and any number of other chores to fill her days. Besides which, she knew that it would be impossible to instil a modicum of obedience in a dog clearly so devoid of breeding.

'He may well be attached to a battalion,' Francois suggested. 'They are using any number of different breeds at the front.'

Their mother blew a puff of air out through her lips. 'I have never heard such rot.'

'But it's true, Mama,' Antoine agreed. 'They have dogs that run messages, dogs to deliver cigarettes to the men in the front-line, and others that locate injured soldiers.'

Madame Chessy did not want to continue this ridiculous talk, yet such extraordinary tales regarding all manner of strange and wondrous things had spread through the French countryside since the war's beginning that at times she was unsure where fact ended and fiction began.

'They say the German mercy dogs are trained to ignore the dead and approach only the injured,' Antoine continued, 'and they carry water or alcohol around their necks or strapped to their chests.'

The dog placed a wide paw on Madame's sturdy lace-up boots and, as if cued, gave a low plaintive whine. The widow furrowed her brow. The noise was not unfamiliar; indeed, she had heard it not twenty minutes ago. She compressed her lips. Here was her fox. 'I doubt this stray has held such a lauded position.'

'He has no identification,' Antoine told his brother. 'Which means we can keep him.'

'Perhaps,' Francois began cautiously, 'he would be a good guard dog.'

Madame Chessy carefully pulled her shoe free of the animal's heavy paw. 'We shall see.'

Antoine smiled broadly, dragged the dog to his side and hugged him.

They sat at the table; behind them the wood fire heated a pot of stream water to wash the plates after their meal. Antoine and Francois were ravenous. The small quantity of bread and soft cheese consumed at noon had long been forgotten. Their mother listened as their stomachs rumbled.

'Slow down,' she chastised, 'you will both be ill.'

Francois paused, a chunk of bread in one hand, a mess of egg on his plate ready to be piled on the dough. Antoine's mouth was crammed with butter-fried wedges of potato and still he tried to place more into his mouth. Only the soft whine of the dog outside the farmhouse steadied both boys while eating.

'The first and second Australian divisions are being billeted in the Saint-Omer–Aire–Hazebrouck region.' Francois' eyes glittered. 'That's good news, I think.'

Madame Chessy did not know much about the Australians, but word had spread of their imminent arrival and that it was a volunteer force. 'It's a long way for them to come. Australia is at the bottom of the world.'

'And yet they come,' Antoine said with fervour, 'to this war to end all wars.'

His mother huffed. 'I've told you to stop listening to the propaganda, Antoine. I pity the Australian women and their families sending their men to the other side of the world to these, these –' she searched for a word that summed up her feelings, '*killing* fields. They have no idea what they are sending them to.'

Her son's cheeks reddened. The pain of their father's death remained raw.

The fire crackled. Antoine poured water from a ceramic jug as the dog barked outside. The noise broke the strained mood about the table. 'What shall we call him?' Antoine asked, his head swivelling towards the door.

Madame Chessy rose to lift the pot of now-boiling water from the fire. Sitting it on the hearth, she sipped her wine thoughtfully. There were only twelve bottles left in the cellar and she savoured her single nightly glass. 'I don't think we can keep the dog.' She dunked her plate in the pot of hot water. 'If what you say about these Australians arriving is correct, then we can only assume the war is nowhere near ending. We must prepare ourselves for food prices to rise again, and no doubt the shortages will grow worse.' She swished a dishcloth absently across the plate. 'We must tend to the soldiers protecting France and our own needs first. With only boys, women and old men left to mind our farms I doubt our ability to produce enough extra food. This dog, I think, will take much to feed.' The woman rested her plate in the drying rack on the hearth.

'I don't agree,' Antoine stated, his voice bold. 'More troops could see an earlier end to the war and then things will get back to normal.'

Francois pushed his empty plate aside. 'Mama, we cannot turn out a defenceless animal.'

Madame Chessy wiped her hands on her apron and rejoined her boys at the table. In the glow of the fire and candlelight the twins looked older than their seventeen years. She had heard terrible tales of fourteen-year-old German boys being sent to the Ypres battleground, and she prayed daily for the war to be over before the authorities came for her sons. It was only a matter of time. Once they were of age they would automatically be conscripted, if they didn't join up sooner. Her countrymen were dying in the pursuit of freedom, and the niggling thought of her only children wanting to prove themselves in battle, to follow in the footsteps of their dead father, was becoming more difficult to ignore. She plied the soft skin of her palm with her fingers.

'I see that you are determined to keep this dog . . .'

The twins waited for her to finish. 'But you must be prepared to hand the animal back should he be claimed.' Her sons nodded in agreement. 'And it is your joint responsibility to look after him, always. Not mine. And,' she added, 'he must sleep outside.'

Francois and Antoine grinned, and despite her misgivings she splashed a little wine into their water glasses to celebrate as they laughed and thanked her and promised to look after their new pet. The discussion of a name for the dog started soon after, and by the time the wine was consumed and the table cleared they were still arguing.

'Roland,' Francois suggested excitedly, as if having made a wondrous discovery.

'Ah,' Madame Chessy nodded with a smile. '"The Song of Roland".'

Antoine looked perplexed. 'Roland? What sort of a name is that for a dog?'

Madame Chessy waggled her finger. 'You should have paid more attention during your lessons, Antoine. "The Song of Roland" is one of the oldest works of French literature.'

Antoine's face was blank.

Madame Chessy shook her head at her younger son. 'About the Battle of Roncesvalles, in the eighth century?'

'In 778, Antoine.' Francois jabbed his brother in the shoulder. 'During the reign of Charlemagne. Don't you remember Mama telling us about it?'

'Well, why didn't you just say Charlemagne?' Antoine complained. '*Everyone* knows him. What?' he asked in response to his mother's smile and the raised eyebrow from his brother.

'Nothing, my dear,' she said. 'However,' she cautioned, 'Roland was a fierce warrior, loyal and trustworthy, and I am not sure this epic name is suitable for your new friend.'

Antoine rubbed at the slight fuzz of stubble on his chin.

'Perhaps with the times we live in, Mama, it *is* a worthy choice,' Francois suggested.

Habit led Madame Chessy's gaze to the vacant chair by the fire. 'I think,' she replied slowly, 'that your father would approve.'

'Good, it's done.' Antoine stood and clapped his hands together.

Outside Roland barked.

'More wine?' Antoine asked hopefully.

'No.' Madame Chessy shook her head, concealing the smile that threatened to stymie her resolve. 'No more wine.'

It was midnight when the squeak of the farmhouse door broke her dreams. She had been sitting by the stream with Marcel, throwing a rag ball at the ungainly dog that had appeared from amid the trees. He was a cumbersome animal; even the way he bounded across the field suggested he was at odds with his limbs. Yet despite the uneven gait and unkempt look, the dog was surprisingly agile and fast. Flinging his body some feet into the air, he caught Madame Chessy's ball with ease and, pirouetting, raced back to her side.

Pushing back the bedcovers, Madame Chessy sat upright and peered through her open bedroom door into the kitchen. The remains of the fire cast a faint glow about the room and revealed Antoine returning to the alcove on the far side of the kitchen table. He sat on his narrow cot, which was squashed tightly next to Francois', and his gaze met his mother's. The dog Roland was at Antoine's feet. Madame Chessy threw back the remaining covers readying to rescue her best-laying hen, her feet touching the cold floor, but the dog only sniffed about the flagstone, barely heeding the hen's presence, before returning to Antoine's side and jumping onto the bed where he pawed the coverlets like a giant cat readying to settle for the night.

She sensed Antoine waiting for words of reprimand, his defiance swelling across the small expanse of the farmhouse and as it grew her own anger subsided. She was weary of being the sole parent, weary of trying to retain a level of normality when only miles away the world was on fire. She lay on her side, one eye trained on the hen, the other partially obscured by the soft curve of the pillow. Finally Antoine slept, his soft snores filling the void left by her departed husband. Adjusting her position until her hip found some comfort, Madame Chessy concentrated on the dancing light thrown by the fire's embers. She had left the firebox door open, allowing the light to stretch along the floor and walls of the farmhouse, illuminating the dwelling with a golden glow. With a sigh she prayed aloud to the Saints, a muttering of blessings for home and hearth and protection for France and her two sons. Most of all she prayed for the Australian soldiers who would take up arms in defence of a country they had never seen.

Miles away a distant rumble, like faraway thunder, echoed across the countryside. The great guns were firing again. The eyes of Roland the dog met hers from across the room. One, she supposed, could never have too many heroes.

≪ Chapter 3 ≫

Sunset Ridge, south-west Queensland, Australia
February 2000

Bamboo flares wafted citronella as the day's remains cast a reddish glow through the garden. Madeleine followed the voices out onto the veranda. Two naps during the afternoon, interrupted by Sonia's mutton sandwich, had left her bleary eyed and restless. It had been years since her last holiday, and she felt strung out, especially after the altercation with her mother. Her brother and sister-in-law were sitting in front of the open French doors that led into their bedroom, where the cooling draft of the evaporative airconditioner made the environment almost liveable. George rose to his feet immediately and Madeleine smiled as they hugged. He pecked her on the cheek, settled her in a chair and poured her a glass of white wine. Rachael blew a kiss in Madeleine's general direction.

'Good trip?' George asked. He was dressed in beige shorts and a striped white and pale blue t-shirt.

'Not bad. I forgot how far it was, and how hot,' Madeleine replied. It was good to see her brother. Although she couldn't understand

George wanting to live out here, she respected his decision. This was his career choice, while she had her own profession and there was no way Madeleine ever would have felt comfortable living out here where their father had died.

Rachael gave a nod. 'If you don't move from the house you'd almost think that life was civilised out here.' Her tone was clipped as she re-tied her long red hair into a ponytail.

Madeleine took a sip of wine. The condensation dripped from the glass onto her sleep-crumpled shorts. 'You've done lots to the house and garden since I was last here.' A fine layer of red dust glazed the rattan chair in which she sat.

'Sorry about your bedroom, sis,' George apologised. 'Rachael packed your things into boxes.'

'There wasn't much,' Rachael replied quickly, 'a few old work-clothes, jeans and stuff and some certificates from school.'

Madeleine wanted to complain about not being told in advance of the renovations, however this wasn't her home anymore, it was her brother's and Rachael's, and her sister-in-law had a tendency to overstep boundaries. 'The nursery looks nice.'

A muscle in Rachael's cheek twitched. 'Unfortunately, Maddy, we're not having much luck on that front.'

'It'll happen when it happens,' George placated, pouring his wife more wine and downing his next beer in a couple of mouthfuls.

'I just feel like everything is drying up, Madeleine,' Rachael continued, 'including me. It's this shocking drought.'

'We've had a bit on our plates,' George agreed. 'Luckily we had that one barley crop last year; it eased the sheep-feeding regime, and all the cattle were sold about eighteen months ago.' He looked at his wife. 'We're still going, just.' He squeezed Rachael's hand. 'At least we're not trying to find feed for the cattle. The stock routes are buggered.'

'But you've done so much to the old house,' Madeleine said. 'And the garden. How could you afford it?'

Rachael plucked at her pink skirt. She still wore makeup from lunch, although her lipstick had long worn off, leaving an outline of pale pink. 'We had to do *something* – the house was falling down around us, and at least the garden is now manageable. It makes such a difference seeing green grass when everything else is brown or dead.'

Madeleine admired the freshly painted veranda. 'And the house?' There were numerous paint catalogues on the table.

'Insurance payout,' George replied. 'Wind storm.'

'Which we added to the extra funds needed for our project. It's been keeping me busy, what with painters and plasterers taking over the place.'

Rachael's skill at avoiding paid employment left Madeleine wondering at her own excessive work ethic. Since university she had immersed herself in her career. She knew it wasn't healthy but work helped to stop her from dredging up the past. 'What project?' she asked.

'Our main concern is ensuring that Grandfather Harrow doesn't appear as if he painted in poverty. We can't have visitors travelling out to the sticks and finding a boring old room with nothing more than a bed, a desk and a cupboard.'

Madeleine shook her head. 'Excuse me? I'm not following you.'

'Well, once the retrospective opens there will be huge media interest. After all, forty works on show that haven't been seen in a single exhibition since the fifties is quite a coup. Naturally the renewed interest in Grandfather Harrow's life,' Rachael continued, 'will extend to his home and upbringing – where he got his early inspiration from, that sort of thing.'

Madeleine held out her glass for a refill.

'When your mother first told George she intended to approach you about holding an exhibition of his work, we jumped to it straightaway. We'd already started the reno, but we knew we'd have to be pretty organised to get things up and running in time.'

Madeleine took a sip of wine. In spite of her earlier hangover she was enjoying the acidic taste. 'Up and running for what?'

'Well,' Rachael replied enthusiastically, 'we thought Sunset Ridge could be promoted during the retrospective as a further area of interest that fans and artists – even critics – could visit.'

'Sort of like a home-stay situation,' George added. 'We could easily accommodate six people in the homestead.'

'The old schoolhouse and governess's room is a bit rustic, but we could certainly fit another four in there,' Rachael said. 'And of course there's ample room for caravans. George and I think we should form a committee to get the district involved. There are so many things we could do: visiting art lecturers, artist-in-residence programs and concerts.'

'My, you *have* given this some thought,' Madeleine said, wondering if she should reveal that the exhibition was barely at the conceptual stage. She knew, however, that the decision would not be hers to make for long: after last night Jude was sure to be on the phone to her son any minute complaining about her attitude to the project, if she hadn't already. 'And you're happy to have strangers living with you, George? When this is a working property?'

'Of course he is,' Rachael answered. 'So, what date came out of the board meeting?'

Madeleine sat the wine glass on the table. 'None. The concept was bumped off the agenda until next month.' It wasn't really a lie.

'Bumped off?' Rachael repeated. 'We've invested a lot of time and money in this project, Madeleine, and I was under the impression that you'd been working on it for a while. Jude said you'd been tracking down the owners of the landscape paintings.'

Madeleine wanted to tell her sister-in-law that she shouldn't have assumed the exhibition would automatically go ahead, but instead she said: 'And I have been, but these things don't happen overnight, Rachael.'

'Do you have any idea of timing, sis?'

'No, George. I don't.'

Rachael turned to her husband. 'I told you, George, that an event of this magnitude should have been offered to a state gallery. I should have taken on the project myself instead of –'

'Instead of what?' Madeleine asked, looking squarely at Rachael.

Rachael sighed dramatically. 'I just feel that Grandfather Harrow deserves something a little . . . grander than a *suburban* art gallery.'

'I see. You know, I never realised you were so interested in him, Rachael.'

In the silence that followed, Madeleine watched creamy moths bash against the veranda gauze. 'Anyway, with *your* art background I'm sure you understand the intricacies that go into mounting an exhibition of this scale.'

Rachael narrowed her eyes. She had been a primary school art teacher prior to her marriage, a fact George felt compelled to mention on the few occasions that he and Rachael were present when Jude and Madeleine chatted about art.

'There's some steamed chicken for dinner if you're hungry,' George offered. 'Sonia cooked it up especially for Rachael.'

Madeleine thought of the mangled chook on the sandstone pavers. 'I'm fine, thanks. I think I'll turn in.' She left the couple sitting in silence on the veranda.

The following morning Madeleine was up early. She could have sworn that the telephone woke her, yet the house was quiet. A soft breeze travelled along the hallway from the open double doors as Madeleine walked the length of the homestead, passing bedrooms, bathrooms and the station office. With the improvements already completed she was unsurprised by the rattan-weave flooring in the now open-plan dining and lounge rooms. The grey fleur-de-lis patterned carpet she remembered was gone, as was the dip in the floorboards and the gap between wall and floor in what was the original sitting room. A deep skirting board now collared the large open space and the floor was level. Madeleine knew that re-stumping houses was a major undertaking, which added to her suspicion that Rachael must have recently received some money from her family. She couldn't believe that George would have borrowed money from the bank for the renovations, not with the drought. The furniture, however, had not changed. It was still a mix of nineteenth-century hardwoods, some art deco-inspired pieces her grandfather had purchased, and a number of shabby-chic chairs and bow-fronted cabinets that oozed Rachael but didn't blend in.

The combined dining and lounge room had two doors on the opposite wall: one led to the old music room, which was empty except for a stack of paint tins and sheets; the other to the kitchen. At least this part of the house was still familiar. Mustard-yellow linoleum squares covered the floor and the cupboards were the same off-white. The rain-water tap in the sink still squeaked on turning and the familiar sound of rattling pipes preceded the red-tinged water. Madeleine drank thirstily, the faint taste of grit on her tongue. Helping herself to Rachael's gourmet muesli, she saw that the fridge was stacked with containers filled with leftovers. Either Sonia over-cooked or George and Rachael were fussy eaters.

Madeleine wandered around the kitchen, bowl in hand. The old Aga still stood at one end of the room accompanied by a gas stovetop and an electric wall oven. She had a vision of her parents dancing to a song on the radio; of George with a paper hat from a Christmas bonbon stuck rakishly on his head. The tall grandfather clock, which once held pride of place in the lounge room, chimed six-fifteen from the corner of the kitchen as Madeleine crunched muesli, the lost family scene melting away.

Inside the pantry the shelves were brimming with tinned goods and a container filled with homemade biscuits. Built on the eastern side of the house, the pantry was a surprisingly cool spot.

Madeleine and George had often hidden there in their youth when their father was having one of his rants. The wooden shelves were long and deep; curled up behind a hessian bag of potatoes and their father's wicker-covered demijohns of rum, it had been easy to stay out of sight.

Looking back, it seemed that anything could annoy Ashley Boyne: bad commodity prices, his noisy children, the weather, the men he and Jude employed to help on the property. Even the most senior of the station hands they were fortunate enough to hire didn't last long. They soon walked under the tirade of abuse that could accompany the smallest error on their part, usually the result of scatty instructions, or after daring to make a management decision in conflict with their employer's less-experienced demands. Madeleine reminded herself, with little comfort, that these days her father would probably have been diagnosed with a mental-health problem, and that this knowledge, had it been available, might have saved his life.

Madeleine's attempts to discuss her father with Jude after they relocated to Brisbane were usually blocked. And for some time George was uncomfortable talking about him as well. Looking back, she guessed his death had been too painful and awkward for her mother and brother to address, yet it was different for her. Madeleine yearned to hear his name, to talk about the happy times before his suicide. She needed to come to terms with why he had taken his own life and in doing so deserted his family. However, as the years passed, their mother only mentioned his name at Christmas and on birthdays, adding to Madeleine's sense of loss.

She knew George shared her misery in his own way and, gradually, after they had been in Brisbane for a couple of years, he began referring to past events on the property when the family was still together. Madeleine would listen intently to her brother on these occasions. Wide-eyed and grateful for any anecdote about their father, she would urge him to share another, and dear George nearly always relented. Although the stories were too few, George's telling of them never waned. Madeleine would always love him for that.

Aged twelve at the time of her dad's death, Madeleine had never understood why he wanted to die, and it was this inability to reconcile her father's taking of his own life that compelled her to raise the topic with Jude when at times her sadness engulfed her. Jude remained stubborn in her refusal to go into detail other than to tell her daughter that she believed stress played a significant role in Ashley's death. Ultimately, Jude thought, he was unsuited to the hard work required to run a rural property. Madeleine spent her formative years – high school and university – wavering between the anger she felt towards Jude for her reluctance to talk about her father, and trying to understand her mother's unwillingness to relive painful memories.

It was George who had set Madeleine straight. Taking her aside one Christmas, he explained that Jude's reticence was due to a mix of disappointment and anger. 'Mum thought she knew the man that she married – instead, he turned out to be a *coward*. They were her words, Maddy, not mine. She felt like Dad deserted her. He left her demoralised and embarrassed and alone.'

Madeleine found it difficult to comprehend such anger, especially against her beloved father, who she believed was clearly hurting and in need of help. The worst of it was that Madeleine glimpsed her mother's harsh attitude in herself. Jude couldn't forgive her husband for his actions, as Madeleine could not accept her mother's hard stance.

Madeleine walked out onto the new bricked-in veranda at the front of the house. Through the window she saw a horse and rider trotting across to the stand of trees in the middle of the house paddock about five hundred metres away. The rider dismounted and appeared to check the horses' hoofs. The man was tall, although with the distance and obligatory wide-brimmed hat he was unrecognisable to Madeleine. He was joined by a dusty white sedan, in which Sonia appeared.

Intrigued, Madeleine moved closer to the oval window as both Sonia and the stockman turned and stared in the direction of the homestead. For a brief moment she felt that they were talking about her.

'What's so interesting?'

Madeleine jumped. 'George! You gave me a shock.'

'Sorry. Did you find everything all right?'

'Yes, thanks. Who's the horseman?' she enquired, gesturing at the window.

'Horseman? I bet you it's old Ross Evans,' George replied, moving to look out the window. There was no sign of anyone outside, although a vehicle was disappearing in a shroud of dust. 'He's an old bloke from the village who rides through here on and off. Don't ask me why. I think he's got a few loose in the top paddock.' George tapped his head. 'Anyway he's harmless. He's helped us out on the odd occasion, unasked. I came across him down by the river about a week after I first took over this place. He was trying to stand an old cow who'd recently calved. Don't you remember me telling you about him?'

'Vaguely. That's a while ago now. I thought it was a one-off,' Madeleine replied.

'Well, every now and then I'll discover a repaired fence or a sheep that's been pulled clear of a drying waterhole. Occasionally I'll see Ross riding through the paddock, but he doesn't want money or thanks.' George looked at his sister. 'Come to think of it, he doesn't even want conversation. Mum reckons there was some bloke who did the same thing after she and Dad first came to live here, although she never got a close look at him.'

'And you think it was Ross Evans?'

'Who knows?' George replied. 'Probably not.'

'Sonia appeared to be talking to him a minute ago.'

'Really? That would be a first. There isn't any love lost between

Ross and Sonia. It was probably Will Murray. He still works here and Ross gives him the creeps.'

'How is Will?' Maddy asked.

'Pretty good. He checks the dams and troughs for me every two days or so across the western and southern country. I do the rest. By the time we've checked the entire forty thousand acres, it's time to start again, in between feeding the sheep, of course. If we don't check the bore system regularly you can bet one of the troughs will go dry from a buggered float or something, and then the sheep will be without water.'

Madeleine noticed the deep frown line etched between her brother's eyes. The drought was taking its toll. It showed in a dull-eyed stare and the flecks of grey speckling his dark hair. Now in their early thirties, they still looked quite similar – both had brown hair and brown eyes and erred on the slim side, although years in an office had given Madeleine an overly rounded backside she could happily have done without. She cuffed him lightly on the shoulder. 'You were the one who wanted to be the farmer.' She smiled; they both knew that wasn't really true – their mother had steered George in that direction. Agricultural college was quickly followed by a stint on a big spread up north, and by his early twenties he was in charge of Sunset Ridge. Madeleine never asked if agriculture was George's calling, probably because his control of the property occurred at about the same time he met Rachael at a Flying Doctor fundraiser. Almost immediately they had become an item, and six months later they were engaged. The rush to the altar reminded Madeleine of the opening line of *Pride and Prejudice*; clearly Rachael decided that George, with his forty thousand acres and boyish charm, was in want of a wife.

'I love the place, Maddy, but if I had a choice . . .' He shrugged. 'Family loyalty, emotional attachment – it's a bit of a bugger, this whole bush heritage thing, but it means the world to Mum.'

'Does it? When was the last time she visited?'

George switched on the kettle. 'She and Rachael don't really hit it off anymore.'

'That wouldn't keep her away, you know that. She still owns Sunset Ridge.'

'And doesn't Rachael love *that*,' George said. 'Coffee?'

'Thanks.' Deciding against making a comment, Madeleine waited as George made coffee for both of them.

'It's just as well she kept it.' George stirred a spoonful of sugar into each of their mugs and passed his sister hers. 'Most women probably would have sold the property after Dad died, especially when she made the decision to leave, however by leasing it she could buy the apartment in Brisbane and still keep the old family place. And, let's face it, we never wanted for anything growing up. She probably sees the place as a bit of a security blanket, and it's a pride thing. Everything Mum's done has been for the protection of the property and, by extension, the Harrow name. She's mighty proud of her family. A number of the older families in the district have come and gone, but not us.'

Madeleine looked at him over the brim of the mug as she sipped the coffee. 'You're angry with her.'

George lowered his voice. 'I would have sold the place four years ago if I could have found a buyer and got Mum's agreement.' He took a sip of his coffee. 'I left my run a bit late, though. I always have been a bit behind the eight ball.'

'Rubbish.'

'No, it's true.' His voice dwindled away. 'Anyway, I'm stuck with it. At the moment Sunset Ridge isn't worth a spit. Besides, now we've got a spotlight on us with this exhibition, we can hardly sell it.'

'I'd always wondered if you'd thought about doing something else for a living.'

'Like what?' George asked with interest, sipping his coffee and swallowing appreciatively.

'I don't know. Barista, perhaps?' George didn't know anything else. And like Madeleine, he didn't have any artistic talent either.

'There *is* going to be a retrospective of Grandfather's work, isn't there? I spoke to Mum this morning and –'

Madeleine gave a knowing smile. 'I was wondering when Jude would call you.'

'She thinks you're dragging the chain.' George took a couple of gulps of coffee and poured the remains down the sink. 'I know you've always felt as though you've grown up in Grandfather's shadow. Remember at school when cranky Mr Masterton used to ride you in art class?' George cleared his throat: ' "*Madeleine, I find it astonishing that a young woman of your pedigree could have such limited ability* . . ." The next minute you're out sneaking a ciggy in the dark room during photography class.'

'Well, I was continually found wanting, wasn't I?' Madeleine crossed her arms. 'Everyone always expected more, and uni was no different to school. People couldn't understand why I wasn't a painter or a sculptor or a potter. People assumed I'd be staggeringly creative in some way. People assumed I would have known my grandfather. Shit, George, I can barely manage a stick figure.'

'Me neither,' he grinned. 'So, what about this exhibition, then?'

Madeleine sighed. 'Like I told Mum, Australiana just isn't popular at the moment, and even if the show gets the green light it will take time to organise, maybe a couple of years.'

George sat down at the table. 'You're joking?'

Madeleine finished her coffee and sat the mug on the sink. 'Each of those forty paintings that we want to include in the exhibition has an owner, some of whom live overseas. Getting permission to borrow and transport valuable artworks for display is a major deal. Then there's the cost. The insurance alone for an exhibition comprised predominantly of loaned material means that this particular display we're considering would verge on the philanthropic. The gallery needs to create some serious buzz to get enough attendees to cover costs.'

'What about sponsorship?'

'I've already approached a number of organisations that are strong supporters of the arts, and the answer's always the same: they're looking for a measurable return on investment.'

'So, why didn't you approach a state gallery? They have more pull with government funding and they've got a better chance of getting good crowds, haven't they?'

Madeleine sighed again. 'Frankly, I don't believe that Grandfather is a big enough name to warrant a state exhibition, especially when none of his work has ever been exhibited before. He was a damn fine artist, but I don't imagine many people apart from serious landscape lovers even know who he is. It will be hard enough getting him into the Stepworth Gallery.'

She didn't want to verbalise her concern that if the retrospective was not successful it may damage her career at the gallery.

'Everyone says he was an excellent artist.'

'And he was. But in comparison to the Streetons and Boyds of the Australian art scene, he's an unknown. That's why we need archival material. If we can build a chronological history of Grandfather's life, it will make the retrospective a far more interesting proposition for the gallery, as well as value-adding to the exhibition itself, especially if we can blend his life and work with the great period of change Australia went through from the 1900s to the 1950s. Heavens, George: two World Wars and the Great Depression! He saw it all, lived through it all – and Mum expects me to stage an exhibition comprised of the forty landscapes he painted after he returned from the war and a couple of sketches. It's not enough.'

'So, do you think that there are more paintings?'

Madeleine nodded. In spite of her misgivings she was beginning to sound like her mother. 'There has to be,' she admitted. 'Jude has those couple of early sketches drawn before the war, so there must be more, and now we know he continued drawing in France. Did Jude tell you about what the War Memorial turned up?'

'Yes, amazing stuff. Mum was pretty excited by it.'

'So she should be,' Madeleine agreed. 'We now have the beginnings of Grandfather's artistic career. Imagine if he *had* been an official war artist; that really would have been something.'

'But Grandfather *was* there, Maddy,' George interrupted, 'and he drew what he saw, what he experienced. Doesn't that make his work just as important as an official artist?'

Madeleine grinned. 'Yes, it does.'

George smiled back. 'You don't sound quite as uninterested in the exhibition as Mum insinuated.'

'I'm trying to be objective, George.'

'Fair enough. So what do you think they were like, the Harrow boys, and particularly Grandfather?'

Madeleine considered the question, thinking of the photograph she studied when she arrived at Sunset Ridge. 'Conservative, polite and well educated, I would imagine,' she said thoughtfully. 'I can only assume they were a product of their time. It's amazing when you think that they grew up in this house, slept in the rooms we now sleep in, and fished in the river like we used to.'

George scratched his head. 'Actually, it's a bit hard to imagine.'

Madeleine gave her brother a soft smile. 'You're riding in their footsteps every day, George, seeing the same trees and red ridges, looking up at the same patch of sky. I should be asking you what you think our grandfather and his brothers were like.'

George gave a crooked smile. 'Well, if they lived through a drought like this one, I reckon they would have been stressed.'

≪ Chapter 4 ≫

Sunset Ridge, south-west Queensland, Australia
August 1916

The wool wagon was being pulled by a team of twenty-four bullocks. Unkempt, lumpy-looking animals with yellowing horns and shaggy coats, they shuffled restlessly, twisting their necks against their yokes as they snorted and bellowed. Dave observed old Harris, the driver, as he came around the side of the wagon, his fingers fidgeting with the buttons on his trousers. He was a short, plump man with shoulders the width of two axe handles and a personality not suited to people. Dave reached out to rub the lead bullock on the nose. The animal shuffled and snorted and the driver, who had begun to climb back up onto the wagon, found the ground instantly.

'Get away with you, boy!' he yelled, waving a whip at Dave.

Dave backed off, scrambling up into the cavernous wool shed, which had been built on solid timber foundations at a height to match that of a wool wagon. In the shadow of the twenty-foot-wide doorway, he looked down to where his father was checking the ropes on the four tiers of bales already loaded at the front.

His tweed coat-tail flapped in the winter breeze as he pointed, the driver's assistant quick to re-tie the rope at his command. Dave had a mind to jump onto the wagon and run across the stacked bales, however he knew such antics would not be appreciated. Their father still held all three of his sons responsible for yesterday's kerfuffle.

While in the village collecting supplies, his older brother Luther had got into a scuffle with the baker's boy, Snob Evans. They had come across him hanging around outside the funeral parlour, his narrow forehead pressed against the curtained window. Snob had a habit of marking his territory like a tomcat, and the results were not always pretty. Although at seventeen he was only a few months older than Luther, Snob was quick to chase Luther down a dusty side street and taunt him about his stutter. In response, Luther had threatened to chop Snob's finger off with his tomahawk. Dave's other brother, Thaddeus, had pleaded non-involvement when reprimanded by their father – at nineteen he was bursting with sibling superiority – but he had sported a torn shirt, while Luther carried his split lip with pride. Snob always won.

Dave wasn't much of a fighter, but he still enjoyed a good showing and his older brothers always provided the entertainment.

Dave jumped aside as Thaddeus helped Rodger – one of the three remaining station hands, the rest having enlisted – roll a bale out of the wool shed. They expected Rodger to join up at any moment, especially because his brother had died at Gallipoli. Timber boards creaked under the weight of the wool as it was manoeuvred across the gap between the shed and the wagon. The wagon rolled back and forth under the moving bale as an extended arm swung across the load from a timber pole. Securing the wool bale with rope, Thaddeus and Rodger stood back as it was winched into the air. The bale hung precariously for a few seconds, haloed by blue sky before being lowered onto the second tier.

'Cold-footer,' Harris hissed at Rodger.

'Don't worry about him, mate.' Thaddeus clapped Rodger on the shoulder as they walked back to retrieve the next bale. 'You can bet he wouldn't be so quick to judge if he wasn't too old to enlist.'

Dave stood back to let the men pass and then jumped to the ground and joined his father. 'It's a good clip, Father.' Having overheard his parents discuss the wool proceeds in the dining room a few nights previously, he was full of knowledge about the British government purchasing the entire 1916–17 Australian wool clip at an agreed rate that exceeded previous prices. 'Lucky for the war, or else prices wouldn't be so good.'

George William Harrow, known by all as G.W., turned towards his youngest son, and Dave felt, as he often did, that he should remind his father of exactly who he was. Instead he smiled as his mother often suggested.

'It's a fine line between fulfilling the needs of the army and profiteering.' His father surveyed the length of the wagon and its precious load. 'However, this is how money is made in the bush, lad. You remember that. Now, go and help Luther stencil the bales.'

Dave squeezed past Thaddeus and Rodger and made his way through the wool shed and the myriad bales filling the cavernous space. Beyond the three slatted wool tables and wooden fleece bins built into the wall, a wedge of sunlight highlighted dust mites floating over the lanolin-smoothed board. He found Luther in a far corner of the shed, kneeling between large wicker wool baskets, rubbing half-heartedly at a bale. Smears of black streaked the bale on which he worked as he stencilled the property name onto it.

Luther dumped the blackening pot and brush on an upturned basket. 'T-take over, w-will you, Dave?' He leaned against a timber upright as Dave began to stencil. The lettering for Sunset Ridge was perfect. 'Not b-bad for a k-kid,' Luther admitted. He pulled his tomahawk free of its leather pouch. 'See that th-there?' Pointing at a piece of rusty iron that was nailed over a hole in the wall some eight feet away, he took aim and threw the tomahawk directly at the wall. The blade whirred through the air to strike the tin dead centre. 'C-cut clean through a m-man, I reckon.'

Sometimes Dave wondered about Luther. The story his mother told of dropping Luther on his head when he was a baby didn't seem to be reason enough for his actions at times. 'Father is in a good mood considering the scrape you got into yesterday.'

Luther prised the axe head free and tucked it back into his belt. 'Th-that w-won't last.'

'It will if we win the Champion Fleece this year,' Dave said hopefully.

His brother scratched a scab on the back of his hand. 'Eighth t-time l-lucky, eh?' He looked unconvinced. 'I heard that C-Cummins is exhibiting another b-beauty and, l-let's face it, he always w-wins.' Luther jumped up on the bales and leapfrogged his way to the front of the shed. On reaching a timber pillar he scrambled up it, swung off a beam and scuttled back along the top of the bales. Dave watched his brother admiringly as thoughts of the fleece competition returned.

The whole family had been present in the wool pavilion at the 1915 Banyan Show. Lily Harrow, dressed in grey with a pristine frill of white at her neck and a hat that brought every other woman's to shame in terms of size, had ensured that Thaddeus, Luther and Dave were at their presentable best. With their smiles pasted on in support of the Sunset Ridge entry, they had stood proudly in line with the podium, the silver winner's trophy within reach. Finally the winners were announced. Sunset Ridge received a forgettable ribbon.

Cummins, the Champion Fleece winner for the eighth year straight, was treated by all with a grudging respect. Although his family had been in the district for twenty years longer than any other, he was not well liked. With a boil the size of a hen's egg on the side of his face and a tendency to arrogance, he was difficult to take to. The Harrows had left soon after the competition, much to their mother's dismay. She had taken a fancy to a piano and had already played two tunes that morning despite their father's consternation. G.W. Harrow was not one for public showings.

Dave positioned the stencil on the next bale and rubbed the blackened brush vigorously across the metal. Beyond anything, he hoped they won this year. Their father had turned purple that day and the colour hadn't faded until the dust whirled behind their dray five miles out of town. No one had dared to speak, except for Luther, of course.

'I'll go r-right over to C-cummins's place and p-punch him square in the nose if you w-want me t-to, 'Father.'

Of course, their father would never allow such a thing to occur, but in the offering Luther set himself apart. In response, their father glanced over his shoulder to where they all sat in the rear of the dray, and with the imperceptible dip of his chin did the rarest of things: he singled Luther out for approval. That Christmas, Dave and Thaddeus received new saddle blankets; Luther, the tomahawk.

Dave finished stencilling the last bale and met Luther in the shade of the engine room where their horses were tethered. All the boys' horses were chestnut geldings out of the same dependable mare, which had finally died – their mother said of exhaustion – last year. They were heading to the river. Soon they would be fishing and talking with Thaddeus's mate, Harold Lawrence.

'What about Thaddeus?' Dave asked as Luther mounted up, his horse whinnying.

'Do you th-think he'd w-wait for us?' He gave his mount a friendly cuff between the ears.

They rode off at a trot, angling close to the sheep yards, careful to avoid the edge of the in-ground dipping trench. Harris bellowed commands as their horses skirted a stand of wilga trees. Behind them the tiers of bales on the wool wagon blocked view of their departure. Dave watched a bale hang suspended mid-air, and then steered his horse into the scrub.

They rode through stringy saplings and mounded ant hills, over late-winter herbage and brittle grasses. The sun warmed his shoulders, and Dave guessed that it was only a bit past one o'clock when they crisscrossed a series of narrow sheep paths that signified they were nearing the river. Only twelve months ago they had been in the grip of a horrendous drought, yet they had fared better than the state of Victoria. With rivers dried up and grass non-existent, ten million head of sheep were thought to have perished down south. Dave couldn't imagine such numbers. Things had been bad enough at Sunset Ridge, with their own sheep lying down on the parched ground, brown eyes gazing into oblivion. Yet the rain had come, as their father said it would. By spring of last year Sunset Ridge was returning to life; the bush was returning to life. Just as a brass band marched down the Banyan main street, calling young men to adventure.

By the time Luther and Dave reached the gently sloping bank of the river, Harold was tying his boat to a tree. He sploshed from the timber craft through ankle-deep water, his boots hanging over a shoulder, a saddlebag in his hand. It was a good two hours' row from the village of Banyan to Sunset Ridge, although the time was cut on the return leg thanks to the westerly flow of the water. A few months older than Thaddeus, Harold was muscular, thick-necked and sandy-haired. His father owned Lawrence Ironmongers and despite being the son of a shopkeeper Harold had been friendly with the Harrow boys since childhood.

With Thaddeus still loading the wool, the three of them baited their lines with worms Harold supplied from a battered cork pot and then spaced themselves apart along the river bank. Dave's patience lasted five minutes. Tying the fishing line to a stick and removing shoes and socks, he clambered up a tree. A gnarled, stubby branch provided the first foothold, a rotted board secured with a rusty nail the next. Below, Harold tugged lightly on his line while further along the bank Luther chopped branches for a camp fire with his tomahawk.

The scent of crushed leaves, distant smoke and tangy dirt and manure carried on the autumn breeze. Sheep grazed quietly on the opposite bank, their swollen bellies carrying the coming season's lambs. To the left the river was protected by a winding row of trees that overhung the water's edge, their branches dipping the surface like a bather readying to swim. Straddling a branch, Dave wiggled from side to side, edging forward until his feet dangled above the water. The westerly course of the waterway stretched into the distance before disappearing into a dense tangle of trees and scrub. Insects hovered over the river, forming miniature rings as they dropped to its surface.

Lifting his hands, Dave formed a square with his fingers. Through the frame a wisp of sunlight speared down on the waterhole. Although the surface of the river was a murky brown, the wintery light revealed the soft swirls of the water's current, tracing the top of it with various hues of green and brown. There was both light and dark below him, space and proportion, pattern and balance. The water reflected almost exactly what Miss Waites had taught Dave and Luther about art composition that week in the schoolroom. Never one for Learners, he had done his best along with his brothers to read and write and add sums – but art was different; he knew right away that he liked it. Especially because their governess did as well. Miss Waites would lean over his shoulder while explaining object placement and symmetry, her oval nail skimming a coloured plate, wisps of pale brown hair curling about her neck.

'Hey, Dave,' Harold called, 'you've got a biter.'

Dave slid back along the branch and half slipped and half climbed down the trunk. Losing his footing, he fell the last few feet, his palm catching roughly against the nail and rotting board.

Biting his lip, he reached the taut fishing line in time for it to go slack in his hand. Blood seeped from Dave's palm as he dug filthy fingernails into the flesh to withdraw a long, thick splinter. He sucked at the weeping wound and spat the blood and grit on the sand as the pop of rifle-fire sounded in the distance. A horse whinnied, followed by the crunch of leaf litter.

'What have I missed?' Thaddeus slid from his horse in a showy manner. He had recently taken to riding bareback, causing their father to ask their mother on more than one occasion if she had planned to breed a circus act. Slipping the rifle from his shoulder, he dropped it on the river bank and joined Harold.

'Joe Barnes died of his wounds,' Harold told them. 'Those blasted Turks got him eventually.'

'Joe was a good bloke.' Thaddeus lifted an arm and bowled an imaginary ball. 'He could run like the wind and bat with the best of them.'

Harold scraped his teeth over a thick bottom lip. 'I'd like to be doing more than selling nails and pannikins. You know, I've heard stories about lads younger than us enlisting.'

Thaddeus clapped his friend on the shoulder. 'By the time your father lets you sign up, mate, the war will be over.'

'I thought you wanted to go,' Harold replied. 'What if we lose over there and the Germans invade Australia? What then?'

'And what about our businesses?' Thaddeus countered. 'We've already lost five station hands since last year, and with Rodger's brother dead I reckon he'll leave soon. That'll leave two. Someone's got to look after the sheep and the cattle.'

'That's a convenient excuse,' Harold sniffed.

'You're just saying that because food and clothing are more important than ladders and lanterns in war time.'

Harold dropped the line he was holding.

'Okay, okay.' Thaddeus held up his hands in surrender. 'I agree that it doesn't seem right, us sitting here fishing while there's a war on, but we're still doing our bit – there's so much beef and mutton being preserved and shipped abroad that you wonder if there's enough meat left in Australia to feed our own people. Anyway, I've been thinking that if the war's still going on next year I'll probably join up.'

'Me too,' Harold agreed.

'It's not our w-war,' Luther argued. 'I'm all for a b-bit of adventure, but I don't w-want t-to fight for the B-british. I'm Australian. B-besides, we would p-probably e-end up over in France and th-there's no w-way I'm eating frog l-legs.'

Harold flicked his line. 'That's just wrong. We're part of the British Empire; we have a duty to the King.'

Luther made a point of swivelling his neck to look at their surroundings. 'I ain't never seen K-king George out the b-back of B-banyan.'

Thaddeus snickered.

'If *we* were attacked,' Harold replied indignantly, 'the King would send troops.'

'If w-we w-were attacked? Out here in th-the b-bush?' Luther let a handful of river sand run through his fingers. 'Dying stock when it doesn't r-rain, drowning s-stock when it does, and l-long b-boring days in b-between.' He tapped his chin thoughtfully. 'I'd tell the invaders they could h-have it.'

A straightening of Harold's shoulders was the first indication that he had a bite. Dave knew the signs by heart and could plot the course of the upcoming battle in his head; the tensing of muscles, the concentration, the battle of wills between fish and man. Harold, never one to be beaten by anything or anyone, treated fishing with the same solemnity Miss Waites gave to their weekly bible reading, and as Harold held the record for the most catches, every fish added to his tally left Thaddeus and the rest of them further behind.

'Keep it t-taut, keep the line t-taut, H-harold, or you'll l-lose him.' Luther jumped to his feet as Harold began to slowly wind in the line.

When Harold took a step forward, they all did; when he paused briefly to check that his catch was still hooked to the line, they each held their breath in anticipation.

'I've got him.' A final tug brought the shimmering yellow-belly to the water's edge.

'He's a b-beauty,' Luther enthused, 'a six-p-pounder.'

The top of the fish was dark brown but once floundering on its side in the shallows the iridescent gold of its body sparkled up through the water. Harold grabbed hold of the fish by moving his hand from the head towards the tail so as not to get lanced by the protruding fins. 'It's a good size. Think I'll keep it.' Carefully freeing the hook, he dropped the fish into a hessian sack and sat the bag in the river's shallows.

'Well, that gives Harold twelve big ones for the year so far,' Thaddeus stated flatly. 'Maybe we should change waterholes.'

'B-bollocks,' Luther argued. 'Th-this is the b-best fishing hole in these p-parts. Fishing's about skill and Harold is th-the best.'

Thaddeus fetched his rifle from where it lay in the sand. Deftly loading a bullet into the chamber, he swept the barrel across the river bank. The target came in the shape of a sulphur-crested cockatoo, which Thaddeus dropped from the branches of an ancient tree with a single shot. The white-feathered bird fell silently to land with a plop in the river as thirty cockatoos took flight, their outstretched wings filling the pale blue of the sky.

'If we do go to war, Harold,' Thaddeus walked towards his horse, 'I don't think your fishing will help us.'

Harold and Luther exchanged glances.

Dave knew that Thaddeus was changing. He had, on more than one occasion, caught Thaddeus checking his reflection in the mirror. Anyone would think he was the one being exhibited at the Banyan Show and not Sunset Ridge's prize fleece. No, Dave didn't think the war was the reason for the changes in his brother. It was something or somebody else.

With the others diverted packing up their things, Dave walked nonchalantly down to the water's edge and, quickly untying the top of the submerged hessian bag, let the yellow-belly escape to safety. He caught a glimpse of shimmering scales beneath the water's surface and smiled.

Lily Harrow fiddled with the cutlery at her place setting. At the opposite end of the ten-seat dining table, her husband twirled a water glass, the finely etched crystal refracting slivers of light from the kerosene lamps on the sideboard. At fifty, G.W. Harrow resembled the grainy photograph of his father. Over the years, watery blue eyes, sunken cheeks and a thick, military-style moustache had replaced crinkled laughter lines and a ready smile. Of course, in fairness she too had lost youth's bloom. If a woman's future was tied to her looks, then fate had been quick to ensure hers would be forever joined to her husband.

The sound of crashing pots and pans emanated from the kitchen. It was hardly the pleasant evening hoped for. The wait for tea was now straggling towards the ten-minute mark, thanks to their wayward sons who had only just managed to join them at the table. They were now being subjected to five minutes' silence, a punishment that Thaddeus, Luther and Dave were quite used to. The boys sat quietly, occasionally flashing covert glances at each other, while G.W. had the familiar tight-eyed expression of a gentleman unused to being delayed.

Although not handsome in the dashing, hero-type mould young women dream of, G.W. had been kind and courteous in the early days of their marriage. Such beginnings suggested a rosy future, and at eighteen Lily had known nothing of life. Her aspirations had centred round an ideal of love, not the reality of it. He had been searching for a bride, and she, eager to escape a coddling, musically inclined yet drink-addled family, was not slow in displaying her interest. It was a pity that their relationship had lost its bloom so quickly. G.W. was distracted by the management of the property and it quickly became apparent that he did not have the patience for children. It was also quickly becoming obvious how little they had in common.

Another crash sounded from the kitchen. Considering Cook's domain was separated from the main homestead by a twenty-foot covered walkway, the noise was impressive.

'This is ridiculous,' G.W. announced.

'I'm sure Cook is doing her best.' Having entered the kitchen earlier to see Cook retrieve the mutton chops from a boiler of fat-laden water, Lily's enthusiasm had waned. Cook detested fat, and her habit of par-boiling every piece of meat before baking or frying left choice cuts tasteless.

G.W. began to drum his fingers on the table. Lily patted the sweep of auburn hair gathered into a low roll at the nape of her neck and thought of the vast acreage surrounding the homestead. At times she loathed the property, at others the land soothed her, yet always it shadowed and controlled their lives, its unrelenting presence serving to remind them all of the great drama that had befallen the family. In a long-running feud with a neighbour over the placement of a boundary fence erected by G.W. Senior in the late 1880s, G.W. had foolishly bet ten thousand acres of the property that the placement was correct. The Lands Department said otherwise and the dirt was lost by way of a gentleman's handshake. Consequently, 1900 was a dire year. They had been in the grip of the Great Drought since 1895 when this calamity befell them, and whether stress played a part in G.W.'s reckless actions, or he was merely exhibiting inherited tendencies passed down from his forefathers, Lily would never know. She did know, however, that life had not been the same since. Her husband lived in the shadow of his forefathers, and they cast their disapproving gazes from the red ridge in which eight of them were buried.

Cook entered the dining room with two large covered dishes and plonked them unceremoniously in the middle of the table. 'I'm not to be blamed for the state of the tatties, missus. I've done me best but a person can't be expected to keep things 'ot and tasty when these young rascals are late.' Cook wiped her hands diligently on a less-than-clean apron.

'I am aware of the difficulties you work under, Cook,' Lily said stiffly, giving each boy a singular stare. 'Had Mr Harrow and I been blessed with girls, your job, I'm sure, would have been far easier.'

The older woman lifted the lids from a platter of gravy-swimming mutton chops and another of vegetables, and then left the room.

As each serving was passed along, Lily added the soft potatoes, burned carrots and a ladleful of cabbage. The end of shearing and the subsequent loading of Sunset Ridge's wool clip should have been cause for celebration; instead the business of eating the unappealing meal merely eased the burden of conversation.

'What happened to your hand?' Lily noticed the bandage on David's palm.

'It's nothing, Mother. I cut it.'

'You better have a look at that, Lily.' G.W.'s cheek bulged with food. 'A cut's the quickest way to get blood poisoning. You know that, Dave. Your fingers could swell up, and then –' he slapped his hand on the table so that everything rattled, 'you're dead.'

'G.W.!' Lily exclaimed. 'There's no need to be quite so brutal.'

G.W. served himself another chop and hacked into it as if he were sawing a piece of wood.

Undoing the bandage, Lily examined the wound. David's palm was pitted by grazes while a jagged cut stretched the length of the soft flesh. 'It appears to be quite clean, G.W.'

'Well, then all is right with the world, David. Your mother clearly believes she has a doctor's perspective.'

Lily dabbed at her mouth with a linen serviette. 'Here's to another fine wool clip and to a fleece that will win the Champion Fleece.'

The boys looked to their father in anticipation.

G.W. raised his head. 'Yes, yes, it may well; the length of staple, the brightness.' He visibly cheered. 'Yes, I do believe it's our best yet.'

By the time Cook's warm custard was consumed, the Champion Fleece trophy was won and G.W. was pouring two glasses of Madeira. Music from the organ and Thaddeus's harmonica filtered through the homestead from the music room as Lily hid a mutton belch with a sip of alcohol. The warmth of the liquid seeped through her like a soak in her precious hip bath, and she wondered briefly at their weekday abstinence until a memory of her father, collapsed over his broken violin, reminded her of the perils of the bottle. The sitting room was a little stuffy tonight. Thick damask curtains were tugged partially across the permanently closed windows and the faint scent of smoke hung in the room. For as long as she had lived at Sunset Ridge these windows had been closed. The red dust was simply too invasive.

G.W. contemplated the oil painting above the fireplace. Years of heat had left the painting's idyllic rural scene strewn with miniature cracks. It remained in pride of place, however; a link to the mother country, Great Britain, home to the Harrows before their emigration in the 1870s. If Lily had her way she would replace it with an ornate framed mirror; it had been thirty years since her parents sailed from London, and they were happy not to harbour keepsakes of the dirty, overcrowded city. Her mother's family had once been wealthy land owners in Devon, until Lily's uncle died and the estate had passed to a male cousin. Lily's mother had never got over the loss of the family seat and the subsequent dwindling of income. Marriage to a financier seemed a good offer, and she was pleased to leave England.

'We'll place the trophy right here in September,' G.W. stated, moving a vase from the centre of the mantelpiece. 'Things are going to be better from now on, Lily.' He joined her on the couch. 'The British Government has finally agreed on the flat rate for the year's wool clip.' He took a breath. 'It's fifteen and one half pence per pound of greasy wool, which is nearly double compared to what they paid us last year.'

Lily clasped her hands, then forced the smile from her face. 'Oh, but I'm forgetting myself. It's for uniforms.'

G.W. patted her arm. 'The Great War machine must be clothed and fed, my dear. With the extra money I've decided to increase our cattle numbers. Eventually they'll be travelling abroad in cans to feed our boys on the front-line.'

In spite of their financial improvement Lily felt a sickness in the pit of her stomach. It didn't seem right to be benefitting when young men were dying abroad. And they *were* dying. The casualty lists were frightening.

'Also, this year I intend to join the ewes again as soon as they've finished lambing. With last year's drought a memory, we'll quickly build our flock numbers up. I expect even bigger things by 1918.' G.W. plucked at his trousers. The habit he had of picking at his clothing had increased since the last drought. Each dry period that decimated their land lingered on in nervous twitches and greying hair and memories that were now slightly blurred at the edges. 'I feel like I've done my penance.' G.W. looked briefly towards the music room where a familiar tune was being attempted on the organ.

Lily squeezed his hand. 'We've had our problems. The seasons have not always been kind.' She faltered. 'There is the disappointment of no more children and –' But the words wouldn't come. The loss of the ten thousand acres sixteen years earlier remained as fresh as if the catastrophe had happened yesterday. The organ music stopped, to be quickly replaced by a harmonica. Uncharacteristically, G.W. began to nod in time to the tune.

'I've heard there is another piano being exhibited at the Banyan Show this year. I could teach the boys,' Lily suggested. 'You know I've always wanted one.'

G.W. considered the contents of his glass. 'Well, my dear, we will inspect it. We may yet find ourselves entertaining in the spring.' Lily couldn't believe what she was hearing. It had been many years since her husband had been so inclined. The bare mantelpiece shone in the lamplight. 'And our sons must marry suitably accomplished women, who will appreciate the refinements that this homestead offers. In the meantime I should warn you, my dear, that we may yet see one of them enlisting. We've been giving the Germans a good push, and I believe we have the upper hand, but one can never be certain.'

'Heavens, G.W., you can't be serious.' Lily sat her glass on the round side table. 'The boys are far too young.'

Her husband raised an eyebrow. 'Thaddeus is already of age, and Luther will turn eighteen next year. The Allies have achieved some substantial gains, however the war is not yet over.'

Yesterday Lily had received word from an old family friend about the appalling death toll suffered by the Australians the previous month during the great battle at Fromelles in France. Mrs Roberts also spoke of the censorship in the newspapers and of a strict no-camera policy for soldiers on the Western Front. This was the opposite to Gallipoli, where many soldiers took personal snapshots, including their neighbour Joe Barnes, who forwarded photographs home. This point stuck in Lily's mind. What *didn't* the Empire want them to see?

'I'm sorry to distress you, my dear, but this must be discussed. If the war drags on into next year at least one of our boys will have to do their duty. If and when that time comes, God forbid, we may well have to make a decision.'

'A decision?' Lily repeated. 'About what?'

'Well, they cannot both enlist; at least one capable son must be safe-guarded to ensure the future of the Harrow name.'

'Oh, G.W.' Lily wrung her hands. She wasn't sure what was worse: the thought of one of her older sons going to war or the indifference shown towards their youngest boy, David.

'The Hardcastles sent their second-eldest. The older boy will inherit the property. And what of the Gordons at Wangallon Station? Is their son going?' Lily's tone was curt.

'Of course he isn't. Angus is the same age as David; he can't enlist for another two years.'

'I have heard rumours of under-age enlistments,' Lily replied.

G.W. sniffed. 'Unfortunately the future management of Sunset Ridge must figure in the equation, and we don't want to see our two eldest boys both in uniform.' He patted her hand. 'Don't fret, my dear. None of this may come to pass. But be assured there is a mighty battle being waged in France, and we must be prepared.'

⋘ Chapter 5 ⋙

Madame Chessy folded the newspaper and placed it on the kitchen table. Sometimes she wished she were illiterate like many of their neighbours – surely it would be better to live in ignorance than to be witness to the rubbish printed in the newspapers. Yet she was unlike many of the peasants dotting the countryside. Her mother's family, the Bonets, had once been part of the wealthy bourgeoisie class. There were also whispers of noble blood in the family, a story validated by her mother. In 1788, a year before the French Revolution began, her great-great-grandmother was said to have been a favourite at King Louis XVI's court at Versailles. Twelve months later, when France descended into turmoil, the entire family went into hiding. The Bonet family had endured so much change over the last two centuries that Madame Chessy often wondered how the line had survived. The family managed to re-establish themselves during Louis-Napoleon Bonaparte's rule, however the glory was short-lived. With the fall of the Bonaparte Empire in 1870 and the establishment of the Third Republic, they never recovered economically.

Marie had been educated by her mother in the family villa, which gradually grew emptier as the furniture was sold off to pay debts. Such an upbringing led to a certain adaptability of character, although Madame Chessy wondered how she would have survived being poor had she not married her beloved Marcel. Having taught her husband and sons to read and write, she hoped future daughters-in-law would not be dullards. She was the last of the Bonet line, and education remained the only form of inheritance she could pass on, although at times she wondered why she bothered with such thoughts.

The edges of the newspaper rustled as a light wind blew through the partially open window. The paper was a weekly extravagance, yet it allowed her to feel in touch with reality, if it could be called that these days. This week the newspapers told her that the Allies were winning every battle and the Germans were on the run. Once again fact was blurred by fiction. The propaganda machines were hard at work. She had no doubt that there was a government office devoted to censoring newspaper articles. Well, they had to, she reasoned, sipping black coffee; the Allied army could hardly note in print which area of the front they were heading to or where they would next engage the enemy, nor could they speak the truth of the battles. The need to ensure that morale was maintained within the military and civilian population, and that the secrecy of military movements was safeguarded had stripped the word truth from the world's vocabulary.

From an early age Madame Chessy learned to project an image of carefree optimism. She had loved her husband dearly, however at times during their marriage she yearned for the life the Bonets had once lived. Such thoughts made her feel guilty, which was why she tried to be positive at all times. Marcel had often criticised her simple enthusiasm, playfully at first, then, as years of physical labour on the farm began to take its toll, he grew impatient and gruff.

The trait her husband took umbrage to was the one that saved Marie following his passing. On news of his death, anger and denial had seeped through her, to be followed by a grudging acceptance. She still grieved for Marcel and dreamed of their years together, but she also learned to be grateful: for her boys, the farm, the food on their table and the life she had lived to date. She did not become bitter, simply realistic. She found it absurd that Marcel did not live to see the change in her.

The final metamorphosis from flirtatious girl to pragmatic woman came with the arrival of a letter. The letter, written by Emmanuel, a soldier friend of Marcel, arrived months after the official notification had been received of her husband's death. The correspondence was a revelation. Unlike Marcel's all-too-few letters from the front-line, this despatch had escaped the censor's watchful eye, and it was brutal in description. In it she learned the details of her husband's death. He had been gassed at Ypres in April 1915. A yellow-green cloud had floated towards the men; assuming it was some type of smokescreen created by the Germans, the French had waited in their trenches for it to pass and the attackers to be revealed. The cloud was poison gas. Madame Chessy recalled the letter falling from her hand. A swift, painless end to her beloved's life was the only one that she had considered. It was some days before her courage returned and she was able to read the rest of Emmanuel's note. In some respects, she wished he had not divulged so much.

Many of their soldiers, he had written, had died in and around Ypres and the carnage had been going on for months. The old town was in ruins and the great Cloth Hall, which dated back to the twelfth century, had been partially destroyed, with a number of civilians fleeing to nearby Poperinge. Despite the artillery bombardments that carried on the wind, the French newspapers spoke only of minor skirmishes. Certainly, few people in the Saint-Omer area, including Madame Chessy, had any idea that such major warfare was occurring only forty miles away.

The worst of it was the number of dead French soldiers Marcel's friend spoke of. The word *thousands* was still imprinted in her mind. One, even twenty perhaps, she could comprehend, but thousands? Where were the bodies? Why were people not screaming in the streets? Did they even know their loved ones were dead?

The author's parting words still haunted her: *'Many still think the war will be over soon. Perhaps it will be. There will be no more Frenchmen left to fight.'*

Madame Chessy threw the newspaper atop the embers in the firebox. As a mother she could forgive the military censors. Part of their aim was similar to hers: a wish to give an assurance of normality and hopefulness in difficult times. These were the same attributes she had worked so hard to instil in her home following Marcel's death, and to that end her twins never saw Emmanuel's letter. It had long ago become ash. Yet as a woman she hated the men who had pushed them into war and now lied and glorified it for the sake of propaganda and military strategy.

The coffee was cold. She sipped at it absently, so lost in thought that when a familiar bash vibrated the farmhouse door the drink splashed the back of her hand. Clucking her tongue at the interruption, she wiped her skin clean and opened the sturdy door to a warm summer morning. Roland the dog sat patiently outside.

'Can you not scratch or paw at my door? Must you fling yourself at it like some marauding animal?'

Roland cocked his head to one side and trotted into the farmhouse. He snuffled about the kitchen floor and then whined.

'I should never have made this for you,' Madame Chessy replied, reaching to where a rag ball sat on the top of a wooden dresser.

Roland took the ball in his mouth and walked outside. Two rabbits watched the dog's progress as he covered the clearing in long strides. Now comfortable with this invader of their territory, the rabbits barely paused in their foraging. Madame Chessy was keeping an eye on them. If they continued being so unafraid she would not even need a trap.

'Don't you disturb Francois and Antoine,' she called after the dog. The boys were easily distracted, and having sent them fishing to a neighbouring pond in the hope of some perch for their midday meal, she didn't want Roland to delay them. Roland looked over his shoulder at her. 'Go on, off you go, then.' Some days she honestly thought Roland understood her. The dog broke into a run and disappeared into the willow trees.

A screech from the chicken pen scattered the rabbits. Madame Chessy lifted her skirts and quickly walked the short distance to the barn. Snatching up a pitchfork, she ran back to the boarded-up yard situated a few feet from the farmhouse. The chickens screeched madly inside, and the rooster crowed hoarsely. A fox rushed past the gate, a smudge of tawny red. A fox in summer was not unusual, but mid-morning? Madame Chessy bellowed her anger, opened the gate and rushed at the animal. She was surprised at its size: it was larger than the one that had stalked them during the winter, much larger than a normal fox. It eyed her as it crouched, two hens already dead at its feet. Tightening her grip on the pitchfork, she pointed it at the animal. Instead of trying to escape through the open gate, the fox held its ground and growled. Lifting the pitchfork higher, Madame Chessy brandished it at the snarling animal.

'Ha, ha!' she said loudly, trying to scare it off. 'Get away with you!'

The fox bared his teeth and continued to growl.

Taking a step backwards, she felt the wall of the chicken pen. The fox sprang towards her –

Roland came from nowhere. A mass of grey hair spun through the air like a missile and slammed heavily into the attacking fox. The animals came together in a blur of teeth, limbs and hair. They rolled around the chicken pen, scattering the feathered inhabitants outside. Stunned by the savage battle, Madame Chessy flattened herself against the wall as the animals bit and kicked. Limbs entwined, they rolled across the ground and slammed into the wooden fence. Minutes later it was over. Roland stood with a single front paw on the fox's neck. The animal kicked and snorted wildly, eyes wide. Gradually the fox gasped, then stilled. Roland snuffled at his prey and lifted his mangy head.

'Mama, are you all right?' Francois appeared.

'We heard the noise downstream,' Antoine added, taking in the sight of Roland still pinning the fox to the ground. 'That fox is massive.'

'It tried to attack me,' their mother gasped. 'Roland – Roland saved me.'

'Good boy, Roland.' The dog growled as Antoine approached. 'It's all right, boy.'

'Is it dead?' Francois brushed grit and leaves from his mother's skirt.

Roland whined and gingerly lifted his paw from the neck of the animal.

Antoine turned to his brother. 'He's dead, all right. Come on, boy.' Antoine held out his hand. Roland slowly surveyed the fenced-in area and, as if finally convinced the attack was over, he ambled across to him.

'Is he injured?' their mother asked, gripping Francois' arm for support.

Antoine ran his hands over the dog. 'A torn ear, by the looks of it.'

Francois steered his mother out of the chicken yard. 'Come, let's get you inside.'

'And you, Roland, let's get you inside as well,' Antoine said.

Leaving the occupants of the chicken yard pecking out in the open, they entered the farmhouse. Francois attended to his mother, offering her a glass of wine to calm her nerves. Roland jumped up onto a chair and allowed Antoine to apply an antiseptic balm to his injured ear. The dog rested his head on the kitchen table and yawned.

Madame Chessy patted him affectionately on the head. 'You have been well named, I think,' she said softly.

The soldiers walked down the road towards the village of Tatinghem. They were a raggedy collection of men. Languid and casual in their movements, they didn't march in formation and were busy talking and laughing, their rifles slung haphazardly across their shoulders. They wore slouch hats and woollen tunics that ballooned over their hips, partly because every man's trouser pockets appeared to bulge with unknown contents. Cigarettes hung from bottom lips and their conversation was loud, full of laughter, peppered with the odd curse as they tried to pronounce French words.

Francois and Antoine observed the approaching soldiers from a copse of trees on the edge of the road. It was mid-morning. They had already visited the markets in the village to sell cheese and eggs in order to buy a little meat from the butcher, and they were about to take a short cut home when the soldiers came into view. Francois patted Roland between the ears and then pointed to the shoulder badges on the approaching soldiers. 'Australian,' he advised. They had already met some of them, either on the roadside or in the village, but the Australian soldiers were yet to be billeted to the Chessy farmhouse.

'What on earth do they feed them in Australia?' Antoine mused as they peered through the trees at the passing troops. The men were tall and strong looking and, by all accounts, a mischievous lot. Antoine had witnessed first-hand that many of these soldiers from the great south land had little respect for British officers, and when not fighting were generally more concerned with gambling, drinking and having a good time than showing any form of military discipline.

The twins then turned to watch as a well-drilled platoon of British soldiers approached from the opposite direction. They marched four abreast, arms swinging smartly, their strides precisely timed. A staff car was in the lead, slowing as it approached the Australian contingent.

'Here's a go,' one of the Australians said with a drawl.

Francois and Antoine glanced at each other. Their English had been picked up gradually over the preceding months from the British soldiers billeted at the farmhouse, but they remained intrigued by the Australians' accent.

The shiny black car drew level with the Australians, who paused and stared as if they were holiday-makers. The British troops were close behind.

The officer in the staff car signalled for his driver to stop. 'You salute an officer, Private.'

The Australian he addressed gave a smirk but kept his hands by his sides.

'I'm a colonel!' the officer stated loudly.

'Best job in the army,' the Australian replied. 'You keep it.'

The officer gave an exasperated sigh and tapped the driver on the shoulder. Francois and Antoine grinned as the shiny black vehicle sped off.

'The war's *that* way,' a dark-haired Australian said and hooked his thumb in the general direction of Ypres as the British troops marched by. 'Not very friendly, are they?' he asked the man standing next to him, when he was ignored.

'Bloody convicts,' one of British soldiers replied from the ranks.

'Bet you're pleased we're here, though,' the sandy-haired Australian replied, laughing.

The Australians walked on.

Francois shook his head. 'They're not like the English.'

'That's a good thing, I think,' Antoine decided. 'They're free men and they came here freely. As long as they fight, what does it matter?'

'An army needs discipline,' Francois countered.

Roland looked from one brother to the other and yawned.

Laughter broke out from the tail of the column of men.

'Bloody hot here. You'd reckon the Frenchies would have a pub nearby,' one Australian said, his slouch hat pushed back off his forehead.

'Too right. I'm as dry as an old Arab's fart,' his friend answered.

The men moved on, their laughter ringing through the trees.

'They say they're fierce soldiers,' Antoine said as they turned to begin the two-mile walk back to the farm. 'Remember that wounded Frenchman at the village last week? Shot through the thigh. He ended up at a casualty clearing hospital about twelve miles from Saint-Omer before he was sent to the hospital there. He talked about the Australians as if they were unafraid of war.' Antoine hesitated. 'Unafraid of dying.' He stopped walking. 'Many of them are like us, you know: farmers and villagers.'

'So, they're brave,' Francois stated with indifference.

'Yes, that's what the people are saying.' They walked over a series of low, lightly timbered ridges until the country opened up and they were among the neat yellow-patched wheat fields of their neighbours. The area sown was greatly reduced due to the shortage of labour, and some of the wheat was yet to be harvested. Antoine ran his palm across the heads of rustling grain as they walked along the edge of the half-acre area. 'I would like to see this Great War,' he continued. 'If we wait until we're of age the whole thing could be over.'

Francois shoved his hands in his pockets. 'I know, but what of Mama?'

'She's safe here. There are many soldiers in this area, and we are miles from the front. It's like we live in another country.' Antoine glanced at his brother. 'I want to go, to see what it is like, to be a part of it, to do what Father did.'

Francois rubbed his neck. 'I don't know. We promised Father . . .'

'*He* promised *us* he would stay alive and come home,' Antoine countered. They traversed another slight ridge. Roland bounded through the grass ahead of them.

'Keep walking or we'll be late,' Francois stated.

They crossed a series of small rivulets. Roland led the way, snuffling and barking at anything of interest, including a wary hedgehog, which quickly increased its speed and disappeared into a hollow log.

'It's not right to feel obliged to stay at home,' Antoine continued, 'not when others have sailed halfway around the world to fight our battles for us. We are French, we have fought for our liberty. Don't forget, Francois, that we overthrew a king.'

'And in return we're paupers.'

Antoine cuffed his brother lightly on the shoulder. 'You've been listening to Mama too much. Those days are long gone.'

His brother gave the slightest of nods. They reached the first of their small fields as the sun travelled to the mid-point of the sky. The wheat had already been harvested and threshed, and the bags of grain had been stacked securely in the cellar with the overflow in the barn. Their mother now worried continually about food, and the boys were just beginning to appreciate her anxiety; two dozen eggs and a round of soft cheese had only given them enough money for a small portion of veal, barely adequate for two people.

At the stream, which weaved its way around the base of the slight ridge on which the farmhouse was situated, Antoine halted. The water was clear and fresh. A single perch rode the current, its body a flash of scales within the glimmering liquid.

'I worry about leaving Mama,' Francois said quietly as he squatted by the water's edge. Roland appeared by his side, nudging his head beneath his arm. 'Who will help with the farm chores?'

'There are neighbours,' Antoine replied impatiently. 'We could speak with old Monsieur Crotet. His eldest daughter Lisette is fifteen; she could come and help Mama.'

Francois nodded slowly. 'Yes, I suppose that's an option. If Lisette took on the role of companion and helper, it would certainly ease my worries.'

'And who knows, Francois?' Antoine clapped him on the back as his brother stood. 'We will have to start searching for brides on our return,' he winked. 'This is an opportunity to have one fully trained. Lisette is quite pretty.'

Francois laughed. 'Always thinking ahead, I'll give you credit for that.'

'I've had another thought,' said Antoine, this time more seriously. 'I think that when we return from the war and we're of age, instead of breaking up the farm we should run it together. One-and-a-half acres wouldn't be enough for each of us to survive on.'

'I don't know.'

'Come on,' Antoine replied, 'you don't really think that a family could exist on such small holdings, do you? Why, we have seen the result of such equality.' Antoine grasped his stomach and held his fingers to his mouth.

Francois grimaced. 'You paint a bad picture, brother.'

'Then it's done. On our return from the war we will be partners, yes? Perhaps we may even buy more land.'

At this Francois laughed. 'No one has added to this farm for over two hundred years. In fact, we've *lost* acreage.'

'Exactly. Time to get it back, I think.' Antoine called Roland. The dog ceased rolling in the grass and bounded towards the brothers. 'Roland could stay with Mama as well,' Antoine suggested. 'He proved with the fox that he would protect her.'

'Yes, I think he would,' Francois agreed.

As they neared the farmhouse Francois gave his customary whistle. Roland ran ahead, springing up the grassy embankment and across the ridge, a flash of muted colours in the midday heat. The farmhouse door opened and the boys watched as the familiar outline of their mother moved to stand in the doorway. Light from the fire glowed softly from within the kitchen as she leaned to greet the dog. Then she was standing again, hands on hips, watching their approach, waiting as always.

Antoine firmed his jaw and met his mother's watchful eyes. 'It is decided then?' he said softly to his brother, although his gaze never left his mother.

'Yes, it is decided,' Francois agreed slowly. He suddenly appeared pale and drawn.

As they neared, their mother saw their faces. Her arms dropped to her sides.

≪ Chapter 6 ≫

Sunset Ridge, south-west Queensland, Australia
August 1916

'My dear, why aren't you up?' His mother's hand was cool against his brow. 'Why, you're burning.' She searched beneath the bed covers for his wounded hand, and then with a cry she raced from the room. Dave was conscious of her footsteps falling away like a coin down a well and then there was only silence, a great emptiness that stretched and moulded itself like a blanket. The bedroom wavered as if it had taken on the rippling surface of the river. Pictures merged into the timber walls to slip through joins, a wooden chair seemed to fracture and then reassemble and the ceiling appeared to be only an inch from his nose. At times it seemed as if the world were cracking while he waited in the midst of the unfolding disaster.

A thick haze surrounded Dave and he no longer knew where he was or if he were alive or dead. Muffled sobs punctuated long stretches of unearthly silence, to be replaced by a stream of hushed, indecipherable conversation. One of his brothers drifted above him. He was conscious of light and shade, of movement.

At times he believed that his mother sat by his side; at others it was Miss Waites, with her wisps of hair and wide-eyed concern. Images wafted: water being squeezed into a basin, a weight on his chest, the click-clack of footsteps.

At one stage a long hallway beckoned, and at the end through an open door a marvellous rainbow settled above the red dirt of the property. He was about to step outside when a firm arm steered him away. He tried to fight them off, whoever they were, but he did not have the strength. Then the coughing began.

When the hallway beckoned again it shimmered with light. His hands travelled gently across the walls of the narrow tunnel. There were figures ahead. 'Wait, please wait.' The words stretched over his tongue but made no sound. Something stirred him, trying to gain his attention. The shaking grew in intensity until in annoyance Dave tried unsuccessfully to brush whatever it was away.

'The fever's broken.'

'Thank heavens.'

His shadow-eyed mother and a young man in black towered above him. Dave blinked at the light streaming through the window. He could smell lavender water, and something pungent. The stranger removed the weight from his chest and placed a stethoscope against his skin. The cold of the metal caused Dave's drowsy eyes to re-open.

'Can you hear me, David?'

Dave wanted to answer but the words lay buried in river sand. He imagined digging up the moist soil and searching for the voice he had lost. Instead, a long, racking cough left him exhausted.

'It will take some time, I'm afraid, to regain his strength. There may also be some initial confusion when he wakes up. The delirium was particularly bad, an effect of the high fever and that cough . . . a most unfortunate coincidence to develop pneumonia. I'll re-dress his hand, Mrs Harrow, and return in a couple of days.'

The man was stippled in sunlight as he unwound a white bandage and dropped the material in a basin. 'It was a severe infection, and David was lucky that it didn't develop into acute sepsis. Your lad here was very fortunate, very fortunate indeed.'

Ointment was smoothed across Dave's palm and then a fresh bandage applied. He grew dizzy watching the white material as it was wound firmly around his hand.

'I suggest at least another week's bed rest, and do try to get some nourishment into him. He's skin and bone. Broth and bread for the next couple of days, Mrs Harrow: a small amount every two hours at first until his strength begins to return.'

'Of course, whatever you think.'

'And tomorrow another four mustard plasters applied for no more than thirty minutes throughout the day. And ensure that the powdered mustard is combined with only flour and egg white, no water. I shall leave some flannel cloth for the dressing.'

'Thank you.'

The snap of the doctor's bag and a swish of his mother's skirt signalled their exit.

Dave woke disorientated. A deep blackness engulfed the space surrounding the narrow bed. He blinked, trying to clear the strange visions infiltrating his brain, aware of his mind growing clearer, his thoughts becoming whole. A dream of Miss Waites pressing her lips to his brow was mixed with strange shapes. With wakefulness came a sudden clarity, as if a bucket of cold water had been tossed over his head. Dragging aching legs from beneath the covers, his numb feet hit the cold boards of the floor and he stood unsteadily. The room tilted and then slowly resettled itself as he took a tentative step, his arms outstretched for guidance. Through the window above the rumpled bed a weave of stars circled the black sky. He stared at them until they began to move, forwards and backwards, side to side. There was a great void between and around them and he reached out his hand as if he could push through the willowy darkness to see what lay on the other side. The pull of muscles startled him and he leaned against the roll-top desk for support while searching for a sketchpad and a stick of charcoal. Then, on a whim, he pulled the bedclothes free from the foot of the bed and moved a pillow to the timber foot-board. Light-headed, he crawled into bed as his breathing grew even.

The star-filled sky dominated the window. He lay awake watching the glittering dots until the first smudge of light filtered across the sky. He wondered what the day would bring. His mother would visit first, followed by Cook and at some stage his two brothers, but what of her? He lay quietly, remembering the feel of those lips on his forehead as streaks of smoky reds and pinks appeared beneath a washed-out blue sky.

The blank square of the sketchpad sat untouched on the bed. Dave lifted the charcoal and drew a square, then a circle. He flipped the page to start afresh, his mind a whirr of images. A cloud came next and then the sky at dawn, except that it looked like a series of squiggly lines. He flipped the page again: a stick figure, a dog, a sheep with a cloud for a body. Another blank page confronted him. These everyday images stifled him. He dozed, his thoughts returning to his night visions. An image appeared behind his eyes: a chair, fractured, skew-whiff, as if someone had pulled it apart and then reassembled it in a series of boxes and squares. It was a chair but not a chair. Lifting the charcoal to blank paper, he drew.

Dave felt like a sissy placed in the middle of the veranda, especially because he was sure that Cook and his mother were holding a competition to see who could check on him the most. Hens pecked their way slowly across the front yard. A handful of poddy lambs frolicked in the tufted grass. Occasionally lamb and chicken would cross paths, and flapping wings and affronted bleats would break the silence that stretched out across the house paddock. The sky was a glazed blue, the stables a shimmering concoction of timber and iron. Dave stared at the hazy structure until it merged with the frill of trees bordering the paddock, then he retrieved the sketch-pad from under the blanket and began to draw a chicken.

'What've you got there, then?' Cook set two warm biscuits and a glass of milk by his elbow. 'A chicken?' She twisted her neck. 'I never seen a hen what looked like that.' Tucking the blanket tightly around him, she compared the hen on the paper with the real thing ten yards from the veranda.

The charcoal hen's body was comprised of many different-sized squares, some of which had been obliterated by blobs of crumbled charcoal. 'I guess you're right, but it's not meant to be in propor-tion. I wanted it to –' He considered sharing some of his strange night visions but thought better of it. 'To be different.'

'I always knew that Miss Waites was a bit off in the . . .' Cook tapped her head. 'Teaching you boys rubbish like that. Argh, a woman that demands sheep's stomach can't be of normal thinking. You know what I mean? Stomach, she tells me; sheep's stomach stuffed. I've told her on more than one occasion that we ain't poor Scots in this household, no-sir-ee. We're edumacated people and we eat accordingly.'

Dave flipped the sketchbook closed and bit into a biscuit.

'That's right. You eat that up. Of course, I can be forgiving a person's differences on account of the fact that her countrymen are fighting in the Great War as well.'

After Cook left, Dave considered what a strangely built woman she was. Thin-waisted and wide-hipped, she had stocky legs beneath a black skirt while her torso was thick and long. It was as if she had been stuck at the waist and then pulled beyond stretching point. Dave thought of the chair and the hen – what if he drew a woman like that? What if he drew Cook?

A scatter of leaves tinkled the corrugated-iron roof as Miss Waites stepped smartly onto the veranda. She wore a long brown skirt and a cream bodice with puffed sleeves and covered buttons that ran from the waist to her neck. 'David, how ar ye? Oh, you're drawing. May I see?' The governess flipped between the pages of the chair, hen and Cook. 'Och! That's guid.'

'Really?' A residue of black dust from the charcoal was smeared across Cook's image. David had relegated her to a one-dimensional figure of sparse, curving lines; a saucepan was the only truly recognisable feature. 'I don't think Father would like them. Mother might.'

At the mention of his mother, Miss Waites looked away for just a second. There was the slightest drop of her chin, before her attention returned to the sketchbook. 'Artists are experimenting in many different ways these days. Would ye like me to find ye some books on the subject?'

'You mean there are other people doing things like this?'

'Yes. There is an artist in Paris who is quite well known.' Her teeth chewed softly on her bottom lip. 'Oh, his name eludes me at the moment, however he is quite modern in style. I recall seeing a reproduction of a nude woman he drew and . . . oh, but you're blushing. Artists quite often draw the male and female form in an effort to understand anatomy, David. It is not lewd in any way, I assure ye, despite what the less educated and the prudish would have us believe.' She patted his hand. 'Where was I? Yes, the drawing of the woman. It is a sketch yet quite absolute in expressive force. Everything in the drawing is flat, like the canvas it was created on. There is no depth to the work yet it is strangely compelling. This is what I see in your work, David. Instead of reproducing visible reality, ye have altered it.'

'Huh?'

'Well, look at your chair. It's a chair, but it's *not* a chair. It is as if we are looking at it from multiple viewpoints. Ye have reassembled it and created something totally different, yet your drawing is a recognisable object. I really dinna understand enough on the subject, but this work seems quite unique to me.' Her fingers drifted across the angular black lines. 'I will write away and order some of the latest art journals for ye. In the meantime, to keep the tip of your charcoal pointed and to stop it from crumbling, ye must rotate it constantly.' She picked up the piece of charcoal and pressed it against a corner of the page. 'Ye see?'

'Yes.' Dave was drawn to the care lines at the corner of the young woman's eyes. As he took the charcoal from her hand, their skin touched. Air caught in the back of his throat.

The moment was ruined by the arrival of Rodger. The station hand was at the back gate, a stockwhip looped across his shoulder. 'I heard that you'd been crook. How are you feeling?'

Dave took back the sketchpad, flipping it shut. 'Better, thanks.' If his father were at home, Rodger wouldn't dare to come anywhere near the homestead. Fraternising was strictly forbidden between the domestics and those employed beyond the back gate.

'What tomfoolery is going on out here?' Cook appeared as Rodger walked down the path. 'Get away, you young buck. You know the rules.'

Rodger turned smartly and hurdled the garden fence.

'He only came to see how David was recovering from his illness,' the governess replied tightly as Rodger waved his hat from the safety of the chicken coop.

'Shouldn't you be in the schoolroom?' A saucepan stuck out at a right angle from where Cook's hand rested knuckle-in on her hip.

'Shouldn't ye be in the kitchen?' Miss Waites replied.

'What on earth is going on?' Lily Harrow asked from the front door; their maid, Henrietta, stood on tiptoe to peer from behind. 'I could hear you at the other end of the house.'

'Rodger came to visit David,' Miss Waites explained, 'and Cook took exception.'

'Well, there are rules for a reason.' Lily gave the governess a cursory glance. 'You should be in the schoolroom.'

'Yes,' the governess agreed, stepping from the veranda, 'I should.'

Three weeks later Dave was unsure how he came to be standing in the sitting room at nine o'clock at night in his pyjamas and dressing gown. Usually he and his brothers were in bed by this hour regardless of whether or not they were tired. He rubbed his right foot against his left ankle as his mother continued with her cross-stitch. The needle poked in and out of the material, a yellow flower emerging in the dim light of the kerosene lamp. Feet away, his father leaned over the round table in the centre of the room. Dave could barely see the thick centre table leg and the root-like scrolling foot. Usually the table was crowded with framed pictures of unknown relatives, a selection of leather-bound books and whatever bush foliage his mother could find and arrange in a vase. Tonight, however, the table was covered with papers. For a number of minutes the only sounds in the room were the flipping of turning pages and the fire crackling in the hearth. Finally his father straightened and twisted on his heels.

'Well, I'm glad you brought this to my attention, Lily.'

'It was only the magazines I was concerned about.' There was an edge to his mother's voice and, although she smiled kindly at Dave, he knew something was wrong. G.W. was rocking on his heels, one sun-browned hand grasping at a jacket lapel, the other tapping at his leg.

'Cook drew my attention to them,' Lily continued. 'She was present when Miss Waites opened the mail and Cook was a little upset by some of the content.'

Dave's stomach grew queasy. What had he done wrong? He knew nothing about magazines and he had hardly seen his father since the illness. In fact, the last few weeks had been spent either on the veranda, in his room or, more recently, under the instruction of Miss Waites once he returned to the schoolhouse.

His father glanced impatiently at his fob watch. 'The tardiness of this household appears to be catching. Must everyone insist on being late?'

A knock sounded on the door and the governess entered. G.W. beckoned her to the table and pointed at the material strewn across its polished surface.

'Guid evening. Oh, David's work.' Miss Waites sounded relieved as she joined G.W., the light from the fire glowing between them.

'Mrs Harrow tells me that it was you that encouraged my son to pursue this.' He waved his hand vaguely above the contents of the table, which included Dave's sketchbook.

Miss Waites nodded. 'Drawing? Yes, it was.'

'And you believe this to be an appropriate occupation for David?' The fire popped and fizzed. G.W. stamped out the errant ember.

'David began sketching while he was convalescing,' the governess explained. 'I felt it important that he recommence some form of learning as soon as possible and that such a gentle preoccupation could hardly do any harm. Ye were aware of this, Mrs Harrow,' Miss Waites said in a pointed manner.

'I think you forget yourself, Miss Waites,' Lily replied, gesturing to David and patting the seat by her side.

Without understanding why, Dave felt like a traitor as he sank down in the flowery material. His father resumed the examination of the table's contents, leaving Miss Waites floundering like one of Harold's fish.

'David is very gifted,' Miss Waites began. 'In fact his drawings are very guid and quite beyond anything I've seen, especially in a student so young. I took the liberty of ordering some of the latest information on –'

'This?' G.W. waved a magazine in the air. 'This pink-covered absurdity titled *Blast*?'

'That is the first issue printed last year in London by followers of the Modernist movement.' Miss Waites's exasperation showed itself in a curtness of tone.

'The what?'

'The *avant-garde*, Mr Harrow. It is a new way of thinking for a new century.' Miss Waites looked to the couch for assistance. 'Traditional forms of art are being revised, reinvigorated if ye like, and that is what David is achieving through his sketches. He is experimenting with form and –'

'And what type of *art* is this?' Another magazine was waved in the air. Dave caught the words 'form' and 'feeling' typed in bold print across the front.

'It is an introduction to –'

'It is an introduction to nudity!' G.W. yelled.

Dave's cheeks pinked up at the word. Next to him his mother began to fidget with reels of coloured cotton.

'David has talent,' the governess persisted. 'We must be open to art in all its forms if he is to learn and grow as an artist. If ye read *Blast* you will see, Mr Harrow, that the contributors reject nudes and landscapes because they tend towards a geometric style, yet David is still learning and so he must be exposed to each of art's many forms. Abstract and Cubinism are new words for myself as well, yet in your son's work I see –'

'Enough. While your interest in David's abilities does you credit, Miss Waites, all of this is quite inappropriate for *my son*.' He dropped the magazine on the table. 'Naked people. Really!'

The governess levelled her chin. 'It is art, Mr Harrow.'

'It is improper, Miss Waites. And as for these . . .' He lifted the sketchpad, flipping the pages over to show Dave's drawings. 'These are just, just an *indulgence*.' G.W. slammed the sketchpad on top of the untidy pile of magazines on the table. 'We are at war, Miss Waites, and yet you have my son drawing dismembered chickens, and chairs that don't look like chairs and all manner of frivolous objects. If he must draw then let it be something correct and proper, something worthy of his time.'

'Like what, Mr Harrow?' Miss Waites countered. 'A corpse? A soldier with a rifle? Or perhaps an idyllic scene such as the one hanging above your fireplace – something that requires little imagination?'

The vein in G.W.'s neck grew and pulsed. 'Enough. You will limit your teachings to the prescribed Learners. Do you understand me, Miss Waites? You are excused.'

Dave kept his eyes averted as the door clicked open and closed.

'David.' His mother gathered all her sewing things and, placing them in a basket, closed the wicker lid. 'We are not angry with you, my dear. You have simply been led astray by a young woman who knew no better.'

His father was staring at the painting hanging above the mantelpiece. 'Throw the magazines on the fire, David.'

Reluctantly Dave gathered the magazines and threw them on the burning logs, watching as the pink cover of *Blast* curled at the edges and then burst into flames. Now how would he understand the images that filled his mind? He had not had a chance to look at any of the magazines, and now he never would.

'Go to bed, David,' his mother said softly. 'Take your sketchbook and go.'

His parents' voices rose in argument the moment the door closed.

'I want her gone, G.W.,' Lily demanded, 'and you know why.'

'She is the only governess who has managed to exert some control over Luther. Despite her free thinking, I believe that she should stay.'

Lily tried to calm herself. How her husband could ignore the facts stunned her. Cook remained adamant that Miss Waites had received a man in her room some nights ago, an action that was strictly against station rules, and now the woman had the affront to think she knew best when it came to David's education. 'Luther's formal schooling is finished, G.W. I only send him to the schoolroom occasionally in the hope his letters may improve.'

G.W. arranged his long limbs in an armchair. 'We are partway through the year, Lily. We cannot risk relieving Miss Waites of her position, as it might be months before we find a replacement.' He sighed as if indulging a child. 'Now, on to more pleasant things: brides for our sons.'

'There's little to choose from in the Banyan district.' Lily's teeth grated at the abrupt change of topic. 'We may well have to advertise,' she finished flippantly.

'I see,' G.W. replied tersely. 'Is there *anyone* in the area suitable?'

'Julie Jackson.'

G.W. huffed. 'A paltry six thousand acres.'

'She may well have to do for one of the others; Luther perhaps. She appears strong-minded and sensible, which is not always a common occurrence out here.'

'There's a whisper that the grandmother is German, so I think we can safely omit her. The family emigrated by way of London and there seems to be a tide of ill feeling against them, which is only natural considering the casualties. But what of Thaddeus? Have you made a decision?'

'I have. I have invited the Bantams down in the spring.'

G.W. raised an eyebrow. 'Seventy thousand acres, plus commercial interests in Brisbane. A sound choice, however –'

'I know what you're going to say, my dear: that they are practically just off the boat. I wouldn't have contacted them, but one would assume that they would be partial to linking their name with an established bush family. You are third generation, G.W., while they have been in our country for less than fifteen years. They are also moneyed,' she enticed, although the Bantam fortune was the least of her interest. G.W.'s land gamble had cost them respectability as well as acreage, for bush society was slow to forget a man's folly. Marriage choices for the Harrow boys, therefore, were limited. 'The Bantam girl has not come out into society yet, so we must –' Lily searched for the right word, 'nab her before one of the larger landed families in Queensland shows interest.'

G.W.'s eyes widened in amusement. 'Do you know much about her?'

'Enough. Meredith is the eldest of eight and thought quite attractive.' Lily leaned forward as if sharing news worthy of confidence. 'Connecting the two families and forging friendships at this early age can only assist Thaddeus's suit when the time comes.'

'You seem quite determined.'

She hadn't been initially. Originally Lily simply wanted Thaddeus to marry well and hoped that some respectability might be restored to their family name in the process. No, it was G.W.'s recent talk of war that stirred her. Although Lily was not naïve enough to believe that an engagement would save Thaddeus from the army, he was the eldest and would one day inherit Sunset Ridge, and a promising union might make G.W. think twice before committing him to battle. She could only be grateful that Luther and Dave were still too young. 'You did tell me to make contact with one of the families that we discussed.'

G.W. plucked at a trouser seam. 'Well, when spring comes we shall see if the young woman is suitable and if so we can make some overtures with regards to joining our two families.' On the far wall, which housed a library of volumes both old and new, the Harrow family bible rested between two brass claw bookends. Carried from London across the sea to the new world of Australia, the bible had been passed down through the male line, with every generation carefully inscribed within its pages. Births, deaths and marriages were scrawled across three pages and stretched back seven generations to a forgotten ancestor who had lived and died in the London slums. It was G.W.'s most precious possession.

'I shall look forward to inscribing another generation in our bible.'

'I thought you would, my dear,' Lily agreed.

⋘ Chapter 7 ⋙

Sunset Ridge, south-west Queensland, Australia
February 2000

George caught sight of Will Murray at midday on his way back to the homestead. The countryside had stilled in the growing heat and a bluish haze eddied through the air as land and sky merged. Will appeared distorted in the harsh light, a slanting line of man and horse that stretched unnaturally upwards as they moved in and out of trees, over fallen logs and around scrubby masses. George waited beneath the shade of a partially dead tree, his attention flicking between Will's steady progression towards him and a large goanna ambling across the paddock. The lizard was broad and fat, well fed on the carcasses the drought provided. George spat on the ground with distaste and resumed his wait. The earth was stifling him today. He could feel her hard heat rising up in complaint. She shrunk his lungs with her parched breath and stung his eyes with her gritty presence. He desperately wished it would rain.

Focusing on Will required effort. Having misplaced his sunglasses earlier in the day, George felt as if his eyeballs were receding back into his head. If that weren't bad enough, sweat poured out of him, drenching his clothes, pricking sun-tender skin until the telltale heat rash reappeared and his vision blurred. George ached to be anywhere but here on the beloved family property.

Running his tongue across dry lips, he silently abused the beer he had consumed yesterday. They'd had dry seasons for a number of years, however two years ago things had become desperate and ever since he had been thirsty; thirsty for water, thirsty for grog. It was as if the land had seeped into him so that he too suffered from her relentless thirst, incapable of quenching his own needs or of tending hers. It was the uselessness that ate at him; watching as the land dried and shifted and melted away. At night he was sure he could feel her calling him, and at times he cried for the sight of green grass, for the caress of her rain-wet body. 'Heat stroke,' he muttered. 'Must be heat stroke.' But he knew better. 'Come on, Will, hurry up.' It was Sunday, God's day, as good a time as any for a drink. Water and grog: one fed the other and now he couldn't live without either. His horse shifted restlessly, lifting first one leg and then the other. 'I know, mate, time to head home.' He wasn't one for riding late in the morning, but with four horses to keep active he had to keep his rotation system going. Sometimes he wondered why.

Will dipped his chin in greeting as he joined George under the tree. At twenty-four, he was a lanky-looking lad with an almost perfectly round face. 'Was there a problem with the trough in the wool-shed holding paddock?' he asked in his usual drawl, the corner of his mouth curling.

Ignoring this latest affectation – last month Will had been partial to rolling over his bottom lip when making a point – George wiped sweat from his eyes. 'Nope. No problems that I know of. Today's drama was trying to get the pump going to fill the water tank. It beats me why women need so much water when it comes to taking a shower.'

'Women, eh? Sonia said your sister was visiting. Said she was real pretty, with a brain, and that you should have married someone like that. Well, I mean, not your sister, just someone like that, someone different.' Will's face grew progressively redder. 'You know someone who –'

'Will!'

'Sorry, George. You know me, sometimes my mouth doesn't connect with my head.'

They urged their horses homewards. 'Now, tell me about the trough,' George asked.

'The trough, yeah. Well, it's been cleaned out and the arm was twisted. Works fine now, though.' Will dropped the reins, unhooked his water bottle and unscrewed the lid. 'Bugger.' The inverted container was bone dry.

George squinted as sweat dribbled down the bridge of his nose. 'Our Good Samaritan?'

'Weird, ain't it? You got any water?'

'No, empty. And you're right, Ross *is* a bit weird.' George turned his horse onto the dirt road and together they began to walk back to the house. 'That's two troughs repaired, the windmill and those three sheep that were pulled free of the dam last year after we got that shower of rain.'

Will scratched his nose. 'Are you sure it's Ross? I've never been one for ghosts.'

'I'm sure, Will. Ross Evans is no ghost.'

'Well, I've got to take your word for it, 'cause I sure haven't seen old Ross out here that much.' Will scratched his neck, rolled his bottom lip and squared his shoulders.

'Well, I have, on and off over the years. I've asked him why he helps out on Sunset Ridge but no other properties, and all he does is mumble something about it being his business and nobody else's. Whatever his reasons, I'm grateful for his help. I just wish he'd let me pay him, but he won't hear of it.'

'Maybe he likes you,' Will winked.

George rolled his eyes.

'Maybe he's bored. He doesn't have a job. I know that much,' Will told him. 'Well, apart from looking after his cranky old mother.'

George whistled softly through his teeth. 'She's a tough one all right, that Mrs Evans. She must be nearly a hundred. They sure bred them tough back then.' The wind rose as he spoke, sending a whirl of grit along the track and into their faces. Both men squinted, their lips cracked and dusty. Even the trees they passed looked exhausted by thirst. 'You know, that old girl would have been around when my grandfather and great-uncles were living here at Sunset Ridge. I went to her house once.'

'What?' Will exclaimed. 'You saw the old battleaxe?'

'Yep,' George continued. 'It was a couple of years ago. I hoped to find Ross and pay him for the odd jobs he'd been doing. Well, she shuffled to the front door all bent over and looking like a relic from the turn of the century in an old-fashioned long skirt and blouse.' George puffed out air at the memory of their meeting. 'At first she smiled, and I remember thinking that she must have been a fine-looking woman in her younger days. Well, didn't the old girl give me what for when I introduced myself and told her why I wanted to see her son? She straightened her spine and abused me like a trooper. She told me Ross was a good-for-nothing do-gooder who wouldn't know right from wrong if it bit him on the arse. Then she told me to bugger off back to Sunset Ridge.'

Will burst out laughing. 'What happened?'

'What do you think? I got the hell out of there.'

'You know she and Sonia don't get on.' Will spat dirt from his mouth. 'My ma says Sonia use to pelt stones through Mrs Evans's window when she was young. They haven't spoken for fifty years.'

'You can bet it'll be over some piddling disagreement.'

'Talking about piddling,' Will began, 'you know, a fella was telling me the other day that's it's so dry the trees are following the dogs in the hopes they'll get peed on.'

'Good one, Will.'

'Sorry, George,' Will said, showing no sorrow at all. 'So, are you going to set me up with your sister?' Will smiled hopefully, displaying teeth that resembled chipped tiles. George could smell him from four feet away. Will rubbed his chin. 'I'd shave.'

'She's a bit old for you, mate.'

'Ah, fair enough. My dad always said the older ones were difficult. Get 'em young and train 'em up's always been his advice.'

Will's father was on his fourth marriage and currently living hand-to-mouth on the coast. 'How's your father going?' George asked.

'Average. At least I get the run of the place now. It's just me and . . . well, me.'

'He'll be back,' George placated.

'When it rains.' Will almost sounded hopeful, but for the knotty sound that caught in his throat.

'Yeah, when it rains.' George understood the loneliness eating away at his young station hand. Will chose to stay on the family farm as a caretaker after his father walked off the property two years ago, up to his hocks in debt. The poor bugger simply didn't know any other life or have any other place to go. 'Well, you can have the day off tomorrow and we'll start the circuit again on Tuesday.'

'Sure. Righto.'

If he had the money George would have kept Will on permanently. They rode on quietly, the creak of leather and the snuffle of the horses breaking the monotonous sweep of the earth.

Madeleine sat cross-legged in front of the open trunk in the schoolroom, her mother's rusty key poking from the lock. She was a little annoyed at being delegated the task of going through the last of her father's possessions, and also unsurprised: Jude wasn't the sentimental type where her husband was concerned. Out of politeness Madeleine had been waiting for George to return from his morning ride before opening it, but after a while she decided to begin – if George was involved, Rachael would be too, and Rachael had little tact when it came to Ashley Boyne's death.

A handful of Banyan and District P&A Society show ribbons lay to one side; small holes peppered the red-and-white bands of material where insects had feasted. The pests' trail of destruction through the trunk included an attack on a tweed jacket and a woollen jumper, among other items that had belonged to her father. Beneath the clothing lay a mass of magazines, cheque books and what appeared to be condolence letters written on her father's passing, all clumped together by a yellow stain of past dampness. Madeleine ran her hand across the thick cable-knit of the jumper before sitting it on the pile of ruined ribbons and clothing. Although she was tempted to hang on to something of her father's, there was nothing salvageable here, and in the end Madeleine knew that her precious memories were more important.

Dust careered around the stuffy schoolroom. Madeleine rose to open the single window, but the church-like mosaic of stained glass refused to budge and she contented herself with the meagre airflow through the partially wedged-open door. It was almost too hot to be cooped up inside the near-airless room, and grit cushioned her bare legs, making her sweaty skin itch. Puffing at the hair sticking to her forehead, she scanned a fan of magazines on the floor. So far she had unearthed old copies of *The Illustrated London News* and *The Bulletin*. The handful of art magazines, mainly dating from the 1930s, were an added bonus. Though they were remarkably well preserved despite the water damage, her enthusiasm waned when she realised they were useless. A quick flip through showed no mention of her grandfather's name. Having hoped for a reference to his work, a profile piece on the artist's life or details of a local exhibition, her disappointment was acute.

Tidying the magazines, Madeleine found a mouse-chewed envelope stuck to the back of a copy of *The Bulletin*. She peeled the letter free and carefully opened it. The contents consisted of a handwritten account noting the purchase price for two separate commissions undertaken for a Miss C. in 1918. They were signed by David Harrow. Madeleine hugged the correspondence to her chest before re-reading them. The works mentioned were titled *Now* and *Then* and were unknown to Madeleine. Her breath quickened. Had she discovered two new paintings that could be attributed to her grandfather?

'There you are. What are you doing?'

Rachael squeezed through the doorway as Madeleine tucked the letter out of sight and began to repack the magazines into the trunk. 'Jude wanted me to go through these things for her. You know, family stuff.' Her sister-in-law had a particular way of pursing her lips when annoyed. 'They were Dad's things.'

'Oh, well, if they're your father's . . . You know, George rarely talks about him.' Rachael surveyed the dusty room with distaste. 'Not that I blame him. I imagine it's quite awkward having something like that happen.'

'Awkward?' Madeleine flicked angrily at the mouse droppings stuck to her leg. Rachael had made similar comments in the past, and each one had stung Madeleine.

'Nothing. I didn't mean to offend.'

'My father had a mental-health problem, Rachael,' Madeleine snapped. 'Untroubled people don't walk into a dam with a rifle and shoot themselves after they've been working in the sheep yards with their kids.'

'Of course,' she soothed.

A few seconds later Rachael's footsteps sounded on the veranda and the gauze door clicked shut. Madeleine tried to remind herself that Rachael couldn't help her scratchy personality, a trait that may have been less obvious if the woman had something to fill the hours. Overseeing sporadic renovations was hardly a full-time occupation for the former primary-school teacher whose pre-marital life had revolved around a busy calendar thanks to her prominent family. In some respects Madeleine could understand her sister-in-law's enthusiasm for a David Harrow retrospective. Such an event fitted with Rachael's idea of acceptable pastimes for a grazier's wife and, apart from giving her an instant role to play, held the possibility of pushing her into the local limelight if the proposed plans for the district events and Sunset Ridge ever came to fruition.

Alone, Madeleine retrieved the secreted invoice. Some artists had work-in-progress titles that were occasionally changed to suit the commissioner of the work once completed, meaning there was a chance that these two paintings from 1918 were already accounted for. Madeleine sucked in her breath. There was also the chance that they were new, unknown works. Tracking them down would be akin to winning the lottery. It was then that she realised that something wasn't right. Glancing at the invoices, she closed the lid of the trunk and sat on it. These were the original invoices, not carbon copies. If her grandfather had been owed money for two commissioned works of art, why hadn't he sent the accounts?

≪ Chapter 8 ≫

Chessy farmhouse, ten miles from Saint-Omer, northern France
September 1916

Madame Chessy served up eggs, chips and a little cured ham and poured three glasses of wine. Despite her best efforts she was continually drawn to the space beneath the window where the twins' equipment was stacked. There were forage caps, canteens, steel scabbards with bayonets, knapsacks and, to her surprise, the same make of rifle her beloved Marcel had complained of in one of his letters home. Joining her sons at the table, she pointed to where their rifles leaned against the wall.

'I am surprised they have issued you with the Lebel,' she said.

Francois and Antoine paused in their eating. They were stiffly correct in their new pale blue uniforms, as if the donning of them and their subsequent weeks of training had changed them to men overnight. Beneath their feet Roland slept; stretched out, he matched the length of the table.

'I have already seen one man off to war from this household. Your father said the Lebel was unreliable. It's old, you know, from the 1880s.'

Francois swallowed his egg. Antoine stopped eating.

'There is a newer make and model. You should ask for it when you get to . . .' Her voice trailed off and she reached for her glass. As yet they had no idea where they were to be sent. The wine calmed her and she poured another. 'At least the uniform has been altered. Sending your father off in those ridiculous bright red trousers and kepi cap.' She blew through her front teeth. 'That was the highest form of stupidity.'

Francois and Antoine stared at their plates.

'Eat, eat,' their mother cajoled. 'I'll not send you off on empty stomachs.'

The twins sipped at their wine, and mopped at their plates with bread. Having arrived home hungry yet excited after weeks of training, they were on their second cooked meal of the day – a luxury in these times.

Madame Chessy kept the sadness from her words. 'You will write when you know where you are headed?'

'Of course, Mama,' Francois promised. 'We're not sure but we have heard whispers of new engagements along the Somme River, and the officers we trained with spoke of Verdun.'

The widow stared hard at her eldest. 'What of Verdun? I thought those rumours were nonsense.'

Francois shrugged. 'The Germans took one of the forts there earlier in the year. We have been fighting them ever since.'

'Verdun.' Madame Chessy closed her eyes briefly. 'I don't believe it. It's protected by a ring of forts. Even Attila the Hun couldn't seize it. It has always been –' she searched for the right word, 'secure.' She lifted her chin. 'Verdun guards the northern entrance to Champagne . . . to Paris.' Her two boys remained blank-faced. Her fist hit the table. 'Do you not realise what this could mean?'

The twins were clearly startled by the passion in her voice.

'I'm sorry.' She shook away the image in her mind of the Germans marching on Paris. Her boys would leave her in the early hours of the morning. 'I have bread and cheese for you to take; a little food to keep the hunger at bay while you march. And I have left extra socks on the dresser. Your father always said he needed socks.' Madame Chessy tried to think of conversation that would steer them away from the subject of war, but always her mind returned to it. 'You should take your woollen scarfs too. The rains will come, I feel it in my bones, and then it will soon be winter –'

Antoine stilled her nervous chatter, placing his hand over hers. 'We will be fine, Mama.'

'Of course you will,' she answered. Ever since the boys' return from the village that August afternoon she had dreamed of their leaving, as if in the premeditated grieving she would find the pain dulled when the day of their departure arrived. It had made no difference. If anything, the terrible throbbing in her chest had been partnered with anger. Francois and Antoine had forged her signature of consent when she had refused their request to join the French army, and she truly believed that if she ever met the French officer who allowed her under-age boys to enlist she would kill him with her bare hands. Of course she could have complained and had the enlistment orders rescinded, but she would rather they went into battle with her blessing, than to run away or depart estranged.

'Lisette will be here tomorrow, Mama,' Francois reminded his mother. 'Don't be too hard on her.'

'Yes, yes, little Lisette. We shall be good friends, she and I, so you boys need not worry.'

The arrangements had been finalised a fortnight ago, Monsieur Crotet happily agreeing to his daughter's employment on the Chessy farm as well as acting as a companion to the widow. In return she would sleep and eat at the farmhouse five days a week, returning to her home on weekends.

'And, of course, you have Roland,' Antoine added.

At his name the dog stretched out a leg, knocking the kitchen table and clattering plates, cutlery and spilling wine.

'Yes,' their mother agreed. 'I have Roland.'

It was still dark when Francois and Antoine rose from their beds. They dressed by candlelight, gathering their equipment together as if it were the most natural thing in the world. Their mother could only watch. The time had come to stop fussing over them. They were young men going off to war, so despite her desperate need to hug them soundly and beg them to be careful, she made them coffee and fed them warm bread fresh from the oven. Roland observed this unusual night-time activity with obvious unease. He whined and whimpered, stalking the flagstone floor in a continuous circle until the hen in her straw-filled box fluffed her wings at him on passing. He gave a low growl but moved to the farmhouse door and sat directly in front of it.

'It's time, Mama.' Francois kissed both her cheeks, held her shoulders tightly. 'You will take care of yourself?'

'Yes, of course,' she replied, kissing him back. 'And you,' she tugged gently on Antoine's ear, 'behave yourself and don't get your brother into trouble.'

Antoine grinned and hugged his mother fiercely. 'We *will* be back.'

The boys patted and hugged Roland, who began to howl uncontrollably.

Their mother knelt by the moaning dog's side. 'Go,' she told her two boys, 'and shut the door quickly.' They blew her kisses and were gone.

The moment the farmhouse door slammed shut, Roland again sat directly in front of it, one paw on the timber just beneath the knob. The kitchen grew eerily quiet. Madame Chessy backed away from both dog and door and turned to the stove-plate where the coffee warmed. With shaking hands she poured a cup and then sat heavily at the table. Tears welled quickly and she let them fall unrestrained. It was better to cry the pain out, she decided, gripping the edge of the table. Her knuckles whitened under the pressure and, as her salty tears spread in damp circles on her lap, she tightened her grasp on the ancient wood.

The memories flooded in: the twins in their crib; tumbling in the grass; playing hide-and-seek in the barn; Francois' first fish; Antoine's fall from the birch tree behind the farmhouse. When the ache in her fingers grew too painful to bear she released her grip. A pale dawn light suffused the farmhouse. Her eyes were dry and the words she wished she had shared with her two boys remained unspoken.

The dog had not moved. The coffee was cold and gritty on her tongue. She thought briefly of the past, five years ago, two years ago, six months, two weeks. So much was altered. She wanted wine and she wanted it to be summer again. She wanted so many things that were impossible to have that her life suddenly felt narrow and empty. But it wasn't, of course, she told herself. She had a farm to run, a new help-mate arriving this morning and she needed to believe that the war would be over soon and that her boys would return.

Leaving his position by the door, Roland jumped up onto the chair opposite where she sat.

'And you, Roland, what do you think of this sorry state we find ourselves in?'

The dog swivelled his head towards the door and then fixed his steady gaze on her, his head cocked to one side.

There was something about the way he regarded her, about the way his dark eyes glittered that cleared the remnants of self-pity from her mind. 'You don't belong here with me, Roland.' The words were uttered without thinking yet she knew them to be true.

The dog gave a whimper.

She rose wearily and ran her hand down the length of the dog's spine, ruffled the lank hair between his ears. Although loath to let him go, intuition told her otherwise. When she opened the farmhouse door Roland bounded from the chair, shaking his rangy body. A clean-dog smell mixed with the fresh morning breeze. He paused to lick her hand before walking outside. She followed him, breathing in her changed circumstances. Everything looked and felt different and now, just when she thought there was nothing else to lose, the stirrings of misery welled up at the thought of Roland leaving.

The dog glanced over his shoulder towards his mistress.

'Look after them, Roland. Look after my boys.'

The great animal gave a single bark and then ran across the clearing, down the soft slope of the ridge and jumped the stream.

≪ Chapter 9 ≫

Banyan Show, south-west Queensland, Australia
September 1916

Opening the drawstring pouch, Luther poured the marbles into his palm. A single glass ball stood out amid the imperfect spheres of the clay old timeys. He tossed the ball upwards, catching it with a determined swipe as snippets of laughter floated across the showground.

'What are you doing with marbles?' Thaddeus asked. He was due to meet Harold outside the tent of the bearded lady in twenty minutes, but he knew that Luther was up to something – he just hadn't worked out what. He raised a querying eyebrow as his brother scrutinised the oxblood in his hand, the streaky patch inside it resembling blood as he rolled the marble around his palm with a grubby index finger. 'Well?'

Slipping the marble into his pocket, Luther turned to the small crowd that had gathered through the showground fence. Beyond the milling kids and teenagers in their short pants and skirts was a circle drawn in the red dust. Thaddeus pictured the girl. She was in there, right in the middle.

'Shouldn't you be with Father in th-the sheep p-pavilion, l-looking at th-the other entries?' Luther reminded him.

Thaddeus scowled. As the eldest, his presence was expected at anything remotely connected to the property. Unfortunately the fleece competition paled into insignificance now his thoughts were centred on the girl at the marbles game, a situation complicated not only by what was undoubtedly another of Luther's hair-brained schemes, but also by the imminent arrival of Miss Meredith Bantam, who was coming to stay at Sunset Ridge. With his mother talking about the importance of the right connections and a young man's future, Thaddeus was feeling decidedly like a cull sheep readying to have its throat cut.

Dave appeared around the corner of the pavilion, a sketchbook under one arm. 'Did you hear the news?' he panted heavily. 'They bought the piano.'

'You're not meant to be running,' Thaddeus scolded, 'or sketching that modern stuff anymore,' he said pointedly.

'Mother said that your Miss Bantam would be needing entertainments,' Dave grinned.

'She's not *my* Miss Bantam,' Thaddeus argued.

'Well, I think a piano is a good thing,' Dave continued. 'Anyway, Harold said he would meet you at the marbles, Thaddeus.' As he spoke, a chorus of yells carried from the direction of the marbles game.

'Great.' Thaddeus scrunched the bearded-lady flyer into a ball. Every year at the show it was the same: he and Harold could stay away for a little while, however eventually they found themselves back at the marbles ring. Although they had never discussed the reason for their semi-avoidance of the marbles championship, Thaddeus knew that it went beyond being beaten by a slip of a girl some years ago.

The three of them walked across the dusty ground to where Harold stood on the periphery of the marbles game. Twenty children were gathered in a tight circle. Some of the older boys were taking bets. Two children visiting relatives in the district made the mistake of wagering their marbles against the reigning champion.

'Of course you won't lose,' a red-headed boy argued, pocketing hard candy. 'She's a girl.'

The girl in question emerged from a cluster of admirers and looked with bemusement at the crowd. Short and slight, her long hair was a glossy blonde accentuating berry-brown skin and snow-white teeth. Hitching up a ragged pair of overalls, she spat on the ground for luck. A murmur rose through the crowd as Corally Shaw lay flat in the dirt and rested her filthy knuckles on the ground. During a split second of silence she flicked at her marble with a steady thumb. The ball hit the glass swirly dead on. Her opponent stamped his foot. The two visiting kids were quickly relieved of their candy.

'Killed!' Corally yelled in a clear, bright voice, pumping her fist skywards.

Harold punched Thaddeus lightly on the shoulder on arrival. 'Isn't she something? She's fourteen now and nearly grown.'

Thaddeus watched as Corally plaited her long hair into a single braid that fell over a shoulder. His breath caught. 'She's a baby,' he answered casually.

Harold hunched his shoulders. 'It's different for you.'

'Different? What are you talking about?' Thaddeus could tell when something was eating at his mate.

'Well, your parents have that Miss Bantam from a good landed family in mind for you. Me, I don't have a lot to choose from.'

Thaddeus felt a streak of something akin to nervousness rush through him. 'I've got no interest in Miss Bantam.'

Harold clapped him on the shoulder. 'Mate, it's not up to you. If your parents and her parents reckon you two are a good match, that'll be it. And you never know, she could be a looker.'

'I doubt it.' Across the milling spectators Corally was polishing a marble. Thaddeus didn't want to ask the question but he couldn't help himself. 'So, so you like her?'

'Well, I ain't coming back for the marbles.'

Thaddeus fiddled with the top button on his collar, longing to undo it. He had known this was coming; two mates could only skirt around the marble-playing technique of a girl for so long before the real reason for their interest arose. The marbles competition at the Banyan Show had begun a few years back when Corally arrived in the district with a bag of glass marbles she had won from a kid down south. Thaddeus never did get the full story of how the daughter of a rabbit-trapper learned to play marbles like a demon, but having paraded around the showground in 1912 as if she carried the crown jewels, Corally discreetly chose an area outside the showground and, with her shiny marbles as bait, promptly began to fleece every opponent.

'In a couple of years she'll be sixteen. If I put in a word now, she'll know my intentions.' Harold cleared his throat. 'So will everyone else.'

'Really? I guess Corally will have something to say about it.' Thaddeus tried to sound casual, as if they were discussing the size of a sinker on a fishing line. He searched out Corally's dark-haired friend. 'What about Julie Jackson? She's a better catch and her parents aren't dirt poor.'

'I don't go much on her,' Harold sniffed. 'All that dark hair and pale skin and . . . well, my father says that a woman has to have a bit of go about her, you know, a bit of ability.'

'How do you know she doesn't?'

Harold ignored him. Although Corally and Julie were the same height, Julie was twice her friend's size. Which didn't exactly make her fat, but it certainly lessened her appeal, despite a pretty face made unusual by thick lips.

'What are you two talking about?' Dave asked, moving to stand beside Harold.

'The Jacksons. You've heard the rumours,' Harold said softly. 'Julie's grandmother was a German. The government are on to those sorts. Her father's got to report to the coppers once a week.'

'What for?' Dave asked.

'Possibility of spying.' Harold lowered his voice. 'Covert activities, my father says.'

Dave eyes widened. 'Gosh.'

Thaddeus scoffed. 'What? Out here? What the hell's bells do you think they'd be spying on? How fast the grass grows?'

Dave waited for Harold to answer.

Harold gave Thaddeus a hard stare. 'Have you forgotten how Fritz stabbed those women and babies in 1915? Anyway, we're better off without their sort in the district, and apparently Cummins has already made an offer for the property. He wants to increase his flock.'

Dave tugged at his brother's arm. 'Do you think the Jacksons are spies, Thaddeus?'

Thaddeus rolled his eyes and lowered his voice so Harold couldn't hear him. 'No, Dave, I don't. The war's overseas, not here in Banyan. You remember that and don't listen to any of that spying rubbish.'

Thaddeus watched as Dave walked away, his thoughts quickly returning to Harold's comments regarding Corally. He consoled himself with thoughts of Harold's parents. He didn't think they would be pleased about their only son outing with the daughter of a washer-woman and a rabbit-trapper, especially with Mr Lawrence head of the local chamber of commerce. Across the crowd Thaddeus watched as Corally and Julie linked arms. The two girls were giggling and when Julie whispered in her friend's ear, Corally gave a loud laugh.

'Who wants to play?' Corally asked the crowd surrounding the circle, as Julie joined the onlookers. 'It's keepsies.' Peering at the swirly just won, she dropped it into the pouch at her waist as two ten-year-olds argued over who would challenge next.

'H-hello, C-corally.' Having walked free of the circle, Luther approached. 'I th-think you d-dropped th-this.' Holding out the oxblood, he sat the marble in Corally's palm.

Corally gave a wry smile and tilted her head. 'It's not mine.'

Her voice reminded Luther of treacle. 'Y-you k-keep it.' Up close Corally was all sun-browned skin and blue-green eyes. Having seen the sea in picture books, he reckoned Corally was as close as he would ever get to the ocean. He took a breath. 'H-how you b-been th-then?'

Corally swatted irritably at a fly. 'Good, and you?'

'G-good, real g-good,' Luther enthused. 'How are your f-folks?'

'You know, the same. We went aways a while when me grand-mother fell ill.'

'How's y-your g-grandmother n-now?'

Corally began to dig around in her marbles pouch. 'Dead.' Tilting her head to one side, she pointed at the sheathed tomahawk on Luther's belt. 'Would you really use that on Snob Evans?'

'M-maybe.' He smiled. 'How'd you kn-know?'

Corally gave a dimpled grin. 'I saw you two fighting outside the blacksmith's and then you took off, lickety-split.' She brushed her palms together. 'You know, I'd like to see Snob get what's coming to him. He called me a rabbit-sniffer on account of the fact my pa's a trapper.'

Luther absorbed this piece of information like a dry rag in a basin of water. He took a breath. 'Do you want t-to see th-the b-bearded l-lady?'

'Why not?' Corally glanced around the ring. As there were no immediate challenges, she told the assembled throng that she was taking a break.

Julie Jackson began to walk towards them and Luther knew he had scant time to get Corally away before the Jackson girl ruined everything. Grabbing Corally's hand, Luther dragged her from the marbles ring, past the sheep pavilion and into the throng of sideshow alley. Just to be certain they were not being followed they detoured around the wood-chopping competitors and backtracked before barging through the queue for the shooting gallery.

Thaddeus watched as Luther and Corally disappeared into the mass of people. Had he been mistaken? Did Luther have Corally by the hand? He mentally reworked the picture in his mind: his younger brother had actually taken Corally by the hand and *she had followed.*

'You better talk to Luther.' Harold followed Thaddeus's gaze and adjusted the waistband of his trousers. 'I don't want anyone getting their noses outta joint.'

'Outta joint?' Thaddeus repeated. This was the third year they had stood shoulder to shoulder at the marbles ring. In the past they had shared everything – fishing rods, rifles . . . Heck, they had even built a billy-cart together, and crashed it together. Now here was Harold, his supposed mate, laying down the law to him about a girl, and not just any girl: Corally Shaw.

'Well, yeah, the sooner everyone knows that I've got my eye on Corally the better.'

Thaddeus wasn't sure why he punched Harold on the nose. Maybe it was because of the way he was talking, like somebody's parent, or perhaps he was angry that his younger brother had more nerve than the both of them. The end result was that his flesh cracked Harold's and his best friend staggered backwards.

Thaddeus was rubbing his knuckles, forming the words for an apology and beginning to laugh at the stupidity of his actions, when he saw Harold's face.

Thaddeus woke up on the ground.

Luther still had Corally's hand in his as they bypassed the carousel and arrived at the bearded lady's tent. 'W-what are you d-doing?' he asked as she broke free of his grasp and ran to the rear of the tent.

'My dad calls it being thrifty,' she winked. 'Now, if they catch us, we'll go our separate ways, right?' Hobbled horses were feeding in the brittle grass. Through the paling fence a line of parked drays and disgruntled horses waited for the day's end.

This wasn't quite how Luther had imagined things. He had saved a little money so they could walk right into that tent, hand in hand, in front of God and everyone, but now they were sneaking in the back. Of course, Luther hadn't planned what was going to happen after they were seated in the front row of the bearded lady's tent – it was the getting-there part that mattered. All Luther knew was that he wasn't going to be like every other boy in the district. They might all lose to her at marbles, but he would win where it counted.

Falling to her knees, Corally lifted a loose tent flap. 'Okay,' she whispered, 'this is right near the end benches where the light isn't so good. Stay close.'

They scuttled in under the bottom of the tent and crawled beneath a bench. Voluminous skirts and trousers blocked their view, while above them the audience members whispered to each other.

'How awful. How could a woman look like that?'

'I don't know, love.'

'Well, I don't think it's real.'

'Of course it's real. I paid good money to see this. They'd hardly troop all the way up here to show something that wasn't real.'

Corally and Luther locked eyes and smothered their giggles. Behind them the tiered seating rose gradually to disappear into the darkened rear of the tent. 'We could wriggle backwards,' Corally whispered, her feet hitting a tent pole as she tried to move. 'I can't see.'

Luther smelled burned toffee and manure and sweat, but most of all he smelled the sweet scent of Corally Shaw. He squirmed in the dirt and squeezed up tightly against her, raising a finger to his lips in warning. His hip bone nestled against hers and the warmth from her leg ran the length of his. It was a strange sensation.

'But I can't see anything,' Corally complained.

In a flash his lips were on her gritty cheek. Luther kept the warmth of her skin beneath his for what seemed like long seconds, before slowly pulling away. In the half-light he could just make out Corally's profile. The curve of her cheek was flushed pink. He hadn't planned to kiss her, hadn't even thought about it. But being with Corally was akin to what he imagined beating Harold at fishing would be like. It was unexpected and exciting, and being by her side made him feel good. This was a prize that could not be forgotten at the end of the day. 'Y-you don't have t-to w-worry about th-that Snob Evans anymore,' he whispered as they crawled from the tent. 'W-when are you c-coming b-back t-to t-town?'

Once outside Corally brushed her clothes free of dirt. 'We moved to the outskirts of Banyan, next to the cemetery, on account of me father's rheumatism. He's figuring to work at the lumberyard.'

'Well th-then, I'll be seeing you,' Luther replied.

Corally shrugged. 'Maybe.'

Thaddeus flinched as the doctor probed the bridge of his nose.

'Broken, I'm afraid, my boy,' he confirmed, wedging plugs of material up each nostril. 'Damn annoying injury. I hope you managed to get one on your opponent.'

'It was his best mate, Harold Lawrence, that did it,' Dave explained from where he sat on a bench inside the tent.

'Well, tell your father I'll be sending Mr Lawrence an account, Thaddeus.' The doctor wiped congealed blood from Thaddeus's face and wrung a wash cloth out in a basin of water. 'It'll be sore for a bit. Best you rest in here until it's time to go home.'

'Does it look bad?' Thaddeus asked, his voice thick and halting.

Dave winced. His brother's nose was bulbous and bloody. 'Why did Harold punch you?'

'You wouldn't understand,' Thaddeus replied, trying unsuccessfully to brush dried blood from his shirt.

'You know, after he hit you he just walked away? He didn't even look over his shoulder.'

Thaddeus gingerly touched the tip of his nose. 'Where did Luther and Corally go?'

'Dunno,' Dave shrugged. Having caught sight of Miss Waites, he had been sorely disappointed when he had found her talking to Rodger. The station hand, all shiny like a new shilling coin, had offered the governess his arm, and together they had walked towards one of the pavilions.

Thaddeus got to his feet a little unsteadily and straightened his jacket. His nose felt as if it were at the back of his head. 'Father will have me if I go out looking like –'

Both boys looked at each other.

'The fleece competition!' Dave yelled.

They rushed from the tent, running in the direction of the wool pavilion, Thaddeus's nose throbbing with every step as they dodged adults, children, dogs and a man on horseback. As they reached the pavilion a burst of applause greeted them. The two boys exchanged worried glances and slipped inside.

Dave's mouth made a wide *o* as Thaddeus craned his neck to see past the burly man in front of him.

'Cummins got it,' Thaddeus revealed.

At the opposite end of the pavilion, surrounded by wooden fleece bins, stood their ashen-faced father. Their mother was greeting neighbours, her face a pale mask.

'Did we get anything?' Dave asked.

Thaddeus winced, the action sending ripples of pain through his head. 'Does it matter? We didn't win. And I can't see Luther anywhere.'

The crowd began to break up. About twenty men clustered around Horatio Cummins. The winner of the Champion Fleece was talking loudly, his booming voice swiftly answering questions about breeding and flystrike and yield as if he were standing in a pulpit.

'Hell's bells,' Thaddeus mumbled, as he stepped aside to let people pass. The thoroughfare cleared in front of him. 'Well, come on, Dave.' His younger brother took a step backwards. Thaddeus grabbed him firmly by the arm. 'Come on.'

Their parents, backs erect, made a deliberate point of circum-navigating Cummins's well-wishers. They skirted the display bins dividing the length of the room, quickly making their way towards the pavilion's entrance. Thaddeus thought that G.W. could have swept the pavilion floor clean, such was the ferocity of his gaze.

'Where have you been?' their mother snapped, manoeuvring them away from the doorway. Her eyes widened when she looked directly at her eldest son. 'And what on earth happened to *you*?'

Thaddeus noted the thick worm of a vein throbbing in his father's neck.

'The holy ghost, *look* at you.'

'Lower your voice, G.W.,' their mother replied softly.

Cummins's admirers turned in their direction.

'Not only do you *not* appear when I specifically asked you boys to be present, but *you*, Thaddeus, behave like some, some *gutter-snipe* and end up in a fight.'

Spittle flew through the air to land on Thaddeus's face. He didn't dare wipe it off. He stepped backwards and was immediately stopped by the pavilion wall, his hand coming to rest on a fleece, lanolin greasing his palm.

'It wasn't his fault, Father. Harold did it,' Dave interrupted, not sure if stepping into the argument was a wise thing.

'It was nothing,' Thaddeus explained.

'*Nothing*! You have a bloodied nose, your shirt is ruined – and you're telling me it's nothing. People don't fight over nothing. *Gentlemen* don't fight at all.'

'It was Harold?' A shadow of disappointment crossed Lily's features.

Dave understood Thaddeus's problem. Harold was his best friend; how could he blame him? Yet if he didn't, Dave dreaded to think what the punishment might be.

'Harold did that?' Their father pushed his hat back off his forehead. 'Why?'

'I don't remember,' Thaddeus mumbled.

His mother laid a cool hand on his skin. 'Dreadful, just dreadful.' She clicked her tongue disapprovingly. 'G.W., there is a time and a place to address this issue, and it is not here. We must load the piano and get Thaddeus home. Heavens, we have Miss Bantam and her companion arriving in a matter of days.' Their mother rested her arm over their father's and spoke pointedly to the boys. 'Your father's fleece won second place. We are very pleased.'

G.W.'s tight-lipped grimace suggested otherwise. Thaddeus held out his hand and reluctantly they shook.

'Yes, congratulations, Father,' Dave added.

'You were meant to be here too; instead you were standing ringside while your brother was hurt.' He stuck a finger in Dave's chest. 'You have *no* excuse.'

'Come now, not in public.' Their mother dabbed a handkerchief at a streak of dried blood on Thaddeus's cheek. 'We have a piano to load.'

Thaddeus's nose was red and bulging and the swelling seemed to be extending across his cheekbones. Combined with the blood-sodden wads of cotton stuck up each nostril and the dried spots splattering his shirt, he looked a mess. As they walked through the crowd in search of Luther, Dave noticed women whispering on their passing. A few men nodded as if in shared pain, while some of the local kids stopped their skylarking and blatantly stared. Dave straightened his shoulders and kept in step with his brother.

'Of course, it was bound to happen,' G.W. said stiffly. 'You can't expect any better from tradespeople. They are much like Cummins,' he continued. 'Who is *he* to lecture the assembled crowd on sheep breeding? Well, I suppose we can't expect much better from the likes of him.'

'Yes, dear,' their mother soothed.

Luther tailed Snob Evans for a good twenty minutes. It wasn't difficult to remain out of sight, for the crowds, although beginning to dwindle, were still thick enough for concealment. He bided his time, waiting for Snob to begin walking to the far end of the showground on his way home. Only feet from the entrance gate, children would be bobbing for apples. There were four barrels in a row filled with water, and beyond stood a number of gnarly-trunked trees and the fence encircling the grounds. It was the perfect spot for a fight.

Snob was engrossed at the shooting gallery, having talked his way into a free second shot. As Luther waited by the Banyan Show Society office he caught a glimpse of Thaddeus and Dave through the crowd. A few minutes more, then he would go to the wool pavilion. As his resolve wavered, he thought of Corally. He wasn't sure what came next where girls were concerned, however a kiss was a fine start. He pondered the feel of her skin beneath his lips, fixing on their conversation at the marbles ring.

'I'd like to see Snob get what's coming to him . . . He called me a rabbit-sniffer on account of the fact my pa's a trapper.'

Luther kept his hand near the tomahawk clipped to his belt and trailed Snob Evans as he left the shooting gallery. He caught up with him near the apple-bobbers. A row of six-year-olds, wet-faced and laughing, were trying unsuccessfully to grab at the floating fruit with their teeth.

'Hey, S-snob.'

Snob Evans swivelled on his heels. 'Well, if it isn't b-bush b-boy b-bandicoot. I see you've still got the tomahawk that Daddy gave you.' Rolling up his sleeves he lifted his fists. 'Come on, I feel like giving you another hiding. Come on,' he beckoned.

This time a round of fisticuffs wasn't enough for Luther.

'What are you going to do, cut my f-f-f-finger off, b-b-bandicoot?' Snob's lips stretched into a semblance of a smile.

'You p-put your finger on th-the fence and I'll ch-chop it.'

Snob laughed. 'You'll chop it, will you, b-b-bandicoot? Come on, boy, every time we have a bit of a scuffle your brother suddenly appears to save you. No, you won't chop my finger off because you're afraid and you can't fight. You're just like that older brother of yours. You know his best mate clobbered him one this afternoon? He ended up in the medical tent with a busted nose, and that runty young brother of yours was there to hold his hand.'

'L-liar,' Luther accused.

'I dare you to cut my finger off. I dare you.' Snob held up his hand, extended his forefinger and rested it atop the paling fence.

Luther ran his fingers across the leather sheath covering the blade of his tomahawk.

'Well, come on, b-b-bandicoot. I haven't got all day.'

Saliva gathered in Luther's mouth. He pulled the tomahawk free of his belt as Snob extended his finger on the splintery upright post. He was grinning like an alley cat.

'That's what I thought. You squatters' kids are all the same: cowards, cold-footers, the lot of you. Holed up on your spreads dodging the war.' Snob spat on the ground. 'Well, not me, I ain't no coward – I'm joining up this week.'

Luther's insides curdled. An image of Corally's sea-green eyes swirled before him. The blade of the tomahawk flashed across the air, slicing neatly through the flesh and bone just below the knuckle.

Snob Evans stood in stunned silence for the barest of seconds before letting out a howl of pain. 'My finger!' Snob screamed. 'You cut my finger off!' The severed finger lay on the upright post as blood seeped across Snob's shirt where he clutched the maimed hand to his chest.

Luther jammed the tomahawk back in his belt and did the only thing possible: he ran. He took the winding back way past buildings and tents, his boots kicking up dirt and sticks, his breath coming hard as he ducked under tethered horses and past clusters of chatting men. His whole body buzzed. He had to tell Corally. He imagined pearly white teeth as she smiled at his news, her slim hand slinking into his. Guessing Corally would be back near the marbles ring trading her less precious balls for anything of equal value, Luther battled want with duty, until reluctantly he zigzagged between tent pegs and headed for the sheep pavilion.

'Where have you been?' Dave asked as he nearly collided with his brother at the entrance to the pavilion. 'We're ready to leave and I've been looking for you everywhere. Mother and Father are furious.'

Luther eyed the rolled red ribbon in Dave's hand. 'N-not second p-place again?' he complained. 'How c-can a m-man keep w-winning year after year? You'd reckon th-that th-they'd give someone else a t-turn. B-besides, our fleece deserved to w-win.'

'Come on,' Dave urged, pulling Luther behind him. 'That's not the worst of it. Thaddeus punched Harold and Harold belted him back.'

'What?' Luther instantly recalled Snob Evans's taunt. 'W-what about?'

They ran past the handicraft pavilion. 'I don't know. Thaddeus isn't talking but he's got a busted nose.'

'A b-busted n-nose?' Luther replied, muttering apologies when he nearly ran into two women. They cut across the main showground thoroughfare towards a side entrance, where exhibitors could park their drays.

'Yes, and Mr Lawrence and Father had an argument about it as they were loading the piano and Mother took to weeping.'

'Hell. Where are they now?'

'Waiting for us. The piano has been loaded and there's a newspaper photographer wanting to take a picture of us with the piano. Father only agreed to it because Cummins'll be getting his picture in the paper again too.'

They ducked under the fence, skirted a row of horses and ran past a family with a bedraggled group of youngsters tiredly bringing up the rear. Among the collection of wagons, drays and two-seater sulkies, a small crowd had gathered around the Harrow dray, the piano sitting aloft. A moustached man with a notepad was talking to G.W. Luther squeezed through the onlookers and stopped a few feet from his father, who immediately crooked a finger beckoning him forward. All of a sudden Luther didn't feel that cutting off Snob's finger or missing the fleece presentation was a smart idea. The reporter was closing his notebook.

'Well, what's *your* excuse?' G.W. was in Luther's face, his breath sour. A few feet away their mother dabbed carefully at his brother's face. Splats of blood dotted Thaddeus's shirt front and his nose was highlighted by a blue-green tinge. Drawing Dave from the safety of the crowd, Lily positioned him next to Thaddeus in front of the piano-laden dray. A photographer fiddled with a tripod, a black cloth over his shoulder.

'Well, speak up, boy,' G.W. persisted.

Looking his father squarely in the eye, Luther apologised for missing the fleece presentation, as a chorus of voices started to yell his name. He imagined the sting of his father's leather strap. 'I-I had a fight with S-snob Evans,' he explained as the onlookers turned towards the commotion. 'He's b-been c-calling me a b-bush b-boy b-bandicoot for years and fighting m-me every t-time I go to t-town. He's b-been –' Luther searched for the right word, one that would appeal to his father's sense of family honour, 'ungentlemanly t-towards C-corally Shaw.'

G.W. didn't blink.

'H-he c-called me a-and Dave and Th-thaddeus c-cowards.'

'Cowards!'

Luther thought that old G.W. might explode.

Looking behind him, Luther saw the local copper, Mr Raymond Evans and a couple of townsfolk walking determinedly towards them. 'There he is,' the baker yelled, increasing his pace.

'H-he dared m-me t-to cut his f-finger off with my t-tomahawk.' An image of severed flesh flashed into Luther's mind. 'S-so I d-did.'

'You *what*?'

The photographer, ignorant of proceedings, steered Luther by the shoulder towards his two brothers. The picture was snapped just as Raymond Evans and the constable arrived. Luther looked at the half-circle of people gathered around them and spied Corally. She stood next to Julie Jackson, who looked astounded.

'What were you doing with her?' Thaddeus asked Luther, his voice nasal and clotted.

Luther barely heard him as he gave Corally a crooked smile.

≪ Chapter 10 ≫

Verdun, France
September 1916

Dear Mama,
We have reached our destination. Ours has been a long trip on foot interspersed by periods of travel via train and at one stage a lorry. Everywhere we go we pass soldiers and automobiles, lorries and trains loaded with men and munitions. The scale of this war must be very great indeed. Antoine and I have found our little free time much taken up writing letters on behalf of others. Most of the farmers who have enlisted cannot read or write and this is equally true of some of the villagers we have met. I must admit we have prospered from your education because we manage to barter goods for our services – wine and cigarettes – although Antoine says I shouldn't be telling you such things.

Roland is with us. I'm sorry that he escaped, for we wished him to stay by your side while we are away. He bounded up behind us not three hours after we left the farm, and he was greeted with much enthusiasm by most of the men when he joined our platoon. Our commander has classed him as a comfort dog, and certainly to date he has been very good for morale. We wondered if he would be allowed at the front when we go into battle, and I have it on authority that a blind eye would be turned in Roland's regard. I must say, Antoine and I are very pleased at this news.

For the past few nights we have been billeted in a barn on the edge of a village not far from the front. Both Antoine and I were very surprised, for the straw was not fresh and there are fleas and any number of small spiders that enjoy feasting on the men as they sleep. Roland has suffered heartily, however this morning we carefully wiped him down with a rag soaked in petrol and managed to ease his itches for a time. Last night we ventured into the village for a drink and had to leave our seats when a group of our countrymen entered the establishment. I cannot tell you how badly they smelled, Mama. The raw stench of them was something to behold, yet their uniforms appeared reasonably clean. We learned later that they were on leave from Verdun. Although we were told that the smell was the stench of death neither Antoine nor I paid much heed to the comment. The villager I queried was complaining of a stolen pig, and food is indeed in short supply.

I guess you would have planted the first plot of potatoes by now. I hope Lisette is a comfort (Antoine thinks she may well make a fine wife for one of us but I'm not in that much of a hurry). Well, I must turn in; tomorrow we head to the front-line. We will join part of the great defensive surrounding Verdun and we are very proud to be part of such an undertaking. Although we are fifteen miles from danger we hear the big guns blazing day and night. It appears the Germans have howitzers that have been nicknamed 'Big Bertha'. Our captain tells us that such guns can fire a single one-tonne shell nine miles, and by the great noise that shudders the very air we breathe I am beginning to believe him.

The Red Cross is here, and one of the medics has offered to post mail for us. Wish us God's speed, Mama, for we go to do our duty.
Your loving sons,
Francois and Antoine (and Roland)
PS Enclosed is a photograph of myself and Antoine taken while in Paris on leave. What a wondrous city – but I will save our sightseeing for another letter.

All around them, men moved back and forth, righting equipment, checking the injured and carrying away the dead. The soldiers were unrecognisable in the dim light. Their features were taut and their eyes hollow. They went about their tasks efficiently as they cleared away debris and tended to the wounded, their emotions betrayed by the odd trembling hand or a voice touched by a faint tremor. Some of the injured moaned softly; a few screamed out in pain; others simply accepted their fate and faded away into the dank earth.

Roland was scarcely noticed amid the aftermath of the battle. He walked carefully between the soldiers. His progression halted as the odd man reached out distractedly to pet him or tweak an ear. Occasionally a resting soldier would call him over and hug him tight.

'Rest easy, Roland,' Louie Pascal said softly as the great dog halted at his side. 'I have seen your masters. I am sure they will return.' Louie tried to sound hopeful even though Francois and Antoine were yet to return from no-man's land. The area of land that separated the two armies was controlled by neither side and divided by a barbed wire fence. Here the countryside was pitted from shellfire and littered with the debris of war: guns, spent cartridges, wooden crates and bodies. Louie squatted beside the dog. Roland licked his hand. 'I think you have a sixth sense, otherwise you would be howling like last time. Remember, when your boys got lost out there for many hours?' Louie nodded over his shoulder. 'But they returned then, as they will return again.' He followed Roland's gaze as a French bulldog barrelled past. Weaving through clusters of men, the dog raced along the trench to where the officer in charge stood with a ragtag group of soldiers. The dog stopped at the officer's feet, sat obediently and waited for the cartons of cigarettes to be removed from the strapping about his body. With the precious cargo unloaded and a brief pat given in thanks, the bulldog was off again, his muscly legs striking the soft soil in an ungainly stride as he began the trek back behind the lines to the supply depot. A gash on the dog's flank glistened with blood.

'Back to work, eh, Roland?' Louie said tiredly. Standing, he watched as Roland took a step backwards, squatted on his hind legs and then sprung up onto the trench wall. The dog gained purchase on the sandbags rimming the top and scrambled over and into the dark.

Louie whistled softly. 'Come, boy.'

The dog turned briefly towards him.

'Damn mongrel, he never listens to anyone,' another voice commented.

Louie whistled again. 'He's never gone out onto no-man's land before.'

The rain had begun during the night, a soft mizzle that threatened never to stop. Louie squinted across the forbidding territory as a pall of smoke drifted across the battlefield. An acrid smell carried on the breeze as Louie watched the dog pad out across no-man's land. The artillery was silent for the moment and across the narrow space between the two warring battlelines Louie could hear the soft moans of the wounded. The voices told of suffering and despair, and of the desperate hope of being saved. He watched Roland spin the length of his body, momentarily disorientated by the need surrounding him. The voices carried clearly across the terrain to merge with the wounded who lay beyond the barbed wire.

Roland continued across the battlefield. Bodies lay strewn across the charred ground, and in the places where they were piled too thick to avoid, he trod gingerly among them. Men with stretchers were picking their way through the dead and wounded, while parties of soldiers joined the search for survivors. The men moved low to the ground, wary of being picked off by a canny German.

'Anything there, boy?' a Frenchman whispered.

Roland looked up from the fallen men he had been sniffing and whined.

'That's what I figured,' he replied, drifting away.

The dog cocked his head sideways. It was still a few hours until dawn and fighting had broken out again to the right of their position. Artillery fire rang across land that had once been a field. Decapitated trees were silhouetted against arcs of light, as flares lit up the area. When the big guns began again Roland cringed, stopping near the rim of a crater. The stench of blood was strong, the scent of death stronger. A tangle of men littered the dank interior. Lifting his head, Roland sniffed the air.

A shell hurtled overhead and Roland flattened himself length-ways next to a dead soldier, burying his muzzle in the ground.

'Roland, is that you?'

The dog pricked his ears and sat up. Francois' expression was grim. A wounded Frenchman was partially slung across his back and he dragged another by a bloody wrist.

'You could be shot, you silly mutt.'

Roland bounded over the fallen soldier, gave a single bark and rested large paws on his master's thigh.

'Shush, boy.' Francois carefully lowered the soldier he gripped by the wrist to the ground and ruffled Roland's head before adjusting the man he carried. 'Antoine is fine. He's helping one of the wounded.

I need you to stay here, with him.' He nodded to the wounded soldier lying motionless on the ground and patted Roland. 'Stay.'

Roland glanced at the man he had been tasked to stand guard over, at the upturned earth and strewn men, and began to follow Francois.

'Stay.' Francois waved a palm at him.

Dropping his head, Roland returned to sit by the man's side as his master merged into the dark. A few minutes later a flare illuminated the pitted, twisted landscape. He craned his head in an arc as the light sheeted the sky. By his side the wounded soldier groaned. He whimpered in solidarity and licked the man on the face. Blood shone on his tunic near the shoulder. The fine spray of rain gradually intensified. Soon splats of rain were hitting Roland's nose and he peered skyward as the water began to seep through the hair on his back.

'Help me.'

The words were barely audible. Roland turned in the direction his master had taken. Another shell ripped overhead and then another. The hair on his back quivered. The big guns were firing in earnest and they appeared to be getting closer. Each strike shook the ground, the vibrations rippling through his body. The soldier gave a rasping cough. Rifle-fire peppered the ground nearby and in an instant Roland was sprawled across the wounded man, the wet warmth of blood matting the soft hair of his belly as he tried to protect him. A shell landed nearby, spraying them with dirt. Then a whistle sounded.

Roland sniffed at the Frenchman. Rifle-fire continued to buzz over the land and then there were fierce yells as hundreds of Frenchmen charged across the open ground. Carefully latching his teeth onto the injured man's tunic near the neck, Roland clamped his jaw shut. Digging his hind legs into the dirt, very slowly the dog began to drag the man back across the soggy ground towards the safety of the French front-line.

119

Each step tore at the dog's jaw muscles and sent ripples of pain down his legs. Every movement was shadowed by shell-fire and hampered by the fallen. Roland reached a shell crater and dragged the man down its sloping walls to safety as the bombardment increased. A filthy hand reached out from the gloomy depths and the unconscious man tumbled to safety, then the same hand reached for Roland and with one quick movement tugged him deep inside. Roland began to slide to the bottom where a stinking sludge awaited. Inches from the crater's pit, the man caught him by the collar.

The dog bared his teeth.

Antoine turned to Roland, his hand outstretched, moisture clouding his eyes. 'My friend,' he cried out softly, 'my old friend.' He pulled the dog roughly against his chest. 'You'll be all right, boy. I think we will have to sit this one out, though.' He hugged Roland as the sky lit up and the ground shook fiercely. Dirt rained down from above and around them as the edges of the crater crumbled. Antoine shielded Roland's face from the flying dirt as the rain caused rivers of filth to run down his own.

Hours later Antoine stirred. Roland's nose was pressed against his cheek, the dog's warm breath reminding him of the farmhouse and their adventures along the edge of the stream. He turned, expecting to see Francois snoring next to him. Instead there was a wounded soldier. Antoine held his hand over the man's face. The puffs of air against his palm signalled life. If he had not seen it with his own eyes Antoine never would have believed that Roland had saved the man's life. Yet it was his dog that had appeared out of the chaos of battle, determinedly dragging the unconscious man into the same crater he had been blasted into.

Antoine's ears still rang from last night's explosion. He had been lucky not to be injured. He scrambled up the side of the shell hole and peered over the rim. The land was damaged beyond repair. Great gaping holes filled his vision, smoke layered the air and the ground was littered with dun-coloured shapes. Antoine blinked, rubbed his gritty eyes and tried to imagine the field that had once existed in place of this hellhole. The first streaks of dawn speared weak sunlight across his field of vision and he grew ill at what he saw: the dun-coloured shapes covering the ground were men, hundreds of men. The mass of bodies, both French and German, were motionless, their uniforms covered in drying mud.

'Time to go,' he whispered hoarsely to Roland. Antoine took hold of the wounded man and dragged him closer to the lip of the crater. He scanned their surrounds again. The groans of the wounded were carried by a soft wind. He checked his rifle, patted his ammunition pouch and, ensuring Roland was at his side, scrambled up the muddy crater wall and out onto open ground, pulling the wounded man along with him. Roland followed and together they began to crawl towards the trench, the wounded soldier between them; Antoine on one side, Roland on the other, his teeth lashed once again into the man's tunic.

'*Sacré bleu,*' a French sentry called out as he spied movement beyond the trench. 'There are two men and a dog alive out there!'

A row of soldiers, including Louie, peered carefully over the trench parapet. A hundred yards away the distinctive pale blue uniform of a French infantryman crawled through the mud, dragging a wounded man. On the opposite side of the prone body the hairy rear end of a large dog was just visible, his hindquarters digging into the wrecked earth of the battlefield as he helped drag the soldier to safety.

'It's Roland the dog and one of the Chessy boys,' Louie called out, breaking the silence and rousing the French soldiers to action. They cocked their rifles and scanned the area for any sign of the enemy as three men clambered out of the trench and, bent double, moved as quickly as they could through the thick mud to render assistance.

Roland was stomach-deep in the water-logged area but still he kept tugging.

'Let go, Roland,' Antoine insisted with a slap to the dog's muzzle. 'There are others here to help.' Prising Roland free, they hurried to safety as the soldiers gathered up the wounded man.

'I wouldn't have believed it if I'd not seen it with my own eyes.' Louie offered water to Antoine. 'That dog was helping you drag him in.' He pointed to the rescued soldier who lay waiting for stretcher-bearers.

Antoine gave Roland a slurp of water from the offered bottle and lay back against the wall of the trench. 'Good boy, Roland, good boy.'

The dog licked his face and lay down by his side.

'There you are!' Francois waded through the muddy trench, patted Roland and grinned at his brother in relief. 'I was wondering when you would show.' He squatted by their side. 'It was a tough one last night.'

Antoine could barely nod.

'Is he okay?' Francois asked, running his hands across Roland's body. 'I left him with one of the wounded.'

'He's exhausted. He helped me bring in one of our men.'

'Really?' Francois raised an eyebrow.

'It's true,' Louie interrupted. 'This dog helped rescue one of our men. I saw him.'

'Then he *was* well named,' Francois decided. He patted Roland thoughtfully. 'Tonight we move back to the reserve trenches.' He began to roll a cigarette. 'I think we have to get Roland away from here. Maybe send him back to field command until we're on leave again and can give him to a villager or a farmer for safekeeping.'

Louie scratched at his hairline as the dog gave the brothers what appeared to be a flinty stare. 'Hmm, I don't like your chances.'

≪ Chapter 11 ≫

'Reform school! You can't send Luther to reform school!' Lily Harrow cried.

Dave picked another sliver of bark from the tree with his pocket-knife. Behind him his father crunched gravel as he paced out five feet, turned abruptly on his heels and stalked back in the opposite direction. It was the tenth time the screech of gravel met with his father's horsehair boots, and Dave was becoming increasingly nervous. He turned from the tree outside the Banyan Courthouse to gaze blindly up the main street of Banyan as he thought of Luther locked up in the cell within the courthouse. His brother had been pronounced guilty for attacking and maiming Snob Evans and was now a juvenile offender.

Dave listened to Thaddeus's stomach rumble as a dray clattered down the dirt road. On the courthouse steps above, groups of people – townsfolk, neighbours, friends and gossipers – waited. A line of boys, all of whom Dave knew, were leaning over the railing sniggering. It seemed that every kid in the district had been dragged into town to witness Luther's humiliation. His brother was being made an example of.

'The whole district's laughing at us,' Thaddeus muttered. A smudge of blue-green still tinged his nose and eyes. 'Look at them standing up there, waiting for the show to re-start. We may as well pitch a tent and hang up a shingle and make a bit of money out of this debacle.' He sat on a bench in the shadow of the courthouse and resumed his blank stare of the street. Dave joined him. They both knew he searched for Harold.

'Lily,' G.W. plucked at his shirt collar, 'right now Meredith Bantam is probably staring out the window of the Banyan Boarding House thanking God that her reputation has not been sullied by association with the Harrows. Can you not see how Luther's actions have tainted the future of this entire family? My God, this country is at war and my own son is disfiguring young men!'

'You've heard Luther's side,' Lily entreated. 'Why punish him further after what he's been through? His judgement may have been clouded, but he was only trying to protect a young lady's reputation and his brothers' characters. And *you*, G.W., would punish him forever for this small matter —'

'Small?' G.W. yelled. 'You think it *small*? When a boy has been maimed and the Harrow name stained beyond repair?'

Dave picked at the splintering wood on the bench and saw his family cracking. Things may not have been so bad were it not for Meredith Bantam. Having been delayed by rain, the young woman had arrived in Banyan the day Luther's trial commenced. Her chaperone, a wily aunt of advanced age, had been quickly illuminated by the townsfolk as to Luther Harrow's shenanigans and immediately booked return passage to Brisbane on the next Cobb & Co. coach. They were due to depart today, having ignored all attempts at communication by the Harrows. 'What do you think will happen?'

'Unless Mr Riggs can do something . . .' Thaddeus's words tailed off, leaving Dave with visions of Luther being carted away, never to be seen again. 'Father thinks Luther should be made an example of for the sake of the family's reputation.'

Dave wasn't sure they had much of that left. Luther's attack on Snob Evans had made the front page of the *Banyan Chronicle* every day for the past week and had warranted a whole column on page two of the *Brisbane Courier*, and the *Sydney Morning Herald* also ran the story. The newspapers had branded Luther a delinquent and the letters to the editor confirmed that this opinion went beyond the printed word. The Harrows' lawyer, Mr Riggs, tried to console the family by explaining that murder and mayhem always led the news. His words didn't help. The war abroad was worse than ever. Brothers, sons and husbands were dying in the hundreds. People were aghast at Luther's behaviour. 'You know,' Thaddeus said quietly to Dave, 'Father's like an old ram in a drafting race. Animals like that, they won't go forwards or back. You can prod them and push them as much as you like but stubborn refusal is all that you'll get.'

The lawyer arrived in a sweep of black cloth with a clutch of papers under one arm. He wore a cropped beard and tufted whiskers that extended an inch beyond his cheeks. Mr Riggs was Luther's last chance.

'I never thought it would be this bad,' Thaddeus continued, as the lawyer spoke quietly to their father. 'Mother said that *trade* people don't take landed people to court.'

Dave would never forget the words spoken within the courthouse over the past few days. Snob Evans's lawyer had accused Luther of affray and assault and malicious wounding and intent to maim. In reply, Mr Riggs argued that Snob Evans's continued bullying of Luther and his penchant for street fights had come to a head when he had verbally abused fourteen-year-old Corally Shaw. Luther had simply tried to safeguard a young woman's honour, albeit rather enthusiastically.

When Corally took to the stand, swore to tell the truth and confirmed that Snob Evans had indeed called her a rabbit-sniffer,

Dave felt the mood of the courthouse change. It didn't last. Ignoring the judge's gavel, G.W. criticised Snob's father, Raymond Evans, reminding the courthouse of the length of time the Harrow family had resided in the district, claiming family reputation and good standing versus a narrow-minded, upstart tradesman.

Dave rubbed his shoes in the dirt until a small mound appeared. He was worried about Luther, and about what would happen if and when they all returned home. During the hearing, Snob's lawyer had tarnished all the Harrow boys with accusations of delinquency and thuggery. Even Thaddeus's fight with Harold was dredged up. Fortunately the Lawrences elected not to get involved. Cook told Dave that the Lawrences were smart people who weren't going to be damned by association.

'Mr Harrow,' the lawyer began, 'all this can be ended quickly and painlessly. In a few minutes the court will be back in session. You need only say the word and Luther will be released into your care. The judge, as you know, doesn't feel the need to make an example of Luther.' He raised a fluffy white eyebrow. 'Not during these arduous times.'

'He has disgraced the Harrow name,' G.W. replied, his lips trembling.

Lily Harrow squeezed her husband's arm. 'My dear, *please*, this is our decision. There is only one to make.'

The lawyer cleared his throat. 'An uncontrollable youth may be brought before a court, which can then duly release the youth on probation, commit him to an institution until the age of eighteen, or to the care of a willing person.' The last two words were said slowly and deliberately. 'When court resumes, the judge will expect you to be that *willing person*, Mr Harrow. Quite frankly I'm surprised he agreed to a recess when you said that you needed time to consider the alternatives.'

'You see, a willing person, G.W.,' Lily said softly. 'That's us.'

'If Luther is sent to an institution,' Mr Riggs stated, with an impatient tug of his neck-tie, 'he may be apprenticed in accordance with the Apprentices Act of 1901.'

'This is ridiculous,' Lily declared, turning to her husband. 'You were the one who gave Luther that tomahawk,' she firmed her jaw, 'so you must accept some of the responsibility.'

Her husband looked as if she had struck him.

'We will be taking Luther home, Mr Riggs,' Lily stated, nodding to her sons. G.W. gave a weak nod of assent, and together they walked up the stairs to the courthouse, the waiting crowds stepping aside to let them pass.

'Splattered across the city papers, we are,' the blacksmith complained loudly to their backs. 'They're saying we're heathens and that we don't know how to bring up our children.'

Dave followed up the rear of their sorry procession, the hem of Thaddeus's trousers guiding him down the centre aisle. Congestion halted their progress, and in the split second that Dave lifted his head he noticed Reginald Cummins. Dave knew that his father would be mortified at the man's presence, and Dave was weighed down by the enormity of the occasion.

At the front of the courtroom, G.W. and Lily moved towards a hard wooden bench, leaving such a gap between their bodies that there was only room for Thaddeus and a pile of legal books. Dave, forced to slink into the row behind them, leaned back against the unforgiving bench. Through Thaddeus's and his father's shoulders he caught sight of Luther. His brother sat at a small table, Mr Riggs by his side. The lawyer patted his brother kindly on the shoulder and for a brief moment Luther looked blankly in Dave's direction.

'He'll go home, won't he?' Corally was at Dave's shoulder, her breath smelling of lemon drops. She wore a dark-coloured blouse and skirt, both of which were ill fitting. Dave turned round on the hard bench. Julie Jackson sat beside her in the third row. 'What are you doing here?' he asked Corally.

'I snuck in. My pa reckons the town had their circus last week and that the baker's boy deserved what he got. He don't need to see a civilised people's idea of justice.'

'I only came to keep Corally company,' Julie said tightly. She sat stiffly, as if she had a broom for a spine. It was obvious that she didn't want to be there.

Dave couldn't believe that Corally Shaw needed support. She was the kind of girl who showed no fear, and although the two girls were always together, he often felt that the friendship was one-sided. Dave rolled his shoulders back, just a little. He hadn't expected Corally to return to the courtroom. 'Were you nervous sitting up there? I mean, putting your hand on the bible and everything?'

Corally leaned forward. She was so close Dave could feel the warmth of her skin. 'No. I told the truth. And besides, no one's ever done something like that for me before. He stuck up for me, Luther did, although I didn't mean for him to chop anyone's finger off. Anyway, all these people here, well they're not so good. See Mr Evans sitting over there? Well, he makes smaller-sized loaves of bread and charges the same coin for them as the proper-sized ones. And see his wife?'

Dave spotted Mrs Evans. The woman now wore black, as if she were in mourning.

'Well,' Corally continued, 'she sleeps with the farrier.'

Dave's ears pinked up as Corally giggled and smoothed her skirt. 'How do you know that?'

'Because my pa works at the lumberyard now. My mother says it's just as well that we're not real townies, otherwise people would be saying bad things about us too. Not that some of them haven't tarred us with the same brush already.'

'Why would they do that?'

Corally rolled her lips together and sighed. ''Cause my pa was a trapper and we live near the cemetery and my best friend,' she lowered her voice to a whisper, 'has a grandma who's a German.'

Dave could see how all those things could amount to a fair bit of gossip. However, he didn't understand how the Jacksons could be called spies just because they were German, and Thaddeus agreed. His older brother thought people were just trying to stir up trouble.

'Your father wouldn't really send Luther away, would he?' Julie asked.

'You never know what your relatives are capable of,' Corally replied sagely. 'That's what my pa says.'

Dave looked at the slight bulge of skin rolling over his father's collar.

Corally rested her arm across the back of Dave's bench. 'Are Thaddeus and Harold still friends?'

'Dunno. They're not talking.' There had been no sign of Harold or any of the Lawrences since the Banyan Show.

Corally rolled her eyes. 'No speakies, hey? That's boys for you.'

Dave couldn't help but laugh. 'Yeah, and you probably shouldn't be talking to me either – people don't like us a whole lot at the moment.'

Corally gave his forearm a playful pinch and laid a hand on his shoulder. 'Oh, I don't give a squat what people think, Dave. Why should I?'

He heard Julie give an impatient sigh.

The judge entered the courtroom. Benches and chairs squeaked as all present stood, then there was a moment of rustling as everyone resettled. A baby whined at the rear of the room. Corally shuffled back in her seat and Dave sat squarely facing the front.

'Mr Harrow,' the judge said flatly, 'where juveniles are concerned I am prepared to give some leeway.' He fiddled with a sheaf of papers. 'You do understand that should you not wish to take your son home today, I will have no alternative but to recommend reform school.'

G.W. stood, slack-shouldered. 'Yes, I do.'

The judge beckoned Luther to stand. Corally's fingers dug into Dave's shoulder.

'I feel sure,' the judge continued, 'that what you have endured this past week, young man,' he looked from Luther to G.W., 'is far and away lesson enough. And you, Mr Evans –' the crowded room swivelled to where the Evans family sat on the opposite front bench, 'should consider your own son's character.'

'But he's the one what was damaged!' Mr Evans called. 'How's my boy ever gonna serve his country now he's maimed?'

The crowd were audible in their agreement.

'Silence!' the judge boomed. He formed a pyramid with his fingers as his order was obeyed. 'This story has become front-page news around our fair country, and it stops now. Mr Evans, you will pay your share of court costs.' He waited until Evans's shouts of protest were silenced and then interlaced his fingers. 'Now, Mr Harrow, Mr Riggs has informed me of your decision. You are going to take Luther home. There he will remain,' he glanced at his papers, 'on Sunset Ridge on probation for six months. As well, you will pay compensation to Mr Evans of an amount to be stipulated that is commensurate with the loss of his son's . . .' the judge read through his papers, 'right index finger above the knuckle.' The judge closed proceedings with a rap of his gavel.

The courtroom erupted. Dave punched the air excitedly as Mr Riggs congratulated Luther.

'When will I see you again?' Corally's slight hand pressed Dave's arm.

'What? Oh, I don't know,' Dave replied, shaking her off. 'I don't think we'll be going out much.' He moved along the bench, intent on reaching Luther as quickly as possible.

'I could come and see you,' Corally suggested, as Julie gestured for them to leave.

People were milling around them and Dave itched to shake his brother's hand. 'What?' he asked. 'You? Come all the way out to Sunset Ridge? Why would you want to do that?'

Corally's eyes grew immeasurably dark. 'Maybe I don't. Forget it.'

Dave overheard Julie Jackson say something to Corally about wasting her time, in response to which Corally told Julie to mind her own beeswax. Dave pushed his way through the crowd. On reaching Luther, they exchanged grins and punched each other lightly on the arm.

'What did Corally say?' Luther whispered.

'She wanted to come and visit us. Bit strange, don't you think, her wanting to come all the way out to Sunset Ridge?'

Luther gave him a lopsided smile as his mother hugged him a second time. Then they were shepherded quickly from the court-house by their red-faced father. No one stopped them, but many stared. Dave had the impression that most of the townsfolk and landholders were disappointed it was all over.

'There's Harold.' Luther pointed to where their old friend loitered on the opposite side of the street.

'Are you going to say hello to him, Thaddeus?' Dave asked as they crossed the street.

'No, he is *not*.' Their father directed them to the dray parked outside the Banyan General Store. Reluctantly Lily accepted her husband's arm and stepped up into the front seat. Dave joined his brothers in the rear and was barely settled when the wagon jolted forward. On the outskirts of the village they passed the Cobb & Co. coach heading to the post office. Here the team of four Clydes-dales would be changed, and both mail and passengers unloaded and collected. The coach showered them with grit in spite of the horses slowing to a trot at the town limits.

'Well, that's one thing I don't have to worry about,' Thaddeus muttered, against a backdrop of creaking wheels and the jingle of harnesses. 'So long to Miss Bantam.'

Dave nudged Luther. 'Bet you're pleased to be going home.'

Luther shrugged. 'Not really. Old G.W. will never speak to me again.'

'Sure he will, won't he, Thaddeus?'

His older brother didn't answer.

'He would have sent me away if it wasn't for Mother.' Luther gripped the timber sides of the dray. 'Nothing is ever going to be the same again, Dave.'

Gravel and dirt spat out across the road as the dray's wheels gathered momentum. Dave wiggled his backside across the splintery seat and hoped his brother was wrong.

⪻ Chapter 12 ⪼

Sunset Ridge, south-west Queensland, Australia
February 2000

A swathe of heat enveloped Madeleine as she stepped outside. It was only 7 am yet the light was harsh, as if the sun were closer to the earth out here in the bush. With vague thoughts of returning to the cool of the homestead she turned her shirt collar up and pulled the cap low over her face. The walk would do her good before the engulfing heat forced her indoors for the remainder of the day. The road from the homestead led past the work shed and the clump of trees where Sonia had pulled up in the sedan to talk to the rider yesterday. The ground was cracked, the soil loose beneath her boots. She envisaged the ground shrinking as each gust of wind lifted the topsoil and carried it away.

Sleep had come intermittently during the night. The excitement of finding the account for her grandfather's two commissioned works had kept her awake: were these works part of the forty landscapes the family knew about, or were they undiscovered paintings or sketches? Madeleine mulled over the cryptic name written on the unsent account: Miss C. The initial meant nothing to her, but she was determined to find out all she could. She finally felt that she might begin to form a real picture of the man her grandfather had been. When sleep did come she spent the night dreaming of the Great War, of scarred earth and mangled bodies and of young men facing oblivion. The images came to her like fractured sketches, and she began to wonder at the strength required to survive such horrors, not only on the battlefield, but after the war. How could a man return to normal life having witnessed such atrocities?

Jude had shared her memories of her father rising at dawn every day to rake the dirt outside the homestead fence. Jude's mother had never queried or disturbed this routine, explaining to Jude that the task soothed him. It was as if by raking the dirt and leaves and twigs, by smoothing the land beyond his home, by tidying it, David Harrow felt equipped to begin his day. David's wife, who had died in 1942 when Jude was twelve following a horse-riding accident, told her daughter that the years on the Western Front staring at the wreckage of no-man's land was the reason David craved such orderly surroundings.

Madeleine pictured again the portrait of Matty Cartwright held by the Australian War Memorial. The young man – a boy, really – was killed a week after her grandfather sketched him; this knowledge led Madeleine to envisage a returned soldier perhaps subconsciously seeking solace from his art. If that were the case then the selection of landscapes as his preferred subject was understandable, except that he appeared not to resume his art until the first landscape was completed in 1935. And why not continue the portrait work, for which he showed such talent?

From memory it was at least four kilometres to the river. As youngsters she and George had spent many weekends fishing its deep waterhole, arguing and laughing in equal measure. A short cut through the house-paddock fence and a tear to her t-shirt from the barbed wire led her to rest under a pepper tree in the middle of the sheep yards. The leaves were pungent between the warmth of her palms and Madeleine breathed in the scent before pocketing the crushed foliage. The wooden yards fanned out from the great tree in a series of squares, before leading to the twin penning-up yards, which fed into a long, narrow drafting race. She recalled running up and down the race when she was twelve years old as she, George and two of the stockmen helped their father draft the rams. Later their mother had told them both that the breeding program had been going exceptionally well that year. They had purchased some stud rams from the Gordons at Wangallon Station in the mid-1960s and the visible improvement in each successive year's lamb drop was marked. Their father had even joked about entering the Champion Fleece competition at the Banyan Show. It never happened.

Blocking out the image from that day in 1980, Madeleine crossed through the wool-shed yards. Skirting the old plunge sheep-dip, the dirt track led south-east and it was in this direction she walked. Once she was on the road, a soft breeze caressed her face, softening the bite of the sun as a scatter of sheep lifted their heads in interest. The paddock was timbered. For years it had been used as a holding paddock during shearing when large mobs were brought to and from the yards. During the remainder of the year it was lightly stocked. The regular short-term over-stocking had kept the native grasses lush and unwanted scrub low, and in a good year the wool-shed paddock appeared park-like. In a good year. Thanks to the drought it currently consisted of sun-baked dirt and dry-leafed trees.

In the distance a line of timber stretched across the horizon, marking the path of the twisting waterway. The ground rose to merge with the atmosphere, the two meeting in a shimmer of heat-held air and trees and shrubs flickering in the harsh light. Madeleine blinked at the bleakness of the landscape. Rivulets of perspiration were already sliding down her back and stomach, and her mouth felt dry. Next time she would take one of George's quad bikes out. Hot, droughty days didn't lend themselves to morning walks, and her idea of walking to the river now seemed foolhardy. A mob of sheep walked off to stand beneath the shade of a tree, while another mob a little further away crowded around a trough. It was difficult to imagine how her grandfather ever became an artist. Sunset Ridge had certainly never inspired her. Even in a good season there was something unruly and wild about the property, which didn't lend itself to the pretty landscapes he later became so well known for. These days Madeleine thought the best thing about the property was its name. Her mother had told the story of the Harrows arriving on the property at dusk when they first settled the land, hence Sunset Ridge.

A large meat-ants nest was nearby and Madeleine felt the nipping insects crawling over her feet. Brushing the ants away, she threw a stick at the mound and watched as hundreds of black-and-red bodies rushed from their home, readying for defence. The sheep scattered at the movement and Madeleine walked towards the deserted trough with thoughts of splashing water on the bites. As she leaned over the trough a hot wind arrived, showering her with grit. The water was cool on her legs and she scooped up a handful, splashing her face, aware of the sheep watching her from the shade. She could almost sense them swallowing in anticipation as the water dripped down her face and neck. On turning to leave, Madeleine noticed a wrench shining in the sun. The metal burned her fingers as she picked it up and slipped the tool into a back pocket.

'That would be mine.'

Madeleine took a step back in fright, tripped and fell on her bottom. Directly above, a man on horseback loomed over her. Scrambling from beneath his shadow, and the horse's inquisitive sniffing of her leg, she stood. 'You gave me a fright. Who are you?' The sun was directly over his shoulder, making his features difficult to see. 'Are you Ross?' She lifted her hand in an attempt to block the sun. 'Ross Evans?'

'I should be asking who *you* are.' The voice was gruff. He held out his hand and Madeleine passed him the wrench.

'I'm Madeleine, George's sister.'

'You look like him.'

'Who? George?'

'No, your grandfather, girlie. Come on, I'll give you a lift home.' He extended an arm the colour of mahogany.

'I can walk.' Light continued to block the rider's features.

'In about ten minutes your arms and legs will be red-raw from the sun. And it doesn't look like they've seen much sun lately.'

'Too much sun exposure is bad for you.' Madeleine felt foolish. She knew the rules: a shady hat and a long-sleeved shirt were vital in the bush if you didn't want to get heat-stressed and burned.

'Bad for everything, too much sun; bad for man and beast, and the land, and *you*. Get up.'

It wasn't so much a request as a command. 'I haven't ridden for –'

'Don't worry, Ned here can smell a newbie for miles.'

Madeleine put a foot in the freed stirrup and was roughly flung up onto the horse's back. She grabbed hold of her shoulder and rubbed it. 'You nearly pulled my arm out of its socket.'

'Well, you looked like you had more spring than that. Hang on.'

She did her best to follow the man's advice, her bare thighs rubbing against coarse horse hair, and perspiration pooling at the waistband of her shorts. By the bony shape of his shoulders and the grey hairs on his neck, Ross Evans was an older man. 'Why do you help us out here on Sunset Ridge?'

'That's my business. Grip with your legs and hang onto me.'

'So you are Ross Evans?' Tentatively taking hold of his shirt tail, Madeleine bobbed up and down as Ned trotted towards the wool shed. 'Did you know my grandfather? You must have. You said I looked like him.'

Ned plodded along the road.

'What can you tell me about him?' Madeleine persisted.

They rode on quietly as the bush settled under a mantel of heat.

'Why don't you want to talk about him?'

Ned's pace slowed. 'I got no reason to.'

'What if I told you I was hoping to organise an exhibition of my grandfather's work and that I'm looking for anything that can help me understand his life better and therefore the choices he made regarding his painting?'

Ahead the iron roof of the wool shed appeared between the trees. Gradually the cavernous building and adjoining yards grew bigger as Ross and Madeleine approached.

Ned stopped abruptly at the wool shed.

'Do I get off here?' Madeleine asked. When no answer came Madeleine ignored his offered arm and slid awkwardly to the ground. 'What was my grandfather like, Mr Evans?' She caught a glimpse of a jutting chin. 'What was he like after the war?'

'Ain't nobody called me mister in a long time.' The horse lowered his head and closed his eyes. The old man crossed one wrist over the other and stared across the paddock, then he pushed his wide-brimmed hat slowly back off his forehead.

His face was wrinkled and sun-brown and the lines at the corner of his thin lips drooped downwards as if he had lived his entire life dissatisfied. In contrast, his blue eyes were still bright. 'He spent most of his time here on the property after the war,' Ross began haltingly. 'When your great-grandfather died in the mid-1920s, Dave took over the running of the place from his mother. I never laid eyes on him until the 40s. Saw him in Banyan one day with your mother. She must have been twelve or thirteen, younger than I was.'

'And?' Madeleine encouraged.

'He sent her away to a fancy school.' The words lingered. 'I saw her once or twice before she married.'

Madeleine sensed loss and longing in the silence that followed until he suddenly spoke again. 'One more thing. Your great-grandparents hated your grandfather painting.'

'How do you know that?'

A glossy rump was the last she saw of horse and rider as they headed back in the direction of the Banyan River. Madeleine gingerly rotated her shoulder and headed home.

That night, dinner was late. Although the airconditioning did its best it was battling the residual heat of a forty-four-degree day and at 8 pm the temperature was still in the mid-thirties. With the house in darkness to avoid using unnecessary heat-emitting appliances, Madeleine joined Rachael in the kitchen, where they shut the doors to contain the cooler air and set up an electric fan on the sink. Madeleine sat at the table probing the sunburned skin on her arms, silently promising herself to never again complain about a stifling night in her studio apartment, with its piles of art books and view of the city skyline. Rachael cracked a tray of ice cubes into a jug of water. The fan whirred noisily, its ancient head clacking ominously as it rotated from left to right.

'Ordinary evening,' George commented on arrival. He was red-eyed and his speech was a little slurred. Madeleine knew that her brother had been cooped up in the station office since returning for a late lunch. However, she didn't think he had been doing the bookwork.

'We should have dinner,' Madeleine suggested as George drained one beer and reached for another.

'I'm not hungry,' George mumbled, opening the bottle and pouring it into a glass.

Madeleine put a hand on his. 'Sure you are; you've just been out in the heat too long today.' She poured some water for him and at her insistence he took a tentative sip.

'I tell him all the time to drink more water,' Rachael began, dishing up Sonia's slow-cooked stew, 'but he always tells me that beer's more refreshing.'

The fan gave a screech, vibrated loudly and then resumed its task. Rachael sat the plates on the table, buttered bread and handed out cutlery. Madeleine began to eat and immediately felt better. Now she knew why the fridge was stacked with leftovers. 'It's tasty,' she encouraged. Although the food was heavy in her stomach, she knew that in a few days she too would be picking at her meals, so it was best to eat up before the heat sapped her appetite. 'Sonia's a good cook.'

'Well, it's taken her a while,' Rachael replied between small mouthfuls. 'I even sent her to a cooking school one weekend. For the first two months she was here I thought she was trying to kill us. It was meat-and-three-veg every night, wasn't it, George? And either mutton or corn-meat sandwiches for lunch.'

George wiped at the gravy with some buttered bread. 'Oh, it wasn't too bad.'

'That's not what you said at the time,' Rachael argued.

'The thing is, Maddy,' George began, 'we didn't have a choice when she applied for the job after Nancy retired.'

'Why? It's only the two of you here. You don't really need a cook-cum-housekeeper.'

Rachael's fork tapped the edge of her plate sharply. 'There have always been staff at Sunset Ridge. And, Sonia being a Jackson,' she continued, 'well, we had to take her on.'

'Why's that?' Madeleine's appetite was diminishing. The hot meal wasn't agreeing with her.

'Because she's a Jackson, and Jacksons have always worked here.' George ran a finger across the gravy-smeared plate and licked it. 'You know that.'

Actually Madeleine had never given the subject much thought. Jude had had help, however that was only after the decision was made for her to work side-by-side with their father on the property, as well as handling the bookwork. Back then they were financially better off employing a housekeeper who could also care for the kids, especially as over the years her father's mood swings worsened and station hands became difficult to find.

George sipped at the water. 'The first Jackson arrived here sometime after the Great War. Julie, I think the girl's name was. Most of them have been cooks or housekeepers and I think there was a maid once.'

Madeleine thought of the account she discovered yesterday in the schoolroom. 'What about a Miss C.?'

'The name isn't familiar. Anyway, after Sonia goes I'm pretty sure that'll be the last of the line, which is a pity,' George conceded. 'The family's been in the district for over a hundred years.'

'What about Nancy, is she still about?' Madeleine had a vision of sitting down to tea with their elderly former housekeeper to discuss family history and perhaps the unknown Miss C. and the missing paintings; it was a thrilling thought.

'Dead.' Rachael placed her knife and fork together, most of the stew untouched. 'Sonia found her in bed and apparently spent a good few minutes trying to wake her up before realising that wasn't going to happen anytime soon.'

'Oh.' Madeleine brushed away the beads of sweat peppering her forehead and began to clear their plates. Although discovering anything about her grandfather – apart from trying to view the land-scape with an artist's eye – had been far from Madeleine's thoughts when she decided to make the trip home, she was now cautiously optimistic. The discovery of the account for the unknown commissioned works was intriguing, and Ross Evans was an unexpected bonus. Madeleine pushed the plug into the sink and rinsed the plates. 'I met Ross Evans this morning. He said he recalled seeing Grandfather and Jude in Banyan in the 1940s. That must have been just after Granny Harrow was killed and before Jude was sent away to boarding school.'

George's eyes bulged. 'How on earth did you get that out of the old fella?'

'It took a bit of prodding. He came around when I called him *Mister* Evans.'

'I'll be.' George looked at his wife.

'Politeness will win every time, George,' Rachael said with approval.

'What else did he say?' her brother asked.

'Well, he wouldn't tell me why he was helping out here. He *did* say that Grandfather took over the property in the mid-1920s when his father died.'

'That sounds about right,' George agreed. 'Mum told me that her grandmother, Lily, stayed on after G.W. died. As she got older the heat really bothered her and she moved to Brisbane in the late 1930s and eventually died in the 50s.'

'It's possible Sonia might know something about Grandfather Harrow, don't you think, George?' Rachael asked.

'I doubt it. It's a bit before her time. Although she's a Jackson, and therefore she must be related to the Julie Jackson who came to work here after the war. It's a pity Nancy isn't still alive.'

Madeleine agreed. Their former housekeeper had been here on Madeleine's last visit home three years ago. A modest woman, she reminded Madeleine of an elderly aunt, pottering in the garden, baking butter biscuits and ironing in front of a portable television in the kitchen. The more she thought of Nancy and her many kindnesses – patting her shoulder at breakfast, cooking her favourite meal of lasagne and salad – the worse Madeleine felt about not saying goodbye to her the last time she left the property. 'You're right, Rachael, it wouldn't hurt to sit down and have a chat with Sonia. You never know what she might know.'

◈ Chapter 13 ◈

Banyan, south-west Queensland, Australia
September 1916

Harold tried not to stare as the Harrows headed out of the village, following the court case. What he wanted to do was turn on his heel and walk away. Instead, he watched the family's departure, a mixture of anger and relief flooding through him.

'Just as well they never accepted our invitation to tea,' Mr Lawrence said in a low voice. 'Otherwise we'd never live the association down.'

Harold turned and faced his father. Having decided to delay opening the ironmongery until the trial was over, Mr Lawrence was ready for business. 'Luther isn't going to gaol, Father.'

Mr Lawrence ignored his son. 'Of course we know why they never paid us a visit; too high and mighty, them Harrows; too good to be mixing with townsfolk.'

Harold knew his mother didn't feel the same way. Although following Luther's arrest, his father had forbidden him to attend the court hearing or mix with the Harrow family, his mother had been inclined to see both sides of the court case. Harold's father

143

on the other hand dredged up four generations of Harrow flaws, both real and imagined, which in his mind had finally culminated in the family's ultimate fall from grace.

'Well it's a work day, lad, even if justice hasn't been done.'

'Yes, Sir.' Harold watched as his father walked down the street to the store.

Although Harold had never been one to hold a grudge, the altercation with Thaddeus at the Banyan Show had soured their friendship. He couldn't understand what had got into his best mate; however, one thing was certain: Harold was not going to put up with it.

'*That Harrow boy probably deserved it,*' had been the standard refrain from many townsfolk upon hearing of Harold's clash with Thaddeus. The fact that some of these well-wishers had never previously spoken to Harold suggested a level of support verging on collusion, however, regardless of motivation, the shared sentiments had buoyed him. Across the road at the courthouse people began to spill out onto the street. The crowd reminded him of meat-ants: a seething mass of occupants scurrying onwards to their next food source.

Although the street teemed with clusters of people and drays coming and going, when the Harrow wagon finally disappeared down the dusty road, a strange remoteness seeped through Harold. He knew he had to head back to the ironmongery, yet the thought of listening to the idle chatter of customers with only one subject on their minds held little appeal. Even heading to the river and the boat didn't interest him – where would he travel to now?

Harold looked back across to the courthouse to see Corally Shaw standing a few feet away from the assembled crowd; just as he had done, she was staring at the empty dirt road. Julie Jackson was talking to her, clearly trying to entice Corally to walk across the road to the general store. In response Corally gave her friend a forced smile and shook her head. Julie walked away, alone. Down the middle of the street a gust of wind lifted spirals of dust, which skittered across the surface to disappear into scrub and red ridges. In its wake, Corally followed. Harold trailed her at a distance, careful to not catch anyone's attention. As he pursued her, he reflected on the conversation he had shared with Thaddeus at the marbles game. Was his old friend interested in the girl? Harold considered the idea and quickly disregarded it. If there was any threat to his interest it was Luther, for hadn't the girl appeared on his behalf in court?

Corally moved quickly. At this rate she would be at the village limits and cutting cross-country to the ramshackle dwelling she lived in before he had left the last of the village houses in his wake. With a rush of adrenalin Harold ran after her. The unmade road was hard beneath the leather soles of his shoes and although he retained a steady pace, soon Corally disappeared from view. At the bend in the road, where civilisation met scrub, he came to an abrupt stop amid a scatter of dirt. Corally leaned against a tree, her skin layered in speckled sunlight.

'What are you doing following me?' Wariness looked out through red-rimmed eyes.

Harold did his best to compose himself. He had intended to wait a month or so before approaching Corally and revealing his intentions – and putting his case forward when he was sweating and out of breath was not the most promising of starts – but seeing her at the courthouse, knowing what she had done for Luther, pulled him from uncertainty to a sense of purpose. 'I wanted to speak to you.'

'Must be urgent then, is it, Harold Lawrence? You running after me and all.' She swayed back and forth against the tree.

'I've been thinking about the future.' Harold rolled his lips together, the action refocusing his thoughts. Corally had always been quick with her tongue. He had seen boys with less experience slink away from her in silence. 'I've decided I should make myself plain so there's no mistake.'

'About what?'

A slight puckering appeared around her eyes. He had her interest. 'About you and me.'

'You and me?' Corally nibbled intently at a fingernail before wiping the unruly nail against her skirt. 'Why, you've hardly given me the time of day, Harold Lawrence, lording it around the place as if you was landed, mixing with them snooty-nosed Harrow boys.'

Harold frowned. 'You stood up for Luther in court.'

Corally crossed her arms. 'He stood up for me. I'd do the same for a dog.'

Harold was not so sure about that. 'So, there ain't nothing in it, then?'

'In what?' Her eyes narrowed.

'In you speaking for Luther Harrow. You're not outing with him?'

'Luther?' For a moment Corally looked confused. 'No,' she said quietly, 'not Luther.'

'Anybody?'

A shadow turned the sea-green brightness of her eyes dark. 'Why? You interested?' She manoeuvred against the bark of the tree, crossing slim legs at her ankles.

'Maybe.' Harold expected Corally to say something, and when she remained silent he realised he was quite pleased with her response. 'So, you reckon you'd out with me?'

Corally's mouth gaped. Harold didn't know if she was weighing up the merits of his question or preparing to bolt into the scrub.

'Well?'

'I'm thinking.'

Harold shoved his hands in his pockets. He had not imagined things would go this way. In fact, he had expected the girl to jump at the chance. 'Well, hurry up. A man hasn't got all day.'

Corally stepped out from beneath the shade of the tree. It was past noon and with spring's arrival a haze hovered above the scrub. 'If there weren't no funny business.'

A red stain seeped up Harold's neck. 'On my honour.'

'Your mother and father won't like it,' Corally said, defiantly.

'I reckon they won't have much say in it. Besides, I haven't ever set eyes on someone like you, not ever.' The words escaped before Harold gained control of his mouth. For a second he worried that he had scared the girl off. Corally had an uncertain look about her, like a person hoping for good but not quite trusting to believe in the possibility of it. Wide, unblinking eyes greeted his thoughts. Treating this as a good sign, he persevered. 'I've been watching you for a while and I figured that you and me, well, that we'd make a good pair.'

'Maybe,' Corally conceded. 'Although I ain't nothing to anyone around here.'

Harold took a step towards her. 'You're something to me.'

'You don't know anything about me, Harold Lawrence. Me and mine, well, we're sure not like you and yours.'

'And do you think the world will be the same place after the war, Corally? 'Cause I sure don't.'

Corally tilted her head to one side. 'My pa always said that it never hurt a person to hope.'

'So, I'll see you then? Next Saturday, noon, at the river behind the ironmongery?'

'Sure, I'll be there, Harold Lawrence.'

Walking away, Harold wondered why he didn't feel more pleased; his eye had been on the girl for quite some time, and they would soon begin outing together. Yet, right now men were dying in defence of the Empire, and here he was working in his father's ironmongery, listening to gossip and chasing the girl he hoped to marry one day. It didn't feel right. *He* didn't feel right. And Harold knew that the hollowness bashing at his innards would not be satisfied by Corally Shaw. There were great battles being waged at this very moment, and he was thousands of miles away.

≪ Chapter 14 ≫

Chessy farmhouse, ten miles from Saint-Omer, northern France
September 1916

The British soldier lay on a stretcher on the kitchen's flagstone floor. His face was pale in the lamplight. The doctor, a sandy-haired captain, was leaning over him injecting tetanus anti-toxin. With each jab of the needle the man squirmed and frowned word-lessly. The injuries to the man's body were incomprehensible to Madame Chessy. Dirt-grey bandages ringed his thighs and torso and a facial bandage was soaked with blood.

'Morphine?' she asked hopefully.

Captain Harrison looked up, his face taut. 'We're out of it, and even if I did have it, there is always someone who needs it more,' the American replied, peering between the other men, before turning his attention back to his patient.

Madame Chessy waited for Lisette to translate. While the older woman was capable of grasping the basics, the dark-haired youngster was reasonably adept with English, having learned the language from an English cousin prior to the outbreak of war. Lisette translated the captain's words quickly and then squared her shoulders against the farmhouse door. She knew a scolding was waiting for her once she and Madame Chessy were alone. She was the one who had taken the lantern outside to guide her way to the toilet, and it was the lantern that had alerted the men to the farm's existence. When Lisette's wary voice had sounded outside the farmhouse walls, accompanied by those of strangers, Madame Chessy knew that duty called yet again.

Sitting on the floor beneath the window were two more wounded British soldiers, dark stains of blood tracing bandages on their thighs. The small farmhouse was heavy with the scent of unwashed bodies and the meaty stink of wounded flesh. Madame Chessy rubbed agitatedly at the neckline of her dress and poked another length of wood into the firebox. She felt both invaded and inadequate and, had she not been cursed with pride, an escape outside, even if it meant standing in the rain, would have been tempting.

The doctor rested his hand on the soldier's brow. 'There's nothing more I can do. He may survive.' The three ambulance drivers and soldier surrounding him took a step back so he could stand. Madame Chessy sat a pot of coffee and some cups on the table, a semblance of control returning. '*S'il vous plaît,*' she gestured at the chairs. '*Oui?*'

The doctor accepted readily and was joined by an Englishman of equal rank. Apologies were given for the intrusion. Madame Chessy inclined her head in acknowledgement although refrained from smiling. The other officer, Captain Holt, was older than the doctor. The puffy bags ringing his eyes and the thinning hair over his temples were matched by a watchful demeanour. The three drivers, men of lesser rank, drank their coffee standing and accepted slices of freshly baked bread with grateful smiles and nods of appreciation. All the while Madame Chessy observed Lisette. Rarely talkative, the girl had been forced to overcome her shyness over the past few weeks. A constant stream of men arrived for billeting or appeared in the field beyond the creek, cautiously crossing the stream and enquiring if they could stay in the barn. Madame Chessy had learned not to ask many questions, for there was talk of the odd soldier simply walking away from the front-line and it was said the British would shoot any of their men who did such a thing.

The doctor smiled tiredly at Lisette, who backed away to stand in the shadows of the kitchen. 'I cannot move him.' He nodded at the man lying on the floor. 'If we'd not been delayed . . .' His voice trailed off. He was a freckled-skinned man with the type of long, thick lashes a woman could crave. His attention was drawn to the rain pelting against the kitchen window. 'Could you please ask Madame if the men could stay in her barn tonight? It's cold and wet and –'

'*Oui, bien sûr,*' Madame Chessy agreed. Some things did not require translation. She pointed at the two wounded British soldiers sitting beneath the window and then at the bunks belonging to Francois and Antoine.

Lisette translated. Captain Harrison understood, gave his thanks and issued instructions. The soldiers consumed their coffee and bread and then helped the two wounded soldiers into the bunks.

Madame Chessy settled the wounded men. '*Oui, bon?*' she fussed, tucking blankets in and drawing the curtain so the alcove darkened. Taking a second lantern from the dresser, she lit it and handed it to one of the drivers. Lisette gave directions to the barn. The men trooped outside leaving muddy boot prints on the flag-stone and a brief silence punctuated by the crackling fire and the wheezing man on the floor.

'How long do you think the rain will last?' the doctor asked.

The older woman grasped the word rain and shrugged habit-ually. Captain Harrison gave a nod of understanding. He had already explained, via Lisette's translation, that he was part of the

American Ambulance Field Service and that his three vehicles had only recently been repaired after being damaged by German artillery fire. They were en route from Ypres to part of the Somme battleground when they had come across a village struck by a stray German shell. The rain had already begun to make roads impassable, and with the delay at the village and subsequent detours they were far from their original route. A severely injured villager had died on the way and lay in the rear of one of the three ambulances bogged on the road leading to Tatinghem. The other wounded – the men currently within the farmhouse – had been on leave in the village when the shell struck.

'You have been here since the start of the war?' Madame Chessy asked the doctor. Lisette was now sitting at the table with instructions to translate their conversation.

'Yes,' the doctor told her. 'I was at Dunkirk and Ypres last year.'

'You were there? At Ypres in 1915?' Madame Chessy scalded her tongue on the hot coffee. 'My husband died there.'

'I'm sorry. Many have died.'

'Yes, a great many. Ypres,' she said, leaning towards him, 'what is it like?'

'Terrible,' Captain Holt answered. 'All war is terrible,' he quickly added as the doctor glared at him.

'I would like to know the truth. Please? Tell me about it.'

The men remained silent.

'We cannot believe the newspapers, the stories, the flyers – nothing. If I couldn't hear the dull thud of the bombs going off at night when I lie in my bed I would be oblivious to the war.' She extended her hands in a supplicating gesture.

The doctor tilted his coffee cup and Madame Chessy poured more of the steaming drink as Lisette did her best to translate. 'You will not like what I tell you, Madame. War is not pretty.'

'Ah, but then life is not always pretty.'

'At Poperinge,' the doctor said slowly, 'there is a railhead.'

'Yes, go on.' Madame Chessy folded her hands in her lap. 'I have heard of the village. Many civilians were evacuated there from Ypres.'

The doctor nodded. 'I have been practising medicine for five years, but never did I believe men could commit such atrocities on their fellow man.'

'It's very bad?'

'Yes, very bad. It was at Poperinge that I finally understood the great machine that is war.' He swallowed. 'The troop trains would come in and the war fodder would be unloaded and begin their walk to the front.'

Lisette's cheeks paled as she translated.

'Yes,' Madame Chessy encouraged, although her chest tightened.

'One day I remember a hospital train arrived.' The doctor took another sip of coffee, his words stilted at the memory. 'It was a great gleaming machine with hundreds of beds and white linen. The field ambulances moved back and forth to the front-line, collecting the wounded and depositing them at the railhead. I did my best for the worst of them while they waited to be transported. They lay on the ground, hundreds of them, until it was their turn to be loaded onto the train.'

'That's good, isn't it?' Madame Chessy replied. 'This efficiency.'

The doctor swirled the contents of his cup. 'Good, no.' His eyes were glassy. 'It was not good. The train was for the English wounded. There was no train that day for the French. They lay as they were left. On the platform. On stairs.' He looked at her. 'On the bare ground.'

Lisette's translation was slow and halting.

'I can still hear them. The ones suffering from asphyxia, unable to catch their breath, and those who moaned from their wounds, their hands grasping the air as I passed.' The doctor stared at the wood oven. The cast-iron cooking plate was slightly warped and a thin curl of smoke sneaked up from the firebox.

'My God; we fight on the same side.' Madame Chessy wiped away a tear with her finger.

Captain Holt interrupted. 'I am sure a French hospital train would have arrived the next day, Madame. Unfortunately in war nothing goes to plan.'

The doctor was readying to speak again.

'Excuse the doctor,' Captain Holt said lightly. 'None of us has had much sleep in the past forty-eight hours, have we, Harrison?'

The doctor ran stubby fingers through his hair. 'The French officers are aggressive, but they make their men –' his gaze met hers, '*brave* men, charge at the Germans with their bayonets at the ready. There is no glory in any war, Madame, and there is certainly no honour in this one. The Germans cut their opponents down with their machine guns. They fire at torsos and legs; anything that will fell them.'

'I think that will do, Sam.' Captain Holt laid a hand on the doctor's forearm.

Fat tears slid down Lisette's cheeks as she translated.

Madame Chessy cleared her throat. 'Lisette, go to the cellar and bring up a bottle of wine.' The young girl appeared stunned. 'Lisette.'

Snatching a candle from the shelf above the wood fire, Lisette slipped through the partially ajar door into Madame Chessy's bedroom. A squeaking hinge was followed by the soft pad of feet on stone.

Interlacing her fingers, Madame Chessy fixed her thoughts on the image of her countrymen lying in wait for the delayed hospital train. Only a matter of weeks ago she had witnessed first-hand the terrible consequences of what Captain Harrison spoke of. She had been visiting the village market when a crowd had drawn her attention. A list of casualties had been displayed at the post office and the street was awash with villagers and visiting farmers craning to see the names. Much later, when the crowd had dispersed, Madame Chessy had read the names immortalised in black ink

– and then checked them again slowly to be sure she did not recognise any. The names that blurred against the cream of the paper symbolised a sacrifice too great to comprehend.

On the journey home she had passed Father Benet on his bicycle. His white collar contrasted sharply with the blackness of his cassock billowing in the wind. Suddenly superstitious at their chance meeting, she had avoided his eyes and crossed herself as they passed on the road.

When Lisette returned with the bottle, her eyes were red. Madame Chessy patted her hand as she re-joined them at the table. The wine was poured and they raised their glasses in silence, the doctor closing his eyes as he sipped.

'My cousin is from Bordeaux. They have tended vines for many years.' Madame Chessy topped up each of their glasses, remembering how not long ago it had been her two beloved boys who sat with her at the table. 'I think business would be good for their wine now.'

'Very good,' Captain Holt agreed.

Madame poured a splash of wine into a cup for Lisette. She was sorry for the girl. Her probing questions had led to a loss of innocence that she would have spared her if she had been able.

The doctor stared dull-eyed at the bottle of wine. It was as if, with his duties concluded for the night, he had shrunk into himself. Madame Chessy understood that both men probably wanted to retire to the barn, but she couldn't let them go, not yet. In receipt of only a few letters from her beloved boys since their departure, she was desperate for news, any news – she knew so little. She only had a name. 'And Verdun?' Madame Chessy asked. 'Tell me about Verdun.'

Captain Holt flattened his palms on the table. 'Madame, it is one of the greatest continuous battles that has ever been waged. The Germans and the French have been fighting in the area since February.'

'And we will win? Yes? The French would fight to the death for Verdun, it is a matter of national pride.'

'From what I hear, the Germans feel the same way,' Captain Holt informed her. 'But I'm not sure there is much to be gained for the Germans, at least strategically.'

Madame Chessy lay a hand on the dark cloth of her blouse. 'In here I believe we will win.'

'But at what cost?' the doctor queried. 'At what cost?'

≪ Chapter 15 ≫

Sunset Ridge, south-west Queensland, Australia
October 1916

On the opposite side of the music room their mother appeared to be dozing in an armchair. Thaddeus, having moved to sit cross-legged on the floor, was tapping his harmonica in the palm of his hand, while Luther continued to rub his heel into the carpet. Round and round his ankle swivelled, as Thaddeus beat the harmonica. Dave ran his fingers across the ivory keys and tapped out the tune to 'My Darling Clementine'. It had been weeks since the court case and the family's disgrace, with the empty days unfolding before them like a dusty road. Each day was marked by silent meals and disapproving glances, and Dave was sure that everything was made worse by the space on the mantelpiece. If their father could only forgive Luther for what happened, if he could only forget the fleece competition and move on as their mother once suggested over dinner. But Luther was right. He couldn't.

Dave thought briefly of Harold and of Corally Shaw and of the six months of punishment allotted to Luther, which their father had extended to include all the Harrow boys. Looking back, Dave wished he had told Corally to sneak them a visit that day in the courtroom, and he wished Harold would write and tell them what was happening in town. Spring, having lasted a paltry three weeks, was over and summer had them landlocked in the homestead or restricted to the house paddock. Thaddeus and Luther were sent out with the stockmen and forced to work like dogs from dawn to dusk. G.W. had decided that Luther would work to pay the compensation due to Snob Evans; Luther moaned aloud that he would be working for the term of his natural life.

How the weeks dragged. Monthly visits to town, fishing trips and swims in the river seemed long ago, and still neither Dave nor Luther knew why Harold and Thaddeus had fought.

The piano keys were cool to the touch as Dave turned his attention back to the music. He was learning that the composition of sound was similar to drawing, every element belonging in a particular place, and music was something he found easy to recall. Melodies flitted before his eyes in a series of shapes; notes were like conversation – some were impatient and angry like Luther, others comforting like their mother, while frustration lurked within his detached older brother. Dave looked out the window as he played, his fingertips almost mimicking the pecking movement of the hens in the dirt. He thought of the sketchbook tucked under the mattress in his bedroom and itched to feel the charcoal in his hand. His drawing was now mainly done in secret. With their father's anger simmering like a boiler of Cook's meat, the slightest broken rule could send him into a fit of rage, and no one in the family could predict what would happen then.

Outside, the bush was glazed with heat. Hot air seeped through the open window. Dave could smell the warm tang of the earth beckoning him outside. The breeze was thick, dense with the heat of a summer too long in coming. At night he dreamed of the river, of swimming through the brown swirl to the other side, of scrabbling out onto the sandy bank. He thought of the craybobs scuttling from their underwater holes, of the fish meandering along the reedy banks and of the trees layering the water's surface with their shadows. His fingers moved effortlessly over the keys. There was now music to accompany his imaginings, and the sounds he created followed him to his sketchbook after dark. In some ways he had been saved by the piano.

The grandfather clock on the opposite wall of the music room struck five o'clock. At that moment their father rode past the homestead on a Bay gelding, a stockman by his side. A straggle of dogs brought up the rear. Having rested during the heat of the afternoon, they were riding out to check Sunset Ridge's newest addition. A mixed mob of two hundred breeding cows had been walked onto the property a week earlier. Purchased for a song from a distressed owner who had lost his sons to the Turks at Gallipoli and his wife to a heart attack, the cattle were currently eating out the paddocks adjoining the western boundary.

Thaddeus walked to the window and, resting his hands on the sill, pressed his head against the glass. 'Damn ridiculous. We're overstocked as it is. Once they've dropped their calves and the ewes have lambed and we're feeding that lot plus the offspring from Father's hair-brained second lambing, we'll have a serious fodder problem.'

Luther swapped ankles and began to swivel his other heel into the floor.

'Stop it, Luther,' their mother snapped. Having spent the better part of the past hour draped across the wing-backed chair, she untucked black patent-leather boots from beneath her skirts and sat upright. 'There is enough discord in this family without you adding to it. Sit down and stop fidgeting.'

'I'd r-rather s-stand,' Luther replied.

Thaddeus continued to stare out of the window. 'This place is a gaol.'

'Thaddeus, please.' Their mother fanned herself with a copy of *The Bulletin*. 'You are not the only one suffering. Now, please, do play something.'

In answer Thaddeus tucked the harmonica in his pocket. Dropping the magazine on a chair with a sigh, Lily shooed Dave from the piano and, settling herself on the stool gracefully, lifted her hands to play.

'It's n-not r-right,' Luther said. 'Keeping us l-locked up here. W-we don't have t-to stay.'

Lily slammed the lid of the piano. 'What do you mean you don't have to stay?'

Luther opened the music-room door. 'S-sorry, M-mother,' he said, walking out.

'Please go and talk some sense into Luther, Thaddeus. I don't want him doing anything rash.'

'Rash?' Disappointment layered Thaddeus's words. 'It's too late, Mother, and you can blame Father.'

'But you know why your father is like this: the land he lost and the fleece competition . . . and now our reputation has been damaged thanks to Luther, *and* there's the Bantam girl who should have been your wife.'

Thaddeus frowned. 'I'm sick of the excuses. And, Mother, when I want a wife *I'll* choose her.'

'How dare you speak to me like that!' Lily quickly softened her tone. 'I only wanted what was best for you, and to protect you.'

'From what?'

Lily held his gaze. 'From life. From the war.' The six-month punishment meted out to her three sons ensured Thaddeus's safety, albeit momentarily.

Thaddeus was halfway across the music room when he stopped. 'We all know what you did for Luther, Mother,' he began haltingly. 'Standing up to Father. I know it's been hard on you too. But you can't expect me to stay and put up with this anymore.'

The colour drained from their mother's face as Thaddeus closed the door. 'What is he talking about?' Lily clutched at the back of the armchair. 'I want you to go after them, David.' She dried her tears with a sleeve. 'Find out what your brothers are up to.' She rubbed her temple. 'Well, go on. Don't stand there gawking. *Run.*'

Dave did as he was told. He ran through the homestead, straight down the wide hallway to their bedrooms. Although not surprised to find his brothers' rooms empty, he was shocked to see their drawers askew. Retracing his steps at speed, he skirted the sitting room and the silver room and continued along the open-sided walkway to the kitchen. At the doorway he slowed. Cook was heaping flour onto the table, her sleeves pushed up to reveal crackly elbow skin. There were pots bubbling on the wood-fire stove and the smell of corned meat cooking in brine. Spying the open bottle of cooking sherry and a glass on the sideboard, he tiptoed carefully behind the older woman. At the rear kitchen door he almost collided with the governess. 'Sorry, Miss Waites.' He ducked his head, eager to avoid her.

'Who's out there?' Cook called from inside.

'My, ye are in a rush,' Miss Waites smiled. 'Where are ye going?'

Dave could smell something soft and flowery. Despite his best efforts the heat rose steadily in his cheeks. Creaking boards announced Cook's approach.

'She dinna like me,' Miss Waites whispered, taking Dave's arm and leading him away to the front veranda. 'I heard raised voices inside. Is everything all right?'

Dave noticed Thaddeus skirting the length of the hedge that bordered the western side of the homestead. The sun speared through the foliage, causing Dave to wince. 'I have to go.'

The governess touched his arm. 'I know things have been diffi-cult, Dave, but that doesn't mean that we can't talk.'

Thaddeus vanished.

Miss Waites lowered her voice. 'I realise I've not broached the subject of art these past weeks with ye. I do wish your parents would see your talent.'

Dave edged towards the front of the veranda. Red dust layered the boards. 'I don't want to get into trouble,' he mumbled. *Or get you into trouble.* He recalled the evening in the sitting room when the art magazines were burned, yet the long days in the school-room since their gaoling had somehow altered his feelings toward her. Dave felt torn between his liking for the governess and anger at her sudden willingness to placate his parents.

'Ye are still sketching?'

'Yes.'

'I'm so pleased. The last piece of work I saw was a sketch on the river bank, it was so guid. I should buy ye oils. I could imagine the pinks and smoky greys of dusk, even within the dark of the charcoal.'

The sensation of having missed her, of having missed their discussions about form and colour and composition grew quickly, yet talking about his art could get them both in trouble and Dave couldn't risk that, nor being cooped up for another six months with the house-paddock fence the prison boundary.

'Ye forgive me, I hope. I came this close,' she pinched her fingers together, 'to being relieved of my position, and I couldn't risk that. But enough, ye don't need to hear of my problems.' She smiled kindly. 'As long as ye still draw.' Her forehead glistened with tiny beads of moisture. 'I would love to see some of your latest work.'

Dave imagined Miss Waites flicking through the sketch-book . . . some of the pictures were of her. The whinny of a horse disrupted his thoughts. 'I'm sorry, I have to go.'

Leaving the governess standing on the veranda, Dave ran swiftly through the back gate, scattering the hens as he high-tailed it from the homestead. He was sure Miss Waites watched as he ran across the ridged ground, and at the thought his leg muscles stretched out as his stride lengthened. His shirt grew clingy with sweat as he spied Thaddeus ducking through the scrub along the house-paddock fence en route to the stables, and Dave followed, zigzagging through the sparse trees until he too was running along the fence-line. Jumping logs and pot holes, he reached the stables as Thaddeus began to saddle his horse. His older brother was in a rush. Blanket and saddle were already on. In the distance a flurry of dust rose into the sky from the direction of the river. Dave checked the stalls. Luther's horse was gone.

'Where are you going?' His breath was ragged.

Thaddeus tightened the girth strap, tied a swag behind the saddle and then threw himself up onto the horse's back. 'Do you know where Corally Shaw lives?'

'Corally?' Dave repeated. Thaddeus wore his good jacket and his boots were polished. 'Near the cemetery. Where are you going? And where's Luther?'

Thaddeus backed up his horse. 'Thanks.'

'But what do you want with her?'

'It's best you're not involved,' Thaddeus replied. 'You take care of yourself, Dave. I'll write.'

'What? But where are you going?'

Thaddeus's horse gave an impatient buck; whacking the animal between the ears, he rode off at a gallop. Dave chased his brother to the house-paddock fence and then gave up. The last he saw of Thaddeus was a flapping coat tail and a rifle slung across a shoulder. Exhausted, Dave waited until the thin plume of dust merged with the darkening sky and then he walked back to sit on the step leading into the tack room. A flock of birds flew overhead as the horizon became a blaze of red against a blue-black sky. Soon his father would be home, and Dave could only imagine the anger that would descend upon the remaining occupants of the household. Picking up a stone, he threw it as hard as he could at the stable's roof. The rock clattered noisily against the corrugated iron.

Dave doubted that he would ever be free again. He would live his life tied to Sunset Ridge, like an old mare tethered to a railing – fed, watered and exercised just enough to be kept in working order – while his brothers took off on grand adventures, caring little about the consequences. Shoving his hands deep in his pockets, he began the lonely walk back towards the homestead. He couldn't believe that Thaddeus and Luther would leave him behind, nor could he understand why Thaddeus would want to see Corally Shaw.

Luther followed the curve of the river as the breeze lifted and the stars traced a path amid the branches above. Having shaken off the heat of the day, the air was refreshing. Midnight had arrived, bringing with it the hum of cicadas and a silvery path created by a waning moon. His horse picked its way carefully through tree roots and the river banks. Luther kept close to the edge of the river where the moon was at its brightest. Having found himself beyond the house paddock, his flighty inclinations had taken some dampening, although Luther understood Scratch's excitement. It was a damn fine thing to be free.

Occasionally Luther stopped to listen to the night noises of the bush. Having done his best to lose Thaddeus in the scrub by keeping his horse at a canter until the river was in sight, Luther didn't want to be caught now, so he stayed attuned to the sound of snapping twigs and the strain of leather, ready to dart into the scrub at the slightest hint of company. He was not driven by indifference towards Thaddeus – in fact, his brothers' suffering for his deed at the Banyan Show was part of the reason Luther felt compelled to leave – he had simply had enough, and he knew that he couldn't live at Sunset Ridge anymore. Telling Thaddeus he was heading to town to find work was easy, and his brother hadn't argued. Surprisingly, Thaddeus had thought it a good idea and they talked about meeting up and heading north; they had spat on their palms and shook on it as brothers should.

Luther hoped for understanding. He was heading south, not north. He wasn't going to be responsible for anyone's life, except his own, and by agreeing with everything Thaddeus suggested he had saved himself the difficulty of saying goodbye.

Patting his horse roughly on the neck, he stretched his shoulders before directing Scratch away from the sandy river flats. A gum tree split by lightning marked the spot where the river twisted towards the centre of Banyan, and Luther spurred his horse up the bank and into the shadowy scrub. The bush was dark where the moon couldn't penetrate the dense woody plants and it took some time before he was certain he was heading in the right direction. His escape was simple; it was what came afterwards that required determination.

After completing his business in Banyan, Luther planned to follow the river to the next town, Whitewood, thirty miles to the east. Here he could catch the Western Mail train to Sydney and his new life: the war. He reckoned he would be suited to that type of undertaking, if they would take him. He was above the required 5 foot 4 inches in height and was fit and healthy. With government posters in Banyan and the newspapers advertising the urgent need for volunteers, Luther figured they wouldn't turn anyone down. Besides, there wasn't much point knocking about the bush for a pittance, not when he could be earning six shillings a day while seeing the world. Becoming a soldier was not something he had planned or even considered until now; he didn't believe in the nobility of the cause the way Harold and his father did, and he wasn't joining for patriotic reasons or the promise of adventure. It was simply a matter of figuring out what a man could do best and then doing it.

The cemetery was a mile and a half from the courthouse, if he remembered rightly. He had been sitting in the rear of the dray as the Cobb & Co. coach passed them and the peeling signpost marking the cemetery road had caught his eye. The idea of calling on Corally Shaw had crept up on Luther gradually. The weeks of boredom allowed plenty of time to contemplate life, and the more he looked back on the previous months, the more Luther came to understand that Corally was the first person to actually care about him. His mother had made a point of standing up to their father's bullying and it was she who had saved him from reform school, but to Luther that was a mother's duty. In comparison, Corally had taken the stand in the Banyan courthouse, placed her hand on the bible and sworn to tell the truth. Just for him. Luther figured that if he owed anyone anything, then that person was Corally Shaw.

The sign for the cemetery was paint-peeled and faded. Were it not for a spray of wilted bougainvillea flowers lying in the dirt, he may well have missed it. Luther tugged on the reins and Scratch nickered softly in reply as they turned down the narrow, rutted road that was fringed by scrub on either side. Luther had never been one for closed-in country and was pleased when the cemetery came into view after just five minutes. The graves stood in neat rows in a long enclosure bordered by a wooden fence. On closer viewing he made out a section of crumbling headstones and broken crosses, and then newer burials gradually filled his vision. It seemed strange to Luther that such a place should be enclosed: who would want to wander in or, for that matter, how could anyone break out?

The moon patched the bare ground with silhouettes, some simple, others ornate granite memorials that seemed out of place amid the more humble remembrances. Dismounting, Luther led Scratch through the graves. The ground was hard, the air dry, yet in spite of his edgy ride towards the cemetery and the dark recesses that lay behind eroded gravestones, Luther felt calm. Walking his horse to the lone tree in the middle of the graveyard, he scanned the unfamiliar surroundings. It was impossible to tell if a house was nearby. Trees skirted the cemetery and in some places twisted scrub had overgrown the wooden fence. At this time of night there was no lonely lamp in a window to beckon him in a particular direction, and the lack of wind offered no scent of a cooking fire. Luther knew that his night wanderings had drawn to an end: it was too early to wake Corally, even if he knew where to find her, and far too late to turn back, not that he was inclined to, for this was a journey just begun. Luther wrapped Scratch's reins around a branch of the tree, slid down onto the ground and promptly fell asleep.

Pre-dawn arrived with an eerie glow. Luther woke to the smell of smoke and a pungent stink that reminded him of sheep guts. The light wind and the scents it carried were blowing directly across his face. Side-stepping headstones and a fresh plot of mounded earth, he jumped the fence and walked through the thick trees that extended from the edge of the cemetery. Birds were already twittering to wakefulness and he scattered slow-moving wallabies as his path took him deeper into the bush.

Eventually the trees began to thin and a shack appeared in the midst of a clearing. It was a small building, barely bigger than the Sunset Ridge kitchen, and for a moment Luther thought the dwelling belonged to the grave-digger. Then he saw the lengths of timber crisscrossed against the side of the building and the ratty hides stretched and left to dry in the sun. Although it wasn't the season for trapping, he counted eight rancid skins; a motley assortment of rabbit, fox and wallaby pelts. There was a wood pile, a copper for washing and a mangy dog tied under a lean-to attached to the front of the house. Apart from the stink of the hides the place was clean. That was something, he figured.

Although Luther was confident that this was Corally's house, he had never caught sight of her parents and was unsure of his reception, so he decided to wait for the appearance of someone from within. Hunkering down behind a tree, he dozed fitfully until the yapping of the dog startled him. The clearing was still layered in gloom as a figure walked out of the hut towards the frill of trees at the rear of the timber shack. Luther would have recognised that blonde hair anywhere as Corally kicked at the dirt before disappearing into the scrub. The sun brightened the landscape as he edged his way through the trees. He came upon Corally squatting in the dirt as sunlight streamed amid the foliage. A glimpse of pale skin showed itself. She was relieving herself. Luther knew he should walk away, but instead he watched the girl as she stood and then very slowly, as if aware of being watched, turned towards him. The morning light shone through the thin material of her gown, highlighting curves Luther had never imagined.

'What are you doing here?' A wild-eyed wariness settled about her. Picking up a shawl from the ground, she wrapped the worn material about her shoulders.

Luther walked forwards, fumbling for words. Corally grasped at the woollen shawl. The dog was still barking in the distance.

'I-I c-came t-to say g-goodbye,' Luther finally replied. They stood feet apart.

The girl glanced over her shoulder. 'You shouldn't have come.'

Considering how awkward he was feeling right now, he thought that she was probably right. 'I-I shouldn't h-have done a l-lot of th-things.'

An easy smile appeared and her sea-green eyes crinkled at the corners. 'What, are you all grown up now, Luther Harrow?'

'M-maybe.' He gave a sly grin.

'Hey, Corally, where's that wood? You got something the matter with your innards or what?' The voice was rough and high-pitched.

Corally cocked her head. 'That's my ma.' She grabbed Luther's arm. 'C'mon, we better get you outta sight. I can afford a belting for taking off for a bit.' Her laugh tinkled like running water as they ran back towards the cemetery. 'But I ain't so sure about you.'

They raced through the trees, skipping over logs and pushing aside scrub until they reached the fence enclosing the graveyard. Scrambling through the railings they headed for the lone tree where Luther's horse, having slipped his tether, was nibbling grass. Corally clutched at her side. 'I've got a stitch,' she panted. Her gown had fallen open at the neck. Luther stared at a shoulder and the rise of her breast, a half-moon of olive brown. He placed his hand on the bare skin and she backed up against the tree.

'Don't, Luther,' she breathed, attempting to right her gown. 'Don't.' She covered his hand with hers as he touched her breast, the shawl slipping to the ground.

Luther could feel the pointed rise of her skin against his palm. He kissed her on the lips as he squeezed the softness of her. Salt laced his tongue.

Corally kissed him back briefly and then turned her face to one side. 'Don't.'

Luther didn't think he could stop. He wanted to feel what the sun hinted at. He wanted it so badly he could taste it. He pushed forward, his free hand gripping the trunk of the tree. The bark was rough as the whoosh of blood pounded in his ears.

'Stop it!'

The slap to the side of his head jolted Luther backwards and he landed heavily on the ground. The sun was warm on his neck and the sound of Scratch rolling in the dirt and snorting carried across on the breeze. Corally looked like a young bird that had fallen from its nest. Strands of damp hair clung to her face and a wide strip of redness highlighted each cheek. Tugging at the gaping nightgown she snatched at the shawl when Luther handed it to her, clutching it to her chest.

'I-I'm sorry,' he said awkwardly. Her sea-green eyes flashed emerald. 'I w-wanted t-to say th-thank you, for what you did at th-the courthouse. I-I didn't mean to upset you.'

'You tried to rut me like one of your pa's precious stud rams. You could've ruined me.' Corally wiped at the tears streaming down her face. 'What have I ever done to hurt you? What have I ever done to hurt anyone around here? Nothing, nothing at all. And what do you do? Treat me like a piece of dirt. I thought you were my friend.'

Luther was mortified. 'O-of course I-I am.'

'No, you're not. First it's Harold Lawrence, then you.'

'H-Harold?'

'Yes.' Corally raised her chin. 'He wants me to be his wife. To wait for him while he goes off to fight the bloomin' Germans.'

'H-Harold? You're m-marrying H-Harold?'

'It's a good offer for a girl like me.' She picked leaves from the threadbare shawl. 'So leave me alone and don't go ruining everything.'

'H-Harold? But you *can't* marry him.'

Corally snuffled back tears. 'Why not? My pa reckons that most likely he'll be blown to bits anyway, but if he isn't . . .'

Luther digested these words. The thought of being injured hadn't crossed his mind. Besides, he was younger than Harold, faster and quicker. There was no way Fritz would get him. 'B-but you spoke for me in th-the c-courthouse.'

'You're going too, aren't you?' Corally eyes were red.

'Yes.' Luther nodded. 'I'm t-taking o-off. I don't go m-much on f-fighting for a l-living, b-but I f-figure I'll see the world at l-least.'

'And your brothers?' Corally asked hesitantly. 'I suppose all of you are the same. All you can think about is rushing off and getting yourselves killed.'

'Dave's t-too young. We didn't t-tell him w-what we were up t-to,' Luther revealed. 'And Th-Thaddeus th-thinks he and I are going north.' He looked at the girl, her toes curling in the dirt. 'I figured after th-them b-being p-punished for w-what I did t-to Snob th-that I should go it alone for a-a while.'

Corally eyes grew moist. 'If I was a man I'd go too instead of being left behind in this place.'

Luther surveyed the rows of headstones fanning out from the lone tree. 'It's not s-so b-bad.'

'Really? And what would you know, Luther Harrow? You with your grand home and miles of land.'

'I b-better g-go.' Corally was getting a crotchety tone to her voice, which reminded Luther of Miss Waites and his mother.

The girl tucked strands of hair behind her ears, wiped roughly at her face and marched past him, her arms swinging fiercely. A jumble of thoughts rushed through Luther's mind. 'D-don't m-marry Harold.'

The girl pointed to where Scratch was lying across a fresh gravesite. The soil forming the mound was rooted up. The horse rolled over the recently buried and whinnied with delight. 'See, even your animals ain't got respect for anybody.' Corally climbed through the fence.

'H-hang on, Corally. Don't go charging off like a b-bull at a g-gate. Won't you write me a-at least? While I'm at th-the w-war?'

Scratch scrambled up onto his feet and neighed loudly.

'Well d-done,' Luther admonished as Scratch trotted towards him. The last he saw of Corally was a slip of a girl merging with the trees.

Dave lay on the floor, staring at the brass knob on the bedroom door. Beads of sweat pooled every few minutes along his hairline to run down the side of his face. Not usually inclined to bathing, he had taken to dreaming of the washstand down the hallway with its cooling water and Pears soap. A suffocating heat had entrenched itself in the room and he was beginning to believe that he would never be cool again. So he remained on the floor, close to the fresh earth below. Occasionally a whisper of air would snake its way through a crack in the boards beneath and Dave would suck in the waft like a cone of flavoured ice.

It had been two days since Luther and Thaddeus's disappearance and still his imprisonment continued. Breakfast and the midday meal had passed; one meal at night was Dave's allocation, that and a jug of water and an old potty in which to do his daily business. He stretched out gingerly, his backside and thighs still stinging from the thrashing given by his father – and G.W. had threatened more if Dave didn't reveal details of where his brothers had run off to. What was he meant to do, he asked himself. Lie? Having never experienced extreme anger before, Dave was at a loss as to how to handle it. He was bored and frustrated, yet his concentration appeared to have been flayed into pieces, much like his wounded skin, and he couldn't draw to fill in the endless hours. In fact, the sketchbook had been dismantled, pages torn out and hidden in case his artwork became another casualty of his father's fury. Chickens now hid in clothes, household furniture in a shoe box, people in an old tin in the manhole in the ceiling, and others in his roll-top desk. Only Miss Waites survived concealment: her images were layered beneath his mattress.

A plan of sorts began to structure itself and as it drew him towards freedom Dave realised that there may well be no turning back if he decided to pursue it. Once he left Sunset Ridge it would be difficult to return and face his father. And then, of course, there was the question of employment. A man had to earn coin to buy food, and what if the worst happened and he couldn't find his brothers? Patches of light angled through the window as evening shadows streaked the garden. Gradually the bedroom grew dark. Rolling onto his side, Dave sat up carefully. Footsteps echoed outside in the long hallway. The doorknob squeaked on turning.

'It's me.' His mother stepped in quietly, then peered back out into the hallway before closing the door.

Dave moved sideways as a meal tray was placed on the dresser. His stomach gurgled loudly.

'We think Thaddeus may be going north,' Lily whispered, folding the cloth that had covered the tray and sitting it to one side. 'He fought with Harold out the back of the ironmonger's store two days ago. The farrier saw the altercation and reported both of them to the constabulary.' Lily lifted the plate of food. 'Here you go.'

'I'm not hungry.'

Lily sighed. 'Suit yourself. Anyway, your brother managed to get away, while Harold spent a night in gaol for disturbing the peace.' Lily fiddled with the cloth, re-covering the food. 'There's no sign of Luther.' She looked at him hopefully. 'Do you know where they are, Dave? If you do, you really must tell us. Please tell us.'

'I know they'd had enough of being locked up here.'

Lily pinched the bridge of her nose. 'So you told your father. You really don't understand the magnitude of this situation, do you?'

'Thaddeus and I never did anything wrong.'

'I know that, but you must understand, your father –'

'I hate him,' Dave said loudly. 'Why are you letting him keep me locked up? Why did you let him flog me?'

'Oh Dave, I'm doing my best. You know how he can be.' Lily gave a sigh. 'I'm worried about your brothers, Dave, and you. Please tell me what you know. It's the only way I can help you and them.'

Dave looked at the floor. His brothers didn't need any help – they were free.

'You can stop this immediately by telling your father what you know.'

'But I know nothing.' He gritted his teeth.

'Please; you boys have always banded together. You do realise that if you continue to refuse what your father asks I will not be responsible for what happens?'

'Fine, keep me in here, then. In the years to come they'll find my bones, like an old cow left to die in the paddock. What will you say then? Then you'll be sorry.'

'If you want to blame someone, Dave, blame Luther. This whole mess started with him, him and that Corally Shaw.' Lily sniffed. 'How ludicrous, trying to protect *her* honour and thinking that maiming the baker's boy was the only way to do it. I'm beginning to think I should have let Luther be sent away to reform school.' Beads of sweat sprinkled his mother's top lip. 'I see you've picked up your brother's tendencies towards insolence, and I must tell you, my lad, it is a most unattractive trait.'

A second later the room was empty again, the key turned in the lock. Dave stood in the middle of the room, his heart racing. He had a dreadful feeling that things were going to get a lot worse. Minutes later a door slammed. His father's voice vibrated through the homestead. Flattening his ear to the bedroom door, he listened to the approaching footsteps and indecipherable voices. At any moment his father could stride down the hallway with his polished leather strap. The footsteps grew louder and Dave glanced at the window. For two days he had been considering the consequences.

Cook's voice cut across the footsteps and then, as if by a miracle, they retreated. Dave slouched against the wall, his mouth dry. He devoured the cold cuts of mutton left over from yesterday's roast and gulped down the glass of fresh water. By midnight he intended to be riding along the river towards Banyan, but first there was someone he needed to say goodbye to.

Dave spread the five drawings of Miss Waites on the bed. His fingers traced the curve of her neck, lightly brushed the indent above the lips. Each drawing showed a different angle, highlighted some part of her that he had agonised over while trying to do justice to her features. He always began with the eyes before checking the positioning of the nose, lips and ears. The whorls of those delicate ears had transfixed him for days, while the soft down at her hairline took hours to perfect.

Gathering up the sketches of the governess and most of the secreted drawings – there wasn't time to retrieve the ones hidden in the ceiling – Dave rolled a clean shirt inside a blanket and, securing it with a leather belt, dropped it through the window. Then he crawled through and slid down the side of the house onto the grass below. The freshness of the air, although still heavy with heat, brought a smile to his lips and he set off with renewed determination, his swag over one shoulder, the roll of sketches tucked under the other arm. He passed the kitchen and Cook's quarters and crossed the yards of dirt and patchy lawn. Despite the heat, Dave sucked in the scent of dry grasses mixed with the red dirt that layered the air and buildings. He could barely imagine life away from Sunset Ridge, and the inevitability of his actions suddenly struck him as if he had been hit. Across the miles of darkness lay the winding river and the animals that gathered at its banks to drink. He could see the sunlight filtering the trees along the river flats and the surrounding paddocks, which fanned out from her as if in homage. Most of all Dave could smell this land of the Harrows; the thick, gritty scent of the decaying drought years and the lush pungency of the good; the decades-whitened bones of their ancestors watching from their red ridge and the tang of manure dropped by cloud-wispy sheep. Sunset Ridge held a palette of possibilities, yet like any great creation in the making there were still flaws appearing in the work. It was these flaws Dave was beginning to see and understand, for they presented themselves in the form of people. It only took the slightest brushstroke or an error in colour to render a possible masterpiece imperfect.

He understood how it felt to be a pebble in a slingshot; pulled in one direction, only to be flung in another. He was readying to say goodbye to Miss Waites, yet worry gnawed at him. How on earth would he find his brothers? Running away from home, from Sunset Ridge, with no firm idea of what awaited him suddenly seemed ridiculous, and now another thought struck him: once he left, there would be no need for a governess at Sunset Ridge. Lamplight shone from Cook's quarters. Dave hitched the swag higher on his shoulder and contemplated the walk back to his room. Was staying worth another flogging? It was harder to leave than he had imagined. A cooling breeze caressed his face. The river beckoned. He was still here, yet the missing had already begun

A murmur of voices carried on the wind. That was all he needed: to be caught outside by his father. Edging along the rear of the schoolhouse, he readied himself for the sprint across the grass back to his room. As he moved Dave became aware that the voices were less audible and appeared to be coming from behind him. Dave followed the voices back to Miss Waites' room, where he peered into the open window.

The soft lamplight made Miss Waites' skin luminous, and her hair was unpinned and fell loosely about her shoulders. Dave took in the sight of the long curling hair, strands of which were streaked with white-gold; he had never seen such beauty. The governess leaned against a dresser, one arm reaching out as if beckoning someone; the image reminded Dave of a picture, an angel rising from a shell. His governess resembled a Botticelli angel, the material of her dress straining against the taut lines of her arm. Dave formed an artist's square with his fingers, racing to memorise the soft hollow at the base of her neck, the gentle tilt of her head.

'Don't do this to me, Catherine.'

The voice was male and all too familiar. At the sound, Dave squatted in the darkness among clumps of spiky grass. He couldn't believe what he was hearing.

'If ye won't marry me now,' Miss Waites replied, 'at least leave me with the memory of your touch.'

'It's not that I don't want to,' the man continued, although his tone was hesitant. 'Oh God, this damn war. I don't want to leave you a widow.'

'I don't want to be left at all,' Miss Waites countered.

'So you'd have me labelled a cold-footer, too afraid to enlist, to do my duty?'

'I just don't want ye to go.' The governess began to sob.

'If I'm seen in your quarters you'll be out of a job.' The outline of a man filled the window.

Dave watched as the man wiped a tear from Miss Waites' cheek.

A crushing weight descended upon Dave. Scrabbling backwards in the dirt he shrank before the single sheet of glass that separated him from the man within.

'You can't honestly expect me to stay? Not after Hughes' referendum on conscription.'

'But it was defeated, Rodger,' Miss Waites argued.

'Narrowly. They're handing out white feathers across the country, Catherine. I'll not have one handed to me, not after my brother's death. The paper is full of the Empire's need for troops. You've seen the posters. Anyway, the guilt would kill me if I didn't do my bit. I've decided to head north first to Brisbane. I'll visit my mother and then I'll enlist.'

The curtains on their wooden reels clattered together as they were drawn across the window, a wedge of light slanting through the material. It was a narrow, weak beam, yet it cut through the dark to highlight the window sill before being engulfed by the night. Dave stared at the outbuildings, at the guttering edging the schoolhouse, the meat-house and the squat laundry with its bricked-in copper. The great trees bordering the eastern side of the main homestead rose proudly into the night and beyond them lay the unknown. Dave crumpled dirt in his palm and let it fall through his fingers. When he finally walked away, the roll of sketches remained on the ground.

⊰ Chapter 16 ⊱

Madeleine sat in the sitting room, staring at the landscape hanging above the fireplace. The oil painting was cracked and crazed from years of heat and was in need of careful restoration. It was difficult for her to be partial towards the work. Of no particular artistic merit, by an amateur artist, the piece didn't deserve such a lofty hanging place yet it had been in this spot for as long as she could remember. No one dared relocate it, not even Rachael, it seemed. It was said that the painting had hung in that same spot since G.W. Harrow's forefathers first arrived in the district and took up the selection that was Sunset Ridge. Apart from her grandfather's roll-top desk, the painting was the only other relic left in the homestead from a time when transport was by horseback or wagon and women's dresses swept the ground at their feet.

'George said you were looking for me.'

Madeleine had been waiting for the housekeeper. She smiled at Sonia in greeting and asked her to have a seat. The older woman hesitated.

'I would be really grateful if you could spare me a few minutes, Sonia.'

Sonia ceased fidgeting and, looking around the room, settled on a high-backed cream chair. 'I hear that sister-in-law of yours is pushing for some sort of local event to commemorate your grandfather.'

'Well, it was my mother who wanted Grandfather's work recognised in an exhibition. Rachael's plans are her own. I get the feeling you don't think it's a good idea.'

Sonia pursed her lips. 'It's my understanding that David Harrow wasn't a showy man. I don't think he would like something being held in the district.'

'Why not?'

'He just wouldn't,' Sonia stated, her hands gripping the sides of the cream chair.

'So, he was a quiet man, then, reserved perhaps?'

'You could say that,' the housekeeper agreed. 'Although he was in his early fifties when I first laid eyes on him. My mother said he was a regular lad before the war, but more . . .'

'Sensitive?' Madeleine suggested. Sonia didn't answer. 'I wouldn't be surprised if he was, considering he was an artist. Sonia, your family has been associated with mine for a very long time. Do you know why there has always been a Jackson working at Sunset Ridge, over the decades? Surely that's unusual in this day and age.'

'To you, perhaps. Loyalty and tradition mean something out here.' Sonia settled back in the chair, clearly satisfied with her answer.

That was similar to Jude's response when Madeleine had rung her mother earlier to ask the same question. Something in Sonia's defensive tone suggested that loyalty wasn't the only reason. 'Perhaps, but I can't help but ask if the Harrows owed your family something back then – a favour perhaps?'

'Don't be ridiculous, girl. The Harrows don't owe us anything. We owed them.'

'How's that?'

'It was a long time ago. Water under the bridge and all that. Suffice to say that my aunt, Julie Jackson, accepted a position here in 1918 and ever since the Jacksons have felt honour-bound to fill any role that's required of us in this homestead.'

'Can you tell me about it?'

Sonia fiddled with the dust rag. 'Nancy and I agreed that we'd never discuss it. Some things are best left alone.'

'Sonia, you've got me intrigued.'

'I knew this would happen, as soon as George told me you were making this trip.'

'What does that mean?'

'Digging up the past. Believe me, although *most* of those involved back then are dead, the older families around the Banyan district have long memories and they won't like it if you open old wounds. *I* wouldn't like it. I'd like to live out my days in the village without the nasty gossip starting up all over again. So, please forget I said anything.'

Madeleine bit her lip. She was itching to know more. 'Okay. While I don't see how telling me *whatever it is* could cause a problem, I respect the fact that you made a promise to Nancy.'

'Good,' Sonia replied. 'What else do you want to ask me?'

'I was wondering if any member of your family may have told you something about my grandfather. You know, a story or anecdote, or their opinion of him? You just said he wasn't a showy man.'

'He was a very fine man.' Sonia removed a dust rag from the pocket of her apron and began to polish the top of a small side table. 'Everyone knows that.' She inclined her chin. 'He deserved better than what he got.'

'What do you mean?'

'Well, firstly, those two brothers of his, your great-uncles – may they rest in peace –' Sonia looked to the ceiling briefly, 'they were always leading him astray. And then there were his parents. Oh, but my grandmother said old G.W. was a hard man, hard as nails.

They say he never got over losing that land in a bet over a fence. He had a screw loose, if you ask me. Who in their right mind bets part of a family property? Not that it was unfair; a gentleman's handshake is just that.'

Sonia certainly had strong opinions. 'Please go on.'

The housekeeper fiddled with the hem of her apron. 'Well, it was on account of G.W. that his boys went to war. Of course, the old man may have regretted the way he behaved afterwards, but by then it was too late. The worst of it was that they got caught up with that piece of white trash, Corally Shaw.'

Madeleine had never heard of the woman, and she said so.

'I should think not. Respectable people don't mix with her sort. But young men get carried away, and back then the pickings were slight. Why, with the way some families intermarried, it wasn't uncommon for cousins to marry.' The housekeeper leaned forward. 'In fact, there are a number of married people around here now who are second cousins, twice removed.'

Madeleine tried to decipher what Sonia meant. 'Was there an illegitimate child? Is that what you mean?' The housekeeper frowned. Madeleine wasn't sure if Sonia was affronted or merely being evasive but she couldn't risk irritating the older woman. 'I do have another couple of questions. Do you know anything about two paintings entitled *Then* and *Now*? I found an account for two commissions and they were made out to a Miss C., but never mailed. Do you know who Miss C. was?'

Sonia resumed her dusting.

'Sonia?' Madeleine persevered.

'I'm thinking. If it was that Shaw woman I'd be mighty surprised. It's more likely it was someone else.' The older woman tapped her chin. 'It could be a surname or a Christian name. Catherine Waites!' Sonia's face lit up like a light bulb. 'Your grandfather had a governess by the name of Catherine Waites. It's a long shot, but it could be her. It's a pity Nancy isn't still with us. I was scrounging through her things last night and –'

'You still have her things?' Madeleine tried not to sound too eager.

'Well, of course. Nancy *was* my cousin, and we lived in the same house on and off for fifty years.' Sonia smiled as she dusted. 'The Jackson house in the village has been our sanctuary for a long time – since just after the war. Family members moved in and out depending on their circumstances; no job, between men, before and after children. Now it's only me rambling about. I don't know why any of us stayed on, really. I guess it was because we didn't have anywhere else to go. Plus, in spite of what some people may think in this district, as I said, we always repay our debts.' Sonia tucked the dust rag back into her apron pocket and stiffened a little. 'Anyway, it's hard to look back on your ancestors and wish their lives had been different.'

Madeleine watched as the housekeeper moved about the sitting room plumping cushions on chairs and straightening already-straight paintings hanging from the picture rail. They were a mismatch of still lifes, flowers and fruit mainly, painted by Jude in the late 1950s. Madeleine had always considered such works as an artist's training-wheels. 'I found some show ribbons for the local fleece competition in the schoolroom. My mother said Mr Cummins won it every year.'

Sonia brought sun-splotched hands to her cheeks. 'There was *such* competition between G.W. Harrow and Mr Cummins. Nancy said the district waited every year for the Banyan Show just to see those two men face each other off inside the Wool Pavilion. Cummins had the edge, though. He knew his sheep.'

'And my great-grandfather never won?'

'Never, and Sunset Ridge stopped entering the competition after 1916. That was the year everything went wrong.' The housekeeper retrieved an envelope from her apron. 'When George told me you were going to visit I started going through Nancy's papers. What with talk of an exhibition I figured you'd be needing anything you could get your hands on. I've seen those shows on television where they talk about an artist's life. Here you go.' She handed Madeleine a manila envelope. 'Nancy wasn't much of a hoarder, but I think these belonged to her mother, my aunt Julie.'

The newspaper articles were from the spring of 1916. The first listed the Banyan Show results from day one of competition. A suited man with an egg-shaped lump on the side of his head was pictured in front of the winning fleece. 'Cummins!' Madeleine exclaimed. There was also a grainy photograph of the Harrow boys standing in front of a dray with a piano roped down on it. 'This is fantastic. Thank you, Sonia,' she said, flicking through the numerous articles.

'Don't thank me until you've read them, my dear. Not everyone's family history is what we would like it to be.'

The next clipping was of a court case. Luther Harrow was accused of affray and branded a juvenile delinquent for chopping part of Wallace 'Snob' Evans's finger off. Madeleine was goggle-eyed.

'I told you,' the housekeeper advised. 'That incident – well, that was the beginning of the end.'

'What do you mean?'

Sonia appeared surprised. 'Well, because afterwards your great-grandfather kept them all locked up here on the property as punishment. Eventually all the boys ran away. Didn't you know?'

That afternoon Madeleine repeated details of her conversation with Sonia to George and Rachael, which led the three of them into the homestead office, where the station books were kept stored in a metal cupboard; it had been years since anyone had looked at them. Both Madeleine and George were stumped by Sonia's revelation. George in particular had wondered at the idea of the Jacksons working on the property all these years in order to repay a debt.

'They've all been paid good money as far as I know, and we pay Sonia the normal wage. It's not like they're working for free,' George added, as he ran a finger down each page of the ledger he was studying.

'Whatever the reason, the Jacksons feel duty-bound to work at Sunset Ridge,' Madeleine replied as she too studied a ledger.

'Isn't there a Jackson family noted on the district land-owners board in the Banyan playground?' Rachael asked.

George removed his metal-rimmed reading glasses. 'You're right, there is. And no Jackson owns land around here anymore.'

'And Sonia said something about it being hard to look back on your ancestors and wish their lives had been different,' Madeleine offered. 'If it's the same family, then Grandfather must have given Julie Jackson a job after the Jacksons hit hard times.'

'So, if that's it,' Rachael argued, 'what's the big deal? The Jacksons fell on hard times and Grandfather Harrow gave one of them a job.'

'Exactly, Rachael,' Madeleine agreed. 'Why the secrecy and why is Sonia worried about old wounds being opened up?'

'Scandal!' George announced, theatrically spreading his arms wide. '*And* it follows Great-Uncle Luther's chopping of the Evans boy's finger in 1916, which, judging by the editorial in those old newspapers Sonia gave you, obviously caused quite an outrage at the time.'

'Evans,' Madeleine repeated. 'You don't think old Ross Evans is related to that boy, do you, George?'

'At this point, anything is possible,' George declared.

'Here we go. Julie Jackson started employment here in the last quarter of 1918.' Madeleine squirreled her eyebrows together. 'Look at this – it's another entry. Isn't two thousand pounds a lot of money, George?'

'It was back then,' he agreed.

'Well, either someone was owed a lot of money or it was a big purchase, not that we'll ever know. The amount is categorised as an incidental expense. And here's another one for five hundred pounds.'

Removing his glasses George sat them on the table. 'Considering all the other entries are so carefully itemised – food, clothing, saddlery items, et cetera – it does make you wonder what these payments were for.'

Later, as she lay on the bed in her grandfather's room and stared at the ceiling, Madeleine thought more about the ledger entries, which they had spent a number of hours going through. The two thousand pounds appeared to be a one-off payment, but each cash-flow book from 1918 up to 1925 showed a withdrawal of five hundred pounds at the same time every year during that period. Madeleine, George and Rachael agreed that these were substantial amounts to be paying out after the war, especially when the world was heading into a depression. George matched stock numbers from paddock books with livestock sale records from the same period and concluded that the property's financial situation began to decline in the late 1930s, and within a decade Sunset Ridge was in serious trouble. He recalled a comment that Jude had overheard her parents make about their great-grandmother Lily Harrow – of her having worn the pants in the family. If that were the case, George suggested, it was possible that as Lily's age increased and her health declined, her role in running Sunset Ridge might have lessened and her son simply may not have been capable of managing the property. Either that or as David Harrow aged he grew less inclined to be a farmer and became more interested in his painting.

There was a substantial gap between the unknown commissions from 1918 and when David Harrow began painting his first landscape, titled *Deliverance*, in 1935, although it was possible that other works could come to light from this lost period in his life, it was equally plausible that David Harrow had simply ceased painting for nearly seventeen years. Why? Was it a combination of things? Had the war affected him so much, did marriage and the business of running the property truly take up all his time? It was possible.

'Your great-grandparents hated your grandfather painting.'

Ross Evans's words came to her unbidden. Sitting up, she dangled her legs over the side of the bed. His statement didn't help Madeleine with the post-war gap in her grandfather's life, but what if Ross Evans was correct and G.W. and Lily Harrow didn't approve of his talents from an early age? Madeleine knew that David Harrow had begun drawing before the war – the river sketches hanging in Jude's apartment were evidence of this – but what if he had hidden his creative side from his parents in the early days? He was a bush boy raised to work the land; maybe his interest in art was considered a little too feminine, and not for public display.

'It couldn't be that easy, could it?' she asked herself. Within seconds she was on her knees tapping the bottom of the desk, removing drawers and checking for false panels. Nothing. Sitting on the floor, Madeleine glanced at the tongue-and-groove walls and then very slowly she looked up to the manhole in the corner of the ceiling. Her mouth filled with saliva as she dragged the stacked storage boxes and shoe-filled milk crate out of the way and positioned the desk chair beneath the manhole. She grabbed an old hockey stick and clambered up.

'Here goes nothing.' She jabbed at the wood panel, loosening it, and then jabbed again. The board flipped sideways, dislodging dirt and leaves, mouse-droppings and paper. Madeleine dropped the hockey stick, rubbed dust from her eyes and looked at the floor. She couldn't believe it. Climbing down from the chair, she quickly unfolded the two pieces of paper. They were a little mouse-eaten and stained but the charcoal drawings were complete. One sketch was of a woman, all angular shapes and distorted lines; the other was of a chair that appeared to have been pulled apart and then reassembled. They displayed all the hallmarks of Cubism and were both initialled with the letters D.H. and dated 1916.

Madeleine let out a scream of excitement that brought George and Rachael running.

Madeleine had always found the village of Banyan an uninspiring destination. Comprised of four short streets, not much had changed in the past hundred years; the original three churches, hotel and post office had been classed as historical buildings.

The heat from the bitumen rose up in a wave as Madeleine left the car and walked across the deserted street. She was still reeling with excitement from having found the two sketches yesterday and she had left George and Rachael checking every crevice, bit of old furniture and manhole in the homestead in the hope of discovering more. The two sketches were wonderful early works, but Madeleine had no way of knowing if her grandfather had had access to art magazines from the period and she could therefore not be sure how much of his skill was raw talent or emulation. If they were drawn without outside influences, then these two early attempts at Cubism would have matched the innovative talents of the greats such as Picasso – an incredible achievement for a young isolated bush boy.

Now here she was, flush with excitement and hoping that a trip to Banyan might dislodge further snippets of information about the Harrow family, specifically her grandfather. A worn plaque noted the destruction of the Banyan newspaper offices from a fire in the 1960s, an event that also destroyed the local court documents from the 1880s that were housed there. It seemed she would have

186

to be satisfied with Sonia's newspaper clippings, which included an opinion piece from 1916 commenting on all three Harrow boys being punished for Luther's crime. She was beginning to form a clear impression of her tyrannical great-grandfather.

Turning left, Madeleine walked down the street to the original post office, which was now a museum. Australia Post had shut up shop some years earlier, citing cost constraints, and the old building was now decked out in a creamy yellow with a brown trim, its signage noting that it was once a changing post for the Cobb & Co. line. Inside, the original mail counter was covered with souvenir teaspoons, tea towels and enlarged laminated photographs of the Banyan River, which in a good season was still a popular spot for fishing enthusiasts. Any spare wall space was taken up with old black-and-white pictures of the village: the time-stained photographs showed a busy place, with varied shopfronts and streets teeming with people and horse-drawn carts.

At the rear of the former post office the building had been extended, and Madeleine was intrigued to find a not-to-scale model of a Cobb & Co. coach laden with mailbags and luggage, with a dressmaker's dummy inside decked out in period costume. Various paraphernalia associated with the turn of the nineteenth century lined the walls, including pictures of a steam engine that had once milled timber in the local lumber yard; and lanterns and ladders and countless other items of hardware were grouped under a sign that said Lawrence Ironmongers.

'What do you think of our museum, then?' The woman was short and had a weather-beaten look. Madeleine guessed she was anywhere between forty and fifty. She held a clear plastic container, the label on which stated that a gold-coin donation would be appreciated. She curled red-and-black-streaked hair around a nail-bitten finger, nodding when Madeleine dropped some coins into the jar.

'Love it,' Madeleine replied. 'I'm wondering, do you have any information on the old families of the district?'

'Sure thing.' They walked to the front counter, where the woman handed Madeleine an A4 photocopied screed. 'Mostly that's on the big families – you know, them with money. The squatters, well, they came first. They're all in there, like the Cummins family. They're the best known in these parts, after the Wangallon Gordons, of course. At one stage the Cumminses gave Waverly Station a run for their money. You know, them that bred the ram that was on the shilling coin for nearly thirty years?'

'Of course.' Madeleine had no idea what the woman was talking about.

'Anyway, the Cumminses are still here. They bought up a fair bit of land early in the piece and they've managed to hold onto it.'

'Anything else you can tell me? Are there any interesting stories about any of the properties, or townspeople – you know, stories from the past?'

'Well,' she said as she lit a cigarette and leaned confidentially across the counter, 'there's a place here called Sunset Ridge.' She blew a puff of smoke over her shoulder. 'People around here reckon the property is bad luck. One of the old people out there lost some of the land in a bet years ago. He was a cranky old bastard, which is probably why his three sons were always getting into scrapes with the townies. Eventually one of them nearly went to gaol, so the old man locked them all up, and then they ran away to the war.'

'Was there a woman involved?' Madeleine tried to sound gossipy.

'Isn't there always? And she was a real looker in her day, Corally was. People around here thought a fair bit of her. She came from nothing – lived near the cemetery in a hut with a dirt floor – and she tried to make something of herself. Every boy for miles about was in love with her.'

Madeleine nodded, thinking how different a picture this was to that painted by Sonia.

The woman took another good drag of the cigarette and dropped the butt in an empty beer bottle. 'Anyway, the story doesn't end there. There was a *murder* out there too, later on, so they say. Then the male line eventually dried up and a daughter married a bloke by the name of Boyne. Ashley Boyne.' Madeleine tried to remain calm, but her stomach began to churn as the woman leaned further across the desk and continued. 'He wasn't from around here – he'd met the daughter at uni, I think, and he came out with her when she inherited the place. He was a drunk, apparently, and there he was out on this big spread. The place was handed to him on a platter, but they say he couldn't take to it, couldn't handle it. Eventually he killed himself. What a loser.'

Madeleine nodded numbly, wondering how much truth was contained in the comment about her father's drinking. Was alcohol the cause of his mood swings, or did he drink to self-medicate? Either way, Madeleine had never realised that he had drunk; maybe it was just gossip.

'After that the place was locked up and leased for ages. There's a son there now, married to a hoity-toity wife. Personally I don't know how anyone can live out there with a history like that.'

Madeleine digested all this information like she was eating a raw egg, feeling an anger welling inside her at the woman's proprietorial attitude towards the Harrow family history. She forced herself to remain calm as she asked: 'And the artist? Didn't David Harrow live there?'

The woman waved away a sticky black fly. 'Yeah, he painted, it's true, although me ma tells me no one liked him much 'cause he was friendly with Germans. Anyway, he couldn't have been very important.' The woman flicked a strand of red hair from her brow. 'So, are you a visitor, then?'

Madeleine straightened her shoulders and stated: 'I'm Madeleine Harrow-Boyne.' She didn't wait for the woman's stuttered apology; instead she left the museum and crossed the street, making for the shady Box tree, where she concentrated on calming her roaring heart. Diagonally opposite was the courthouse, to her right a peeling signpost that directed visitors to the site of the old blacksmith's forge and the path to the Banyan River. Madeleine's brain hurt as the information percolated through her skull, raising questions and shattering long-formed ideas. Was her father an alcoholic? And what was this about murder? She needed to speak with George, immediately.

⋘ Chapter 17 ⋙

Verdun, France
October 1916

W hen the guns began, Francois woke with a start. Roland nestled close to his chest and twitched nervously. Pinpricks of light, the glowing tips of cigarettes, punctuated the shadowy recesses of the trench, yet Francois took little comfort from the men around him. At a right-angle to where he sat a slither of sky was just visible. Stars sprinkled the narrow void.

Make it stop, make it stop, make it stop, he whispered silently through clenched teeth. The noise haunted him day and night, echoing in his brain whether he was asleep or awake. He couldn't go out there again; he knew he couldn't. The land was gone. It had simply vanished, reduced to a mass of boggy ground filled with bodies and bits of bodies. Only yesterday he had reached for a hand extending up from a shell-hole, only to have the arm it was attached to disintegrate. No, Francois decided, he wasn't going back out there.

Roland nuzzled his neck as Francois hugged the great animal closer to his body. He had fallen asleep perched on two munitions crates, his dog beside him, his backside and rotting boots free of the water moving sluggishly along the bottom of the trench. The trench had been cut through a ridge, and it was this slight height that prevented the area from becoming a complete bog hole. Pulling at the fingers of his right hand to straighten them, he blew on the tips and with cold-stiffened hands began to roll a lumpy cigarette. For two days Antoine had been missing. 'Do you think he's still alive?' Francois whispered, puffing on the cigarette, his free hand resting on Roland's back. 'If anyone can survive out there, surely it's Antoine.'

Roland pricked his ears. Further along the trench six men carried a single stretcher between them. They waded through the knee-deep mud of the trench, their progress desperately slow.

'Have you found many?' Francois queried when the men staggered past. 'My brother, Antoine Chessy?'

The stretcher-bearers greeted Roland before one shook his head in answer to Francois. 'I'm sorry, this weather . . .' The sentence remained unfinished.

Francois knew the danger of wounds exposed to the putrid water that filled shell-holes and covered the ground. Nearly all the men in his platoon were reinforcements; few of the original faces were left. How long had they been here? Two weeks. This, then, was Verdun.

'Keep your dog safe,' a stretcher-bearer called.

Francois drew heavily on the cigarette and tossed it in the soupy mud. If they all died today Roland would probably survive. Neither side fired purposely on the battalion dogs, with the majority of wounded animals simply caught up in the maelstrom of war. It seemed that there was a limit to man's cruelty. Francois straightened his legs, feeling the click of bones. How he wished they were back in the flea- and spider-infested barn they wrote to their mother about. The last village they had stayed in had no straw and was rank with the stink of death. Although they were only there for one night en route back to the front, it had been a long night: before they arrived, the village well had been struck by a German shell, and they had been forced to drink water from a shell-hole that also held a dead body.

At least their time here was soon to end. Their captain had informed them last night that General Nivelle, the new commander of the French Second Army, was carrying on with General Pétain's habit of ensuring that troops were rotated regularly. Where possible, every Frenchman was to be put through the wringer that was Verdun. After mere days here Francois had comprehended the reasoning behind this tactic: the casualties on both sides were enormous and the Allied and German bombardments rarely stopped – no man could sustain such horror for long.

Taking a swig of water from his canteen, Francois poured some of the contents into his steel helmet. 'Sometimes I think Antoine is still alive.' He stroked Roland's head. 'Then at other times I imagine him sitting and talking with our father. I envy him then.'

The dog slurped up the cool liquid. All along the trench men checked their equipment, reaching for rifles and ammunition. Francois' heart began to race. He clutched at Roland's back.

'I keep thinking of the farm and dear Mama. I think perhaps it would have been better for you and me if we'd not listened to Antoine. It would have been better not to be a soldier. Imagine if we were at home now: we would be asleep in the farmhouse; in a little while Mama would be up checking the fire and putting water on to boil.'

Roland yawned. A fog was forming. Trails of moisture began to streak the air. Francois leaned wearily against the trench wall. 'Do you think they know we are attacking again?' he sighed and then gave a weak chuckle. 'If Antoine was here, he'd tell me to stop asking so many questions. Have a look, will you, boy?' he said softly, nodding upwards. 'I don't trust the sentries. We're all exhausted.'

Francois watched as Roland scrambled up the earth wall to a cavity that had been hollowed out for him. It was barely deep enough for the dog's body, yet by scrabbling forward Roland could balance quite well. The sandbags along the top of the trench had been repositioned and from this vantage point the dog could peer through a gap out across the battlefield. Francois stood and leaned against the trench wall as Roland curled his tail beneath him and then rested his chin on the cold ledge of compacted soil. As Roland sat quietly for long minutes, Francois grew aware of the men either side of him waiting for a warning sign, a low growl or a hurried bark. Above them shells whistled and thumped as the fog thickened.

'Nothing, eh?' Francois commented when Roland re-joined him. 'Good.'

The word was passed along the line. Francois drew Roland back to his side.

'I'll have to go out again,' Francois said softly. 'I know I talk about not doing it, about not obeying orders, but I have to. I've reconciled myself to it, Roland. I don't have any choice.' Francois laughed mirthlessly. 'Imagine, Roland: I am French; our people rose up during the revolution and deposed a king, yet now I have no say in whether I live or die.' He scratched Roland's head. 'The worst of it all is that we're to be relieved tomorrow and I can't bear the thought of leaving Antoine out there, alone.'

Roland stretched and whined softly as if he were standing by the stream on the farm, bored and impatient while the boys fished. Francois gave the slightest of smiles as the rangy animal left his side and padded along the edge of the trench, trying to keep clear of the worst of the mud and water. Occasionally he would stop and a soldier would pet him or offer a kind word.

'He's good luck, he is,' a boy not much older than Antoine stated to the man beside him, touching Roland on the head. 'They say he's rescued many men, dragged them from out there in no-man's land in God's view and everything.'

'I don't believe it,' the soldier argued. Nevertheless he patted Roland's head.

'You will when he has you by the scruff of your neck,' an older man interrupted. 'I was knocked off my feet by a shell. The next minute I'm being dragged by this mutt of a dog across no-man's land, then I wake up in a bomb crater with Antoine Chessy and,' he nodded towards the dog, 'Roland.' He knelt on the ground, accepting Roland's lick on his hand. 'Both of them dragged me to safety.'

Roland pricked his ears at the mention of his master's name.

'Where's this Antoine, then? Why didn't the dog rescue him?' the disbeliever asked.

'Weren't nothing left to rescue,' the soldier answered dryly, patting Roland. 'I wish his brother would accept it. Everyone saw it happen. One minute he's advancing with the rest of us, the next a shell lands right on him. Probably blown to smithereens.' He looked fondly at the dog. 'You can't rescue a ghost.'

'You there,' the captain stated firmly, 'ready yourself, we'll be moving in five minutes.' Roland ran to him and the captain, partially squatting, ruffled the matted hair on his back. 'And you keep out of trouble, eh?' He waggled a finger at the dog and then rubbed at his collarbone. 'You've got a good grip, boy.'

Roland retraced his steps as the gunfire stopped. The silence unnerved the dog and he broke into a run, his thick hind legs springing along the side of the trench as he rushed past soldiers. Sniffing the still-warm patch where Francois had sat, he looked up towards the top of the trench. All along the walls the men were readying for action, rifles were loaded and ammunition was checked.

'Where's Chessy?' a soldier whispered.

Louie Pascal slid the bolt on his rifle. 'I don't know. He was talking about Antoine again.'

The captain positioned himself against the trench wall with his men and drew his revolver. 'God bless,' he muttered as he lifted the whistle to his lips.

The piercing screech propelled the mass of men forward. Simultaneously Roland let out a blood-curdling howl. Spinning his body length, he gained traction on the far wall of the trench and bounded forward. His long limbs flailed the air as men scrambled over the top of the sandbags to attack. The dog weaved through the attacking force as machine-gun fire peppered the boggy ground and shells whizzed overhead. Still he ran as the men fell around him, his paws sinking deep into the mud, his muscles rippling as he barrelled onwards.

Roland left the first line of the French behind as a new barrage of shells flew towards the men, and, with a grunt, he disappeared into the encroaching fog.

≪ Chapter 18 ≫

Banyan, south-west Queensland, Australia
Late October 1916

Corally sat in the shade on the eastern side of the hut. Sticky flies buzzed the air as she tied a knot and then bit the cotton, spitting the stray thread in the dirt. As she examined the patched blouse, her father's mangy dog sniffed at the globule of saliva before beginning to dig in the exact spot. The dog's front legs gradually built up speed as a spray of dirt trailed out from behind him. Corally pelted a handful of dirt at the animal and the dog ceased digging and stared at her, one ear bent and floppy, the other pricked skyward.

There was a stain on the blouse and the collar remained stubbornly grubby despite three washes in the copper, however it would have to do. Corally contented herself with the thought of the fine woollen shawl she had snatched from a dray during a burial this morning. It would do well enough for a bit of frippery, and she was sure Harold's mother would appreciate the quality of it when Corally appeared with it wrapped about her shoulders.

'Have youse finished yet, Corally?'

At the sound of her mother's voice she gathered up the blouse and ducked around the side of the hut. She had not yet done the washing or searched for kindling, the latter a chore that took her further afield every day. She had a mind to head for the cemetery again. With this morning's service well over and the nob concerned now buried, she was sure there would be some flowers to gather up. Sacrilege it was: wasting good money on flowers or rooting them out from your own garden only to let them wilt in the sun, especially when they looked fine in a glass jar beside her bed.

'There you are, sitting in the dirt like one of them poor townies.'

'I was fixing me blouse.'

'What, to see that Lawrence boy? How a girl like you got it into her head that he'd hook up with youse has me beat.'

'He said I was special to him. That he wanted me to wait for him when he went to war.' Corally folded the blouse, shaking the cuffs free of dirt.

Edna Shaw leaned against the gappy timber of the hut. 'Has he told his parents? Has he given you a token or a ring?'

'No, but –'

'Will you marry before he leaves?' Edna slouched against the wall. 'Not too young for an engagement.' She cocked an eyebrow in emphasis.

In spite of her mother's doubts, Corally knew Harold was keen. They'd met ten times since the day he'd first declared his interest in her.

'Mother, it's up to me and Harold to work things out.'

'And him in love with you, eh? In my day if a man had a hankering for a woman he'd make it known soon enough.' She squinted. 'You've not been up to any funny business?'

Corally blushed. 'Of course not.' She tried not to think about Luther, about what he had attempted to do and how she had *almost* let him.

''Cause if a man has his way,' Edna clucked her tongue, 'used goods.'

'Harold's not like that, Ma.'

Her mother waggled a finger. 'You're gettin' above yourself, girly. Ain't no store-owner gonna let his son marry the daughter of a trapper.'

'Pa's got a respectable job at the lumberyard.'

'Sure, sure, and the sins of the past are wiped away forever.'

Corally screwed up her nose. 'What's that meant to mean?'

'That people don't forget where a person comes from.' Edna spat a fly from her mouth. 'Ever. Just take that German girl, Julie Jackson. Why you let her hang around is beyond me.'

'She's my friend.'

Edna snorted. 'When you feel like it. Mark my words: if she does manage to wash away the stink of her grandmother you can bet she'll drop you like a rotten apple when it suits. And if she doesn't you can be sure it's because no other right-minded person would be seen dead with her, not these days, not with the war and all. Women don't need women friends. Not out here where men are scarce and a jealous tongue can ruin the best-laid plan. And best you forget the Lawrence boy too and set your sights on your own kind. One of them boundary riders from out west will be needing a wife. They're always looking for someone who can cook and keep a place a bit clean.'

'I'll get the kindling.' Corally dropped the blouse through a timber shutter onto a table.

'You do that,' her mother called after her. 'Anyway, when your pa comes back tonight we'll know what's what. He was going to the ironmongery on his way home to speak to the Lawrences. Just to make sure everything was above board and all.' She sniffed. 'Beats me, but he reckons you'll be taken advantage of. Not her, I said. Not me own Corally. I brought her up with smarts. At least I thought I did.'

Corally walked through the scrub surrounding the hut. The pathway to her special spot was lined with gum and wilga trees, which gradually gave way to towering pine as the hard earth underfoot turned to sand. A fallen log made a fine seat and the close-growing trees left the air cool, even on the hottest days. Digging her heels into the soft ground, she breathed in the scents of the bush. Ever since the morning in the cemetery with Luther, Corally had relived his kiss constantly. It wasn't that she liked him or didn't like him. In fact, her feelings for Luther equalled those she had for Harold. And therein lay the problem. She didn't love either of them. One was her friend, the other her chance at a better life. She liked Harold and Luther, but a girl in her position had to be smart about things, even if it meant she might end up sad. When she thought of Harold's solemn declaration and Luther's rough handling, an overwhelming sense of loss engulfed her. There was love in Corally's heart, but it was for somebody else; someone who barely saw her and who didn't care. She counselled herself to accept that this was her lot; that she was nobody, with what her friend Julie Jackson called *limited prospects*. Being Corally Shaw was a little like emptying your pockets and finding a shiny pebble and a bit of string. All she had were her looks to trade on and it wasn't enough. Not when others had land and money and names that meant something to others. Not when parents decided whom their sons could marry. Corally knew that in the end it didn't matter if the boys liked her or wanted her; if their parents didn't think she was worth a spit, she didn't stand a chance.

It was as her father had once said: she would have to settle for dry bread – serviceable, reliable, plain old bread – while others dug their wedges into dripping. It was a hard thing, realising that people could treat her like a bit of blow-away grass on the side of the road. It was a hard thing being nobody. 'God save me,' she whispered to the trees, 'I sure would have liked the dripping.' So, she hadn't really minded Luther kissing her because it would be the closest she would ever get to a bit of dripping, and she would marry Harold because there wasn't anyone else around mildly interested in her who wasn't dirt poor and whose parents would allow the union.

When the last of the sun's rays streaked through the trees, Corally gathered an armful of wood and wandered back to the hut. In a week's time she was due to meet Harold again; a whole week. By then he planned to have told his parents that he wanted to enlist and that he also intended to get married. And if he hadn't got around to telling them yet, it sounded like her father would soon set the Lawrences straight.

As she approached the hut she saw that her father was home, splashing water from a bucket onto his face and greying hair as the dog growled and nipped at his ankles. He wiped his hands and face on his dirty shirt, prodding at an earhole with a finger. Satisfied at what he had prised free, he flicked his finding into the air and then proceeded to dunk the shirt up and down in the bucket before laying it across the rack among the drying hides. 'Your boy's been in gaol for fighting with Thaddeus Harrow.'

Corally dumped the wood at the entrance to the hut. 'Gaol? Why? How?'

'Steady on. Give a man a chance.'

They ducked beneath the water bag swinging in the hut doorway. A pot hung over an open fire at the opposite end of the room. Three pannikins and a large frying pan dangled from nails on the wall.

'Did you tell her?' Edna turned towards them, her dress patched with sweat. The ladle in her hand dripped brown water onto the dirt floor.

'I'm trying. Sit, girl.' Stewart Shaw threw his hat on the sagging bed that was partially concealed by a length of hessian strung from a makeshift rod.

The three of them sat around a narrow wooden table as Edna carried the pot across and thumped it down. The single-room hut was fiercely hot. Corally rounded her fists until her palms smarted from the bite of her nails. Why couldn't her father just spit out his news instead of behaving as if he were sitting down to a feast? The scent of last night's mutton stew was plain enough, and a second night on the same pot meant the best of the meal was already long gone.

'So, about this fight,' her father began, accepting a wedge of bread from his wife. 'No one knows what it was about but it seems Thaddeus high-tailed it out of town.'

'Go on, then,' Edna encouraged, handing the plates and spoons around and dishing out the meal.

'There's more. All the Harrow boys have taken off from Sunset Ridge, including young Dave. There's talk he was locked in his room for a time.' He turned to his daughter. 'And it seems the Lawrences didn't know about their son's pledge to you.' He blew on a spoonful of stew, his concentration directed on a single, lumpy piece of meat. 'Although they do now. Mr Lawrence was pretty straight in telling me that there weren't no union happening between their only son and –'

'And the daughter of a rabbit-trapper.' Corally finished her father's sentence.

'I told you so, Corally.' Edna brushed her hands together. 'Didn't I tell you? Anyway, look at them Harrows, eh? There's no future with them that have a few coin. They're all the same, Harrow or Lawrence. When I think of you being dragged into those legal wrangles when that wild Luther chopped off the baker's boy's finger, well it just doesn't bear thinking about you getting tied up with any of those lads.'

'I'm sorry, girl.' Her father patted her hand roughly. 'I'd like to be telling you better news.' He sucked on the spoon before delving into the mound on his plate.

Corally glanced at the blouse lying on her bed. 'Did you see Harold?' she asked hopefully.

'No, there wasn't any sign of the lad, but the copper gave me a note to give to you.' Her father searched his trouser pockets. 'It's from Harold.'

'Where is it?' Corally's stomach was beginning to churn.

'I'll just find it.' With a guilty look he walked outside.

'Good man, your father.' Edna held a spoonful of stew mid-way to her mouth. 'Thinks the world of you. No point dropping that bottom lip of yours, my girl. I've told you more than once to stick to your own kind.'

Her father reappeared. 'Here you go, girly.'

Corally took the wet envelope, which had obviously been left in her father's shirt. Opening it carefully, she smoothed the note on the table. This was something at least, she decided, as she flicked a look of *I told you so* at her glowering mother. Although the letter was blurred and smudged from being dunked in the bucket, the letters were still distinct. Corally imagined Harold writing it; his thick fingers with their large oval nails carefully constructing a secret message just for her.

Edna spooned more stew into her mouth and then cut another piece of bread for her husband. 'Just a pity,' she said, her mouth crammed with food, 'that none of us can read.'

Dave woke coughing. The stench of manure filled his nostrils as he spat out whatever was lodged in his throat. He turned over stiffly, conscious of the complaints that seemed to come from every bone in his body. Overhead, sunlight filtered down through a wooden-slatted ceiling, the weak light highlighting dust that hung as if suspended in water. There was straw beneath him, the smell of sweat and urine and horses. He felt woozy, as if he were moving. Dave clutched at his head. His body *was* being jostled from side to side. Hell, he *was* moving. Through the cracks in the timber walls the countryside whooshed past him. There were hills in the distance, and a rising sun. The clickety-clack noise battering his aching head came from the train he was aboard. Dave crawled into the corner of the carriage. Around him men slept or muttered among themselves, while at the far end a number of horses lifted their legs restlessly as the movement of the train pushed the occupants from left to right.

'I don't reckon you're meant to be here, mate.' The man talking to Dave had a black eye and a cut lip. He sat cross-legged a few feet away, a length of straw clamped between his teeth. He nodded at the opposite end of the carriage where four soldiers passed a silver flask between them. 'What were you doing in McInerney's old shed anyway?'

Dave's memory was hazy. He recalled riding through the bush in the dead of night, of getting lost and bunking down. 'I didn't know whose shed it was.' He was dying for a drink. 'I was trying to get to Banyan.' He thought of his mad dash to the river on horseback, of the moonless night, which darkened the bush, turning the trees murky with shadows.

'Well, you were headed in the opposite direction.' The man clucked his tongue. 'Ain't the time for travelling, lad, nearing the dark of the moon. That's the time for hunkering down.'

Dave's head vibrated against the carriage wall. The old shearing shed he had found had seemed as good a place as any to camp the night he had fled Sunset Ridge – once he had realised he was lost. He had hoped that after a night in the nondescript shed the following morning's daylight would allow him to get a better sense of the country he was in, to find some sign that would lead him on to Banyan. So, he had bedded down at the end of the lanolin-smoothed board where a draft of wind had teased him into a restless sleep as he tried to reconcile what he had seen back at Sunset Ridge between his friend Rodger and Miss Waites.

The crack of a rifle sounded, once, twice.

'That's some young nob shooting kangaroos out of a carriage window. They're letting him shoot 'cause he's giving the train guards a shot as well and the men are placing bets, so the sergeant over there tells me. Four from four; a crack shot, he is.'

Dave had a sudden and unpleasant recollection of being dragged along the board by the ankle and then punched and kicked until his face hit dirt.

'Seems like you got caught 'cause of me.' The man gave him a guilty look and chewed the inside of his cheek. 'They wouldn't have got me except I helped myself to a bit of food from the local store and the owner had the coppers onto me right fast. I never realised you were in the shed. Anyway, next minute the both of us are in the hands of the army. Those soldiers,' he gestured to the end of the carriage, 'were out bush following up on a lead from a farmer. Riley and Turtle over there,' the man pointed to two men seated nearby, 'joined up a few months back but jumped before they were due to set sail. They've been holed up in an empty water tank for weeks, living off the land. Near dry-boiled, they were, in this heat.'

'Why?' Dave asked.

'Why? 'Cause they changed their mind. They don't want to go and fight the bloody Hun, especially since the bastards are killing us like we're the rabbits in a rabbit shoot.'

Dave looked at Riley and Turtle. Both men sat with their arms locked around their knees. Their faces were red and peeling. 'So, they were running away?'

'Everyone's running from something.' He eyed Dave carefully. 'Thing is, a few months back you might get a white feather, but a man could live with being a cold-footer, especially if his mates had already been blown to bits back in '15. But now, what with so many dead and maimed and that bloody Billy Hughes and his referendum on conscription, well the whole country's arguing. I thought I'd go bush, get meself a job and lie low until the toffs had finished blowing everyone up over there. Turns out the folks out in the scrub want everyone to be a hero as well. Anyway, they bundled us both up and the next thing we're on the Western Mail heading to Sydney. I got a choice – gaol for stealing or a job with army pay. Them fellas were real convincing.' He rubbed his jaw, wiggled a tooth. 'It's a pity. Normally the women would cross the road for a better look at me, but I ain't at my finest at the moment.'

'Sydney,' Dave repeated. He had heard of the city often enough but now that he was travelling towards it, it didn't sound so appealing.

One of the soldiers walked the length of the swaying carriage. His hat was propped on the back of his head and an unlit cigarette appeared glued to his lower lip. 'Name?'

'David Harrow.'

'Stand up when you're being spoken to.'

Dave got to his feet unsteadily.

'That's better. Now, what were you doing with Marty in that wool shed?'

Dave swallowed. 'Nothing. I got lost. I was heading to Banyan to find my brothers.'

'Well, the army takes no responsibility for runaways who find themselves in the wrong place at the wrong time.' The sergeant lit the cigarette and peered at Dave through the smoke. 'You look familiar. What did you say your surname was?'

'Harrow,' Dave repeated.

'Bugger me.' The sergeant took a drag of his cigarette and then nodded his head back in the direction he had come from. 'This way.'

Dave sidestepped Riley's and Turtle's now outstretched limbs as he battled the shuddering train with legs unaccustomed to movement. He squeezed past the horses, and was greeted by a blast of fresh air and harsh daylight as he followed the sergeant from one carriage to the next and then on up a centre aisle lined with bench seats. This carriage was packed with young men of varying ages.

Groups were huddled together, laughing and joking, some smoking and playing cards, others betting on a game of two-up. Towards the rear of the carriage, fifteen or so men were gathered in a semi-circle around a carriage window. A rifle shot rang out and a chorus of cheers went up.

'You lot,' the sergeant called out, addressing the group.

'C'mon, Serg,' one of the youths commented. 'We're only having a bit of fun.'

'You Harrow boys breed like flaming rabbits,' the sergeant announced to the two occupants kneeling on the bench seat. 'I've found another one.' He pushed Dave forward, his hand gripping his shoulder.

'I'll be damned, Dave, what are *you* doing here?' Thaddeus asked, lowering his rifle.

'Dave?' Luther was bug-eyed.

'Likely the same as the rest of us,' the sergeant said, looking at Dave, 'considering he's part-way to Sydney.' He glanced back to Thaddeus and raised an eyebrow. 'Brother?'

'Yes. What happened?' Thaddeus asked.

'Holy frost,' Luther frowned, 'you're bl-black and bl-blue.' He reached for the tomahawk at his side.

Thaddeus stayed him with a cautionary hand.

The sergeant looked the three of them up and down like they were week-old bread and bared pointed teeth. 'The lad here got caught up in a kerfuffle that likely wouldn't have happened if he'd not been out wandering the bush in the middle of the night, apparently searching for you.' Finally he let go of Dave's shoulder. 'Well, he's your responsibility now.' He waved a finger at Luther. 'And I know who *you* are. You're the lad that maimed that boy. So, you behave yourself, Chopper Harrow.'

Luther grinned.

'What happened?' Thaddeus asked again when the sergeant left them and the assembled crowd lost interest in the conversation.

'Father belted me and locked me up because I didn't know where you two had run off to and he thought I was lying. So I ran away.' He sat heavily on the bench seat. 'Do you have any water?' he asked tiredly.

'C-crikey.' Luther passed Dave his water bag. 'The old fella'll h-have our h-hides.'

Dave drank thirstily. 'What are you two doing here?'

Thaddeus scratched a fuzz-covered chin. 'When I didn't meet up with Luther I figured I might as well get the train to Sydney. And, bugger me, if he wasn't sitting up in the first carriage when we stopped at Whitewood.'

'What w-will we d-do with him?' Luther asked Thaddeus.

Thaddeus looked out the carriage window. The countryside was a blur. 'Well, he can't go back. G.W. will go near to killing him after everything that's happened. He'll have to come with us.'

'With us?' Luther repeated. 'You've g-got to be j-joking.'

'Have you got a better idea?'

Luther scowled. 'T-talk about th-things not going t-to plan.'

'What's that meant to mean?' Thaddeus asked.

Luther ignored the question. 'He'll n-never get through. He's t-too young.'

Thaddeus studied his younger brother. 'He's tall enough, and if he's with us there's a good chance they'll take him as well.'

'For what?' Dave's head was pounding.

'The sergeant reckons the British are pushing the government for five-thousand-odd Australian reinforcements a month,' Thaddeus continued. 'They'll take him.'

Luther shook his head. 'I d-don't know, Th-thaddeus.'

Dave took another slug of water. 'What are you talking about?'

Luther turned to his brother. 'War, D-dave. He's t-talking about going to war.'

≪ Chapter 19 ≫

Banyan, south-west Queensland, Australia
Late October 1916

Catherine Waites stared out the window of the Banyan Post Office and thought of the life she had left behind. It had been days since Dave's disappearance and two days since her position as governess on Sunset Ridge had ceased to exist. Her former employer, G.W. Harrow, had spent every afternoon following his youngest son's desertion on the homestead veranda. He sat there from midday on, a lone figure tapping anxious fingers. Around him station life continued. Sheep were rotated into different paddocks and checked for flies, fences were inspected, and repairs made where necessary, and watering points checked. The recently purchased cows now appeared to be G.W.'s primary concern. Rodger revealed to Catherine before he left that an old boundary hut was being rebuilt where the cattle were running, and a man well past his prime had been employed to watch over them. If the stockmen thought anything amiss with the boss's constant vigilance, they never uttered a word. All living on the property knew that the Harrow boys had run off; they went about their duties with quiet efficiency, arriving at daybreak for their orders and retreating to their quarters at dusk.

And still G.W. Harrow sat. It was an image Catherine would carry for the rest of her life; a middle-aged man, sitting on his homestead veranda, waiting for his three sons to ride in from the scrub.

Catherine remembered once again the last conversation she'd had with Rodger.

'What will you do?' Rodger's hand was warm on hers the morning he came to say goodbye.

'Try and find employment in the village,' she replied. 'I just feel the boys will be back.'

Rodger pinched her cheek lightly. 'I'll write you care of the Banyan Post Office.'

'Cook's taken to the bottle,' Catherine revealed as her arm looped through his. 'Dave was her favourite. She told me she thinks he fell to harm in the scrub.' Her lips puckered. 'Injured and eaten by wild pigs, she says. Och, no wonder she screams in her sleep.'

Rodger pressed his lips to her brow. 'Don't think the worst.'

Catherine wasn't convinced. 'Ye will be careful?' Her cheek was against his, the scent of him filling her so completely that Catherine wondered once again how she could ever let him go to the other side of the world.

'I thought we weren't to speak of war?'

'You're right, we weren't.' She brushed her lips against his. 'Just the same,' she said softly, 'be careful and . . . come back to me.'

Outside, a dray trundled slowly past the ironmongery, waves of gritty dirt blowing the length of the unmade road. The dust swirled in through the window, and as Catherine slammed it shut, perspiration trickled the length of her spine. The post office – now her place of employment – was an uninspiring edifice of timber, with a narrow veranda and four constricting wooden pillars. It was deceptively bright inside the square building and unceasingly bland. A long counter cut the room in half; a row of chairs lined the customer side, while behind Catherine were the wooden mail pigeonholes and behind that desks and postal bags. Were it not for recent events, Catherine never would have accepted the position advertised in the local newspaper by the postmistress, Mrs Dempsey. Her options, however, were limited if she wanted to stay in the district. The local school had no vacancies and the larger outlying stations either already employed governesses or sent their sons away to board at city schools.

Catherine blew her nose on a linen handkerchief. An eerie noise was keeping her sleepless at night in the boarding house, and if she had not known better she could have sworn it was the sound of someone wailing. She was so tired and worried. She couldn't stop revisiting the night Dave ran away. It was Rodger who had found Dave's sketches lying outside on the grass and, try as she may, Catherine couldn't help but blame herself. Somehow, perhaps quite unwittingly, she had played a part in the boy's decision to leave and guilt gnawed at her.

'You all right then, Miss?'

Catherine stepped behind the wooden counter and pasted a smile on her face. 'Guid morning.'

'One stamp, please.' The man wore a white apron; flour speckled his clothing. 'I know you. You're the governess from out at the Harrows' place,' he said, sliding a coin across the counter.

'Was,' Catherine admitted, picking up the coin and putting it in the tin change box. The man was stringy looking with a knob of crow-black hair on the crown of his head. She selected a stamp from the stamp book in the counter drawer and stuck it on the letter.

'Well, never mind. Probably just as well to be out of the place. Mob of hoodlums, those boys. Cut my lad's finger clean off, that Luther did. Bugger of a boy, excusing my language, Miss.'

Catherine bristled. Flipping the lid on the stamp pad, she inked the round postage stamp and bashed it on the letter. 'Well, Mr Evans, as I believe ye have just purchased a share in the funeral parlour with the compensation due your son, it certainly wasn't all bad, was it?'

Evans's bottom lip flapped open, revealing three spaces where teeth should have been. Dropping the letter into one of the gaping postal bags slung over a wooden frame, Catherine watched him leave the post office.

Across the street the Imperial Café opened its door, followed by the general store. The village came alive gradually, although the clanging of metal from the blacksmith and the distant sound of the steam-driven saw at the lumberyard had been disturbing the otherwise sleeping village since daylight. Catherine wondered again at Dave's disappearance. The entire station knew that the youngest of the Harrow boys had been soundly whipped and locked in his room and yet somehow his sketches had ended up abandoned in the dirt outside her quarters. She thought back to the early hours of that morning, when Rodger stepped outside and found Dave's sketches lying in the dirt.

'He's in love with you,' Rodger announced. Having gathered the sketches up in the dark of pre-dawn, he had delivered them back to her room, and they had studied them side by side.

'Don't be ridiculous; he's a child.'

The sketches said otherwise. Rodger gazed at the portraits of Catherine. 'These are,' he looked at her, 'beautiful.'

She knew that the images were indeed masterful, yet were they her? No, every detail, every attribute had been heightened, refined, rendered beautiful. Catherine knew she may have been the subject but she doubted that anyone could ever guess the sketches were of her. With a twinge of delight she realised she had inspired him. She was the artist's muse.

'Perhaps he saw us through the window,' Rodger suggested, turning a sheet of paper upside down, absorbed by a sketch of a dismembered chicken.

'I dinna understand. What would he have seen?' she asked. 'The curtain was drawn.'

'Enough?' Rodger replied. 'Was it drawn enough?' He gathered the sketches together. 'You keep them,' he suggested. 'If he comes back –'

'When he comes back,' she corrected, 'I wouldn't know what to say.' In the end, she had not taken the precious sketches. She had left them behind.

'Miss Waites,' Mrs Dempsey said unnecessarily loudly. 'Nothing to do, is there? Time to daydream out the window, have you?' The postmistress jangled a brass ring of keys in Catherine's face and then slid them across the counter. 'Second cupboard. Two parcels for Mrs Marchant, thank you; she has just arrived in the village.'

Catherine retrieved the parcels and sat them on the counter as three gentlemen walked past to line up for the services of the telegraph office.

Mrs Dempsey observed the clock hanging on the wall behind the counter. 'Well, get ready, girl. We are approaching rush hour. Remember?'

Catherine checked the penny stamps and the day's postmark and rearranged the selection of writing paper and matching envelopes displayed on the polished counter.

'And?' Mrs Dempsey asked.

Catherine double-checked the counter's contents once again. 'Och, I'm sorry I don't –'

'Well, you wouldn't, would you? Stuck out there in that big fancy house oblivious to what's going on in the world.'

'I'm not oblivious to anything, Mrs Dempsey.' Catherine's nostrils flared.

The three older gentlemen lined up at the far end of the room turned in their direction.

'No, of course you're not,' Mrs Dempsey replied tartly, greeting the waiting men with a polite nod. 'The scales? Don't you think there will be mothers sending comfort parcels to their boys at the front? Once a month I sent something to my lad. Soap, a book, socks or a flask of brandy – anything to get him through the worst of it.' Her voice trailed off.

'Och, yes. Sorry.' Retrieving the scales from the cupboard, Catherine sat them on the counter.

'Now, the Cobb & Co. coach comes through Banyan once a week at noon and there's a mighty amount of mail to be sorted and dispatched onwards, the majority of which is then delivered to the outlying stations. I'll be depending on you to handle this quickly and efficiently.' She looked Catherine up and down again, as if suspecting she had missed something on first inspection. 'This isn't some soft job, if that's what you were expecting. This isn't some squatter's homestead with a cook and maids to be at your beck and call.'

'I do realise that, Mrs Dempsey.'

'Do you? Well, I don't expect to come in here and find you staring out the window.' The older woman balanced a pair of spectacles on the bridge of her nose. 'Now, I've some errands to run.'

The customers arrived soon after Mrs Dempsey's departure. 'Neatly timed,' Catherine muttered as the queue reached fifteen. She sold twenty one-penny stamps to a red-eyed woman with a pile of black-rimmed funeral cards.

'Her husband, dead at forty,' the next customer explained. 'Never should have been accepted. He had a gammy leg.'

After that, the morning became a blur. One strange face was replaced by another and then another. The majority of the customers introduced themselves, eyeing her with interest. She was learning that word spread quickly in the village. All the women knew who Catherine was and where she came from and most had comments to make.

'Shame about those poor boys running away.'

'Young rascal; that boy should have been sent to reform school.'

'You're better off with us, love, with your own kind, eh?'

'That's what happens when a man lets his wife make the decisions.'

'Don't mind them,' a portly woman commented.

'Guid morning, how are ye?'

'Good, my dear.' Mrs Marchant introduced herself and signed the ledger on receipt of her parcels. 'Not much happens in the village and any gossip takes people's minds off things.' She handed over a package wrapped in pre-used brown paper and string. The word 'France' was written in a bold hand.

Catherine positioned the scales and sat the parcel in the weighing pan hanging beneath the beam. In the opposite pan she placed weights until the scales balanced. She checked the postage cost in a tattered book. There was a special section for overseas deliveries, with the required postage for the AIF and the locations for troops stationed abroad underlined in pencil.

'My Joseph's been there for nearly six months, and not a scratch. I put it down to my prayers at night and the weekly parcels I send him. It's not much, sometimes a nip of rum or new socks. "Can't get enough socks, Mum," he tells me, bless him. But this time I made a fruitcake. Wrapped up good and tight, it is. Made the mixture real dense and sticky and added some extra rum to keep the chill out. It will be winter over there soon. Nasty time in them northern places.'

'Well, I'm sure he will enjoy it, Mrs Marchant.' Catherine dabbed the stamps on a dampened sponge and stuck them on the paper. 'My fiancé, Rodger, has gone to enlist,' she revealed. Her cheeks pinked up as she stamped the parcel.

The older woman stilled Catherine's hand with her own. 'I'll pray for him.' And with a kindly smile the portly woman was gone.

When a lull in business finally came, Catherine listened to the soft metallic beeps sounding from the telegraph office while she stared at the neat labelling above each pigeonhole lining the wall. The area was divided into two sections: Banyan residents and those who lived beyond the town limits. Each section was arranged alphabetically, and each square represented a business and family; each slot a microcosm of joy and sadness, life and death, hope and despair. Telling Mrs Marchant, albeit briefly, about Rodger had loosened something within her. It was the first time Catherine had spoken of him in a personal manner and it reminded her that there was no confidante in her life, no close friend.

She thought of the funeral cards that were sitting in the bottom of one of the mailbags and of Mrs Marchant's parcel bound for France. Catherine had no doubt that boys from her home village in Scotland would have enlisted, but with no cordial relations existing with what remained of her relatives she would never know which of those families were affected. Today was the first time she had been confronted with the actualities of war, with the women left behind to pray and hope. More importantly, Catherine realised that she was now one of those women. If she had ever wanted to crawl into a hole and wait out the war in desperate isolation, she had chosen the wrong occupation. The post office was the centre of life – and particularly of all things pertaining to the war – in Banyan. At the thought of Rodger and the Harrow boys, Catherine clutched the counter for support. Perhaps Mrs Dempsey was correct. Maybe she had been oblivious.

At day's end Catherine walked outside into a stifling heat. A handful of horse-drawn drays shuffled impatiently in the street, while at the far end of the dirt road the Banyan Hotel was ringed by horse-drawn vehicles. Dabbing at the perspiration on her brow, Catherine crossed the street to the single Box tree and sat beneath its shade. The street was quiet, the leaden heat forcing everyone indoors. Spirals of dust floated down the middle of the road as she wished for a zephyr of air to rustle the leaves overhead. Catherine felt like a fool, burdened by a dislocated life; a girl at odds with her family; a governess without a governess position and three charges who had run away. Worst of all, she had kissed her lover goodbye, and surely sent him to his death.

'Hello.'

A winsome young girl stood before her. Catherine absorbed the dated skirt and blouse, both carrying the remnants of old stains. 'Do we know each other?' she asked the girl, who had a fine woollen shawl tied absently about her waist.

'Well, maybe if you've been to the Banyan Show, you might have seen me there.'

Catherine placed a hand to her chest. 'Corally Shaw, of course.' She paused. 'I'm sorry. I'm not really myself today.'

The girl inclined her head to one side. 'Out of sorts, are you?'

'Yes, I guess ye could call it that.'

'You were the one that taught Luther and Dave, weren't you?'

'And Thaddeus for a time, yes.'

Corally bit her lip. 'Have you heard from them? I mean, I know they've run away from home and all, but do you know where they've gone?'

The girl looked as if she could burst into tears at any moment. 'No, no I don't.'

The girl wiped at her nose with the back of a hand. 'I thought you might have heard something. That's why I waited. My pa told me you were working here now and I figured if there was anything to know, well you'd know it; especially with handling the mail and all.'

'I wish I did.'

The girl eyed Catherine for a good few seconds. She was clear-skinned with extraordinarily coloured eyes that instantly reminded Catherine of the sea. Some would think her beyond pretty, and for a moment Catherine almost understood Luther's rash act of chivalry.

'Do you know why Dave left?' The girl's voice was velvety, almost a caress. 'Was it really because his parents locked him up and beat him?'

'I dinna know.' The gossips had been busy. Catherine stood and began walking back to the boarding house.

'How can you not know? You lived out there,' the girl countered.

'I was only the governess,' Catherine replied. Guilt made her wary.

'So, one minute all the boys were at Sunset Ridge and then they were gone,' Corally stated simply. 'So, they didn't tell anyone out there what they were up to?'

'No.'

'Dave would have been too young to join up, wouldn't he?' Corally asked, matching Catherine's measured walk as she headed absently down the street.

'I would have thought so,' Catherine agreed. 'But from what I hear the British government is desperate for volunteers, so I dinna know. He may have gone.'

Corally tucked her arm through Catherine's. The familiarity surprised the older woman yet she was quietly grateful for the companionship. 'I have this letter, you see. It's from Harold Lawrence. We was promised, but now Mr Lawrence tells me that Harold's gone to war and that it's my fault on account of the fact that he couldn't face his parents after he'd been bold with me.'

'Bold with ye? Ye and Harold were *engaged*?'

The girl stiffened and pulled her arm free.

She hadn't meant to sound surprised. However, the little Catherine knew of Harold Lawrence, based on his frequent visits to Sunset Ridge, suggested that not only would the boy be wasted in an ironmongery, but he could do far better than a girl such as Corally Shaw.

'I thought you'd be different,' Corally said flatly.

'I apologise. I didn't realise Harold was outing with anybody.' The girl had a defiant look about her, one that reminded Catherine of Luther. 'What were ye going to show me?'

Corally was not one to be so easily fooled. 'You're not so much older than me, you know, and being a governess doesn't make you better.'

'I never said it did.' Catherine guessed she was a good five or six years older than the girl, although Corally did seem to have a confidence beyond her years.

The girl appeared to weigh up both Catherine's answer and whatever quandary that had led her to seek the older woman out. 'Come on.' She led Catherine down the alleyway, the lingering scent of smoke hanging in the air as they passed the blacksmith to cross the dirt track that bordered the Banyan River. A slight breeze drifted up from the waterway as the girl wove through the trees, her clothing merging with the dull browns of the bush. Catherine lifted her skirts as she skittered across the sloping ground in pursuit. Finally they arrived at a clearing part-way down the bank of the river. Catherine's heels slipped in the leaf litter as she caught glimpses of Corally through the trees. She came to a sliding stop against the thick trunk of a tree.

'Here will do,' Corally announced, sitting in the leaves and dirt beneath a shady tree. She patted the sandy earth by her side, flicking at the ants trundling across the dry ground. 'It's about the coolest spot, and apart from the ants there's nothing that bites, unless a snake appears.'

Dabbing at the sweat on her upper lip, Catherine sank to the ground.

'The thing is, I reckon Harold hasn't gone anywhere, on account of the fact he promised he'd see me this week and he's always been true that way, you know, saying something and meaning it and he said nothing to me about going to the war straightaway.' The girl unfolded the letter carefully. 'I have a friend. Her name's Julie, but I didn't want her to know what was going on.'

'Why ever not? That's what friends are for.' The girl didn't answer. 'Don't ye trust her?' Catherine asked.

Corally considered the question. 'Well, this is important. I couldn't risk asking anyone in town about Harold because they might run and tell his parents and all hell would break loose.' She glanced at Catherine. 'Sorry about the blaspheming. Anyway, most of the folks around here think they're hoity-toity and they ain't got time for the likes of me.'

Catherine was loath to agree. Unfortunately, she had seen clearly how well developed the class system was in the Banyan district. The property owners were king, followed by the shop owners, while domestics, pastoral workers and shop staff had their own pyramid of importance that firmly placed the poor and the unemployed at the bottom. Catherine had seen the distinct have-and-have-not attitude at its worst during Luther's trial.

Corally smoothed a letter gently across her knee. 'The thing is, when I heard that you'd left the Harrow place and come to live in town I figured you'd be the one to ask on account of you being a governess and all and not being –' Corally chewed the words over, 'one of them.' She nodded towards the village. 'Or them,' she finished, gesturing over the river.

'I see.'

'Do you?'

Catherine knew that she had been found wanting, and shame flooded her cheeks.

Almost reluctantly Corally passed her the letter. 'I can't read,' she admitted, her gaze directed at the sloping river bank and the curl of water below.

The paper was water-stained, the words smeared. Holding the note to the light, Catherine studied the curve of the writing until letters formed into a semblance of understanding and most words could be deciphered.

'Tell me.' The girl pulled her knees to her chin, her face open and eager. 'I reckon he's out bush and that the letter has directions to join him.'

'It's badly damaged. I can't make out some of the words.'

'It doesn't matter,' the girl answered in a rush of enthusiasm. 'Just whatever you can read, it'll be enough.'

Catherine began.

My dear Corally,

My father is against our union. Although I tried to persuade him, he remains adamant. He talks of water finding its own level. You and I know different, and it's the knowing which counts in the end.

I have decided to enlist immediately. I believe in doing one's duty for the Empire and so I join the great struggle. It's long been on my mind as you know and now I see war as a means to an end. Soldiers make money and with the war heading into its third year I can't possibly see how it could last much longer.

So my question . . . will you marry me tomorrow? Once we are joined and I'm at war . . . well, simply put, it will be too late. We have talked of this briefly and without the benefit of our parents' consent, but believe me I would be ever so proud to have you by my side.

Meet me at dawn tomorrow at the Presbyterian Church. I have spoken to the Reverend and he has agreed to marry us at first light. Should we not be joined by the time I ride northwards mid-morning tomorrow, I will assume that you do not feel as I do. In that case I miss you, I want to wish you a grand life.

Yours,

H

The letter was warm in Catherine's hand, the girl's eyes moist.

'Is that all?' Corally whispered.

'Yes.' Catherine refolded the letter.

Tears slid down the girl's cheeks. Picking up a stick she tossed it towards the river. The branch wavered in the sand before falling on its side.

'Would ye like me to re-read it?' Catherine offered. Instead, the girl retrieved the note and tucked it into a skirt pocket. 'How long have ye had the letter?' It dawned on Catherine that 'tomorrow' had probably come and gone. 'Corally?' The girl's right hand curled and uncurled itself.

'Too long.' She gave a muffled sob.

'Och, I am sorry.' What else could she say? It was bad enough kissing your lover goodbye and sending him off to war, but for a man to leave on such terms and for the girl who loved him to suffer so terribly . . . 'Ye could write to him, Corally, care of the Australian Imperial Forces, and explain what happened. If he has enlisted the letter would find him eventually.'

'How?' Corally sniffed. 'I can't read and I can't write.'

A green-and-yellow bird settled in a branch above them. It tweeted prettily, causing both women to trace its movements among the foliage.

Catherine considered the young girl's plight. 'I could help ye.'

The two women shared a conspiratorial smile.

⋘ Chapter 20 ⋙

Verdun, France
Late October 1916

Francois opened his eyes to a steel-grey sky and a blurred land-scape of dark, uneven shapes. Movement caught his attention and he reached for the rifle by his side. His hand scrabbled air and he sucked in a painful breath. It was as if something were astride his chest, pushing his body downwards into the after-world. There was no rifle by his side, no bayonet, nothing. The thought of lying unarmed in the muddy debris of the battlefield filled him with dread. Saliva caught in his throat. He tried desperately to work it forward but even the muscles in his mouth were against him. He was so thirsty. His tongue felt overly large, too large to moisten his cracked lips. The pain struck at him as if a knife. Something wasn't right. Maybe it was him? Maybe his body was lying in two in the muck that was Verdun and his brain was yet to comprehend the inevitability of his destruction. Could he will death before compre-hension came to him?

There it was again: the same flicker of movement. 'Germans,' Francois mouthed, clenching his teeth against another rippling sting. They must be Germans approaching. He had heard that the Red Cross had access to the German hospitals; maybe he would be captured and sent for medical treatment behind enemy lines. It was the best he could hope for. He lay perfectly still. It was possible that the Germans would pass him by. It was possible that his own men would find him. He needed to scream. A terrible throbbing tore at his body causing his limbs to shudder and his brain to float into the ether. Images flickered like a kaleidoscope merging horror with snatches of life before the war; the trickling stream, the curl of smoke above the farmhouse, the broad shoulders of his father that he once rode as a child.

Breath wheezed in and out of his lungs. What had happened? Francois wondered. How did he come to be lying out here? He could only recall fragments: night, cold, the wet slick of water, or was it blood? There had been a burst of artillery and then he had fallen. His arms were outstretched to break the impact but instead he toppled over and over. He was a boy again, having tumbling competitions with Antoine. Over and over the two of them rolled, their parents sitting in the dappled light beneath the willow trees, laughing in delight.

The pain throbbed and pushed and pulled as if a living being.

Antoine. He had ventured out one more time to look for his brother. What had Francois been thinking, running out across no-man's land while the shells flew overhead? When the whistle sounded from the trench it was too late to turn back and so he had continued onwards, a lone man leading a futile attack.

Francois expected the Germans to be on him at any minute. He guessed that if it came to the worst he could still stab one of them with his dagger, if he could find it. He was cold now, very cold. Above, planes flew overhead, their engines threatening him with a growling whirr, and all around the noise of the shelling continued. When the pain came again he screamed.

'Next.' The male voice was harassed yet firm.

A blur of people moved back and forth. Beyond them the flapping sides of a large marquee opened out onto lines of tents and rows of prone soldiers, and still the roar of battle hummed in his ears.

'I really can't see the point of taking up valuable ambulance space with these cases. I'm sure the main dressing stations just don't want to deal with the dying.'

'Shush up, Nurse, this one's conscious. And wipe that M off his forehead. He was one of the lucky ones to receive morphine. Most have to manage with opiates.'

As if a bystander, Francois watched as his muddy tunic was cut open and his chest was prodded. A man and a woman stood over him. One wore a Red Cross armband.

'I don't think we'll be able to manage them all, Doctor, there are too many.'

'Remember your training, Nurse. Assess the patient, label and then move on.'

'But the shelling. I can't stand the shelling. It's too close.' The woman raised a hand to her nose, leaving a streak of blood on her pale skin as she passed the remnants of Francois' kit and uniform to a waiting orderly.

'Anna, remember your position here.'

The nurse sniffed and began to cut at his rotting boots, before the scissors sliced away at his trousers.

'He may make it,' the doctor deliberated, dressing the chest wound quickly. 'Attach a chest label and – no don't. Look at his leg: gas gangrene. Mark him urgent.'

'And the head wound?' the nurse asked as she pinned a label to Francois' chest bandage.

'Superficial by the looks of it and . . . What on earth is that? Are those *teeth* marks on his shoulder?'

The nurse leaned over Francois. He felt her breath on him and smelled the sweet scent of her. Flowers, spring flowers; he had been saved by a woman who smelled of flowers.

The nurse shook her head. 'I have seen others with this mark. The men talk of a dog rescuing them.' Her fingers traced the deep purple bruising that surrounded the bite mark.

The doctor raised an eyebrow, peering at the puncture marks. 'The Red Cross uses dogs to find the fallen, and of course the German dogs are trained to locate the wounded. But I have not heard of the French having a dog that would drag a man to safety. No, no, there must be another explanation. Give him some brandy and then get some orderlies and clear this space.'

The nurse poured a measure of brandy into a tin cup and, lifting Francois' head, forced the burning liquid down his throat.

Francois swallowed. 'Where am I?' he murmured.

'A casualty clearing station, soldier. Next,' the doctor called.

Francois felt his body lift upwards. The tent opening revealed neat lines of bodies, some bandaged, some partially naked. Why had they been left out in the cold? He craned his head towards the scene outside, but his view was quickly obscured. A hard coldness seeped into him as feet pounded by his head. Black boots, brown boots, lace-ups, thick-heeled hiking boots, boots being dragged. He gazed into the glassy eyes of a soldier clutching at the stump where his arm should have been and watched as dollops of blood dripped onto the duckboards covering the earth beneath. Wounded were resting in every available space, both in cots and on the ground. When the familiar stab of pain coursed through his body, Francois began to weep.

'Move him out of the way.'

The air rushed.

'Have you seen all the ambulances?' The voice belonged to one of the men carrying him. The fair-skinned youngster's features moved in and out of focus. Francois squinted and tried to concentrate.

'The brass have given the doctors two days,' the orderly continued. 'Those who haven't been moved on to a base hospital by then will be dead.'

Nurses weaved to and fro between the wounded, as doctors yelled for assistance.

'Those three are dead,' a nurse called out.

Francois felt a whoosh of air and then the grey of the sky pressed down on him. Overhead, planes buzzed and the firecracker zip of artillery fractured the atmosphere. A work detail of four men flicked cigarettes on the ground and picked up shovels leaning against munitions crates. A shell sped over the clearing hospital to land a mile away. The boom was deafening.

'That was close,' the fair-skinned orderly commented. 'I don't go much on working only nine miles from the front.'

'Any further away, Andre,' his assistant at the other end of the stretcher commented, 'and most of these poor men would already be dead.'

Francois felt the steady creep of hurt readying itself for attack. Why would they not give him anything for the pain? Orderlies rushed past carrying empty stretchers. They were in some form of queue; a woman was giving instructions. He stared at the boggy ground, at a single spray of greenery that edged its way up from beneath the wet soil. Further away, two men walked to the line of prone soldiers. They hesitated for a moment and then picked one up. The body sagged in the middle as the men carried the soldier away.

'Nurse Valois is back,' the one called Andre said. 'She arrived last night.'

'She's too old for you, my friend, too much of a woman for you.'

'Rubbish,' Andre retorted. 'Age makes little difference to me. All that long brown hair and those dark eyes. We would be a good match.'

His friend laughed.

Francois felt the palpitations grow in his chest. They passed a row of tents fanning out in a circle and for a minute he thought he was to be laid with the dead. 'Don't put me there with them.

I'm alive, I'm still alive.' Did the words leave his lips? He couldn't be sure.

'He's in shock,' Andre's friend explained. 'Look how much he's shaking. You'll be all right,' the orderly said to Francois. 'You're being sent to a base hospital. Bloody hell!' His attention returned to his friend. 'Have you seen his shoulder? Look at it. Bite marks.'

The orderlies ducked their heads as they walked into another tent. Francois floated above occupied cots before being deposited on the floor. The jolt caused a shocking pain to ripple through his body and the tent went dark.

'See that: those teeth have gone clean through his uniform.' The excitement was evident in Andre's voice. 'That's the third I've seen. And that dead captain. He had marks on both shoulders. One lot appeared to be healed. I heard one of the field medics talking about a mongrel dog that rescued thirty wounded men during the night.'

'That's enough nonsense.' Nurse Valois waited for the orderlies to move out of the way. With a strange calmness she wiped bloody hands on her apron. 'You should be too busy for gossip.' Screams sounded outside the tent. 'Well, go on, someone needs help.'

The orderlies stood to one side of the tent flap as more stretchers were carried in, the occupants deposited hurriedly on the floor.

'All hell's broken loose in the marquee – there's a wild animal in there,' one of the orderlies told Nurse Valois as he placed a patient on the ground.

At the other end of the tent, which housed forty cots, a second nurse, Nurse Duval, suggested he concentrate on the task at hand.

Nurse Valois agreed, waving the young man away. 'I've enough to contend with here,' she replied with obvious irritation as she washed her hands in a basin of bloody water. 'Wild animals? Ridiculous.'

'It's true,' a soldier with a bandaged head said croakily. 'The dog's name is Roland.'

'Delirious,' she muttered. Nurse Valois found those cases the hardest to deal with. The gaping wounds she could attend to, but the mad ranting caused by wound shock and a poor reaction to morphine – for those fortunate enough to receive it – bordered on the unbearable. Next to Francois' stretcher she set up a frame upon which hung a saline solution. 'Now, let's see if we can't get this tube into one of those veins of yours,' she said softly, kneeling beside him. With the task completed, she began to clean the chest wound. The shrapnel appeared to have missed his heart, but the three crescent-shaped gashes were bleeding. Nurse Valois pressed a bandage to the injury and then turned to attend to three other patients. Two were the victims of machine-gun fire through their thighs. Amputation appeared unavoidable for both young men, while the third was already dead from a stomach wound. How was it possible, she wondered, for men to inflict such wounds on each other? How was it possible for human beings to sit behind polished desks and make decisions that led to such carnage?

'Where are the ambulances?' she heard her voice cry out. 'These men need to be moved immediately.'

Nurse Duval lifted her head from the man she was bandaging. 'Are you all right?'

'I'm fine, and you?'

The younger woman continued to stitch up a gash on an arm. Nurse Valois observed the precise way in which Duval drew the surgical cotton through the wound, her wrist giving a little flick as she tightened each stitch. They were like machines, she reasoned. Trained and then conditioned to the terrors of war, they were just one tiny cog in this great horror created by mankind. There was nothing to do but continue. When she swallowed, the acrid taste of bile rose unbidden. At twenty-eight she had witnessed far too much suffering. For two years she had served at the front; during the past twelve months she had been rotated through the casualty clearing stations eight times. Doctors praised her for the meticulous approach with which she went about her duties and for the display of steady nerves so vital when they carried out such bloody work under shell-fire. Few nurses could sustain such continued exposure to the horrors of war, particularly when they were working so close to the fighting.

'Which ones?'

An ambulance driver stood before her. His tunic was patterned with dark stains and an arcing scar down the side of his face showed at least forty stitches.

'You should have that wound covered,' she said. 'Let me bandage it for you.'

'Nurse, which ones?' he asked again, ignoring her concern. 'I can take only eight from this ward. Two of the horse-drawn ambulances were hit by shell-fire, so now we are even more short-handed.' When no answer came he cleared his throat. 'I'm sorry, it's the best I can do.'

Nurse Duval appeared and with a slight cough of interruption led the driver away by the arm and began to point out the men who were to be transferred immediately. Nurse Valois observed this random selection with weary detachment. It was the same out on the battlefield. The stretcher-bearers were ordered to bring in the least badly injured, with the critically wounded left until last, often to die in the cold from infected, unattended wounds. Trenches could not afford to be clogged up by the movement of the wounded. Priority was given to moving the dead, the troops and the munitions.

As those who were deemed to have the greatest chance of survival were stretchered out of the tent, Nurse Valois resumed her ministrations. The young man with the crescent-shaped shrapnel wounds was shivering. Draping a blanket over him, she checked Francois' pulse. His breaths were interspersed with soft moans.

'Rest,' she soothed. There was further damage to his body to attend to, namely a bulbous foot with a seeping wound. Her brow furrowed briefly before smoothing into a practised smile of comfort. From a table she selected swabs and disinfectant and slowly began to clean the leg, before irrigating the suppurating wound. The stink of rotting flesh was hard to ignore. There were two phials of morphine in the tray on the bench behind her. They were continually running out of morphine and she knew she should save it for the more critical patients, but as she reached for the hypodermic needle and administered the painkiller she was conscious only of the suffering she would ease in that moment. The man on the ground was so young and Nurse Valois was certain he would not survive. She glanced at the second phial of morphine. By ending this soldier's pain forever would she not in fact be saving him?

A Red Cross volunteer appeared in the tent with a crate. 'The plasma has arrived. And one of the doctors said to tell you he is beginning to disperse nurses from the receiving marquee to the different wards now the initial rush has passed.'

'Thank heavens.' Nurse Valois dropped the second phial of morphine into the pocket of her uniform and, taking the box of plasma, placed it on a table. 'Help me set this up. I have fifteen patients who need plasma immediately.' When she turned around the volunteer was gone. Very slowly she began to unpack the crate; gradually her practised speed increased. 'Plasma,' she called over her shoulder to Nurse Duval. The younger woman joined her and together they swiftly hung plasma bags on frames next to the neediest patients and attached tubes to veins.

'You should take some leave,' her friend suggested. 'You are exhausted.'

Nurse Valois waved away her concern.

'Why do you not go and see your family in Paris?'

'Why do you not visit your mother?' Nurse Valois countered.

They were joined by three more nurses, who quickly turned to the as yet unattended patients. Habit made Nurse Valois check each plasma recipient until she was back at Francois' side. He was young, too young. 'Right,' she said as she squeezed the plasma bag and checked the tubing running into Francois' arm. 'Let's have a look at that head wound of yours. And what is that?' She glanced thoughtfully towards the tent opening before calling out to Nurse Duval. 'I have another with those strange marks.'

'And I,' the younger nurse replied.

Nurse Valois resumed her task. 'Well, we might try to get you into a cot, my lad; displace one of your companions who haven't got quite so many wounds to contend with.' The nurse rose wearily, holding a hand to the small of her back. 'I'm sorry I cannot do more for you.'

A massive animal stood in the tent's doorway. Matted with blood and mud, it lifted its wolf-like head and sniffed the air.

The nurse scanned the surrounds for anything she could use as a weapon. 'Marianne?' she called out to Nurse Duval at the far end of the tent.

The second nurse caught sight of the animal and backed away. 'What is it?'

'Keep still.' Nurse Valois stood rigidly by Francois' side and, with a stay of her hand, bade the three new nurses do the same.

The creature padded into the tent and began to walk to each cot. He sniffed briefly at every occupant before finally turning in the senior nurse's direction.

She stood firm by Francois' side, a hypodermic clutched between her fingers as if a stabbing knife.

'He won't hurt you.' An ambulance driver filled the tent's entrance. 'That dog chased us nearly halfway here from the front.'

The nurse backed away as the dog sprang to Francois' side. He sniffed him from head to foot, circled his prone body and then stretched out by his side and howled.

'I knew it,' the ambulance driver stated.

Nurse Valois looked at the dog and then turned back to the man before her. 'What do you mean by allowing him in here? This is a hospital not a –'

The ambulance driver walked towards the nurse and held out his hand. In his palm lay a set of identity discs. Intrigued, the nurse picked them up and examined the owner's name.

'They were in the dog's mouth when the ambulance picked him up.'

The nurse stared at the name written on the discs. Antoine Chessy. The exhausted dog snored at her feet, his great pink tongue strung out across his paws, his hips angular and lean beneath the matted hair.

'But how did –' Nurse Valois turned to the sleeping dog, then looked in confusion back to the driver, who smiled and nodded.

'No one thought it possible,' he said, 'but that's because we're not out there, with them.' He gestured to the men lying in the cots and scattered on the floor. 'We can't contemplate the horrors nor the possibilities, and so we don't believe. Check his identity discs,' the ambulance driver suggested, tilting his neck to where Francois lay. 'Apparently the dog belonged to two brothers.'

The nurse leaned over and tentatively lifted the discs from Francois' neck. The dog raised his head and then, assured the woman meant no harm, lowered his shaggy muzzle onto the floor.

'They –' She looked at the ambulance driver. 'They say Francois Chessy.' She double-checked the discs she still held.

The ambulance driver nodded again. 'And that is their dog.' Taking Antoine's identity discs from the nurse, he hung them around the great animal's neck. The bite marks were clearly visible on the soldier at her feet. Despite her disciplined, scientific training, Nurse Valois's eyes grew blurry. This was not the first time such marks had been presented to her. There was no other explanation. Kneeling at Francois' head, she studied the puncture wound. The shape of it was indeed representative of a deep bite, and the surrounding bruising and tearing of skin suggested that the creator had latched on forcefully. Her cheeks burned with the enormity of the realisation. 'So, this animal, he dragged them to safety?' Confirmation was important to her. Such a feat conjured a word lost in a world at war: hope.

The ambulance driver nodded. 'The men say his name is Roland.'

Nurse Valois stared at the war-weary dog at her feet. The animal's hair was coarse, crusty with mud, his long muzzle bloody. Beneath the plain garb of her uniform a cross nestled in the soft indentation at the base of her throat. She reached for it now. The boy at her feet was dying and his dog was by his side.

⊰ Chapter 21 ⊱

Sunset Ridge, south-west Queensland, Australia
February 2000

They were driving back from the western boundary. Every time Madeleine got out of the utility to close a gate the sun bit at her skin. The land lay heavy and silent in the afternoon heat, glazed silver by the sun's rays, as if some other-worldly potter had slipped the earth into a giant furnace, turning the land into a ceramic rendering of silver-strewn browns and beiges. The sun moved to rest momentarily on a distant tree line, sending tendrils of red across both sky and landscape. She slid back into the vehicle, relishing the airconditioning yet aware that she was becoming more attuned to the environment around her.

George was still processing everything the woman at the museum had shared earlier that morning, and Madeleine could tell he wasn't happy. Neither of them was. After the excitement of discovering their grandfather's two hidden sketches, a further search of the homestead had proved futile. They both knew they were lucky to find anything at all, and they believed that the location of the sketches showed that David Harrow's talent was far from appreciated in the homestead when he was growing up – an important fact that would create interest at any exhibition. The idea of an artist suffering either mentally or physically or both in the creation of their work was a powerful image.

They still should have been running on adrenalin after the discovery of the sketch; instead, they were driving around the property as Madeleine tried to understand why neither Jude nor George had told her about her father's alcoholism.

'I'm sorry you had to hear all that, Maddy. Talk about a gossip.'

She looked at him. 'Was Dad really an alcoholic?'

George turned down the radio. He had been fiddling with it for the past few minutes. 'I don't know when it started. He never drank that much in the homestead as far as I know. Sure, he had a rum-and-water before dinner, but that's about as much as I remember, unless he got stuck into the grog after we went to bed.'

'I don't believe it. All these years I thought he had a mental-health problem not an addiction.'

'Can't they be one and the same?' George replied.

'I don't know,' Madeleine answered irritably. 'Why didn't anyone tell me and how did it become common knowledge?'

George changed down gears as they drove over a stock grid. 'I guess one of the station hands knew, probably by being in the wrong place at the wrong time. That's how I found out.'

'What do you mean?'

'I was riding past the cattle yards one day – I think you and Mum were in Banyan shopping for groceries – and I heard this noise, and there's Dad sitting cross-legged by the cattle crush. I knew he was drunk as soon as I saw him. He was singing and laughing and there were two empty rum bottles on the ground beside him. He didn't see me, so I backed off and left him alone.' He turned to her. 'I didn't know what to do. I was eleven at the time. Three years later he was dead.'

For a moment Madeleine was too surprised to speak. 'Oh, George. I'm so sorry, I had no idea.'

'He probably had stashes of rum around the property. He wasn't the first grazier to fall foul of the bottle, Maddy. There are many stories about bushmen, isolation and grog. I remember asking him for a drink out of his waterbag once and he said it was empty. I think it was probably filled with rum.'

'Why didn't you tell me? Why didn't Mum?'

'What would have been the point? You adored him, Maddy.'

'I had a right to know.'

'Mum didn't want either of us to know. When I told her about what I'd seen at the cattle yards she said that Dad was just going through a rough patch. She made me promise not to tell you. It was important to her that you were protected. I'm pretty sure that she intended to tell you at some stage in the future, but let's face it, Maddy, after he shot himself would you really have wanted to hear that he was a drunk?'

'So, his mood swings were caused by his drinking?'

'I don't know, but they certainly got worse as we got older.'

'I thought his suicide was the reason Jude didn't want to talk about Dad, and I always thought her attitude was selfish. Maybe I've been too hard on her. It must have been so tough for her, so stressful, with a property to run and two young kids to look after.'

'How Mum and Dad ever thought they would make a go of the property still amazes me. It was already an albatross by the time Mum had inherited it. It still is, I guess.' George changed gears and reached for the packet of jubes he kept on the dash. Even as a child he had liked them warm and squishy. He sighed as he chewed. 'Sunset Ridge should have made a motza out of the wool boom during the fifties, like everybody else in the business did.'

'But it didn't; that was plain in the ledgers you showed me.'

'Exactly. The property was riding a pretty thin line, and when it was left to Mum she had to make a decision: sell it or try to get it back on its feet. I've often wondered if it was a conscious decision to have us both later in life or whether it was something that just happened naturally.'

'I know the rest, George,' Madeleine responded sharply. 'She sold Grandfather's legacy to keep this lump of dirt. *Why*, I will never know.'

'Why? Because Mum couldn't support herself with her painting, Maddy, and the man she adored was an unemployed charmer – her words, not mine.'

Madeleine's bottom lip dropped.

'Anyway, I don't know if she had an inkling into Dad's character then, but in the end she chose security, her childhood home, deciding it was better to sell the paintings and use the proceeds to get the property back on track. At least then they would have a roof over their heads and the property to manage.'

'They could have sold the property and kept the paintings.'

'Jude was an only child. To her, Sunset Ridge was the only security she had left. I understand her thinking, Maddy. Here she had a home and a ready-made job for her husband.'

Madeleine slumped back in the seat. 'I can't believe that Jude never told me any of this.'

'Mum said when we were still both under five Dad became obsessed with winning the Champion Fleece competition at the Banyan Show. She guessed he wanted to please her, to do something to repay the Harrows for what he couldn't provide himself. So, they spent a fortune on stud rams, and the flock did improve substantially. When they finally bred a showable fleece, Dad said it wasn't good enough to be entered in the competition, and no amount of argument would sway him. Mum thought he was afraid of opening himself up to public scrutiny. After that episode he began to lose interest in Sunset Ridge, and a year later she began to notice subtle changes. He wanted to sell out and move back to the city. Dad couldn't understand why they couldn't just live off the sale proceeds. Soon after, the mood swings and drinking began.'

They drove on in silence as the sun sank and a slight breeze stirred the trees as they passed. 'So considering everything Mum has done to retain the property why doesn't she come back to visit, George?'

'Because even though she loves Sunset Ridge, the memories will always be too raw.'

It was past seven o'clock, and while neither mentioned it, they both knew that Rachael would be annoyed by their late return. Madeleine watched the evening star emerge from a darkening sky as the faintest smudge of crimson fell away over the horizon. A pool of sadness had gathered in the pit of her stomach as she thought of Jude and of her flawed yet beloved father and the all-too-few years they shared.

'So, Maddy,' George said with forced brightness, 'any other news from the village?'

She wiped her nose. 'Well, the gossip at the museum said that Corally Shaw was admired by all the local boys, and that Grandfather liked Germans.'

Switching on the headlights, George slowed as two kangaroos crossed the road in the halo of light. 'Not exactly a popular sentiment, I would have thought, after the dreadful casualties the Allies suffered during the war.'

'Are there any German families around here, George?'

'Not that I know of.'

'Well, Grandfather must have said or done something at the time for the subject to still be considered gossip.' Madeleine hesitated. 'There is one more thing that the woman at the museum mentioned.'

George turned to her, watching her for a moment before asking, 'What?'

'She said there was a murder out here.'

'A murder?' George repeated incredulously. 'When?'

Madeleine shrugged. 'I didn't get specifics.'

George laughed. 'Next thing you'll be telling me that there's a ghost on the place.'

Madeleine punched him lightly on the arm.

'Don't believe everything you hear, Maddy.' As they neared the homestead George shifted through the gears, finally parking outside the house. 'So, do you feel more confident about an exhibition now?'

Madeleine thought of the three Australian War Memorial portraits, the two river drawings hanging in Jude's apartment and the drawings discovered in the ceiling of her grandfather's bedroom. Most of all, she thought of her mother and the legacy Jude had lost in her attempt to provide for her family. 'Yes,' she answered, 'I do.'

After another late dinner, Madeleine sat down at the roll-top desk in her room and began to craft a letter to the director at the Stepworth Gallery. Every few sentences she paused and a doodle would form in a corner of the page, then she would lift the pencil and resume, noting the reasons why the retrospective should be held. With the addition of the work from the Australian War Memorial and the Cubist examples, the argument for an exhibition was now far more compelling. There was also Jude's original 1950s sale catalogue, Sonia's newspaper clippings and the photograph of the three Harrow brothers in their First World War uniforms.

Madeleine coupled the facts with an outline of her grandfather's life, reminding the gallery director that the landscape works only surfaced after his death. No one could doubt his ability as an artist, for David Harrow's landscapes, some in watercolour, others oil, drew favourable comparison to the early Impressionists. She re-read the draft letter. It was newsworthy stuff, but would the director think David Harrow had the pulling power to ensure both sponsorship and crowds? Typing up the letter on her laptop,

Madeleine connected the telephone line and then hit the send button on the email. Hanging on the wall above was the picture of the three Harrow boys. It seemed to Madeleine that they looked at her with pride.

≪ Chapter 22 ≫

Chessy farmhouse, ten miles from Saint-Omer, northern France
November 1916

The cleaver sliced neatly through the rabbit. Wiping the blade on a towel, Madame Chessy turned to the stove and shook the large pan. The frying bacon sizzled and spat, greasing the pan with fat and sending an enticing aroma through the kitchen.

'Do you think more soldiers will come today, Madame?'

The older woman turned to Lisette and shrugged. 'I hope not.' The rabbit lying quartered on the table had spent the last week indoors scurrying safely around the farmhouse and out of the hungry reach of billeted troops. It was not that she was averse to sharing food – she hoped some kindly woman was doing the same for her own sons – yet nor did she intend for her and Lisette to starve. This rabbit would last them for four or five meals and the leftover juices would form the basis for a rich potato soup laced with cream if the milking cow obliged. 'That British officer thought we would continue to see more soldiers until Christmas,' she reminded Lisette. The last troops had left the relative warmth of the barn only days previously. They were heading back to the muddy freeze of the Somme, grumbling about luckier soldiers from other battalions who would probably be granted furlough in London now the festive season was less than six weeks away.

Lisette's fingers nimbly tied string around the bouquet garni of dried thyme, parsley and bay leaves and presented it for inspection.

'Very good,' Madame Chessy praised, before scraping the cooked bacon out onto a plate and dropping the rabbit into the pan to brown in the leftover fat. Lisette began to chop onions into wedges. 'Good, if it is too fine the onion will melt away while cooking.' She observed the girl with motherly pride as Lisette flattened two cloves of garlic with the blade of a knife. The girl was proving to be a good companion and, more importantly, had been excited by the opportunity to be taught to read and write. Lisette soaked up their evening lessons gratefully, although she was easily distracted. Every time even a small improvement revealed itself in a thoughtfully read paragraph or a questioning gaze of approval, there would be a knock at the door and Lisette's dreamy gaze would follow a young soldier's meanderings outdoors.

The older woman knew she should not be ungrateful for the men's presence, but they did intrude. One British soldier, who introduced himself as his officer's assistant, requested a visit to the cellar in order to peruse the available contents; Madame Chessy was quick to chase him from the door with a broom. And she was still uncomfortable with the British habit of writing in chalk on the barn door the number of men that the barn would accommodate. It was bad enough to have the Germans edging their way onto French soil – she didn't need the British to exert ownership tendencies as well.

With the rabbit browned, she added a cup of wine and two spoonfuls of flour, followed by the remaining ingredients. The bouquet garni was poked into the liquid and the lid placed on firmly before the pan was slid into the oven.

Lisette's nose twitched. 'It smells very good.'

Madame Chessy wiped down the table with a dishcloth and washed her hands in a ceramic basin. 'Two hours and it will be cooked perfectly, I think.'

Outside, the afternoon shadows were creeping across the countryside. Normally the curtains would already be drawn against the cold, but a vision of the twins returning from over the fields haunted her daily and hope kept the curtains open and the view unrestricted. Angling a chair towards the window, she pushed the cork back into the neck of the wine bottle. It was her last. Lisette's father, Monsieur Crotet, had promised to buy wine on her behalf when he next took her produce to the village market. Until then she would measure out the meagre supply by adding a little water to her nightly indulgence.

'It's a long time since I have eaten rabbit,' Lisette said in her quiet voice. 'Papa prefers fish and pork.'

The girl no longer retreated to the corner but sat instead in Marcel's chair, winding skeins of wool from a fleece grown by her family. The fleece had been washed and dried in the sun before being combed out, and every Monday morning for the past few weeks Lisette had arrived at the farmhouse with a basket of spun wool under one arm and explicit instructions as to the lengths of wool to be included in each ball. Madame Crotet knitted outerwear, and there was talk that her warm clothing was popular on the black market. Madame Chessy was less concerned with the extra francs her neighbour may make over the winter months than the thought of a cut of the tasty meat hanging in the Crotets' cellar. Yet despite the many kindnesses she had shown towards their daughter, she was yet to benefit in this regard.

'You are fortunate, Lisette. No doubt you have enjoyed lamb these past weeks on your visits home.'

Lisette nodded. 'Some,' she admitted. 'But I like pork.' The rhythm of her fingers barely changed as she looked quickly but shyly at Madame. 'All my family like pork.'

Alerted by a distraught sow grunting in alarm, Madame Chessy had foiled pilfering soldiers with a piglet under an arm on a number of occasions. Despite her vigilance all but the sow and one, the runt of the litter, were taken. With the distinct possibility of awakening one morning to an empty pigsty, she had slaughtered the remaining piglet last month. Cut and cured, it hung from the wooden beams in the chill of the cellar.

'Really?' Madame Chessy replied eventually to Lisette's statement. She calculated the cost of obliging such an obvious request. There were six people under the Crotet farmhouse roof and two beneath hers, besides which she was already feeding Lisette. She could do without lamb, she supposed. Besides, Marcel's remaining sow was living on borrowed time; her safety could not be guaranteed and she too would have to be killed and cured before winter's end. Some of the meat could be bartered for produce in the village and would keep well in the cellar for a number of months.

Lisette rolled the wool precisely, her right hand looping the growing ball as the home-spun yarn continued to rise from the basket at her feet. She sat skew-whiff in the chair, one side of her face yellow in the dwindling light, her fingers deftly plying the natural fibre. She had talked recently of joining one of the many textiles factories, as if immersion in such a trade would offer a better life away from the drudgery of farm work. 'After the war,' Madame Chessy had cautioned, 'wait until after the war.' Last week's paper talked of strikes in some of the factories, with workers complaining of poor wages and the loss of jobs as owners sought more efficient production through the increased use of machinery.

'Finished.' Lisette dropped the last ball of wool into the basket and, flicking irritably at a strand of dark hair, rested her leg over the arm of the chair.

Madame Chessy opened her mouth to protest and then thought better of making a comment. Initially she had been perturbed to see the casual way in which Lisette took ownership of her husband's chair. Now she welcomed it. Exhausted by the day's end, Lisette often fell asleep after their evening meal and lesson, her lips slightly apart, softly snoring. Such a scene of youthful domesticity would have pleased Marcel.

'Madame?'

'Yes?' Madame Chessy replied.

'You will write again?' Lisette asked.

The black-and-white photograph of her uniformed sons sat in a wooden frame on top of the dresser. Antoine and Francois appeared suitably serious in the studied pose, and more than once she had caught Lisette running her finger across their faces. The picture had arrived during October and was accompanied by a brief note from Francois. She had been thrilled to have evidence of their good health. Since then, she had been in receipt of only four letters from her boys. Three were heavily censored and, judging by the postmarks, were mailed at village post offices; the fourth, penned en route to Verdun and mailed through the Red Cross, miraculously escaped the censor's pen.

'Madame?' Lisette queried.

Outside the land darkened. The willow trees began to lose their form as night bore down on the farmhouse. 'Tomorrow. I shall write again tomorrow.' She shared a smile with Lisette, conscious of a previous sharp edge to her tone. There was no point in burdening the girl with fears that were as yet unfounded.

Lisette hovered her palm above the stove.

'Yes, another piece of wood, I think,' Madame Chessy agreed. The kitchen was not the warm fug of earlier, and the rabbit required constant heat. Selecting a length of timber from the neatly stacked pile on the floor, Lisette poked it into the firebox. The wood crackled and fizzed and when Lisette took possession of Marcel's chair again Madame could feel the girl's eyes on her. Madame Chessy knew that Lisette wanted to talk about the twins, but she could not bear to. Her previous letters had gone unanswered. Optimism rallied her spirits during the day and chores kept them both busy, but at night it was becoming increasingly difficult not to believe the worst.

'Madame?'

'I'm sorry, Lisette, what did you say?'

'Last Sunday Mama and Papa were talking about Christmas.'

The older woman frowned. Everyone, it seemed, was talking of holidays. 'We are yet part-way through November.'

'It's good to have something to look forward to,' Lisette persevered. 'I was asking if you will be joining us to celebrate Noël? Mama and Papa insist. First we will walk to the village to celebrate midnight mass and then we will have such a celebratory supper. Oh, I love that time of year.'

'I don't think so. What if Antoine and Francois return home and find the farmhouse empty? What if a thief should steal the last of the chickens or the sow or –' Madame Chessy stopped herself. Lisette was clearly disappointed. 'You do understand?' she said more gently. 'Please thank your parents, but I must be here.'

'But it's a celebration,' Lisette insisted. 'The little ones place their shoes on the hearth for Father Christmas to fill. Papa has promised escargots and Mama is going to make a little foie gras from wild duck.'

Madame tried to smile. 'I am past broaching the cold at midnight, Lisette.'

'But, Madame, it's a celebration,' Lisette repeated dejectedly.

Above the stove Christ on his fractured wooden cross stared vacantly into space. 'Not for everyone,' Madame Chessy replied.

A knock on the farmhouse door stilled further argument.

Madame Chessy lifted her palms upwards in annoyance. 'So, once again the cow, hens and my little pig will have to share their space with soldiers. This time we must tell them that the barn must be cleaned out and the hay burned before they leave.'

Lisette nodded intently, causing her hair to come loose from its ribbon. 'Yes, Madame. Last time it was terrible. The fleas were so bad all the animals suffered.' Her fingers scratched her arm automatically.

'And only eggs and potatoes are for sale, no other produce,' the older woman waggled a finger, 'alive or dead.' Lisette had fancied a young British private billeted with them last month and came close to being coerced into parting with a round of their precious cheese before Madame Chessy intervened.

'Yes, Madame.'

The rap of knuckles on wood sounded again. Madame Chessy looked out the window. 'Coming, coming,' she replied sternly. 'It's nearly dark,' she called out, crossing the short distance. Sliding the bolt on the door, she opened it just a little. A blast of cold air swept into the cramped room.

'Who's there?' Lisette asked, walking forward.

Madame Chessy staggered backwards, her progress halted by the kitchen table.

Father Benet dipped his chin apologetically, stepped inside and closed the door.

≪ Chapter 23 ≫

Sunset Ridge, south-west Queensland, Australia
November 1916

The front door slammed. Lily rose from her mending as G.W. strode through the homestead, leaving a trail of mud in his wake. Flinging open the door of the sitting room, he marched to the shelving that housed their library, his filthy hands coming to rest on the Harrow family bible.

Lily followed her husband into the room. 'My dear, your boots.'

Unhearing, he selected the large leather-bound book and thumped it down on the oval table in the middle of the room. The vibration rattled the porcelain knick-knacks and tipped over the crystal specimen vase with its single native flower within. Water seeped across the table.

'Eight hours we have been out in the paddock. Eight hours in this abominable heat.' Dragging a chair to the table, he sat heavily.

'Please, my dear, don't distress yourself so.'

'We are stretched beyond capacity. There are sheep bogged in dams, sheep that need to be mustered in and checked for flystrike.'

Lily lifted her skirts above the dirt on the floor. 'Let me get you some water.' Mud reached to G.W.'s thighs and splattered his torso and arms. As the heat slowly crusted it, tiny pieces flaked from the clothing onto the floor and table.

'I have the books to balance and accounts that require payment. And what am I doing? Wading in mud and filth while your sons gallivant about the countryside, shirking their duty to the family business.' Pointing a mud-caked finger, G.W. snarled at her. 'This is *your* fault. I never should have allowed you to sway my decision regarding Luther.' He slammed a fist on the table. 'He should have gone to reform school, and the others with him.' He unlatched the silver hinge and opened the bible. 'Instead I allowed you and your mollycoddling ways to interfere.'

Lily grew alarmed. The man before her was turning purple and a large vein on the side of his neck was pulsating and increasing in size.

'Painting and pianos indeed, woman. You birthed boys, not the weaker sex. Mark my words, Lily: it will be the first and the last time you meddle in family business. Do you hear me?'

Lily backed away from the harsh tone. 'I understand that you are upset, my dear, but please remember that our sons cannot be blamed for the season or for our lack of staff. The war has brought many changes and –'

'Don't interrupt me!' G.W. shouted. 'Those boys ran away with scant regard for anybody except their own misplaced sense of injustice. Who did they think was going to work this place in their absence – *you?*' Reaching inside his jacket, G.W. withdrew a notepad, which he threw on the floor before locating a stubby pencil.

'What are you doing, G.W.?' Lily took a step closer to the table. The bible was open on the first page of the substantial Harrow family tree. Dirty fingerprints smeared the page.

'Seven generations,' he muttered. 'Seven generations and we've come to this.' He met Lily's horrified stare. 'I should have chosen more carefully,' he announced. 'Clearly our blood was not meant to mix.' Turning to the last page of entries, G.W. lifted the pencil and drew a thick black line through each of his sons' names.

Lily mouthed a silent *o*.

With the obliteration complete, he closed the bible, snapped shut the finely etched silver latch and pushed the book aside.

Seconds later he fell to the floor.

⫷ Chapter 24 ⫸

Sunset Ridge, south-west Queensland, Australia
February 1917

Lily rested the rifle butt on the veranda. The barrel was cool to touch, a distinct contrast to the heat of her husband's shoulder. 'G.W.,' she whispered through clenched teeth, shaking him. There was drool at the corner of his mouth. 'G.W.,' she said more firmly, 'we have a visitor.'

The man in question was sitting astride a horse beyond the back gate. It was difficult to decipher where the rider finished and the animal began, such was the paraphernalia that hung from man and beast alike.

'What's the matter with *him*, then?' The man's voice was deep, his physique nuggety. A long beard and moustache covered part of his face, a wide-brimmed hat the rest. Lily noted a swag, two rifles, a quart pot, saddle-bags and a stockwhip.

'Nothing is wrong with him.' Lily's fingers gripped the cold steel of the barrel as the stranger dismounted.

'Right, and the Hun have all been beat and the war is over.' Unlatching the gate, the stranger crunched dirt beneath cracked boots.

Lily lifted the rifle as the man continued towards her. Although aged in appearance, he walked energetically. 'Who are you?' The rifle bolt slid into place with a metallic click.

'Don't get uppity, missus.' He raised a palm against the rifle's aim. 'The boss there employed me to look after his cattle.'

Lily lowered the rifle, just a little. Her husband was asleep.

The man propped a boot on the edge of the veranda, the movement dislodging myriad smells including grass, horse sweat, cow manure and camp smoke. 'If you put the rifle down I'll be thinking you don't mean no harm.'

The glint of sunlight on a silver spur distracted Lily. 'I think I'll leave it be for now. What's your name?'

'Taylor.' He scratched at his beard. 'You here by yourself?' His eyes swept briefly over Lily before returning with interest to his employer.

'No. I have Cook and a maid.'

The man's eyes skimmed the homestead. 'What about men? Who's running the place?'

Lily lifted her chin.

'Well, I'm here 'cause I'm out of supplies.' He paused as if expecting argument. 'No one forgets supplies unless there's a problem, and it looks like you've got one.'

Lily finally lowered the rifle. 'Heavens, supplies. I'm sorry.'

The stranger appeared relieved. 'Well, I figured something was up.' He nodded at the weapon dangling in her hand. 'You might want to uncock that thing.'

Lily's brow wrinkled as she slid the bolt back. 'My husband would hardly forget such a thing normally; unfortunately, he's not been himself since . . .'

Taylor tipped his hat back to reveal a white forehead untouched by the sun. 'Since his boys cleared out?' He raised a hand for silence. 'One of your station hands told me. How many men have you actually got left, missus?'

'Enough.'

He twirled a hat between thick fingers. 'Look, I can walk out of here tomorrow as well, if you like. By my reckoning that will leave you with one boundary rider.'

Lily met his unblinking gaze. Her predicament was painfully obvious. Either she trusted this unsavoury-looking individual or wake in the morning with not a soul left to run their vast holding.

Slowly, his crinkled-eyed frown smoothed. 'Might be worthwhile advertising for an extra couple of stockmen. Do you reckon you could do that?'

'Yes,' Lily agreed slowly, letting the rifle barrel rest on the veranda.

'And station stores? Who's in charge?'

Lily pressed her lips together.

'I ain't here to steal, missus.'

'Cook has the keys,' Lily relented.

'Well, if you're willing, I'll double-check what's there and make out a list of requirements.'

'Very well, as you seem intent on assistance.'

'Has a doctor seen him?' He nodded at G.W., whose face was flaccid.

'No. That is, yes, some weeks ago. Melancholy was diagnosed.'

'Looks to me to be a bit more than that.'

Lily ignored the inference. She was hardly going to sprout forth that her husband's stroke had rendered him incapable of managing Sunset Ridge. If word got out that there was a female on a remote property with not the slightest idea of how to run it, well, who knew what could befall her? 'Where are you from, Mr Taylor?'

'Nathanial Taylor is the name.' He gestured vaguely northwards. 'I was thinking of enlisting, except they turned me down not two year ago because I'm flat-footed. Now they say a man nearing his fifties is too old to fight. Lucky for me your husband needed an extra hand.'

Nathanial Taylor was the most objectionable individual Lily had laid eyes on. The red dirt of the bush appeared embedded in his skin, hair and clothing and he stank as only the long-unwashed can. Yet he was an older man, which was something of a comfort, and he clearly knew enough to have been hired by her husband. A thought came to her. 'Mr Taylor, would you be interested in taking over the management of Sunset Ridge while my husband recuperates?' The rashness of her offer was tempered only by the quick, if temporary, solution the stranger presented.

Turning on his heel, he surveyed the land. It was a hot, dry day, one that didn't inspire confidence. Lily felt the familiar pang of exhaustion at the back of her eyelids. She was beyond coping. It was all she could do to get her husband out of bed and dressed every day, and even then G.W. ranted and complained until he had staggered out onto the veranda and resumed his vigil.

Taylor faced her. 'I reckon I could be of service to you,' he replied. 'Have you heard from your boys?'

Lily bit the inside of her cheek. 'No.'

'I'll set up camp, then.' He touched his hat, turned and walked down the gravel path.

'Well, we have a manager,' Lily advised her sleeping husband as Taylor led his horse away by the reins. Although there were chores to attend to, a slip of white cloud hanging forlornly in the west held her attention. Lily remained convinced that somewhere on the other side of the world her errant boys were staring at a different sky. In desperation she had written to the Lawrences late last year in the hope of news. The ensuing terse note informed her only that Harold had enlisted, and on the strength of her children's friendship with the Lawrences' son, she guessed that they too had joined up. So, she wrote to them care of the Australian Imperial Forces and prayed they would reply. She wrote to them weekly, her words never varying. Although bitter at the selfishness of their leaving, she craved news of them, especially of her youngest, and she begged God nightly for a reply. Everything – the property, her future, G.W.'s health – depended on her sons. They simply had to survive.

◈

'Camped out on the flat, he is, like a blackfella. Got all his gear circling him as if he expects someone's going to steal it in the dead of night.' Cook mashed the potato uninterestedly. 'I don't know, Mrs Harrow. It just don't seem right, a man like that camping in the middle of the paddock, especially if he's going to be running things, for a while at least.'

Lily sat her husband's partially eaten meal on the kitchen table. Nathanial Taylor had been camped in the house paddock for three weeks and the only time she had seen evidence of Sunset Ridge's new manager was when he returned to the campsite at dusk. A spiral of smoke silhouetted against the reddening sky signalled his existence. On the plus side, the stranger's presence had led Cook to consume the monthly supply of cooking sherry in three days, rendering the woman grumpy yet a touch more amenable to direction.

'Of course, he's a hard worker,' Cook commented, 'and he knows his stores, to be sure. Had the store house itemised within the hour. But, a man like that, well, you never know who they are or where they've come from.' Cook tapped the side of her nose. 'Or what they've done; if you get my meaning, Mrs Harrow.' Cook spooned the lumpy potato beside the cold cuts of meat. 'Down on his luck and all, looking like he does. I've been keeping the locks oiled and the windows bolted.'

'I don't believe that my husband would have employed Mr Taylor if he weren't capable,' Lily replied. 'But I agree he can't continue to sleep under the stars. It's not as if we can't accommodate him.'

'Begging your pardon, missus, but where are you going to put him up?'

Lily wiped splatters of potato from her blouse. G.W.'s frustration at his inability to hold a knife was growing worse. 'The governess quarters.'

'What? Just there? Not a wink and a step from me?'

'Yes, Cook, just there,' Lily answered, walking out onto the veranda. 'There is little point employing a manager and having him camping out on the flat. I need to know what he's doing every day. I need to be able to keep an eye on him.'

Cook shook her head. 'It's more than likely,' she muttered under her breath, 'he'll be keeping an eye on us.'

Lily left the homestead and walked across the featureless house paddock as daylight began to slip over the horizon. She thought that dusk probably wasn't the time for a social call. However, with no opportunity over the past week to discuss things with Taylor, there was little alternative. Oblivious to the red dirt gathering on the hem of her skirt, Lily headed directly to the clump of trees in the middle of the paddock. The countryside was strangely quiet. In the dwindling daylight a mob of sheep were feeding in the distance. With the resident top-knot pigeons, willie wagtails and soldier birds settled for the evening, a baker's dozen of kangaroos bounding across the dry dirt of the property was the only sign of life. Lily breathed in the heat that shrouded her every step and tried not to think about tomorrow. She had enough to contend with just getting through each day.

A thin line of smoke crept into the air, marking the spot where Sunset Ridge's manager camped. Lifting her skirts, Lily criss-crossed the grass and fallen timber until the smell of smoke and roasting meat directed her through the trees. The camp spot was deserted. Two horses whickered softly as they grazed nearby, while mounds of gear and supplies, intermingled with stacked logs, circled the fire. The manmade embankment almost resembled a defensive position. The fire was hot and an indecipherable chunk of meat was sizzling in a battered skillet. Lily surveyed the site for some minutes wondering what to do next. On closer inspection, she saw that the unfurled swag was neat in appearance and a book lay in the dirt to one side. Somehow, this link with the world of the educated unsettled her. She sighed irritably, and turned to leave.

'Yes?'

The man in question was but a foot behind her.

'Must you sneak up on a person like that?' Lily retorted, quite undone by not only Taylor's sudden appearance but by his shirtless torso.

'I'm camping here,' he reminded her. 'You're the one doing the sneaking.' He brushed past her. 'Ever thought of knocking?'

Disconcerted by his reproach, Lily stepped clear of the smoke, which he appeared to fan in her direction. 'I wanted to ask how things were going.'

He sat on a fallen log, one knee bent, the other leg flung out before him in the dirt so that the holey sole of a leather boot was visible. 'Well then, ask.'

She was sure that their conversation should not be conducted like this, she standing awkwardly and he partly unclothed and squatting in the dirt. With difficulty she recalled the garbled conversation she and G.W. had attempted to share. In the end, forced to make good with single words and confused snippets, she had decided on her own list of instructions, most of which were based on the information G.W. had chosen to share with her over previous years. 'I'm concerned about the waterholes, if there is sufficient —'

'The boys have begun checking everything. They are young, those two lads you hired, but willing enough.'

His long hair was wet and freshly combed.

'And the cattle? With you here, there is no one to watch over them. I'm worried —'

'I already rode out and checked on them today.'

'Oh.' Lily doubted she had ever seen so much hair on a man; it literally spread like a carpet from his face down his neck, shoulders and chest. Realising she was staring at the youthfully formed body beneath, she continued briskly, 'The sheep will need to be brought in and checked for fly.'

'There's a mob in the yards already. Anything else?' He poked at the fire, and turned the chunk of meat roasting in the pan.

'Yes: we usually join the ewes in March.'

'Where are the rams?' He dished up the meat and sat the plate on the swag.

That was something she had neglected to consider. 'In the ram paddock.' The statement sounded more like a question.

He smiled. 'Well, then, everything is on track. I know what I'm doing, missus. Besides, you offered me this job, remember?'

'I was thinking that, for propriety's sake, you should move into the quarters at the homestead,' Lily suggested, her voice strong even if her legs were shaky.

'Propriety's sake?' He sounded amused. 'Why? Are you expecting somebody?'

'Well, no. But it seems ridiculous, you camping out here. The governess quarters are free.'

'Guess you've not much use for one of those now.'

His words stung. 'I can't be expected to walk out into the bush every time I need to speak with you, Mr Taylor.' Lily felt his gaze on her dirt-layered skirt. She brushed a twig free from the folds. 'Well?'

'I can see that you're the type of woman that man invented the door for.' He rubbed his matted beard.

Lily blushed. 'So, it's agreed?'

'And you'll feed me as well? That will be a bonus.'

She thought of the lumpy, cold potato and stringy meat awaiting her back at the homestead. 'Yes, I'm sure you'll appreciate some good home cooking.'

'Mrs Harrow?' The manager's voice was sombre.

'Yes, Mr Taylor?'

'Your boys, did they enlist?'

Lily closed her eyes briefly. 'I have no idea.' Leaving the camp fire, she walked back through the trees into a day grown dark.

⋘ Chapter 25 ⋙

En route to Saint-Omer, northern France
May 1917

The small stones hit the windowpane. A group of young children were running along the train platform, the station master shouting and raising his arms in pursuit. As the train pulled through the French village, Dave pressed his nose squarely against the cold glass. Sitting in the cramped confines of the wood-panelled dog-box, he could never have imagined that this perilous descent towards war would prove to be quite so provocative. He loved the fresh new sky and the bracing air of the slowly unfolding countryside, and the heavens both intrigued and unsettled him, for there was no great Southern Cross, no evening star dangling above the red crust of the earth – at least not one that was familiar. Just last night he had lifted the rattling train window and sucked in the windless fragility of a night dark amid the unknown. It was then that it struck him: what he had done in leaving Sunset Ridge; where he was going.

No one talked of war, not now they were in France. This war they were going to, this rabbit shoot as Luther jokingly referred to it, was now only days away. On the opposite bench seat, Thaddeus and Luther snored in tandem. Three other recruits filled their allocated seating: the man from McInerney's wool shed, Marty, and the water-tank runaways, Riley and Turtle. All six of them left England with the rank of private. The brass had decided that the Harrow brothers needed some older men with them, although Thaddeus told Dave that he wondered who was looking after whom.

Dave believed that he could be a good soldier, one disciplined thoroughly in obeying his superior's orders if they were orders worth following. And therein lay his problem. On revealing his concerns to Marty, the older man had shoved a pointy finger in his chest and reminded him that such a thought was incompatible with a soldier's reality. He had a moral duty, Marty reminded him, to obey his superiors. Yet were he to be tested, Dave doubted his ability to blindly follow another's bidding. Hadn't he left Sunset Ridge to escape such things? That detail aside, Dave reckoned that he possessed some of the qualities needed to take part in a war. He was adept at running and digging, the latter leading him to receive a great deal of ribbing from his platoon of twenty-five men. This latent talent was eventually forgotten, however, when a new, more important ability came to light. The instructor at Lark Hill on the Salisbury Plain in England scored him perfectly on the rifle range, much to his brothers' surprise. The intensive training had proved him to be an excellent marksman; a result Dave begrudgingly admitted was probably important if they were going to be killing Germans.

Through the window unfamiliar trees spread out across a landscape that was soft and rounded. The gentleness of the countryside reminded Dave of a woman. Delicate green slopes folded away into the distance and every few minutes another pond or stream glimmered in the morning light. At times the blur of trees fringing the railway line grew so thick the dog-box darkened, yet when the great woody plants thinned, a curl of smoke would be silhouetted against a blue sky and he would glimpse a farmhouse and the neat fields that fanned out from the dwelling. Dave was beginning to understand what it meant to fight to protect what you loved, and he was unexpectedly proud to be helping the French defend their beautiful country. This new land the Australians entered, so old in terms of civilisation, was so unlike his home that it drew comparison immediately. Sunset Ridge was a tangled expanse of rugged bush interspersed with great swathes of land that rippled with varying grasses. It was flat country of mixed soils and numerous red ridges, as if the innards of the earth had been spewed upwards. It was rarely green and lush. Such changes to the land came infrequently, following flooding rains that gouged out the river and carried their precious sheep into oblivion. Yet such devastation brought life to Sunset Ridge. Dormant seeds would sprout from the ground, their livestock would grow fat and smiles would return until the season changed. Then the land would shrivel once again and the animals would melt into the cracked ground. Maybe that was the reason for their father's fractious personality. At times G.W. too was at war, with the land he loved.

The breast pocket of Dave's uniform contained the last letter the Harrow brothers had received from their mother while in training. It was sparsely addressed, care of the Australian Imperial Forces. When it arrived at Lark Hill all three brothers had stared at the postmark, as they had her previous notes. Their eyes had met above the familiar looping letters and for a few seconds they had passed the envelope around their small circle, suggesting one or the other to open and read it first. Finally the task had fallen to Dave.

'We should have written back before this,' Dave had commented, his fingers carefully peeling back the envelope. He had lost count of the number of letters their mother had written. The first few had been angry and accusatory in tone and, although the contents remained the same, he could sense a growing sadness as the silence stretched on between them. The arrival of each letter made it more difficult for the boys to put pen to paper, and his older brothers grew more sullen with the arrival of each new note.

'But we decided not to,' Thaddeus had reminded him. 'We agreed on that. We said we'd write after we arrived in France.'

Luther had nodded. 'Don't l-look l-like that, D-Dave. If w-we'd told th-them before w-we sailed it's just as l-likely they would have p-put th-the c-coppers on our t-tail to b-bring us home.'

Dave sighed and then read aloud.

Boys,

I hope this letter finds you. With only the scantest of information I have presumed you have joined up and so I write, once again, as you have not.

How difficult you have made these past months with your silence. Do you not give a thought to how worried we are? Do you not think about the parents you have left behind and your heritage that is Sunset Ridge? I never expected such indifference and I am at a loss as to how to reconcile your combined actions.

Forgive me. I am told I should be proud at your eagerness to join up, if that indeed is what you have done. I am not. I know I should forgive all three of you for your careless attitude. I cannot, not when your silence continues.

I would care to know if you are indeed alive and together. As your mother I am owed that courtesy, and if you have dragged David into some foolhardy adventure, then his safety is in your hands, Thaddeus and Luther. God help you that you do not fail in this regard as well.

Your mother

The train rattled onwards. Dave didn't need to re-read the few lines; they were already memorised. When the boys eventually replied, they shared only a brief paragraph noting they were about to leave for France. It was Luther's idea to enclose the photograph of the three of them taken at Lark Hill, and Dave knew that in spite of their mother's anger she would be proud when she saw them in their AIF uniforms. Yet despite the righteousness of their actions, a whiff of guilt hung about them like stale food. Dave wished he could throw the letters away. At times he felt as if they would burn right through him, yet they remained the only tangible link to Sunset Ridge and his mother. Quite simply, he missed the land and her.

They entered a lush valley, the fields undulating away from them like small waves impatiently waiting to lick fields and hedgerows. Villages dotted the landscape every few miles as the troop train meandered across the countryside and flocks of birds fled from nearby trees. Dave craned his neck to follow their ascending path until they left his field of vision and then he reached for his kit bag. Having managed to purchase some new sketchpads while in England, he was determined that not even war would prevent him from drawing.

As the Banyan River came to life on the page, his senses conjured up the ancient trees inspecting their stately reflections in the blue-green calm of the water. The charcoal deftly traced the grass-softened banks, scattering fallen timber, darting water fowl and a kangaroo nibbling tender shoots on the far bank. If he had paint he could capture the blue haze of the eucalypts, shadow the stalking long-legged water birds, and cause a shaft of light to dapple the morning-dew leaves of a large gum tree.

Luther awoke and, leaving his seat, squashed in between Marty and Dave. 'Th-that's a b-beauty,' he remarked loudly, elbowing Dave in the ribs. 'It's exactly as I r-remember it.' Luther ran his hand across the drawing, as the occupants of the dog-box stirred amid a series of grunts and coughs.

Thaddeus yawned and reached for the sketchpad. Marty, Riley and Turtle peered at the drawing in turn.

'What'd you know?' Marty exclaimed. 'We've got an artist with us. You kept that quiet.'

'Always did want me portrait done,' Turtle said, straightening his slouch hat. 'This is me best profile.' He turned sideways, displaying a nasty scar that he claimed to have earned in a bar fight.

Riley smirked and leaned towards Dave. 'Fell against his mother's copper, he did, when he was a little 'un.'

Dave closed his eyes and imagined the river bank.

'Did not,' Turtle said.

'Did so,' Riley persevered.

'Anyone would think you lot were going on a round-the-world trip, not to a war,' Marty complained as he stretched his shoulders and left the dog-box.

'Don't mind him,' Turtle yawned. 'His girl left him for a younger fella. Told him she was embarrassed about him shirking his duty and ending up a thief. He only got word from her the day we left England.'

Thaddeus stared out the window. 'Well, it's not like she's the only woman on earth.'

Dave wondered if his older brother had turned sour on women. When questioned about his need to see Corally Shaw the day he left home, Thaddeus had clamped his lips together. 'There wasn't any need,' came the sour reply. Then there was the pretty girl in a village near Lark Hill. Bethany was as keen as mustard on Thaddeus, but Luther joked that Thaddeus had only outed with her to get some experience before telling the girl it was just a bit of fun. That wasn't the older brother Dave knew. Besides, Marty told him that there were women who would take coin to relieve a man's need, although, he cautioned, near everyone ended up with venereal disease.

'You never have t-told us w-why you and Joe joined up and th-then b-bolted into th-the scrub, Turtle,' Luther said, rolling shreds of tobacco between his palms.

Very slowly Turtle straightened his long neck. The skin on his face had not recovered from the hot summer days spent hiding in the iron water tank; it was patchy with burn marks. 'I figured it for a bit of a lark,' Turtle began, 'until Mother told me about the wounded following a big push back in '16. Newspaper after newspaper, and the names just kept on coming. She heard from the minister's wife at her church group that there was a big advance at Fromelles. Well, the lists of the dead and missing and wounded . . .' Turtle shook his head. 'I just wondered if it was worth it.' He looked at Dave. 'You know, to die over here for another man's war.'

Luther slid the cigarette between his lips and pulled his tomahawk out from beneath his tunic. 'Ain't no one d-dying on m-my w-watch.'

'Sure there ain't, kid,' Turtle said softly. 'Anyway, we're here now, so we'll have to knuckle down and make the best of it.' He turned to Dave. 'Have you got a sweetheart?'

Dave felt heat rise in his cheeks at the thought of Miss Waites. 'Nuh.'

'Well,' Riley interrupted, 'I reckon that's somewhat of a bonus – for her at least, if you get knocked.'

'Hey, Riley, lay off the kid,' Turtle protested.

Riley lit his second cigarette in as many minutes. 'If he's old enough to be a soldier, he's old enough to know the score.'

Dave had enlisted with the help of a wooden crate, a stuck-on moustache and the threat of his brothers refusing to volunteer if he wasn't allowed to join up. Marty tried to talk him out of it, but that wasn't going to happen, not with his brothers by his side. On arrival at the Lark Hill training camp the sergeant-major only cocked an eyebrow and mumbled something about the desperate need for reinforcements.

Overnight, Dave had been launched into a man's world and treated as such. He missed Sunset Ridge, but as part of a platoon he experienced a strong sense of belonging. There was no pecking order, no favourites and no mother to baby him. He was his own man. Wedging the sketchpad between the seat and the wall of the carriage, Dave pressed his forehead against the train window. The glass was cold on his skin, the sky slate-grey. When the train stopped momentarily at a siding the low rumble of thunder hovered towards them. A belch of smoke appeared on the horizon, then another and another. Dave's stomach knotted.

'Well then,' Luther clasped him briefly on the shoulder, 'looks like we're here.'

Sister Valois tucked a stray piece of hair beneath her cap and stared out the window of the ground floor ward in the temporary field hospital. The chateau was a stone dwelling belonging to a wealthy textiles merchant. Requisitioned by the French army, its eight bedrooms and substantial public areas provided space for a hundred patients. The local villagers believed that the owner had been killed by a shell when his Ypres-based factory had been hit the previous year. There were two sons at the front who were also presumed dead, and a wife and daughter who were thought to be living in Paris. Sister Valois had never resided in such style and wondered at the circumstances that would cause a woman to desert such a building.

Often she would pause during rounds to stare at the parquet floors, gilt mirrors and ornate clocks sitting on mantelpieces, and wonder at the lives of the owners and the architect who had constructed such a place. The two-foot walls held deep recesses, and there were corners everywhere, as if the builder could not make up his mind as to the direction it should take. A set of stairs to the upper level creaked and groaned even when not in use, and the younger nurses and aides swore to repeated sightings of shadowy shapes.

Sister Valois's quarters adjoined the large kitchen. Into her room she had dragged one of the ornate gold Louis XIV chairs from the dining room and a bow-fronted writing desk, while a tapestry wall hanging pulled from one of the salons took the chill from the flagstone floor. No other senior nurse was afforded such privilege. Most rented out houses in the village or were forced to bunk down in the tents attached to the converted estate. But Sister Valois was now in charge of the hospital, an improbable promotion during peacetime and one only made possible by the recommendation of the doctor she had served with at the Verdun casualty clearing station.

Through the open window the warming scents of spring carried on the air. Never had she been so happy to see the end of winter. Typhoid, trench foot, frostbite and gas-gangrene battled for supremacy amid the shell and shrapnel wounds, and at least here they were no longer cutting bloodied, muddy and rotting uniforms from maimed bodies. If a patient made it this far he had already experienced both a dressing and a casualty clearing station and perhaps another field hospital. This temporary field hospital was the last stop for the majority of the wounded within its surrounds. Most would eventually be sent back to the front. Others were here to die. Some things, however, had not changed. The hospital staff still waged a continual battle to keep lice under control in the wards. Then there were the shortages: bandages, dressings, sheets, towels, disinfectant.

Sister Valois's fingers caressed the tiny leaves that edged their way from the springy vine on the exterior of the building against the windowsill. Outside, two elderly male villagers tended a straggly vegetable and herb plot. The remains of a substantial garden showed itself in the flowering bulbs sprinkled amid stone footpaths and overgrown hedges, and although the grassy stretch between house and estate buildings had been trampled by the business of daily life, Sister Valois took some comfort in knowing that perhaps one day, when the war was over, both house and garden would be restored to their former splendour.

The chateau was located on the edge of woodland, and a number of trees had been thinned in a circle that fanned outwards from the rear of the hospital for more than a mile. The cleared area housed a patchwork of buildings, including the caretaker's farmhouse and stone barn, which had been joined by rows of white tents. Young women walked quickly to and fro, their long skirts and white aprons marking them as volunteers. Some of the girls were undisciplined yet Sister Valois could not fault their enthusiasm. They took on myriad roles, from ambulance drivers and nurse's assistants to cooks, canteen workers and laundresses.

'Sister?'

Private Gregory McNeil was the son of a French woman and a Scotsman. He should have been convalescing in a London hospital by now. However, like many of the amputees in this ward, he suffered from an infection of the bone. She walked towards his cot, one of forty in the converted dining room. Some six feet above him, on a painted screen, was an idyllic forest scene of dancing nymphs. Forming a smile, she tried not to look at the flatness of the white sheet where his legs should have been. Like many of the soldiers lining this beautiful room, little by little more of his skin and bone were cut away, until the disease went beyond the surgeon's skill.

'Yes?' she said brightly, taking his pulse. He was grey today. Together they had composed a letter to his wife and daughters. She had mailed it a week ago at his insistence, and he still lingered. She had to remind herself that it was a terrible thing to grow used to death, yet here in this ward they lost at least one patient a week. There was a new cemetery filling with neat white crosses just half a mile away. 'Yes?' Nurse Valois repeated. Too exhausted to move, the private's eyes slid to the right.

Patting his arm, she checked the patient next to him. Francois Chessy's breathing was ragged. With practised movements she swiftly adjusted his pillow, easing him upwards so that he was partially sitting. 'Better?'

Chessy nodded as his breathing gradually improved. 'Water?'

He held the glass weakly as she positioned the thinnest surgical tube she could find between his lips. Chessy was at his best in the early morning. He could drink unaided and consume eggs or a nourishing soup, albeit slowly. With his leg lost to gangrene below the knee, damage to his heart and a lung shredded by shrapnel, how he still lived seven months on was staggering. Especially with the bone of his amputated leg infected. It was true that some of the amputees managed to fight off infection, however multiple injuries lessened the chances of survival. One of the volunteers was assigned to sponge bath him daily and Sister Valois knew that massage was vital to ensure circulation and alleviate bedsores. There was little else they could do for him.

She checked the large gilt clock that sat within an alcove at the far end of the room. 'One hour,' she advised him. His course of opiates kept him mildly sedated and, she hoped, would gradually ease his suffering while he waited for death to claim him. She took the glass from his hand.

'No.'

The strength of his voice startled her. Drawing a stool to the side of his cot, she thought back to the day at the Verdun casualty clearing station: she wished now that she had given him the morphine overdose. 'It will help.'

'No. How can I fight what I cannot feel?'

'Would you like to write to your mother, Francois? I am sure she would like to hear from you.'

The young man glanced at the Highlander lying four feet from his cot. 'I am not dying.'

'Of course you're not.'

Chessy had been difficult since the morning of his arrival at the hospital two months ago. He refused to believe that his brother

Antoine was dead; refused to write to his mother; refused to accept the severity of his injuries and appeared to be concerned about just one mortal thing in this world – his dog, Roland. The majority of the patients in the ward accepted their fate with stoic resignation, using the few moments of clarity and strength left to them to pass on some final words to loved ones; but not Francois Chessy. Sister Valois reached for the notebook in the pocket of her apron. 'You are being unfair to your mama.' A pencil was poised above the thin paper.

'No.' Chessy lifted a hand. 'I have told you: I will write when I stand again.'

'Then I will write a few brief lines on your behalf.' The fine skin between her eyes knotted. 'A priest, then?' Sister Valois had learned that a man of the cloth could speak some sense into even the hardest cases.

'No. You think I will die, Sister, and maybe you are right, but what if you are wrong?'

What could she say? 'Then I would be very pleased,' she soothed.

'Have you heard anything of Roland?' He asked the same question every day.

'I have already told you all I know. When you were transported out of the casualty clearing station near Verdun your dog travelled upfront with the driver. At the first temporary field hospital you were sent to, Roland was looked after by some of the staff. Then you arrived here, alone.' Sister Valois hesitated. False hope could be more detrimental to a patient than the truth.

'Yes?' Chessy encouraged. 'There's something else?'

She interlaced her fingers. 'Yesterday,' her words were halting, 'when another intake arrived, one of the Red Cross ambulance drivers told me that there are stories about an American Field Ambulance doctor travelling with a dog.'

Francois struggled upwards in the bed.

'They say that the animal is a large, rangy beast; wolf-like, I am told.' She locked eyes with his. 'They say he has saved lives.'

'It's him.' The young man wiped away a tear.

Sister Valois cleared her throat. 'We can't be sure.'

'You were there that day I was injured. You told me you saw Roland. You know what he did at Verdun.'

'I can't be sure –'

Francois shook his head, his face filled with pity. 'Why do you find it so difficult to believe?'

Sister Valois could not answer. Of course some people doubted the stories surrounding Roland, if indeed it was the same dog, yet there was also truth at the heart of the tale. She looked at the young man propped up in bed, with the crescent-shaped shrapnel wounds on his chest, and observed the faraway look in his eyes. For the first time in weeks, he smiled.

✢ Chapter 26 ✢

Banyan, south-west Queensland, Australia
June 1917

Catherine's eyelids drooped. There had been no chance of sleep last night. For a few blissful periods she had drifted off, only to be woken by the eerie howling. She had waited and listened as a low wailing sound drifted about the boarding house, haunting her under the covers until a nervous perspiration layered her skin. Twice she had risen to peer through the grimy window, expecting a westerly wind to be the cause of the peculiar noise, but the night remained still, the wind non-existent, the unsettling noise continuing for over an hour.

Adjusting the shawl wrapped about her shoulders, Catherine leaned back in the threadbare armchair. The days grew shorter. The boarding house, already shadowed by the timber dwelling next door, was cold. She wondered if Corally would maintain their evening visits once winter was upon them in earnest, for the time they shared filled the long evening hours.

After Catherine had taken on the role of correspondent on behalf of the illiterate Corally last year, eventually her young charge had been the recipient of a number of letters from Harold Lawrence. Although the tone of these initial letters verged on brusque, Catherine persevered in her replies and eventually Corally's absence from the village church on the morning of Harold's departure last year was forgiven. Concealing her inability to read, Corally simply blamed her father for failing to pass on Harold's letter in a timely manner. Mr and Mrs Lawrence of Lawrence Ironmongers were unaware that their only son was now engaged to Corally Shaw.

During this time Catherine had also offered the young woman her services as a governess. It was an arrangement of mutual advantage: Corally Shaw was receiving a most needed education and Catherine now had a project to fill the evenings. Their agreement, however, was not without difficulties. The girl's reading and writing skills were slow to develop, with significant improvement showing only over the past few months. Initially Corally remained convinced that she was left-handed until Catherine threatened to tie the offending arm behind the girl's back. Eventually she was capable of forming letters with the hand God intended. Theirs was a fractious relationship, one that Catherine tired of within ten minutes yet missed once her young charge left. This evening, however, would be different.

The Cobb & Co. coach had delivered mail from France. Finally there was a letter for the forgotten inhabitants of Sunset Ridge, as well as another from her beloved Rodger. Instantly recognisable also were the letters addressed to Corally. Catherine knew the respective handwriting by heart. Had she not leaned over their shoulders, urging them not to press too hard on their nibs as they formed words in their ledgers? Rearranging the mail on the narrow writing desk in her room, she wondered why Thaddeus and Luther had written to Corally. Although her resentment at their communication with the young girl was tempered by relief at finally having proof of their whereabouts, Catherine was saddened that they had not thought enough of her to pen a few brief lines.

Corally was late as usual and Catherine used the time to re-read Rodger's letter. He wrote once a month, scanty notes that talked briefly about his new life. Having delayed enlistment due to his mother's poor health, he had knocked about in Brisbane for a while and then, following her passing and burial, had waited for the will to be read. Eventually he had sailed aboard a troopship that carried him to Great Britain, and in between his training spent his leave in London. He wrote little of the sights and sounds of this great city yet appeared to receive much entertainment observing the toffs shopping at the fancy department stores. Rodger's voice in his all-too-few letters was at times quite foreign to her. He was clearly enjoying his freedom and, as he was yet to finish training, rather hoped he wouldn't see action. Great Britain, it seemed, was too much fun. In comparison, Harold Lawrence was now a Lewis machine gunner and had already seen action in France.

Catherine rearranged the envelopes on the desk. She could only imagine the joy Mrs Harrow would feel on receipt of a letter from her sons. The village gossips talked of G.W.'s continued illness, with Sunset Ridge now being run on a skeletal staff with an unknown quantity at the helm. By all accounts, Nathanial Taylor – he had been pointed out to Catherine when he was in the village collecting station supplies – was the boundary rider placed in charge of the Harrows' cattle last year; now it appeared he ran the entire property. The proof of this stranger's ability would come to the fore at shearing time, the matrons of the village informed her at the post office. It was one thing to oversee livestock in the paddock, quite another, the locals mused, to arrange a shearing team and the sale of the clip in a timely manner.

There was a knock on the window and then a bare leg hoisted itself over the sill. Corally landed lightly on her feet and casually said hello. Barefoot and dressed in cut-off pants and a shirt tied at the waist, her one concession to femininity was the fine woollen shawl she was rarely without. The girl could well have been mistaken for a boy.

'Ye could use the door,' Catherine chided.

'What, and have that mousy landlady turn her nose up at me?' Corally sat cross-legged on the timber boards at Catherine's feet.

'Ye know ye will have to do something about your dressing before Harold returns,' Catherine said pointedly.

The girl rubbed at her nose with the back of a dirt-smeared hand. 'You need coin for that.'

'I have a white blouse and dark skirt that could be cut down to size. We may well be able to sew a second blouse for ye from the material.'

'Goodo,' Corally grinned. 'That's one thing I can do, sew. You look done in.'

Catherine pinched the bridge of her nose. 'I've not been sleeping. There's this howling noise that's keeping me awake at night.'

'And you've got Mrs Dempsey giving you strife during the day,' Corally observed.

Catherine agreed, reluctantly displaying the letters like a fan of playing cards.

'What, all for me?'

With a tight smile, Catherine opened each letter and scanned them briefly. 'They are from the Harrow boys. They're in France.'

'Really?' Corally beamed. 'So, they're all over there, even Dave?'

'Och, I'm not sure. Let's see. Let me tell ye the general news and then I'll read each one separately.'

Corally drew her knees up beneath her chin.

Thaddeus and Luther talked of the training camp at Salisbury Plain in England, of the things they had seen on arrival and of the great adventure they were having. They also explained why they had run away and the joint pact they had made not to write to their mother until they were in France. Thaddeus also wrote of how they met up with Dave.

'Guid, he's with them,' Catherine said with relief, picturing the discarded sketches abandoned outside her quarters at Sunset Ridge.

'I prayed for him. My pa says that praying is a waste of time, for people still get sick and die whether you do or you don't, but I prayed for Dave anyway, on account of the fact that God's meant to look after young ones, isn't he?'

The rush of words left Catherine momentarily speechless. 'Yes, I suppose he is. Let's continue.'

Dave, the poor lad, Thaddeus wrote after a stilted introduction, *had the worst of it. He was roughed up some by the local coppers when he ran away from home. Luckily he ended up on the Western Mail with us. We had to take him with us considering all that had happened, and Luther and I are keeping an eye on him.*

'Ridiculous,' Catherine complained. 'Those two should have known better.'

Still, it could be worse. I hope you'll write to me, Corally. I know Harold has been persistent in his attentions towards you, but you are not yet married and I would put myself forward as a possible suitor should you be inclined. I tried to see you before I left last year but I ended up in an argument with Harold and had to high-tail it out of the village. He told me you and he were outing. I guess I'm writing now because we're going into action and I wanted you to know what I thought.

Corally looked slightly abashed. 'I never knew he wanted to out with me before he went to the war, honest. Harold told me I was in demand because there weren't a whole lot of girls around – well, apart from Julie Jackson, but no one wants her 'cause of the Germans in her family.'

'Corally!' Catherine was askance. It was bad enough that the Jacksons were being refused service in the village, but Corally was supposed to be her friend.

'It's true. I saw her with her mother in the main street and people crossed to the other side.'

'Well, I do hope that ye are not behaving in such a bigoted manner. Ye told me once that Julie Jackson was your closest friend.'

Corally ignored the comment. 'It's not like I see her that much anymore. They rarely come to town.'

Catherine shuffled Thaddeus's letter behind Luther's and read it aloud.

Dear Corally,

The war isn't what I thought it would be, but we're making our mark over here. The boys in our platoon are top drawer and although we've lost quite a few already it only makes us more determined to see this thing through to the end. Thaddeus has turned out to be a fine leader. Dave and I think he'll make an officer in no time, especially as he's pretty tight with Captain Egan. As for Dave, he has become something of an artist. The boys like his sketches and it's a real sight to see him drawing in the trenches.

I think about that day in the cemetery, Corally, and I know you were unhappy with me, but I want you to know that we're peas in a pod, at least that is what Mother would call us if she could see us together. That's why I decided to write to you. We made a pact not to tell anyone where we were, especially our parents, but now we've been in the thick of things I figured it was best not to waste another day. I'll not forget the kiss we shared, nor the way you stood up for me in court that day. I knew then there was something between us.

Catherine's hand fell to her lap. Corally offered a wan smile and opened her mouth to speak. 'Don't say anything,' Catherine warned. Heavens, she thought, the girl in front of her was not yet sixteen. 'This letter is from Harold.' The governess cleared her throat.

My dearest Corally,
We are about to go into battle. I'm scratching these few lines
waiting for the whistle to blow. I don't think I'm scared, more
concerned that I do my part and not let the men down around
me, nor they me. I am here to do my bit yet it doesn't stop me
worrying about what will become of you should I not make it
through this next scrape. I would be with you now if I could.
Yet I am one for duty. Knowing that you did not desert me
that morning makes the time easier. I have something to look
forward to on my return. I have our life together.
With deepest affection,
H

Corally swivelled on her bottom and glanced at the writing desk. 'Is there not another? Is there not one from Dave?' Her disappointment was palpable.

'No, there isn't.' Catherine folded the letters and handed them to the young girl. 'I think ye had better tell me what's going on, Corally.'

The girl rose and began to pace the oblong room. At the far end she stopped at the washstand. A bottle of lavender water sat next to a face cloth and a cake of Pears soap. Corally ran her finger absently across the soap and sniffed at the faint smell it left on her skin. 'Haven't you ever wanted something so bad that you could taste it?' Turning on her heel, she faced the governess. 'I have. I've wanted lots of things.' She raised her eyes briefly to the ceiling. 'A good feed, a mother who wanted better for her daughter, and a good man to take care of me.'

Catherine interlaced long fingers in her lap. 'Corally, ye are still very young. There is no rush.'

'I didn't go looking for them, Miss Waites.' She jammed her fists in the pockets of her trousers. 'I just made the best of my situation. I've always had a dead-eye dick aim. At least that's what me pa calls it. Spit clean through the eye of a needle, he reckons, when I was just a wee thing. So, I began playing marbles and I beat every boy I had a mind to beat, and in the beating I realised something.'

'What was that?'

'I'd got their attention. Oh, not like a lady in a fancy dress or with a pretty face. It was something else.' Corally raised her chin. 'Respect. That ain't something I ever had until I fleeced every boy in these here parts.' The girl gave her a challenging stare. 'Harold told me that there weren't any other girls around the district like me.'

'He admires ye,' Catherine told her.

'Yeah, well, admiration sounds real nice but in the end it doesn't buy you squat.'

'It gave ye Harold.'

'Yes, it did. I've got smarts, Miss Waites, and smarts go beyond a fancy house and a name that means something to others. And I ain't living my life in a fallen-down shack with nothing but a brood of little 'uns to show for my trouble because some hoity-toity parents don't think I'm good enough for their boys.' She swallowed. 'So, that's why when Harold Lawrence came knocking I said yes.'

'I see.' Catherine sat back in the armchair. It was nearing the time for supper and although she loathed the cramped communal dining room, her own quarters were bordering on claustrophobic. The young girl, standing so defiantly before her, drew so much energy that Catherine was beginning to feel flushed. 'Ye don't love him, do ye?' She thought of Corally's eager gaze as each letter was read aloud and the sheer disappointment that had emanated from her slight body upon realising there was nothing from the youngest of the Harrow boys. 'It is Dave ye care for, isn't it?'

Corally scuffed at the floor as if she were standing in the dirt. Her nose turned pink. 'You know, sometimes I look at the moon and I think that if I could just grab hold of it, if I could just have all that light shining down on me for just a moment, well, then maybe Dave would see me.'

Catherine lit a candle in the darkening room. 'All those boys are at war now, Corally.'

The young girl crossed her arms across her chest. 'So?'

'Well, ye must write back to each of them.' Catherine rubbed at her temples. 'Ye must tell Thaddeus and Luther that there can only ever be friendship between ye. Ye have pledged yourself to Harold, after all, and it would be wrong to give the others false hope.'

Corally chewed her bottom lip.

'Ye have to do the right thing. Ye simply can't lead young men on like this.' For a moment Catherine thought the girl would refuse. She observed the set of Corally's shoulders. 'Come back tomorrow and I will help ye write the necessary letters.'

The girl reluctantly agreed. 'Can I have some writing paper to take with me tomorrow so I can practise my letters?'

The request was surprising yet Catherine was pleased. 'Of course, and there is something else worth considering, Corally. On Harold's return he will have seen things that ye can only imagine; the great cities of England and France, different foods, architecture, clothing, language and women. European women.'

'What do you mean?'

'Well, as ye are so determined to marry quickly and, well, don't ye think it is time to start behaving and dressing accordingly? Ye don't want Harold to come back and be . . .' Catherine searched for the right word.

'Disappointed?' Corally challenged. 'No, I don't.' The girl studied Catherine's dress and then her hair. 'I suppose I'll have to learn from you, even though you are still unmarried.' With a curt goodbye she left through the window.

Corally edged along the side of the building. Dry grass cushioned her progress and at the end of the boarding house she peered down the ill-lit street. Half a block away a single lamp light opposite the courthouse broke the gathering dark. Large creamy moths flew into and around the light, filling the halo of brightness with movement. At the far end of the street a number of horses were tethered to the hotel hitching rail. The remainder of the street appeared to be deserted. Corally's nose twitched; mutton, potatoes and the fatty scent of dripping made her curse the miles back to her parents' shack by the cemetery. The polite people of the village were sitting down to their supper behind the soft glow of illuminated windows.

With a final glance at the deserted street she began the walk home. There was no real reason why she chose to sneak to and from the boarding house. Mainly it was because Corally didn't want the townsfolk sticky-beaking into her business, or that of Miss Waites. The governess was helping her, after all, and her pa said to be nice in return. It was a pity then that the governess had become like everyone else. Corally was yet to meet anyone who didn't feel obliged to lecture her. With a little skip she left the outskirts of the village and walked into the scrub. Tomorrow she would sit patiently while Miss Waites dictated what she wanted her to send to the Harrow boys, then with the letters safely in her pocket she would take them back to the hut and burn them and then write her own. The only good thing about being offered advice was that you didn't have to take it.

Nathanial Taylor wiggled a horse-weary backside against the lumpy mattress cushioning the floorboards and stared at the narrow bed upended against the wall of the governess's room. The novelty of being indoors and having his arse lifted two feet off the ground had not lasted long. Ever since Mrs Harrow requested he be bedded within the confines of the homestead garden some months ago, the walls of this new dwelling had been steadily closing in. Nathanial rolled sideways, pushing his riding boots out of the way. His old faithfuls were nearly past their prime. The leather was beginning to pull away from the sole. Some repair work was in order if they were to see him through another winter, especially as he had never been one for socks. He had run with the blacks up north for the first twenty years of his life and had learned to ride and to work livestock bare-foot. In pursuit of a woman nearly ten years ago he had relented and purchased his first pair of leather boots. The ones smelling up the place next to his head were his second.

Through the open door the bush grew dark as the sun was consumed by the earth's rotation. The scene was accompanied by the tinkle of piano music, a nightly occurrence and one that he enjoyed. Although the tune was unknown it rekindled memories of long nights by lonely camp fires and the odd woman who had passed his way, like diamonds from heaven. Lily Harrow's touch was deft, and the nightly music became a backdrop to his musings and the unfolding nights. Turning on his side he watched a flock of white cockatoos wing their way towards the river. The birds left a gun-metal grey sky smeared at the edges with a purple hue as the bush quietened.

He had been bashing about the outback for long enough to know when man and beast were in for a cold winter. G.W. Harrow's cattle were already showing signs of healthy hair growth, a sure indication of a lengthy cold spell. At least the feed would hold out till spring now he had finally reached agreement with Mrs Harrow.

They were to start shearing in a couple of days. With Sunset Ridge's normal team unable to accommodate the changed date, Nathanial had called in a couple of favours and wangled a team from down south. Once the clip was sold he then intended to sell two thousand head of Sunset Ridge's breeding ewes. That would ease the pressure on the pasture and allow them to receive the full benefit of the highly anticipated spring rains. While he was loath to overrule G.W. Harrow's management style, he had never been one for overstocking.

Nathanial had expected a battle from the stoic Lily Harrow when it came to bringing the property's shearing date forward, but it seemed the woman's hands were full caring for her ailing husband and running the homestead. A man such as himself couldn't ask for better circumstances; who would have thought he could slip into the role of managing such a property? Yet notwithstanding the fact that he had fallen on his feet, his current accommodation was less than satisfactory and he yearned to be back out in the bush. 'She's trussed me up like a broiling hen,' Nathanial muttered, scratching at his neck hair. Lily Harrow had promised good food if he shifted camp to the old governess quarters, and he had been led in from the scrub by his stomach. It was soon apparent, however, that everything that lived and breathed was killed three times in that room they called a kitchen, and by the time it reached his plate in the evening Nathanial found himself sizing up his portion as if he were about to do battle. He would put up with the poor food for as long as it stayed chilly and he enjoyed the novelty of keeping the missus happy. That would last till spring, he reckoned.

In spite of Cook's limited ability Nathanial was not immune to the more pleasant side of his employment. The boss was not unattractive, and he admired her tenacity; indeed if the old man kicked the bucket he harboured ideas of cleaning himself up and edging a boot into the homestead. A man could not be blamed for having needs. And there was always the possibility that Lily Harrow would not be averse to a brief undoing. She wouldn't be the first better-bred woman to take a fancy to him, even if such affairs were short-lived. For the moment, however, there was a live if decrepit husband and absent sons for Mrs Harrow to concentrate on. Nathanial wondered if the missus would sleep a little better tonight. Cook informed him at supper that the Harrow boys had finally written to her. This long-awaited information was divulged with folded arms and a tone that suggested he better not get too comfortable as manager. That was one thing about women, Nathanial mused: they courted death by assuming all would be well. He didn't have the heart to wipe the sanctimonious look from Cook's face by telling her that if all three Harrow boys were in France, their parents would be lucky to see two return to Sunset Ridge.

The screech and rustle of flying foxes sounded from the gum trees behind the quarters. For small animals they sure made a ruckus. He had a mind to fire his rifle into the trees, but he knew that the ungainly feet-hangers would regroup within seconds, making any attempt to dislodge them futile. Nathanial sat upright and groped in the darkness for his roll-your-owns. The night was eating away at the station outbuildings. Little by little they disappeared to merge with the gloom of a moonless night.

'Damn it all,' he muttered when the tobacco pouch remained elusive. Scrabbling to his feet, he ran his hands across the dresser in the dark. A stub of candle and a box of matches were quickly located, but the ensuing light was weak. The candle box was empty and he had neglected to refill the kerosene lamp this morning. With a huff he jerked at the wooden drawers of the dresser, searching for a spare candle that would see him through the evening. With his few belongings thrown over the back of a chair or piled on the floor, there had been no need to rummage through the dresser drawers or narrow wardrobe; it had been a long time since he had hung or folded clothes.

Nathanial ran calloused palms across the base of each empty drawer. About to give up, his search revealed a stack of papers. Lifting them free he flicked through the pages in the wan candle-light. They were a collection of sketches: strangely shaped people and animals and something that looked disturbingly similar to a chair. Nathanial itched at his beard and drew his formidable eyebrows together. Each drawing bore the initials DH in the lower right-hand corner. He guessed that one of the infamous Harrow boys was the artist responsible for the peculiar collection.

Only a couple of the drawings appealed. They reminded him of Miss Waites, the young woman who worked in the village post office. Although a bit on the skinny side for his liking – he preferred a woman with bits he could hang on to – she wasn't a bad sort. The sketches of the woman were pretty good. Nathanial could not recall when he had last seen the curve of a woman's lip or the whorl of an ear close up. In fact, the images were so realistic they were almost indecent.

Sitting the candle on the floor beside the sketches, he rolled a cigarette. The tobacco filled his lungs as he sorted through the drawings. The ones of the woman he left by his swag; the others were less enticing. He began to fold some of the animals and people into foot-long oblong shapes, as smoke trailed across his eyes from the cigarette dangling between his lips. On completion of his task, a pile of folded paper sat before him. Stubbing out the smoke, he flicked the remains out the door and began to line his boots with the paper. He pushed and prodded at the inside of each shoe until the drawings were moulded to the shape of his foot and the worn leather was reinforced by the new inners. He returned the unused sketches in the drawer. When eventually the task was completed Nathanial gave a satisfied nod. He too could appreciate art.

Lily rode out through the house paddock and followed the track that led to the river. The air was cold. Ice crystals latticed the frost-crisp ground. It was many years since she had ventured out to this part of the property, and a good five years since she had last sat on a horse. In the days when her marriage was still soft and pliable, a weekly ride with G.W. was something of a treat. He was hers then, his attention yet to be stolen by the many responsibilities that gradually had drawn him from her side.

There was a sense of freedom that came with riding, a sensation that had flooded back as soon as one of the young stockmen saddled up the bay mare. The boy barely spoke and had remained silent when she announced she would not be riding side-saddle. These days Lily had neither the time nor the inclination for a leisurely, ladylike trot around the paddock. She wanted to sit astride like a man, to feel the winter air on her face and to gallop headlong into it as if there were no tomorrow.

It took time for Lily to settle into the animal's natural gait. Her body felt cumbersome in the saddle and she was self-conscious about her old riding habit. The white shirt and tailored jacket were paired with riding pants hastily purchased from a catalogue a number of years ago and rarely worn. The mare plodded through the trees. Lily let the horse have its head, her gloved hand caressing the woody plants as they passed. Birds twittered prettily in spite of the frosty morning as they darted through the foliage, and it was with anticipation that Lily clucked the mare onwards.

She steered the horse between the wide-girthed trees until the gentle slope of the river bank appeared. The mare halted and lowered her head and Lily let the reins slip through her fingers as the horse began to nibble at tufts of grass. She breathed in the tranquil surroundings, her breath white puffs in the cold air. Ahead, the slow chug of brown water wound its way along the waterway to disappear among trees and scrub and lignum.

The mare walked forward grazing amid fallen timber, the crackling of fragile twigs and grasses disturbing a mob of sheep. The animals were strung out along the edge of the river, their heads dipping into the water as they drank. One or two lifted their heads and sniffed the air, then turned towards Lily, stamping their hoofs in annoyance. The mare swished her tail lazily as the sheep began to move, before they began to run along the bank in the opposite direction. River sand and dirt puffed up in their wake as the mob crossed a grassy verge and disappeared around the next bend in the waterway.

Lily breathed in the morning scents of earth and animal and thought back to her life twelve months ago. How things had changed. She now knew that her three sons were engulfed in the greatest war mankind had ever seen and her once-robust husband was no more. He barely acknowledged the letters their sons wrote when she read them aloud, and if he did care when she tried to convey her concerns for their safety, he never showed it.

The mare whinnied. Above the tree line the white glow of a winter sun was mottled by a wisp of cloud. Lily clucked her tongue, urging the horse down to the water's edge. Now the cold of winter was with them G.W. was not so adamant in his need to rise early, which was why Lily had decided to go riding. She'd been house-bound for too long. The doctor's original diagnosis of a gradual deterioration of G.W.'s health was slow to materialise. Her husband remained stubbornly resistant to his predicted downfall. He made a point of walking every day, and his shuffle had improved so much that he could now amble about the homestead with the help of a sturdy silver-knobbed mahogany walking stick. While his speech remained slurred it too showed progress, and quite often he could be found silently forming words. Unable to write, he spent much of his time reading. There was no limit to the man's willpower and, although Lily said nothing for fear of reproach, she was proud of G.W.'s fierce determination. If only the doctor were not more positive and she more patient. If only her husband still behaved as if he cared.

Lily was torn between the resolve shown by her husband and the doctor's prediction of an eventual worsening of his condition. With the prospect of an invalid to care for, she knew her days of freedom could be limited, and therein lay the most immediate problem. Lily needed to ensure that if the worst happened, the property would continue on as always. Sunset Ridge had been her life for so many years she could not foresee a future without the comfortable expanse of dirt swathing her in safety. If she could rely on Nathanial Taylor her reflections would be less worrying, but fate had made her realistic.

Sunset Ridge's manager was an unknown quantity, and no amount of searching through the station office had calmed her fears. G.W.'s response to her queries remained unhelpful, although it was clear he was not happy with Taylor's promotion. There were no written references for Nathanial Taylor and no paperwork noting next of kin; in fact, the ledger entry stating the manager's starting date and terms of employment was scant on detail, apart from a street address for a residence in the town of Charleville. Lily had penned a letter of enquiry, hopeful of obtaining a list of previous employers. Such lack of formal paperwork was hardly cause for concern, yet now her days had settled into a more regular routine she queried whether Nathanial Taylor was qualified to manage such a large holding.

Initially his arrival at the homestead was a timely fix for her immediate problems, and outwardly the man appeared to be doing an excellent job. But what did she know? A woman in her position with an ill husband and three sons fighting abroad needed to be assured of both the suitability and ability of the property's manager. She needed more than his word. Should her enquiries show him unsuitable for the job, Lily intended to advertise for a new manager in the spring. When her sons returned they would barely be experienced enough to take over the management of the property, and she faced the probability that her husband would never fully recover.

'Morning.' Nathanial Taylor appeared around the river bend, his gelding at a trot. 'I wondered what startled those ewes.'

'Sheep are not known for their steady nerves,' she replied, noting the curve of his thigh and the ease with which he held the reins.

He stretched cold-stiffened fingers. 'Actually, Mrs Harrow, I've always found sheep to be incredibly intelligent. It's all in the handling.'

The gelding trotted to the mare's side and snorted playfully, tossing his head sideways. Lily noted that the shaggy beard Taylor favoured had been cropped and his neck-hair trimmed. She could smell soap beneath the familiar scents of horse, leather and perspiration. It was a welcome change. The gelding walked forward, pressing the length of his warm body against the mare's. Lily's leg touched human warmth and she caught a glimpse of grey eyes as she quickly reined the mare away until some distance separated the two horses. Taylor leaned back in the saddle, watching her watching him.

'What are you staring at, sir?' A twinge of nervousness settled in her throat as the mare pulled on the reins.

Nathanial Taylor rested his hands on the saddle. A rope and stockwhip hung close by. 'Why, at you, Mrs Harrow.'

Lily looked away but then inexplicably found herself returning his smile. Her response confounded her. Flicking the reins, she steered the mare up the bank and away from the river.

'I didn't realise you could ride, and without a side-saddle, I see.'

Lily gripped the leather reins.

'Very modern,' he drawled, walking the gelding after her. 'You should do it more often.' His mount crushed leaf-litter. 'It becomes you.'

Lily turned the mare so that she faced the manager. 'Mr Taylor, I –'

'Yes, Mrs Harrow?' he interrupted, urging his horse forward. 'I was simply stating the obvious.'

'It's not your place, sir, to say such things.'

The manager walked his horse slowly towards her until he was by Lily's side again. 'It's the truth,' he replied.

Lily wasn't one for blushing if it could be helped but nor was she immune to the unknown sensation of having a conversation with a single man in the middle of the bush. 'I have to go.'

'Of course.' Mr Taylor tipped his hat. 'If you must.'

Lily hesitated and then turned the mare back in the direction of the homestead. The scrub closed in around them. She wanted to look behind; instead she clucked the mare onwards, noticing that every tree looked the same, every nubby bush similar. Commonsense told her there was little need for concern; the mare would find the trail home. Once or twice Lily looked over her shoulder, as the mare zigzagged through the dense bush, convinced she was being followed. 'Ridiculous,' she muttered. 'You've been alone in that rambling house with a nearly mute husband and a sullen cook and housemaid for too long.' The scrub behind her was empty, save for the twittering of birds and the startled dash of kangaroos and wallabies as they bounded across the mare's path.

'Steady, girl,' Lily cautioned, rubbing the horse's neck when the mare shied at a wallaby. Her tiredness was mounting, and an ache was building in Lily's lower back; any number of unused muscles were readying to complain once the morning ride came to an end. To the right, a noise echoed through the timber. The snap of twigs and branches and the rattle of leather and brass confirmed her suspicions. He was out there, perhaps not following, but close by.

When the trees began to thin and the countryside was again spread out before her, Lily relaxed. There was no rider poking out from the fan of trees, no sign of Sunset Ridge's manager. Soon she would be home and the dull domesticity of homestead life would resume with regular monotony. At the moment it was a pleasant thought, in spite of the difficulties that awaited her. It was just as well she had firmed her decision with regards to advertising for a new manager. Nathanial Taylor had unnerved her this morning and the worst of it was that she had found their brief conversation strangely compelling.

⋘ Chapter 27 ⋙

Tapping the horse's flanks with the heel of his boots, George dodged through the trees in pursuit of Ross Evans. With dawn trickling light across the countryside, George had risen earlier than usual, having spent most of the night awake. The entire homestead was awaiting the response from the Stepworth Gallery and, with a good few days having passed since Madeleine sent the email, they were hopeful that the project was being given the consideration they believed it deserved. George had more riding on the exhibition than his sister, wife or mother knew. He was overdrawn at the bank, and with the manager most supportive of the Sunset Ridge renovations in light of the planned David Harrow retrospective, George hoped for a confirmed exhibition date that would keep the bank happy. And that date needed to happen soon, because if the drought continued he would have to borrow even more money within months.

The horse zigzagged through the trees, startling birds and kangaroos as George tried to follow the rider ahead. Every time he drew near the trees would close in about him and it would be long seconds before he caught sight of Ross again. With his horse beginning to sweat, he slowed their pace. There was little point tiring out his mount for the sake of a man who may well be unhinged – as Rachael reminded him, who in their right mind worked for free these days? At the Banyan River, George gave up the chase. There was no sight of horse and rider, and the mad dash had only succeeded in disturbing the bush creatures at a time when every animal was trying to conserve its strength.

'You don't have to give chase.'

The voice echoed along the dry riverbed. George stood up in the stirrups and looked about. 'I know that, Ross. I mean, Mr Evans,' he said, hoping the polite route might work for him as well. 'It's just that after you talked to my sister the other day, well, I thought you might be willing to have a chat with me.'

'You young people just can't accept a good turn. You always have to have a reason.'

George swung his head in the opposite direction. 'Well, I apologise if we come across that way to you. I guess it's hard to believe that a person would lend a helping hand these days without expecting something in return.'

'Believe it.'

'Fair enough. I know one thing for sure: your mother certainly doesn't like you coming out here. She gave me an awful roasting the day I visited your house a few years back.'

'You went to Mum's place?' Ross asked. He nudged his horse out from a clump of trees and crossed the sandy bed of the dry river, halting twenty feet from George.

'To say thanks and to offer to pay you for some of what you'd done,' George replied, hoping to prolong the conversation. 'You've been a real help to me over the years, especially since this God-awful drought started.'

'She never told me you came looking.'

'Well, I got the impression I wasn't wanted, so I left real quick.'

Ross gave a rough laugh. 'She's ballsy, my mum. Always has been. She's one of the reasons I'm here.'

'Sorry?' George said, confused.

Ross scratched his ear and dismounted, straightening his back with effort. For a seventy-year-old he was still pretty agile, even if his movements were slow. 'It's a long time ago, George.' Dropping the reins so his horse could graze, he leaned against a tree and then reached for the packet of cigarettes in his shirt pocket and lit one.

George dismounted and tied his own horse to a stump and then joined Ross on a fallen log. They sat companionably, the smoke from Ross's cigarette wafting about them. After a minute's silence, Ross spoke.

'I guess I sort of figured it was better to just go about my business and do what I thought was right. And I did. Then your wife started spouting around the district about this art thingy she wants to do for your grandfather, and your little sister turned up. After her visit to the Banyan museum, most of the district wants to know more about your grandfather's life and the few left who remember the old days wish you would all bugger off.'

'Why?' George asked.

Ross took a deep puff of the cigarette. 'Because not everyone has a high opinion of your grandfather. He did something when he came back from the war that riled a lot of people, and back then not everyone wanted to see his point of view. He made a lot of folk feel real guilty, the rest, angry.'

George thought back to what Maddy told him after her visit to the museum. 'Did it have something to do with Germans?'

Ross swivelled his neck and stared at George, then stubbed out the cigarette in the dirt. 'What he did was draw attention to a number of families, and his actions made a lot of people in and around Banyan feel mighty uncomfortable. Some of the folks involved have descendants living in Banyan today. But all that aside, he did the right thing by my mum, and despite the fact the old girl's been in a bad mood for as long as I can recall, your grandfather looked after her for a time when her situation was real tough. Of course, there's a cost to everything, and Mum never could forgive your grandfather.'

'I don't know what you're talking about,' George admitted.

'Well, of course you don't,' Ross replied. 'The Harrows made sure it was all kept quiet and Mum agreed to it. I understand there's a pecking order in society. Mum doesn't, but I sure do. Anyway, me helping you and your mother is just a way of repaying your grandfather's kindness.'

'So, it *was* you all those years ago. My mother said she believed that someone was giving her a helping hand when she and Dad were running the place.'

Ross nodded and looked away. 'She was a good woman. It was the right thing to do. Actually, I probably wouldn't have kept on poking about the place after your father died and Sunset Ridge was leased, but I got used to coming out here. I'd rather be riding through the scrub feeling useful than sitting in a chair like most of the retirees watching television or down at the club playing pokies.'

'How come you didn't just tell me years ago?' George was flummoxed.

'Because it would have got around the district eventually, you know that. Now, I'm not having a go at you, George, but either you or that wife of yours would have said something, even in passing, and I'm not a believer in people having to know everyone's business. Some would have said I was off my rocker.' Ross stretched out each of his legs before standing. 'My heart's not as sound as it used to be. In fact, I reckon this will be one of my last rides around Sunset Ridge. Don't look like that; I'm not a bloke that needs pity. Anyway, when you turned up this morning, I figured you deserved to know why I've been rambling around here for so many years, and it seemed the timing was right.'

'Hang on.' George watched as Ross mounted his horse. 'You haven't told me what Grandfather did for your mother.'

Ross pulled his hat brim low over his face. 'Son, that's not my story to tell.'

The ride home took George through a desolate landscape. Although intrigued and pleased by his conversation with Ross, his good mood soon ebbed. The country felt flat and lifeless, as if all the energy had been sucked from it. At times it was as if the tired heart of the land strained beneath his horse's hoofs. No grass remained to bind the soil together. Little by little the vegetation had simply melted away, leaving the paddocks devoid of ground covering. Manure stippled the pock-marked ground that was crisscrossed by the narrow indentations of sheep tracks leading to and from water. Here and there the white bones and animal hides of the dead swept in and out of George's field of vision. And still the great trees waited for rain.

George understood that he was only a custodian for the next generation, and yet at times he was almost beyond tending the property anymore. The inadequacy of his daily rounds reminded him of a doctor unable to treat the dying and he was unsurprised at his depressed mental state. In some respects he was fortunate to have endured for so long; however, the inevitable was approaching. In a few months they would no longer be able to afford sheep feed and he would have to approach the bank again, cap in hand. He knew that any goodwill had already been consumed by the loan for the homestead renovations.

Were it not for the fact that he hoped the project would lift his wife's spirits, George never would have agreed with Rachael's plans. It was not as if the home stay would bring in thousands, nor did he suspect that Rachael would be the one to clean the house and make the beds and cook the food for the paying guests. The honeymoon was definitely over and in its place he was left with a whinging wife and a drought that threatened to push them off the land. If the retrospective did not eventuate, he would have to ready for the worst.

They would go to Rachael's parents. The thought of the small granny flat behind the weatherboard Queenslander in Brisbane terrified him. He could feel it now: the bricks-and-mortar reminder of a life lost and the accusing wife who married a grazier and ended up with a busted-arse farmer. What would he do for a living? What would he tell his mother? Despite the fact he considered selling up four years ago and had said as much to Maddy, the reality of moving on was very different. He was skilled with horses and sheep, and in a good season he was adept at managing the untameable land of his ancestors. The bush was his office, the sky his ceiling. The thought of a patch of lawn and square of sky designated by the life of the urban dweller gave him palpitations. Having tried to explain these feelings of heritage and identity to Madeleine, the expression on her face only served to reinforce Rachael's complete lack of understanding. This may have been his sister's childhood home but she was as removed from bush life as was the barrister's daughter he had married. They had no attachment to Sunset Ridge. To them it was merely a piece of dirt.

One thing kept his pride intact, kept him from losing himself in grog and a niggling sense of uselessness. It was true that there were times when he wanted to run away from the land of his forefathers, yet a greater responsibility kept him tethered to it. Many others had walked this crusty shell before him and they were of his blood and they had not given up. He thought of his mother doing the best for the family and he knew that it was time for him to make a few adjustments. No one could control the elements and the bitter war waging between land and sky, however George could ensure that he did everything in his power to keep the property in the Harrow family.

❖

Madeleine and Rachael were sitting at the kitchen table with cups of coffee when George walked in the door.

'The Stepworth Gallery is not interested in the retrospective,' Madeleine advised. 'They were quite blunt in their assessment of the "economic viability of such an exhibition".' She chose not to share the rest of the terse yet polite email, in which the director suggested that Madeleine spend her time more fruitfully and that if she were looking for a project during her holiday they could easily forward suggestions.

George went straight to the fridge and opened a beer.

'It's a bit early, isn't it?' Rachael snapped.

'Tell George the rest, Rachael.' Madeleine cradled her head in her hands.

George looked across as his wife spoke.

'I have been trying to organise a district meeting in the town hall for next week and I received word today that the Shire Council doesn't want anything to do with the retrospective.'

Madeleine lifted her head and looked at her brother. 'I don't understand. The Shire Council wouldn't be staging it, the Banyan district would and as a district event we could create a not-for-profit organisation and could probably even obtain funding.'

'The problem isn't so much the council as *one councillor*,' Rachael continued. 'He's a heavyweight in this part of the world and he's dead against the idea. Everything from the mobile preschool to the local cricket club relies on him for sponsorship. You can imagine how important his contributions have become with this drought dragging on.'

'Are you telling me –' George began.

299

'Yes,' Rachael said. 'Horatio Cummins.'

Madeleine listened as George and her sister-in-law rehashed the Harrow–Cummins pre-war history. Then George repeated his conversation with Ross Evans.

Madeleine couldn't believe it. 'That's incredible. No wonder Grandfather went broke – he was trying to help the Jacksons and Ross's mother.' Madeleine turned to George. 'Well, don't you agree that he must have been giving Mrs Evans money as well, based on what Ross told you and what we found in the ledgers?'

'I guess it's possible, Maddy,' George replied.

'And he wouldn't say what this dreadful thing was that Grandfather did?' Madeleine asked her brother.

'Not a peep,' George said. 'And now that I know about Grandfather's compassion, I have to wonder why old Mrs Evans was so rude to me that day, even though her son said she never forgave Grandfather for what he did. I don't think Grandfather did anything wrong, Maddy. Ross said his actions made people feel guilty. So, it sounds to me like he was trying to right a wrong.'

'One that might have involved the Cummins family?' Madeleine said thoughtfully.

'And the Jacksons,' Rachael added.

George took a sip of the beer. 'And Ross Evans's mother.'

'That sounds like some triangle,' Madeleine agreed. 'Do you know Horatio Cummins, George?'

'Not well,' George replied. 'He lives on the outskirts of Banyan. There was a falling out in the family and the business was split in half. His son Douglas now runs Cummins Farms here at Banyan while Horatio has a large spread further east.'

'Would it be worth approaching Douglas?' Rachael asked.

'What for?' Madeleine asked, deflated. 'With a negative response from Stepworth's, I will have to start approaching other galleries and, quite frankly, based on the Stepworth response I don't like our chances of success.'

'Damn it.'

'Yes,' George agreed with his wife, 'damn it all.'

Her brother's tone was terse and as Madeleine watched him place the cold beer to his brow she knew that there was more on his mind than the David Harrow retrospective.

'Rachael,' George said after he had drained his beer, 'I'm sorry to add more bad news to our increasing pile, but we're going to have to make some changes. Sonia will have to go.'

'What? But –'

George raised a hand for silence. 'And the renovations will have to stop. We simply can't afford to spend the money now the chances of an exhibition are unlikely.'

Rachael gritted her teeth. 'But you agreed to it.'

George nodded. 'Yes, and now I'm disagreeing.'

'You can't be serious,' Rachael replied.

'I most definitely am.' George opened the fridge door. He reached for a beer but then changed his mind and selected the water jug and poured a glass. 'And one more thing, Rachael: you will have to get a job. Please don't look so stunned; this is our home and we have to work together to keep it going.'

Madeleine decided against remaining for the rest of the conversation. As the voices in the kitchen rose, she walked back to her bedroom. There was nothing left to do but pack.

⋘ Chapter 28 ⋙

Flanders, Belgium
July 1917

They marched in single file along the duckboard, passing troops returning from the front-line. These men, dirty and bloodied, trudged silently. The odd soldier raised a clenched fist in salute, but most looked steadfastly at the back of the man before him, eyes glassy. Dave marched on, his mind blank. They were returning to the front and the thought of what lay ahead deadened his soul. The brass talked of the success of the battle of Messines last month, yet Dave, thrust from a training camp immediately into battle, could scarcely comprehend his changed circumstances. Messines haunted him.

Regardless of how he tried to forget what he had witnessed, his artist's eye impregnated his mind with filaments and fragments, much like the bodies strewn about this damaged land. Dave recalled the deep underground mines exploding and the sky lighting up like a pillar of fire. There had been whispers of the noise being heard in England, such was the strength of the explosions. The tremendous blasts had been detonated after ten days of a sustained preliminary artillery bombardment. Guns and mortars had spun over their heads into the German lines while they sat in their trench, nerves fraying. When the order to attack had come they were supported by tanks and the new Livens projectors that were designed to throw gas-canisters into the enemy trenches. Dave had walked through no-man's land with his brothers as a creeping artillery barrage maintained a curtain of fire just in front of them. At the time he thought his chest would explode from fear. Only his brothers' presence stopped him from turning around and running back to their trench. Turtle had been blown to pieces in the first hour; a casualty of their own guns and his impatience. Timing was everything.

Dave recalled long periods of terror contrasted with snatches of wonder. Death had been all around, yet the casual gallantry of the men he served with as they dragged the dead into shallow holes was as inspiring and as bittersweet as birdsong on a clear, crisp morning. One night he had lain fear-frozen under the body of a digger as Fritz stood about smoking and talking, kicking absently at the fallen. Expecting the worst, he had listened to the sweet strains of a nightingale and wondered at such impossible beauty amid so much decay. On the fourth day of the battle, when their battalion was due to pull out, Marty and Riley had simply vanished. There weren't even body pieces left for identification.

Their route to the reserve trenches this morning had bypassed the casualty stations and bulging graveyards as the whispers of staggeringly high casualty lists continued. They were running behind time, which meant that as a pre-dawn glow spread across the landscape they were still marching rather than being hunkered down safely. High in the shell-blackened air Dave spotted a German observation balloon. For a moment he considered waving at the idiot, signalling his re-entry into this lost world. Minutes later there was a cracking sound overhead and the balloon dropped slowly from the sky.

'Six-shilling-a-day murderers, that's what they're calling us.'

Dave stopped walking, throwing the column of men behind him into disarray.

Thaddeus thumped him on the shoulder. 'Dave, come on.' Further back along the line men began to complain.

'That voice. Didn't you hear it? It sounded familiar.'

A digger waiting behind Dave sniggered. 'Maybe it was Mother.'

'If you don't keep walking,' another soldier called out, 'I'll be turning back and heading home.'

Dave didn't budge. To his right another snaking road sheltered a group of men.

'Bloody pacifists.'

Dave headed to where the group of soldiers sat on the edge of a shell crater. Although it was still dark he knew it was Harold Lawrence. Huddled in the dirt amid soldiers, their old friend sported a week's growth on his face. 'Harold, it's me, Dave.'

Harold lifted his head. For a moment Dave thought the iron-monger's son had lost his sight and he took a step closer until he was sure Harold could see him clearly. The man's squint turned to a frown, which deepened the cut in the shape of a question mark around his right eye. The lines on his skin were caked with grime. By his side was a stubby butted Lewis gun and rounds of ammo. The diggers with Harold appeared old and wiry. A couple had their limbs bandaged and the chalky whiteness of the French soil coated their uniforms.

'That one shouldn't have been taken away from his mother,' one commented, coughing up something slimy from the back of his throat.

Dave felt Luther's restraining arm across his chest. They had both seen that wild-man gaze before. One had to be careful that surprise didn't lead to confrontation, especially with men coming straight out of battle. Not every digger shut down automatically after the fighting finished.

'Good t-to see you, m-mate.' Luther selected a pre-rolled cigarette from the band around his slouch hat and lit it. Thaddeus loitered a few feet away.

The men sitting around Harold looked to him for direction. In the distance, howitzers and Lewis guns rang out across what was left of the French countryside. Rifle fire sounded periodically.

Their old friend focused on them. There was a glimmer of recognition.

'Get up, you l-lazy b-bastard,' Luther encouraged with a grin. 'Say g'day to your m-mates.'

'Jeez, I didn't recognise you; any of you.' Harold shook hands with Dave and Luther. 'It's good to see you fellas, but you shouldn't have brought *him*.'

'I brought myself,' Dave replied. Despite his best efforts the cough that struggled up from his chest was noisy and thick. He had been told it was the effect of the gas and dendrite fumes and that a condition similar to bronchitis was the outcome, no doubt made worse by last year's illness.

'Fair enough,' Harold replied. 'You lot are late, you know.'

Behind them the column of Australian soldiers moved onwards. In a brief break in artillery fire, squeaking leather was audible.

'Give them what for, you chaps,' a soldier called out from a retiring British battalion.

Luther gave the soldier the thumbs-up sign. 'We'll do our b-best.'

'Thaddeus,' Harold said. 'Last time I saw you, you were spitting blood.'

'I wasn't the one carted off to the Banyan gaol,' Thaddeus retaliated.

Dave had expected arm punches and grins between the two childhood friends, not this surly stand-off.

'Well, since then I've been knocked over by a shell,' Harold countered, 'buried twice and spent twenty-eight hours in a crater with five dead Huns. Eventually me and me mate had to cut them into pieces and throw them out of the hole, they stunk that bad. So, I can't say that bit of fisticuffs left much of a mark on me.'

Thaddeus shrugged. 'Welcome to France.'

'Never took you for a fighter.' Harold's statement was directed back to Dave. 'My folks wrote me and said that they'd reckoned all you lads took off from Sunset Ridge. I didn't believe that you would have joined up though, Dave. Thought your parents would have had more sense than to let you go.'

Thaddeus hitched his thumb through the leather strap on his rifle. 'It's a long story.'

'Well, who knows if there will be time enough to tell it?' Harold picked up the Lewis gun and shouldered it tiredly. 'Looks like what's left of our mob will be joining up with yours. We're to support you lot in the reserve trenches until more reinforcements arrive. And apparently you're down on guns, so here I am. One slightly buggered Lewis gunner, at your service.' Harold displayed a row of busted teeth. The partially congealed wound near his eye began to bleed. Saying farewell to his wounded mates, Harold introduced his number two on the Lewis gun, Thorny, and two blond-headed blokes nicknamed Trip and Fall. The Harrow boys were understandably confused.

'They're brothers too,' Harold explained as they all shook hands, 'and their names are self-explanatory.'

'Th-this should be interesting,' Luther commented as they re-joined the stragglers at the rear of their column.

'On the plus side,' Trip said as he stumbled on the rutted track, 'neither of us has been hit yet.'

'Which is a positive, I reckon,' the red-haired Thorny said drily.

Harold's expression turned sour. 'You boys would've heard what they're calling us back home. "Murderers." Can you believe it?'

'Harold's plan,' Fall revealed, 'is to kill as many Germans as possible, end the war and then go home and kill the pacifists.'

Luther grinned. 'Works for m-me.'

Adjusting his kit, Dave tagged along behind the others. Thaddeus walked ahead, leaving Luther and Harold to chat about bludgers and would-to-Goders, the politicians back home who enticed young men to volunteer while spouting forth that they too would enlist, would-to-God they were able.

'You all mates then, eh?' Thorny asked Dave. 'You and Luther?'

Dave nodded. 'Thaddeus too. He and Harold were pretty tight back at home.'

Thorny shifted the pouches of Lewis gun cartridges that hung from both shoulders into a more comfortable position. 'Well, if they were they don't look so friendly now. It must have been some fight they had, by the sounds of it.'

Harold and Luther were laughing and joking while Thaddeus had merged with the column of men up ahead. 'Yeah, it must have been,' Dave reluctantly agreed.

They halted in a section of the reserve trench directly behind the front-line. Decaying corpses protruded from the earthen walls as a work detail tried to rid the winding channel of the newly dead. The platoon stood aside to let the remaining troops they were relieving straggle past as dawn broke.

'Nice of you to show up,' a British soldier complained.

Their platoon, now with only thirteen old faces of the original twenty-five men, began to tidy the area. Captain Egan, who had been with them from the beginning, waited patiently. Originally a farmer from near Newcastle in New South Wales and a qualified accountant, his short stature and ungainly waist hid an athlete's quickness and a propensity to be at the front in the thick of battle.

'Get to it, lads,' he encouraged. 'That dug-out needs to be reinforced as well.'

'If Messines was an outright Allied victory,' Fall said to no one in particular, throwing a wooden crate out of the trench, 'why do we have to keep fighting?'

'The front-line still needs to be held, soldier.' Captain Egan kicked a shattered rifle to one side and watched as the dug-out entrance was cleared of debris.

Luther righted sandbags atop the trench parapet. 'Yeah, from B-Belgium t-to Switzerland.'

'There are only minor skirmishes expected in this sector,' Captain Egan revealed.

'M-minor, m-my arse,' Luther muttered. 'If th-they were minor I'd still b-be sitting in th-that *estaminet* drinking plonk and t-taking those nice green dollars from th-the Americans in a game of two-up.'

Thaddeus grunted. 'And then this section of the line would be overrun by Fritz and we'd be back to square one.'

'Listen to Thaddeus,' Captain Egan encouraged as he entered the dug-out. 'Now make yourselves useful, all of you, while we've got the chance.'

Broken and useless equipment was tossed up and out onto the pitted ground above, and fallen sandbags were re-positioned. Dave peered over the top of the trench and saw the front-line thirty feet ahead. Seconds later, a whistle screamed.

Shells and mortar bombs showered forth, each fresh wave increasing in duration so that the concussion made ears ring and minds blur. Dave searched for Luther and, diving for the spot by his side, crouched against the trench wall. 'I thought Captain Egan said this section was relatively quiet.'

'You'll b-be right, Dave.' Luther gripped his shoulder. 'Stick with m-me.' He pushed Dave's helmet firmly down on his head and adjusted his own.

Thaddeus, close by on Dave's right, rested against the earthen trench wall and waited. Chunks of dry dirt sprayed their bodies. Dave's heart began to pound savagely.

'Got room for another at this party?' Harold slammed into Thaddeus, the Lewis gun gripped tightly in his hands. Beside him the red-haired Thorny grinned, clamping an unlit cigarette between his lips. 'They're giving us a fair kick up the you-know-what today.'

'We'll k-kick 'em right b-back,' Luther growled.

The dug-out was hit in the first two minutes, collapsing the entrance and trapping its occupants. Amid the heavy barrage, Luther and Thaddeus pulled away dislodged sandbags before digging fiercely at the piled dirt. Fall and Trip joined them, digging with their bare hands as shell-fire grazed the tops of the trenches. Captain Egan was pulled free, and Thaddeus smacked him hard on the chest to get him breathing again.

'I'll live,' the captain spluttered.

When the barrage finally ceased five minutes later, Fritz attacked in earnest. The enemy was well entrenched and the crossfire from the machine guns kept the Allied trench subdued.

'Waste of ammo,' Luther snorted as he crouched against the trench wall. Bullets slammed into sandbags and whizzed over their heads. Amid the noise, two distinct bombs could be heard. 'Grenades,' Luther said loudly as a battle cry went up from in front.

'Someone's having a go!' Thaddeus yelled.

Captain Egan took a quick look through his field glasses. 'Two German machine-gun nests have been blown.'

Dave watched as the Australian front-line charged across no-man's land. His stomach tightened in anticipation as he gripped his rifle. Next to him Thaddeus and Luther were staring at Captain Egan, waiting for the order to attack.

'We've got to give them a hand, sir,' Thaddeus yelled.

Captain Egan lifted his whistle and blew.

Hopping the bags, they rushed towards the front-line trench as Germans swarmed the area. They shot, stabbed, punched and slashed at the oncoming invaders, only to be pushed backwards by a fresh wave of artillery fire and dead and wounded Australians.

Harold, perched to one side rattling his Lewis gun, did his best to protect retreating Australians, Thorny replacing each empty magazine cartridge oblivious to his own safety. Finally the enemy retreated and the remaining Australians fell back into the trench.

'It's a grand war this one, Thorny.' Harold spat dirt from his caked lips, and rested against the trench wall. 'The side that wins will have the most dead.'

Thorny looked at his cigarette. The tip of it had been shot off. 'Light?' he asked casually.

Dave felt an insistent tugging at his body. There was something warm and wet on his skin.

'Is he all right, d-do you th-think, Thaddeus?' Luther asked.

His brothers were patting him down, checking for wounds. Dave noticed that Luther's tomahawk was slick with blood.

'Had the wind knocked out of him, I reckon,' Thaddeus replied. Picking up Dave's helmet, he dropped it on his head. 'You might try and keep that on,' he admonished.

All along the trench system the call for stretcher-bearers rang out. Slightly concussed, Dave examined the lifeless soldier by his side. It was not the first time he had been saved by fate. Over the last few weeks men had been blown to bits in front of him, effectively shielding him with their own flesh and blood. But this time it was different. Dave knew this particular digger well.

Smudges of exhaustion circled the fading irises and highlighted the curved lashes; the tender face recalled images of cherubs. Grasping the boy by the shoulders, Dave pulled the dead weight into an upright position against the trench wall. He imagined it to be someone else's hand when his own reached out and closed the still-warm eyelids.

'Cartwright, isn't it?' Captain Egan asked, nodding towards the dead soldier.

Dave looked up at the officer. The captain had a bloody cut

running the length of his cheek and his uniform bore the white-chalk remnants of his recent burial in the dug-out.

'Yes, sir. Matty Cartwright was his name.'

The captain shook his head, writing the name in a notebook.

'They shouldn't have let him join up, sir.' Dave searched Cartwright's pockets. Most of the men carried a final letter; a few brief lines to loved ones in case their time came. 'No letter, sir.' He patted another pocket. 'Nothing. Oh, hang on.' The paper was un-bloodied despite the black-red liquid oozing from the gaping wound in the boy's chest.

'Well, hand it over, son.' Captain Egan unfolded the wad of paper and studied the extraordinary likeness of the dead boy. Cartwright was immortalised in crayon. 'Is this your work, Dave?'

'Yes, sir. I did it as a favour. He was a mate and he wanted a sketch as a present for his mother.'

Captain Egan stared at the drawing.

'You'll send it back like he wanted, sir?'

The captain folded the drawing. 'I'll see she gets it.'

All along the trench, men righted themselves, checked the wounded and regrouped in case of a counterattack. A number of soldiers were tasked with making running repairs to sections of the damaged trench; others carried the dead further along the trench system to where they would be collected by a work detail and taken away for burial. Captain Egan trailed this latter grisly task, noting down the names of the dead and ensuring the men were kept busy. Stretcher-bearers reached their section and quickly ascertained the worst cases. Bow-legged, with backs and heads bent to escape a canny sniper, they collected the injured. Dave willed himself to movement and joined his brothers, who were stacking bodies. Harold collected the remains of a hand: he held the lifeless flesh mid-air until, at Thorny's suggestion, they watched it sail through the air into no-man's land.

Bile rose in Dave's throat and he vomited into the dirt. Someone slapped him on the shoulder and asked if he was all right. Dave nodded and wiped his mouth with his sleeve.

'N-now I've seen everyth-thing.' Luther nudged Thaddeus in the ribs. Coming towards them were two stretcher-bearers, a field doctor and a great mangy dog.

'American Field Ambulance,' Harold explained. 'They're handy blokes.'

'And the dog?' Dave asked. They had heard the stories of animals attached to battalions, but many were mascots and few lasted long on the front-line.

As they talked, the Americans passed, stopping a few feet away to tend to other wounded. The dog trotted up and down the trench, snuffling the ground and sandbagged walls with interest. At a bend in the trench where a pile of dead bodies awaited collection, he gave a single bark and sat patiently on muscular hind legs.

'Well, hurry up!' the American medic yelled at them from where he tended a soldier with a gunshot wound. 'If the dog says there's a live one, there must be.'

The Harrow boys exchanged glances with Harold and then rushed to the pile of corpses. Gingerly they turned each of the five men over and checked for signs of life. There were limbs missing, and the deadly crossfire technique of the German maxim gunners had shot one man almost in two.

'Jesus,' Harold uttered, 'they all look buggered to me.'

Squeezing between their legs, the dog smelled each prone body and then placed a large paw on the leg of one of the men.

Thaddeus held his palm above the bloodied face. 'God's holy trousers, he's breathing!'

They carefully but quickly pulled the soldier free and stood back as the medic knelt by the man's side. The soldier's coat was swiftly unbuttoned and the shoulder wound prodded. The doctor rolled the man onto his side.

'Bullet's still in there. Missed his heart.' Placing a field dressing over the wound, he rose.

The dog shook his hairy body from head to tail. 'Good job,' the captain praised, patting his companion.

Dave fell on one knee and hugged the animal. Despite the stink around them, the smell of the dog reminded him of home. 'Hey, he's got an identity disc around his neck. It says Antoine Chessy.'

'They're enlisting dogs now!' Harold said, rubbing at his cheek stubble.

'Keep safe, Antoine,' Dave said quietly, running his hand along the dog's back as more stretcher-bearers arrived. Noticing the rank on the American's uniform he asked, 'Is he yours, Captain?'

As if understanding their conversation, the dog looked up. The captain only smiled. 'I wish,' he answered, before following his men to another section of the trench.

The dog disappeared around the next bend as sporadic artillery fire continued to sound across no-man's land. In the all-too-few moments when the gunfire eased, the brief silences were filled with the groans of the wounded.

'There are men out there.' Harold's palm slid up and down the magazine of the Lewis gun.

'Haig's standing orders say no rescues,' Dave replied as he scratched at Matty Cartwright's dried blood on his face. 'Besides, we tried it once and Egan nearly tarred us he was that mad. He threatened to write us up on charges.'

Thaddeus gave a snort of disgust.

'B-bugger Haig,' Luther retorted. 'I h-haven't l-laid eyes on him since this b-bunfight started. I didn't come all th-this way to listen to our b-blokes die.'

Thaddeus quickly organised a rescue party, comprising himself, Luther and Trip and Fall. The latter were passing along the trench with bags of lime, throwing handfuls of the stuff on blood and flesh, their approach advertised by the blaspheming of diggers who found themselves either kicked or inadvertently bustled aside. The brothers dropped the lime on the duckboards at Thaddeus's order.

Thaddeus cuffed Dave on the shoulder. 'You stay here. If the worst happens – well, three of us would be a bit hard on Mother.'

Harold positioned the Lewis gun and scanned no-man's land. The enemy soldiers were clearly visible in their trenches. 'It's too risky, we should wait till dark.' He looked directly at Thaddeus as diggers positioned their rifles along the earth wall. There was a mumble of agreement from some of the assembled men.

'Bollocks,' Luther replied. 'You l-lot cover me.' Scrambling over the top of the trench, he waved a filthy rag in the enemy's direction.

'Bloody hell,' Thaddeus muttered, cocking his rifle. He peered through the rifle sight, scanning the scarred, open terrain as his brother walked into no-man's land, the handkerchief fluttering in the cordite-filled air. 'You cover the right, Dave. I'll do the left.'

'We've got his back, Thaddeus,' Fall and Trip answered in unison.

Dave took a deep breath and steadied himself. There was movement in the German trench, movement across no-man's land. Bulbous rats scurried around purulent corpses. He tried not to think of the rats or the Germans or the odds of Luther surviving such a reckless action. Everything would be all right. *Please let Luther be all right.*

Harold patted his tin helmet. 'That boy never was one for worrying about consequences.' He ran his hand across the barrel of the Lewis gun. 'Be ready, my lovely.'

All along the trench, men took aim, watched and waited. 'It's Chopper Harrow,' someone remarked.

Luther walked carefully through the dead, dying and injured. Hands reached to pluck at his legs, men raised themselves upwards before falling back into oblivion, and at every carefully placed step the cries of the maimed carried him onwards. Occasionally a lone shot rang out and a spray of dirt rendered Luther motionless. Fritz was having a bit of fun. In a single window of silence the wind carried a plaintive voice: 'Don't forget me, cobber.'

The forty men in Dave's section of the trench lifted their rifles as one in response.

Captain Egan rolled into the front trench, anger furrowing an already lined brow. 'Who is it?' he snapped.

'Luther, sir,' Thaddeus replied.

'I should have bloody well known it would be one of you Harrow boys.'

Two hundred yards out Luther was met by Fritz, his own scrappy bit of material wrestling with the rising wind.

'Well, I'll be,' Captain Egan muttered. 'Stand to, stand to,' he called along the line.

'They already are, sir,' Thaddeus replied. His finger was poised on the trigger, the rifle's line of sight centred on the flag-waving Fritz. 'If the worst happens,' Thaddeus hissed at Dave, 'cover me. I'll not leave him out there.'

Dave held his breath to steady his aim.

Captain Egan drew his pistol. Across the field of battle, German heads popped up all along their trench.

The two men stood a foot apart, silhouetted by haze and debris, their bodies melding together in a shimmer of sunlight. Dave watched the two lone figures, squinted upwards into an uncaring sun and waited. Minutes later Luther and his counterpart walked their separate paths back towards armies that prayed to the same God.

'Bloody idiot,' Thaddeus chastised, pulling Luther down into the relative safety of the trench.

'Holy Ghost!' Harold exclaimed, clapping Luther on the shoulder.

'Th-they've agreed to l-let us get our w-wounded and dead, sir,' Luther addressed the captain. 'And I agreed th-that Fritz could get th-theirs.'

'Did you, now?' the captain responded.

Luther held his gaze.

Captain Egan grunted. 'Well, then, you men, you heard him. Get yourself into working parties of four. Wounded first and then the dead. So, you were out there for long enough, Harrow – have a nice little chat, did you?'

'Yes, sir.'

'And are you going to share this friendly conversation with the rest of us?'

'Yes, sir.'

'Well?'

'I said it was a l-lovely day for a w-war, sir.'

Egan appeared stunned. 'You said *what?*'

'I said it was a lovely day for a w-war, sir.'

'I heard you the first time.' Captain Egan shook his head. 'Go on, then. Get going, the lot of you.'

'What did Fritz really say, Luther?' Dave stepped carefully between the fallen bodies strewn across the ground as they scoured for wounded.

Luther lit a cigarette and spat a shred of tobacco from his mouth. 'I th-think he said,' he answered softly, 'th-that he w-wanted to go home.'

When the last of the injured and the dead were carried off the scarred dirt to await stretcher-bearers, the men collapsed into the trench. For long minutes they simply sat, arms dangling by their sides, smokes clinging to dry lips as stretcher-bearers moved to and fro. One damaged digger, laid out on a canvas stretcher, was set down for a moment by Luther's side. With difficulty he lifted a bloody hand. Luther clasped it strongly.

'I knew you wouldn't forget me, cobber,' he muttered before being carted away.

Thaddeus took a sip of water and ran the edge of his harmonica across his tongue. When he placed it to his mouth, the first few strains were shaky but recognisable. It was 'My Darling Clementine'.

Luther arched his neck so that the earth wall of the trench was firm against his skull. Very slowly he rocked to and fro. 'Hey, Dave. You got th-that p-picture on you? You know, th-the one of the river?'

Dave fumbled about in his uniform. The sketch was dog-eared and torn in places but it clearly depicted the four of them in their old fishing spots by the Banyan River.

Harold cleared his throat. 'Jeez, that's a beauty. Good on you, Dave.'

The men were silent as the sketch was passed around to the strains of the harmonica.

'Do you have more of these?' Thorny asked.

'He's drawn half the battalion,' Thaddeus elaborated, 'and everything in between.'

Luther ran the blade of his tomahawk against a sharpening stone. 'Regular ar-artist, he is. He'll go w-without rations t-to carry his sketchbook.'

'You know,' Harold began, 'you're like a big bush spider.' He studied the drawing. 'You wind us up in your sticky web and hold us fast. I can almost imagine we're back there.'

'Put me in your drawing, will you, Dave?' Thorny asked quietly. 'I'd like to be there too.'

'Sure thing,' Dave agreed.

'Pipe down with that music,' Captain Egan called from the mound that was his dug-out. 'We don't need a whizz-bang landing on our heads.'

Thaddeus gave a defiant squeal on the mouth organ and hunkered down to rest.

In no-man's land the strains of an answering harmonica floated unexpectedly across the barren landscape. Then it too was silenced. Dave closed his mind to the morning's images and narrowed his thoughts to the only things worth remembering: Luther's bravery and a great mangy dog named Antoine.

Thaddeus waited at the entrance to the dug-out. Unlike the men's cramped hole in the ground, it was reinforced with timber and spacious enough to accommodate a table and chairs. Two camp bunks were pushed hard against a rear wall; dirt fell onto them intermittently from the low ceiling. At the table a seated Captain Egan read the note the messenger had presented and ran a finger across what appeared to be a map. Above him a kerosene lantern hung from a timber beam. The vibrations from the intermittent shelling caused the lantern to swing to and fro.

'Very well, tell the brass we'll move out after dark.'

The messenger saluted, leaving Thaddeus alone with the captain.

'Drink?' Captain Egan asked, beckoning him forwards.

Two rats were fighting on top of one of the cots. With barely a glance in their direction the captain flung a book at the rodents, which quickly took flight. 'That's about the best use I've found for the rule book.' He poured rum into stubby glasses and offered one to Thaddeus. 'Sit, Harrow.' He took a sip and then, placing the glass down, folded the map of the battlefield and tucked it into a leather compendium. 'Well, we're to be relieved tonight.'

'What, already?'

Captain Egan drained the glass of rum. 'Five days, Harrow; we've been in the front-line for five days – nine if you count the time in the support trench. Although we've little to show for our efforts, the Germans have been constant in their defence.'

'They are well dug in, sir.' Thaddeus studied the contents of the glass in his hand. The days were blurring together, broken only by a tin of bully beef and the endless monotony of sitting uselessly in their trench until the next engagement with the enemy. And still the guns fired, shuddering both man and land until Thaddeus doubted he would ever again sit tranquilly without expecting some type of torment to rage down on him.

'Harrow?' the captain frowned.

'Sorry, sir.'

'I said that I'm promoting you to sergeant.'

Thaddeus accepted the grimy envelope and enclosed stripes and saluted Captain Egan. 'Thank you, sir.' His advancement came at a cost. The previous sergeant was dead.

'At ease, Harrow. Have a seat. You've a cool head in battle, which is more than can be said for your brother Luther.'

'He's a damn good soldier, sir.'

'Relax, Sergeant, I'm not disputing his fighting qualities, merely making an observation.'

'The men would follow him anywhere, sir.'

Captain Egan nodded. 'You as well, Harrow.' The chair squeaked as he crossed his legs. 'We're on furlough for a week. I asked for two but it appears we've been drafted for a work detail.' Pouring a splash more rum for both of them, the captain slid the platoon mail across the desk. 'I've also received orders that Harold Lawrence is to be transferred across to us, as well as the three other men that were part of the temporary relief.'

'Yes, sir.'

'Good.' Captain Egan sat forward. 'We don't bring petty arguments to war, Sergeant.'

'No, sir,' Thaddeus agreed, swallowing the remains of the rum. He gathered up the mail, unsurprised that the captain knew that he and Harold were barely on speaking terms. War hadn't changed Harold. He was just as arrogant. Thaddeus could have forgiven him for his attitude regarding Corally, but they had fought twice and while Thaddeus had been prepared to right the situation, Harold wasn't. It was as if they were kids again, bickering over who had the best sling-shot or who could run faster. The competitiveness that had always marked their friendship now served to pull them apart. The worst of it was that Thaddeus was not one to be beaten either, but now they were in the thick of things he simply wasn't interested in confronting his old friend. There were other things to worry about. All Thaddeus wanted was to survive the war and make it home to Sunset Ridge with his brothers.

Dismissed, he left the dug-out and passed the word along that they were to be relieved at dark. It was quiet this morning and the men were lined up along the wall of the trench. Some wrote letters home, others cleaned equipment. Dave sat sketching the mongrel dog that had sniffed out the wounded digger. The animal was depicted sitting in the trench, the identity discs dangling from his neck. Luther, airing his bare feet in the sun, was heating a tin of bully beef over a small makeshift fire, careful to fan the smoke so as not to give away their position. Thaddeus passed the mail to Trip, who quickly sorted through it and began to hand the letters out. Dave was the first recipient.

'Let's hope they don't get lost,' Harold quipped in reply to Thaddeus's information. He sat on a munitions crate cleaning the Lewis gun. Beside him, Thorny set lice alight on his arms with a cigarette. 'A month or so back we waited eighteen hours for our relief to show. Got lost, didn't they, Thorny?'

Thorny rolled his eyes. 'Bloody new chum officer, couldn't find his way to a whore-house, that one.'

'You lot are being transferred across permanently,' Thaddeus continued through the men's sniggering.

'W-what? Joining us?' Luther punched Harold in the arm. Dave added his approval to the chorus of voices.

'Well, looks like you won't be getting rid of me so quickly, eh, Thaddeus?' Harold's words had an edge to them.

'War isn't the place for petty grievances, Harold,' Thaddeus replied.

'You're right, mate. A man should know when he's bested,' Harold retaliated. Accepting a letter from Trip, he brandished the envelope for all to see before making a show of smelling the paper as if it were scented.

Thorny gave a low, appreciative whistle.

'That's enough,' Captain Egan interrupted, singling each man out with a hard stare. 'And put that blasted fire out, Harrow, before you have Fritz on top of us. Now, you've heard the orders: we will be moving out tonight, and not before time.' He gestured to Thaddeus. 'Harrow has made sergeant.' The announcement brought enthusiastic as well as ribald comments, soon silenced by a wave from the captain. 'Keep your heads down, men, and we'll be out by nightfall. Post your sentries, Sergeant.'

Thaddeus accepted the men's congratulations, aware of a new wedge between him and Harold. He now outranked his old friend.

'Can I have your boots, Luther, if you get knocked?'

Luther stopped wiggling his toes and considered Trip's request. In comparison to Trip's regulation issue, his boots were well cared for.

Trip squatted opposite in anticipation. 'Oh, and this is yours.'

Luther stared at the letter before tucking it inside his uniform. 'I t-tell you w-what,' Luther replied, 'you give me t-ten quid and a p-packet of smokes now and th-they'll b-be yours.'

Trip searched his pockets for the money and cigarettes and was about to hand them across when a thought came to him. 'But what if you don't get knocked?'

'Don't be b-bloody silly,' Luther replied, taking the bartered goods. 'Of course I w-will.'

⋘ Chapter 29 ⋙

Temporary field hospital, France
July 1917

Sister Valois directed the walking wounded up the creaking stairs of the chateau. The least able were assisted by volunteer orderlies who also offered words of encouragement. At the end of the line a soldier faltered on the first step. Placing a hand on his elbow, she urged him onwards. The blind always proved difficult to accommodate but at least the worst of this young man's injuries were nearly healed. The men moved stiffly, grateful for the support the age-smoothed banister provided. On the landing above, framed by a six-foot-high tapestry of seventeenth-century huntsmen on horse-back, three nurses in their pristine uniforms waited to take the men to their respective wards. Sister Valois lingered a little longer than necessary at the foot of the stairs until the last of the men reached the second level. The receipt and care of the wounded may have given her greater satisfaction if she did not have to send them back to the hell from which they had only recently escaped.

Yesterday nine men had been released from her care only to be returned to the front following their allotted leave time. Although

Sister Valois's emotions never overtook the professional and somewhat aloof attitude she had so carefully cultivated since the beginning of the war, she found it increasingly difficult to feign indifference. The soldiers had been driven away in a civilian bus, and one of them, a Parisian, had pressed a palm against the rear window, his narrow face staring coldly at the chateau until the bus turned out of the long driveway.

The soldier had taken part in General Nivelle's April offensive at the battle of Aisne and complained bitterly of having to return to the battlefield. Nearly all of his friends were dead, he had told the occupants of the ward upon his discharge, and following the failed April attack – which was supposed to have ended the war within forty-eight hours – thousands of his fellow French soldiers had mutinied. Waiting at the end of the ward with clipboard in hand, Sister Valois had been stunned by the news. It was the first she had heard of such cowardly behaviour, and she worried for the men listening to such dispiriting tales. When on the Parisian's leaving she protested at the impromptu address, he cited the continuing high French casualties. They only wished for a decent amount of leave, the Parisian claimed, as they were being forced to stay at the front-line for weeks on end.

'Excuse me, Sister Valois, the other ambulances have arrived.'

Thanking the male orderly, she crossed the parquet floor and walked through the interconnecting reception rooms. In the main salon, with its mirrored doors and gilt chandeliers, she surveyed the neat rows of cots housing the convalescing soldiers. Those who were able wrote to loved ones or played cards, while a curtained section at the far end of the room provided a wounded junior French officer privacy from the enlisted men and access out onto the chateau's grounds.

The entrance hall bustled with the arrival of stretchers. Red Cross staff, American medics and French drivers were being disgorged from the ambulances, which were reversed up under the portico to escape the light rain. A French orderly was doing his best to stop the forward movement of the wounded until Sister Valois's arrival, and he smiled in relief at her approach. As the queue grew, so did the mutterings of discontent from the ambulance staff. Joining the throng were a number of volunteer aides, while a handful of junior nurses assembled quietly and awaited instruction.

'We cannot possibly accommodate all these patients.' Sister Valois counted five more wounded than space allowed. Her complaint, addressed to the head of the ambulance convoy, was met with apology.

'I have my orders, Sister, and to be frank, where else would I take them?'

The stretcher-bearers waited patiently, their arms taut with the strain of the injured they carried.

'Very well.' They could hardly be turned away. 'We will make do.' Her orders were quick and precise. The volunteers were assigned to bring extra cots from storage and squeeze them into the already cramped converted bedrooms upstairs while the incoming patients were assessed. The worst of the injured would be assigned to Ward A, the dining room, with those patients not expected to survive. It was against Sister Valois's rules – she firmly believed that placing a wounded man next to another with little chance of survival did nothing for recovery – but Ward A contained spare cots, and bed space had to take priority over mental-health concerns.

When the last of the wounded had streamed into the chateau, Sister Valois stood in the entrance hall, arching her right foot. Hours walking across the chateau's parquet floors gave her aching cramps in both ankles and all toes, a condition heightened by sheer exhaustion. The rattling of cots and the steady clomp of boots echoed through the old building, occasionally interspersed by a female voice of complaint. She wondered if the ghosts the junior nurses and volunteers spoke off would finally be evicted from the building with this latest influx of wounded. Certainly there was barely a corner unused. Next on the agenda would be to inform the kitchen staff of the extra mouths to feed, and she would have to cancel all leave for this coming weekend now they were at capacity again.

'Are you the nurse in charge?'

Already thinking of the extra sheets required, she stared blankly at the man standing in the doorway of the chateau. Behind him ambulance drivers leaned on their vehicles, smoking and laughing.

'I said, are you the –'

'Yes, Captain, I am Sister Valois. I speak English.'

'Good, because my schoolboy French is limited.' He strode towards her. A freckle-skinned, sandy-haired man of middling height and weight and a cautious smile, he introduced himself as Captain Harrison of the American Field Ambulance.

'We have seen very few Americans here.' Sister Valois ushered him forward, noticing the thick lashes framing pale kindly eyes. 'You will have to walk with me, I'm afraid, Captain, we are rather busy today.'

They arrived in the first of the reception rooms in which volunteers were placing clean linen on a number of cots. Captain Harrison gave a low, appreciative whistle as his gaze travelled beyond the occupants of the makeshift ward to the frescos on the ceiling and the gilt-framed portraits of unknown men and women hanging on the buttercup-yellow walls. 'Very nice.'

Sister Valois checked the contents of a clipboard passed to her by a junior nurse and inspected an ulcerated leg belonging to a Frenchman aged in his forties. 'It needs to be lanced and drained,' she advised the nurse in French.

The owner of the leg winced. 'Not again, Sister.'

'What is a little scratch compared to what you have already endured?' she reminded him kindly. The soldier nodded reluctantly and she turned to the captain, who was observing her with interest.

'I won't hold you up,' he began. 'Although it is a rather long story. I'm currently on leave and I thought I would pay you a visit.'

'Me?' Sister Valois queried in English before moving to the next new arrival and switching back to French. 'A saline drip and, Nurse, redress this wound.' She pointed at the bloody head bandage.

'Well, a patient of yours, actually,' the captain said almost sheepishly. 'This is going to sound a little strange, but –'

'I assure you, Captain,' she interrupted, 'I have heard and seen many strange things. Please excuse me.' Scanning another clipboard, she turned to the nurse hovering at her side and addressed her in French. 'This soldier should be in Ward A.' She tapped the clipboard. 'Can you not read? He has been burned by gas. Call the orderlies and tell the nurse on duty in Ward A to exchange one of the lesser cases with this young man.'

The chastised nurse nodded. 'Yes, Sister.'

Captain Harrison cleared his throat. 'As I was saying, Sister, the reason for my visit today . . . it's about a dog.'

Sister Valois stopped prodding at a distended abdomen. 'Did you say a *dog*?'

'Yes.' Captain Harrison waited until the examination had been completed and then drew her aside.

She found herself remembering what it was like to be touched by a man. A single word came to mind: comforting.

Captain Harrison continued: 'A dog and a French soldier by the name of –'

'Francois Chessy.' Sister Valois raised a hand to her throat. 'He is here.'

'So, he's still alive? I have to say, it was some task tracking him down.'

'Francois is strong in the mind, stubbornly strong. This strength may yet be his saving, for he has been in hospital since his wounding last year at Verdun.'

Captain Harrison considered this piece of information. 'And he had a brother, Antoine?'

'Yes. Antoine died at Verdun. But the dog you speak of, Captain, have you seen him? Have you seen the war dog they call Roland?'

'Roland,' Captain Harrison repeated. 'I didn't know his name. Some orderlies at a field hospital near Amiens asked if I would take the animal, and for some reason I agreed. But, you know this animal, this "war dog" as you call him?' He thought of the great mangy dog and found it difficult to equate such a lofty description with the wolf-like mongrel he knew.

'Yes,' the woman replied.

He could sense the expectation bubbling up within her. Perhaps the rumours were true, Captain Harrison thought. Certainly the animal was graced with an uncanny sixth sense when it came to differentiating between the wounded and the dead, but dragging soldiers to safety in no-man's land? That was a stretch.

Sister Valois touched his sleeve. 'You have not answered my question, Captain. Have you seen Roland?'

'Yes,' the captain answered slowly. 'Yes, I have.'

❧ Chapter 30 ❧

Chessy farmhouse, ten miles from Saint-Omer, northern France
August 1917

'**G**'day. I'm looking for the artist.'

Harold stopped dunking his smalls in the water trough and inclined his head to direct the soldier towards the open patch of ground in front of the farmhouse. Dave had the best spot of the billeted diggers: dappled sunlight from nearby trees, the cool stone of the house behind his back, and an admiring Frenchwoman who treated him to titbits from her kitchen. None of them could top Dave's gift of a sketch of the farmhouse with the owner standing in the doorway.

'Over th-there, next to the b-bloke shaving,' Luther added. This boy appeared younger than the last, a skinny, flea-bitten sort who was likely to get blown back across the Channel to England if a shell landed near him. The young soldier glanced around and then walked through the groups of resting diggers. Some played cards or slept, others cleaned the dishes from the portable field kitchen, while a handful played cricket with a cloth ball and a length of timber.

'Sixty-six and *still* not out,' Thaddeus yelled as he lobbed the ball into the trees. Trip and Fall rushed after it. Thaddeus sat down in front of the wicket – a broken bird cage – and grinned.

'Show-off,' Harold mumbled in Thaddeus's direction before turning back to watch the newest subject head off to find Dave. 'More stray soldiers have been here than I've had cooked breakfasts.' Stripping off, he clambered into the animals' watering trough, his knees close to his chin. 'We can thank Captain Egan for Dave's new-found celebrity. Not that we're making much out of it. A man can't live on smokes. We'll pass the word along that from now on it's a bottle of plonk or a chicken in return for one of his sketches.'

'F-fair enough.' Luther hung his shirt to dry over a branch and sat on the ground. The men were lethargic this morning. They had spent the past few days loading cut lengths of timber onto carts to be used to reinforce trenches. The week prior they had been transported on buses from Tatinghem to Saint-Omer and on arrival had helped another work detail load munitions for transportation to the front. It was obvious that the brass had a new push coming. 'Have you t-talked to Thaddeus yet?'

'No,' Harold stated.

To be fair, trench life since Harold's arrival had not allowed much time for chinwags. 'Isn't it t-time you t-two made up?' Luther suggested. 'What are y-you fighting about, anyway?' He thought back to the day Thaddeus was promoted to sergeant and the antagonistic way in which Harold had sniffed appreciatively at a letter received in that day's mail.

'It's between us.' Harold's words were clipped. 'Best you stay out of it.'

Luther wasn't inclined to stay out of it, especially because he couldn't get a word out of Thaddeus either. What he did know was that there had been two fights between the former best mates last year: one at the Banyan Show and another out the back of

Lawrence Ironmongers a couple of days before he met up with Thaddeus on the Western Mail.

'There *is* something I want you to know, though, if you can keep it a secret.'

'What?' Luther asked.

'Corally Shaw and I are engaged.' Harold leaned back in the trough. 'Does that bother you? I know you and she had something going for a while back at the show last year, and she stood up for you in court.'

Luther was slow to respond. There were two letters from Corally secreted in his pocket and neither mentioned anything about Harold. He thought back to the day at the cemetery when Corally first told him that Harold had asked her to wait for him until after the war. It wasn't possible, was it? 'Really? You kept th-that quiet.'

'Well, I had to. Actually, if you want to know, that's one of the reasons your brother and I fell out. That and what my mother would call a personality clash.'

'Are you t-telling me you two were fighting over C-corally Shaw?' Luther could not believe it. First Harold was telling him that he was engaged to Corally and now he was saying that she was one of the reasons Harold and Thaddeus were avoiding each other. 'Does Th-thaddeus know about you and Corally?'

'Not that we're engaged.'

Luther's head spun. Something was very wrong. Corally was writing to *him*, and as for Thaddeus . . . Luther was sure that Harold had his wires crossed. Everyone expected Thaddeus to marry well, and if he was promoted in the field again, he would return to Australia with the pick of the graziers' daughters to choose from. Hell's bells, Luther would bet his rum ration on Miss Bantam resurfacing. Lighting a cigarette, he concentrated on controlling the trembling in his left hand. It was as if his stutter had taken up residence in this new yet unscathed part of his body, for his speech was much improved.

Harold splashed water on his face. 'Are you going to tell me who you've been writing to?'

Luther drew on the cigarette. 'A friend.' As he blew out a ring of smoke his thoughts turned to Corally's last letter.

I shuld ave written soonir, Lu, but Im not real good at putting pen to paper. I just want you to no that you were rite that day in the cematary. We are like peas in pods and I liked your kiss. Weve got somthing speshal. I hope you come home soon.

Whenever he thought of Corally's words Luther felt stronger, taller. He was cloaked in the bond they shared, and that letter, tucked protectively against his chest, carried him safely through the worst of the skirmishes they endured. When he hopped the bags, snipped at barbed wire or led night raiding parties into German trenches to discover which divisions were against them, Corally was there, her words reminding him of another, better life.

'A friend, eh?' Harold soaped his hair and disappeared underwater.

Obviously Corally and Harold did step out together before the war, Luther decided. After all, he and his brothers had been confined to Sunset Ridge for weeks, leaving Harold at a loose end. But an engagement? Luther remembered clearly the day in the courthouse when Dave had repeated Corally's wish to visit them at Sunset Ridge. That didn't sound like a girl who wanted to out with Harold.

Harold reappeared from under the water, shaking his head like a dog. 'You have to give me more than that.'

Luther flicked the cigarette butt into the air. 'I m-met a girl in Sydney before w-we sailed.' The lie slid off his tongue.

'What's she like?'

Luther pictured Corally the last time they were together, crimson-cheeked and wet-lipped. 'She's d-different, I guess. Th-there are no airs and graces with her and she's p-pretty, p-prettier than any girl I've laid eyes on.'

'Like my Corally.'

Luther told himself that it would be a hard-hearted female who broke a man's heart in wartime, so it was likely that Corally still wrote to Harold. Luther considered telling Harold the truth about his relationship with Corally, but it was easier to say nothing, especially with another big push in the wind. He could only guess at Harold's sadness and Thaddeus's shock if they discovered that the woman they were supposedly fighting over was actually keen on him. No, it was far better to wait for Corally to clear up the misunderstanding. Luther didn't want to be in the middle of an argument when they next fronted Fritz.

'Engaged, eh? Well, I'm not surprised at anyth-thing a w-woman agrees to during wartime,' Luther said cautiously. 'A mate of ours b-blown up at Messines reckoned th-they change their mind like the w-weather. Why, he had a girl and she wr-wrote and t-told Marty they were over the day b-before we left for France. Makes it easy, you know,' Luther picked at the lice trailing through the hair on his legs, 'l-letters. You can say one th-thing and mean th-the other.'

Harold snorted water up his nose. 'Not my Corally. Anyway, what's happening at Sunset Ridge?'

Luther was pleased to change the topic. 'Mother's still p-pretty riled and she never m-mentions Father, it's all about the p-property. Anyone would th-think she was in charge of it now. Shearing is over and they sold two th-thousand ewes at a good p-price.'

'My parents say you have a manager, some bloke called Nathanial Taylor, and that your father's ill.'

Luther disagreed. 'If he was th-that sick she w-would have told us, I'm sure.'

'I guess. Anyway, I feel sorry for them. At least I told my parents what I was doing, but you lot just buggered off.'

'And I t-told you why. Anyhow, you w-would th-think Mother would have calmed down a l-little by now. It's nearly nine months since w-we left, b-but every letter is th-the same. She's always accusing Th-thaddeus and m-me of dragging Dave t-to war and reminding us th-that his l-life is in our hands.' Luther sighed. 'I didn't w-want him to come.'

'She's angry,' Harold agreed.

Luther listened to the splash of water against the side of the tub. 'Wash my back, Luther.'

'B-bugger off. Come on, hop out b-before th-the w-water turns black.' Luther stepped out of his long underwear, revealing a muscular, taut physique. They swapped positions.

Luther settled himself in the tepid water and began to scrub himself. 'Do you th-think it's a good thing, this painting of Dave's?'

'What do you think? Sketching the likenesses of the soon-to-be-murdered.'

Luther washed his face. 'Well, remind m-me not to get *my* p-picture done.'

'The ones of home, of Sunset Ridge and the Banyan River, they're the ones I like. Now he's too busy drawing soldiers.' Harold pulled on his trousers and stretched out on the ground.

'W-well, *you're* his b-business manager, Harold; and let's face it, th-there isn't too much demand for p-pictures of t-trees.' Luther scrubbed the nape of his neck; the men never seemed able to rid themselves of lice. Giving his head a final dunk, Luther stepped out of the trough and shook himself dry before dressing.

'Lovely; a man can't even dry off in peace,' Harold complained, wiping at the droplets sprayed across his chest.

A couple of hundred yards away Dave sat cross-legged opposite another young soldier, his stare intent. It was the type of look that took in a man's face, broke it apart and then reassembled it piece by piece. Such visual interrogation unnerved Luther – it was as if his young brother could see inside a person's soul. Although he had not voiced an opinion, Luther agreed on the governess Miss Waites being reprimanded for encouraging such feminine inclinations; painting simply wasn't a good pastime for a man. Yet he had to concede that the sketches gave the men something to talk about, and if Dave's drawings helped take the men's minds off where they were and what they had to go back to, well, then that wasn't such a bad thing, he supposed. Not that Luther would ever have his own portrait done. That was for men like Thaddeus who deserved to be officers.

His decision had nothing to do with the men Dave sketched who now lay dead.

At the rickety table where diggers played cards, a fight broke out.

Harold jumped to his feet. 'That'll be Thorny. His blood's worth bottling, but give him half a mo and he's backchatting the best of them.'

Cards were strewn across the ground and the table was upturned. Thorny was backed up against a tree, muttering something unintelligible, a bottle in one hand, his impressive eyebrows an unbroken line.

'He just went off,' one of the shocked diggers explained as he gathered up the playing cards.

Thorny took a glug from the bottle. The liquor ran down his chin, leaving splats of darkness on his tunic. Very slowly he slid down the tree trunk.

'Come on, mate,' Harold cajoled. He turned to Luther. 'I've never seen him like this. He's always been a straight shooter with the bottle.'

'L-let him sleep it off. He'll b-be right,' Luther suggested.

'Will he? He's my number two on the gun, Luther. He's my responsibility. And he's a good bloke. He follows instructions, never argues and he's a brave little bastard.' Harold prised the bottle from Thorny's grasp and threw it aside. 'I've lost two number twos and Thorny knows it, so I made a pact with him that I'd watch his back.'

Luther thought of his own mother's wishes regarding Dave and stretched out his aching shoulders. War wasn't the place for expectation.

An appreciative whistle stirred the billeted soldiers' interest. A dark-haired young woman was walking up from the stream carrying a bucket of water. A blue headscarf framed her pretty features and matched her long skirt, which swished across the grass. Three soldiers rushed to her aid, one managing to take the bucket. The men shadowed the girl up the slight incline, chatting and joking along the way. A short distance from the farmhouse the girl retrieved the bucket of water and gave a coy thank you.

'*Bonjour*, Lisette.' Dave waved as the girl retreated into the farmhouse. He looked at the sketchpad resting across his legs. It was filled with images of his mates. Most of them were pretty life-like, although he knew he had a long way to go before he could be considered a proper artist.

'You w-won't have any joy there,' Luther advised, walking towards him with Thaddeus in tow. 'The m-missus keeps her under l-lock and key.'

'Very funny. Anyway, I'm hungry,' Dave complained.

'Th-the kid's got worms,' Thaddeus replied.

'Well, as long as he doesn't start dragging himself across the ground in front of Madame Chessy.' Luther's nose twitched. The door to the whitewashed farmhouse was ajar. Light struck the flagstone floor of the kitchen, highlighting the low wooden beams within. 'I smell eggs.'

The crashing of pans and a male yelp was quickly followed by the appearance of Trip and Fall emerging from the farmhouse with Madame Chessy in pursuit.

'Leave off, missus!' Fall complained. 'We was only after a few eggs.'

'No eggs for you. *Comprenez!*' Madame Chessy threw a rolling pin at Trip, striking him in the middle of his back; the missile off-balanced him, throwing him sideways so that he veered into his brother. Two sets of arms and legs twisted and fell.

Thaddeus and Dave flinched.

'We should p-put her in the front-line,' Luther recommended.

'You will eat me out of the 'ouse and the 'ome,' Madame Chessy responded to Thaddeus's attempts at placation, her floury finger waggling like a thick worm. 'If you want extra food you must find it. I have no more to sell.'

Luther rolled his lips into a smile. 'There's a nice little chateau on the edge of T-tatinghem village. Word is a bunch of Scots have set themselves up th-there for a fortnight.' He rubbed his hands together. 'Anyone interested in a l-little reconnaissance mission t-tonight?'

'Count me in,' Thaddeus answered. 'We'll dine on meat and plonk tomorrow.'

'Plonk?' Madame Chessy repeated with interest, wiping her hands on her apron.

'Yeah, plonk: wine, th-the grape, *vin blanc*,' Luther enthused.

Madame Chessy smacked a kiss on Luther's cheeks.

'I think she understands what you mean, Luther,' Thaddeus told his brother. 'But in the meantime we're going to need something to eat. It's nearly midday.'

Luther winked at his brother. 'L-let's go fishing.'

≪ Chapter 31 ≫

Temporary field hospital, France
August 1917

F rancois sat on the edge of the bed massaging the thigh muscle above his amputated leg. At times he wondered what cruel tricks the saints played on him, for at night the phantom foot ached and his toes cramped horribly. At least today he could sit upright for more than the usual hour and his overworked lung was steadier, making his breathing more consistent. The improvements in his general health were excruciatingly slow yet they were visible and progressing. Three operations and a further six inches taken from the stump and the doctor seemed certain that the bone infection had been eradicated. For the past few weeks Francois had concentrated on strengthening his remaining whole leg. The exertion he experienced initially from even the most basic exercises, such as pushing down on the floor while seated, was evidence of the long months spent inactive as he had lain caught between life and death. However, there was much to spur him onwards, for Sister Valois had agreed to his transfer to a ward for the living, once space could be found.

The cot next to his was vacant again; at least seven soldiers had come and gone from the bed to be interred in the cemetery at the edge of the woodland – and they were the ones Francois could remember. Yet he still remained struggling back towards life. He could taste his growing survival in the bread and soft cheese that liquefied softly in a grateful belly. A soldier's rations – biscuits and coffee tainted by the petrol cans the water was carried in – were gone forever. He had lost a leg, but his injury had set him free and he was far from being ashamed at his good fortune. As he plied the weakened tissue of his thigh, two young nurses moved around him checking on the day's arrivals. The empty cots that had given up their occupants so easily to the soil beyond the chateau now contained a new batch of maimed who were undergoing the usual routine of sharply folded sheets and the taking of weakening pulses. Francois wasn't sure who benefited the most from these simple tasks, but these procedures and the daily rounds under-taken by Sister Valois and the doctor broke the monotony of the long days. Watching the men and women work also took his impa-tient thoughts away from the set of crutches that leaned against the wall next to him. He had asked for the crutches and deter-mined that very soon he would stand again, walk again. In defying the odds he grew more resolute.

The large double doors to the ward opened and Sister Valois arrived. She clapped her hands. 'Out, if you please,' she said to the nurses.

They stopped their tasks immediately and filed down the middle of the ward, their intrigue evident. Once alone, Sister Valois stood at the foot of Francois' cot. 'How are you feeling today, Francois?'

Surrounded by prone bodies, Francois felt little excuse to be miserable. 'Better.'

'Good. I don't wish to get you excited, Francois, however –' Her words were lost amid shouts of confusion and the sound of running feet.

Francois looked towards the door. An American captain strode towards him, weary delight evident on his features. Francois didn't recognise the man, indeed he was slightly alarmed by such a visitation. 'Le Capitaine,' he said, snapping off a salute, the first in many months. The action off-balanced him and Francois struggled to remain upright, at pains to ensure both respect for his superior and his own dignity.

'Relax, son, I've brought a friend,' the captain said in stilted French.

Gripping the sides of the cot, Francois waited. There were any number of soldiers who might appear, yet uppermost in his mind was the possibility of Antoine walking through the door. 'Have you found him? Have you found my brother?'

The American captain and Sister Valois exchanged a brief glance.

'He is missing in action, Francois, presumed dead, and with the time that has passed . . .' She placed a hand on Francois' shoulder. 'We've talked of this. Your mother received notification of your brother's death last year. She has spoken of this in the letters she writes to you.'

Francois' eyes glittered. 'You think me wrong to hope?'

'Only when desire clouds reality,' she replied softly.

Francois fingered the edge of the blanket beneath him.

'We have your brother's identity discs,' Captain Harrison explained, waiting for Sister Valois to translate.

'So then, he is gone.' Francois looked at the empty cot next to him. 'I knew it, Sister.' He wiped a tear from his eye. 'I just didn't want to believe.'

'There's more.' The captain's voice brightened. 'As I said, I've brought someone to visit you.'

It was then that Francois heard the noise. The sound of running, the sound of an animal, the sound of –

Roland tore through the ward door and slid across the parquet floor, slamming into a soldier's cot. The wounded man moaned as the dog regained his footing and in great lumbering strides headed for Captain Harrison.

'Roland!' Francois called, his voice muffled by emotion.

A few yards from the American, Roland slid to a halt and began to keen softly, his shaggy head lolling from side to side as he realised who sat before him. Moving tentatively towards his wounded master, Roland jumped on the bed beside Francois, shaking the cot so violently that Francois fell sideways onto the blanket. The dog barked excitedly and covered Francois with noisy saliva-filled licks. Those among the seriously ill who could, looked across to see what the commotion was about.

'I told you,' Francois said breathlessly to Sister Valois. 'I told you. It's Roland, he's come back.'

The captain wiped a hand across his nose. 'Highly irregular, eh, Sister?'

Sister Valois stared at the scruffy animal, recalling what this ugly dog had done. 'If Roland is to visit with the patients,' she cleared her throat, 'then he will have to have a bath.'

From a cot in the ward came the soft sound of a breathless whistle. Roland pricked up his ears.

Captain Harrison smiled at the sister. 'Well, I think Francois will have some competition for Roland's attention.'

'Thank you, Captain, thank you.' Francois buried his face in Roland's shaggy coat.

'After what this dog has done,' Captain Harrison said, 'well, I can honestly say it's my pleasure.' He watched as Sister Valois patted Roland, speaking to the animal in French.

'I remember you, Roland,' Sister Valois said. 'I remember you from Verdun.'

The dog gave a single bark and then cradled his head beneath Francois' arm, his body quivering in excitement.

⋘ Chapter 32 ⋙

Sunset Ridge, south-west Queensland, Australia
February 2000

'You made quite an impression at the museum the other day.'
Madeleine stopped tapping at the laptop keys. She had been so engrossed in her work that Sonia's entrance had come unannounced. The older woman carried an empty string bag in one hand and a collapsed removalist's cardboard carton in the other. Saving her work, Madeleine swivelled in the rickety wooden chair and greeted Sonia, a little embarrassed at the messy state of the room. After yesterday's negative response from the gallery and the resulting argument between husband and wife, Madeleine had elected to spend the remainder of her time on the property secluded in the bedroom. There was a half-empty bottle of chardonnay on the roll-top desk, along with the partially eaten remains of last night's dinner. The rest of the space on the desk was covered with paperwork while a fan of material formed a circle at her feet.

'Well, I thought a visit to town might help with the research into Grandfather's life, which it did, especially when added to what Ross Evans told my brother yesterday.'

Sonia raised a wiry eyebrow. 'Ross Evans spoke to George?'

'There's far too much cloak-and-dagger stuff going on, Sonia. George and I know that your aunt, Julie Jackson, as well as old Mrs Evans, benefited from my grandfather's compassion, and it would appear that that kindness came in the form of money. How the Cummins family got caught up in all of this is beyond us, and whether or not this turn-of-the-century drama involved Germans in some way is unclear. What I can't understand is why in this day and age you all still feel so compelled to hide the truth.'

Sonia twisted the string bag. 'I'm sorry you had to find out about your father the way you did, Madeleine. That was wrong.'

Powering off the laptop, Madeleine felt inclined to tell the housekeeper to mind her own business. 'Well, now I know,' she replied tersely, 'although you can imagine how I feel learning that the district knew about my father's drinking problem and I didn't. Anyway, are you going to answer my question?'

Sonia pressed her lips together in thought. 'Sunset Ridge is not the best property in the district, Madeleine. Your father took on something he was not born and bred to because he loved your mother, and your mother made the best choices she could at the time. You should be proud of both of them.'

'I am,' Madeleine answered. She had already telephoned Jude and explained what she had learned about David Harrow over the past few days. Discussing her father proved to be more difficult, although by the end of the conversation her mother had sounded relieved and they'd parted on good terms.

Sonia looked around the bedroom. 'George tells me you're leaving soon.' The housekeeper sat the bag and box on the end of the unmade bed.

'It was meant to be this morning.' Madeleine glanced at her watch. 'I guess I lost track of the time.' She eyed the bag and box on her bed. 'You're going?'

'For the moment,' Sonia told her. 'I told your brother that I would stay on for another couple of days each week but he wouldn't hear of it.'

'That was generous of you.' Madeleine thought it interesting that the housekeeper considered the job loss to be temporary.

'Well, there have always been Jacksons at Sunset Ridge.'

Madeleine began to shuffle papers. 'So I've been told.'

'George tells me the exhibition probably won't go ahead.'

'It is looking doubtful, which is really disappointing. I've just received an email from another owner of one of Grandfather's landscape paintings confirming that they are happy to loan the work for the exhibition. Now I'm going to have to contact everyone and tell them it's on hold.'

'That's a pity.'

'What I don't understand is why some people around here don't want to see any form of commemorative event in recognition of Grandfather's art.'

Sonia sat on the edge of the bed. 'Am I right in assuming Horatio Cummins is against the idea? Wait, don't answer that, Madeleine. Just tell me: why do *you* want the exhibition to go ahead?'

'It was my mother's idea. When she first asked me to investigate the possibility of a retrospective I didn't want to be involved. I couldn't see the point. Not when all those beautiful paintings, his legacy, were sold decades earlier and scattered across the globe. I was bitter, I guess. I spent three years at university with lecturers and classmates who were amazed I never knew him and also equally stunned at my lack of artistic talent, so for a time I was also angry at Grandfather, misplaced though it was. I wonder now if I haven't just been angry with everyone since my father's death, especially Dad.'

'But why do you want the retrospective to go ahead *now*?'

Madeleine thought about the letter forwarded to the Stepworth Gallery; of Jude's desire for recognition for her father; and of George and Rachael's varied reasons. 'I never knew him, and this will sound strange, but I miss not knowing him. Maybe I just want to believe that my grandfather was a great man.' Madeleine tucked a strand of hair behind her ear. 'No, it's more than that. I *know* he was a great man.'

'Go on,' Sonia enticed.

'Being here, looking at the property through his eyes, I'm intrigued by what he drew from his surroundings. I don't find it a very inspiring place and yet he found beauty in it. He loved Sunset Ridge, and you can see that devotion in his landscapes. He loved it in such a pure, almost religious way, and it's that respect, that love that shines through in his work. Every twist in the river, every scent, every streaky golden dawn – my grandfather saw it, loved it and rendered it real for the world. I'm proud of him and in awe of his talent, and I'm just beginning to understand a little of his life, and somehow I think it was sad.' Madeleine cleared her throat. 'Then there's my professional opinion. We have a number of sketches now, which I'm sure George has told you about?'

Sonia nodded. 'Yes, he has.'

'I still think there's more of his work. There has to be more. I've even advertised in local French newspapers in the hope that someone may have one of his drawings tucked away following his time in France. When I think of Grandfather's known body of work I feel the depth of his ability, his emotion, his struggle, and still I return to the beginning, to the sketches hanging in my mother's apartment. This is the artist who piques my interest, the young man at the beginning of a career whose simple view of the world was limited to boys sitting on a river bank. These two early charcoal works suggest an artistic ability rare in one so young and they speak to me far more than the celebrated forty pieces that can be found on any serious landscape collector's wish list.' She glanced out of the bedroom window, stirred by her own emotion. 'I understand form and composition, art history and acquisition, and I firmly believe that had my grandfather's developing years not been cut short by the war, his work may well have developed into something unique. The two

Cubist pieces I discovered are proof of this, but I don't have enough material to convince the Stepworth Gallery to exhibit his work. And, Sonia, Grandfather deserves an exhibition, he really does.'

Sonia patted her hand. 'I think you'll find that there are a few people around here who agree with you, my dear. Not everyone is against honouring your grandfather's life and work.'

'Maybe not,' Madeleine frowned, 'but I'm not getting very far.'

'Sheila Marchant is the descendent of a Mrs Ruth Marchant whose son died in the Great War. She was bequeathed two paintings by her great-aunt, who apparently became good friends with Catherine Waites, your grandfather's governess.'

'Miss C.!' Madeleine gripped Sonia's hand. 'That's the initial on the invoice. Where is she? Can you help me find her?'

'Yes, my dear. I gave her a lift out here. She's in the kitchen.'

Sheila Marchant sat at the kitchen table, her hand resting protectively over a ratty old blanket that was wrapped around an oblong object. She was a slight woman, aged in her fifties, with manicured nails and a mousy brown bob that suited her oval face. Madeleine noticed the white shirt-dress yet barely heard the introductions Sonia gave. Her attention kept returning to the rust-coloured blanket. Finally the housekeeper cleared her throat a couple of times and then pulled out a chair so Madeleine could sit down.

'Where's George?' Madeleine asked. 'He should be here.'

'I really can't wait, Madeleine.' Sheila lit a cigarette, glossy pink lipstick leaving an imprint on the filter. 'I explained to Sonia that I have to be back at the bank in a couple of hours.'

'Thank you so much for coming. You don't know how important this is to my family.'

Sheila took a number of long puffs of the cigarette and smiled when Sonia produced an ashtray for her. 'I have a fair idea,

Madeleine. If I had someone gifted in my family, I'd want people to know too.'

Madeleine beamed. 'May I?' she asked, gesturing to the blanket.

Sheila stubbed out the cigarette and brushed her hands together. 'That's what I'm here for. I should tell you first that one of them is damaged. It came to me that way.' Unwrapping the blanket, she positioned the two paintings side by side. In matching gilt frames, both were under glass, slightly faded and marked by the odd insect spot. 'The names are on the back of the mounts,' Sheila explained. 'This first one is entitled *Then*, the other, *Now*. Your grandfather even wrote a description on the back of each. That's his governess, Miss Waites, who ended up working at the Banyan Post Office after the Harrow boys went to war.'

Madeleine looked gratefully at Sheila, lost for words, and then turned her attention back to her grandfather's work. The first showed Miss Waites positioned in front of the blackboard in the Sunset Ridge schoolroom. She was an attractive woman, her slight figure accentuated by a long blue dress with puffed shoulders. Her blonde hair was upswept and there was somewhat of a beatific, Botticelli-inspired smile on her face. Scattered on the schoolroom floor were curled pieces of paper that appeared to be covered with drawings. The governess's lone student, a young David Harrow, was depicted in profile. Although appearing to be listening to Miss Waites, his attention was drawn to the view beyond the school-house window, the Banyan River and two figures, presumably his older brothers.

The second work was painted using the same mediums as the first, yet there all similarity ended. Where the first work radiated an almost dreamy quality, this one was stark. The governess wore a light-brown dress and sat stiffly in a chair by a window. Although her hair fell loose about her shoulders, she had become plainer, perhaps a more genuine version of the real person. A letter lay on her lap, while an envelope gave the appearance of having just been dropped to the ground. Outside the window stood David Harrow in a heavy overcoat. He appeared to be looking straight past the governess, a pained expression adding age and gravity to the face of an otherwise good-looking young man. On the left-hand corner of the painting a section had been torn away, leaving a pair of women's lace-up boots as the only hint to what may have been painted there.

'My mother says that your grandfather is wearing his army-issue great coat in that painting. As for the part that's missing, no one in my family has any idea who it might have been.'

'These are incredible. How did you come by them?' Madeleine asked.

'They were part of my great-aunt's estate and she left them to my brother. Harry passed away a couple of years ago and he willed them to me.' Sheila accepted Sonia's offer of coffee and lit another cigarette. 'I only came back to the district to go through Harry's things, but I liked the place and decided to stay. Anyway, I dug these two paintings out of the spare room a couple of days ago. Some of the bank's customers have been talking about the possibility of a David Harrow exhibition and that's what reminded me about these pictures.'

'They're marvellous,' Madeleine told her. 'Do you know anything else about them?'

Sheila took a sip of the black coffee Sonia handed her. 'Only what Mum told me yesterday. A few garbled stories have been passed down through the family. Whether there's any truth to them is another matter. One story is that Miss Waites died of a broken heart; another is that she left Banyan in the 1920s after your grandfather married. She was engaged at one stage, but I don't think she married locally. She did live in the Banyan boarding house for quite a while and it's said she kept to herself and didn't have many friends, except for a young girl by the name of Corally Shaw, whom she taught for a couple of years.'

'What happened to Corally?' Madeleine asked, aware of Sonia's eyes on Sheila.

'Who knows? That's about all I can tell you, Madeleine, but I would like to loan these to you for the exhibition if it goes ahead.'

Madeleine walked around the kitchen table and hugged Sheila. 'How can I ever repay you?'

Sheila grinned and lit another cigarette. 'Send me an invite to the opening night. I love a good party.'

They shook hands. 'You're on,' Madeleine promised.

≼ Chapter 33 ≽

Chessy farmhouse, ten miles from Saint-Omer, northern France
August 1917

Thaddeus and Dave stood at the edge of the pond, camouflaged by the drooping branches of a willow tree. It was cool beneath the canopy and they waited patiently, enjoying the soft feel of the air and the scents of still water and stacked hay.

'How come you and Harold aren't mates anymore?' Dave could tell that the question caught Thaddeus off guard. It wasn't the first time he had broached the subject. 'You barely talk to each other, and the other day in the trench I thought you two were going to have another fight.'

'It's a bit hard for him, I expect. We've always been –'

'Competitive?' Dave suggested.

'And now I outrank him.'

That didn't seem to be a good enough reason for Dave. 'But you were friends first.'

There was a scuffle to the left of them and the brothers squatted at the tree's base, expecting an angry Frenchman to appear. Branches rustled and Dave reached automatically for his pistol.

Thaddeus placed a hand over the barrel and lowered the weapon to the ground.

'We're not at the front now, Dave,' he said gently, as Luther and Harold appeared through the tight knit of woodland.

'Anything?' Thaddeus asked once Luther and Harold joined them.

'Nothing,' Harold replied. 'Not even a farmer.'

They were half a mile from the Chessy holding, on land belonging to another farmer. 'It beats me how they manage to produce so much off such small acreage,' Thaddeus said as they looked across the surface of the pond. The water was pale green, with a third of its surface covered in water lilies. Birds darted across the water to the far bank, where thick trees fringed the lush herbage leading to the water's edge.

'It seems a pity to ruin it,' Dave observed as they walked free of the willow tree. 'It's so peaceful.'

'Yeah, it is,' Harold agreed, 'but I haven't had a decent feed of fish since I arrived over here.'

'It's a bit different to th-the B-banyan River,' Luther admitted. 'Prettier. I bet th-they don't have floods and droughts here.'

'No, they've got wars,' Dave reminded him.

'I still l-like it here,' Luther argued, 'war or no war.'

'That's because you're good at it,' Dave told him.

'Good at what?' Luther replied.

'Killing,' Dave said softly.

'Stop talking.' Harold pointed over the water. 'Did anyone hear that?'

Thaddeus scanned the far bank. 'It could be an animal.'

Harold looked doubtful. 'Something is moving over there.'

'There'll be hell to pay if we get caught.' Thaddeus sounded testy.

'Spoilsport,' Luther scoffed. Taking two grenades from a haversack, he walked to the edge of the pond and, after briefly checking the surrounds, pulled the pins and threw them into the water.

There were consecutive bangs and then two great plumes of water broke the surface and speared the sky. The men watched as birds took flight and the liquid arced upwards and then fell back to land with a loud splash. The water rippled in concentric circles as dead fish rose up to float on the surface.

Luther turned to his mates, clearly pleased with himself. 'D-dinner is served.'

From across the water they heard a series of yelps and then a group of naked men ran out from between the trees and dived into the pond.

'Bloody hell,' Harold complained. 'They're Aussies.'

'Well, come on, th-then,' Luther yelled, pulling off his boots, 'they'll be nothing l-left!' They dived into the water fully clothed and swam towards the floating fish.

'Grab as many as you can!' Thaddeus spluttered, shoving a fish down his shirt front.

Great splashes of fragmented silver sprayed up into the air as the men tried to rescue their catch. Shouts and laughter sounded as fish slipped from lunging hands, until finally a punch was thrown. Harold emerged from the water with his slouch hat filled with fish. The other boys pulled fish from inside shirts and tunics, letting them drop at the edge of the pond.

'You b-buggers!' Luther yelled at the retreating men. 'You're m-meant to be on our side.'

'Thanks, cobber!' a voice called from the far bank as five skinny buttocks disappeared into the foliage.

'B-bloody Australians,' Luther muttered, before he burst out laughing.

❧

Dave sat at Madame Chessy's kitchen table and deftly added a number of strokes to the defiant jawline. The Frenchwoman sat perfectly straight, her fine patrician nose and clear oval eyes immobile. A fire crackled in the hearth. Water bubbled in a pot swung across the flames. The room, although clammy, smoky and claustrophobic, was warm and safe. It was with reluctance that Dave added the finishing touches to the portrait. On the other side of the kitchen, Lisette sat quietly in a faded floral chair. There was a laying hen in a box at the girl's feet and although she pretended not to be interested Dave knew she examined him. He added a little shadowing, an effect that gave further contour to Madame's face.

Dave still wondered at the few brief lines recently received from Corally Shaw. He had written back immediately, assuring her of his wellbeing and thanking her. Although unexpected, it was nice to receive a letter from someone other than his mother, with content that didn't need to be shared. Both his brothers had received mail the day Thaddeus made sergeant, as well as Harold, and although Dave longed to query who their letters were from, a sense of privacy stopped him. They lived their lives like rats only feet from men who wanted to kill them; every day was spent in the company of others where nothing was private and life was a game of chance. Corally's note reinforced and fed his need for normalcy, and Dave silently thanked her for that.

David,
I wanted to tel you that I wory for you. I care for you.
Plese rite, Corally

'Fini.' He slid the sketch across the table as the vibrations from the Allied bombardment continued to shake the few possessions on cupboards and shelves that encircled the room. Madame Chessy admired the work, pouring him a second glass of wine. Dave waved away an offer of more eggs and potato but drank the wine grate-fully. It had surprised him how quickly he had developed a taste for alcohol. Despite his age it was accepted that he would drink as much as the rest of the men.

'You are very good,' Madame Chessy announced in her heavy accent. She sat the sketch on the kitchen cupboard next to a picture of two boys in French uniforms.

'Not so good.' Dave wiped slivers of charcoal from table to floor, recalling the day on the veranda at Sunset Ridge when Miss Waites had explained how to stop the fragile charcoal tip from falling to pieces. He had not thought of the governess for many weeks. 'I'm still learning.'

The Frenchwoman's gaze lingered on her sons' picture. 'I think you go soon, *oui?*'

Through the grubby window flashes of light haloed the horizon. '*Oui,*' Dave agreed. 'In the morning, I think.' The Allied guns, which had been hammering away for a number of days, sounded as if they were only down the next road. There was a new offensive in the wind and although no one as yet knew the details, the whispers suggested a much larger push than that of Messines. Passchendaele lay on a ridge east of Ypres, and Thaddeus talked of a railway junction five miles away from this spot at a place called Roulers, a vital part of the supply system of the German Fourth Army. But first they had another work detail.

The Frenchwoman sipped her wine. Their raiding parties had produced two bottles of Scotch, a crate of wine and a side of veal. Combined with some potatoes and three chickens, which Lisette complained to Dave bore an uncanny resemblance to the hens from her father's farm, the takings had been good. Madame Chessy was overjoyed with the shared hoard.

'You come back, *oui?*' the woman encouraged. 'Then you draw Lisette.'

Dave longed for the opportunity, although the chance to sketch Lisette was secondary to his desire to touch the curve of a cheek, perhaps even press his lips against the redness of hers. It seemed such a small thing to want, yet it had become extraordinarily important to him since his receipt of Corally's letter. He didn't want to die never having kissed a woman.

'Now?' he asked hopefully, the charcoal warm in his hand.

The Frenchwoman twirled the glass on the table. Dave suspected that she guessed his motives. Lisette glanced at the older woman.

'Why did you come here?' Madame Chessy asked in French, gesturing with her hand for Lisette to translate. 'You live so far away.'

'To help. If the Germans were to invade France, where would they end up next?'

Lisette shifted forward in the chair. 'My papa says we will be saved by the Allies, especially by *Australie*. You are very brave soldiers.' She repeated the sentence in French for the benefit of Madame Chessy.

Dave sat the piece of charcoal on the table. 'We are no different from the rest.'

'My boys thought you were,' the older woman disagreed. 'They fought at Verdun.' She clucked her tongue. 'Young men die for old men's mistakes.'

Lisette rose and, taking the picture from the mantelpiece, pointed out the Chessy twins to their visitor.

'They say Antoine is missing in action, presumed dead. Francois is wounded.'

'I'm very sorry.' The Frenchwoman's sons could not be much older than him. A distant memory interrupted his thoughts; a pile of bodies and a feral-looking dog. 'Did you say Antoine? Your son is Antoine Chessy?'

Madame Chessy looked hopeful. '*Oui.*'

What was he to say, Dave wondered: that her son's identity discs had ended up around the neck of a dog? 'I think I met someone who mentioned him,' he said slowly. 'They said he was very brave.' He felt Lisette's eyes on him as she translated.

354

Madame Chessy sighed. 'They say Francois may not survive. A nurse wrote to me from a field hospital many days' travel from here to tell me of his wounds. He has lost a leg and there is an infection of the bone making his recovery difficult.' She looked away while Lisette translated.

'I'm very sorry,' Dave repeated, at a loss for something more effective to say.

'Your Captain Egan tells me there are still passenger trains running but there are also many delays due to the movement of troops and munitions and other supplies. I would visit him but I cannot be sure I would only be gone for one week, and if I went, what would I come back to? And I could certainly not expect Lisette to stay here alone.'

Dave waited for Lisette to translate and then agreed that the times were difficult. An empty farmhouse might well be stripped of its contents if word leaked that the owner was away. The Allied soldiers were adept at scrounging for small comforts. As for Lisette, while there was always the chance of a wayward soldier taking advantage, she was fortunate not to be in an area closer to the front. The Germans took their occupation rights seriously and were not averse to raping French women, although it was equally true that some women acquiesced to their advances in order to survive.

'I have nothing except this farm.' Madame Chessy's hand trembled as she brought the wine to her lips.

'You can send him this drawing and perhaps the one of the farmhouse. Most of the soldiers I sketch send their portraits home to their families. You could do the same,' Dave suggested.

Madame Chessy clapped her hands and replied in English: 'This I will do. Thank you. *Oui, oui.*'

Lisette topped up their wine glasses and poured water for herself. 'There were explosions last month. They were very big.'

'Messines,' Dave explained. 'It was a series of underground mines. Tunnellers worked for months to lay the mines beneath the

German trenches. The whole place lit up like a Christmas tree and the brass reckoned Fritz was blown to bits.'

'Good.' Lisette cupped the water glass between her palms.

Dave was no tactician, however it seemed silly to him that Messines hadn't been followed up immediately with another major strike. Instead here they were, weeks later, twiddling their thumbs as their gunners bombarded the Germans. Luther furiously argued with anyone within earshot that Haig's noisy calling card was allowing Fritz to muster their forces in anticipation of this next push. None could say he was wrong. While the usual brave faces were evident around the farmhouse, a sense of foreboding was building among the men. Fierce fighting had broken out again at Ypres and battles continued to be waged through an area collectively known as the Somme.

Madame Chessy clucked her tongue. 'The rains will be heavy this year, I think.'

'How do you know?' Dave drained the tumbler of wine.

The woman rose. Only after she had rinsed their dishes in the simmering water and sat them in a plate rack to dry near the fire did she reply. 'I know this land. It is a feeling I have.' Navigating the cramped room, she rested a hand briefly on his shoulder. 'You come back? *Oui*?'

It wasn't like him to tear up. Dave blinked away the moisture and began to rip finished sketches from his pad. 'Will you look after these for me?' he asked. 'If you are right and there is a lot of rain they will be ruined if they get wet.' He would be sorry to leave them behind. The drawings spoke of better times and it was becoming increasingly difficult to draw beauty from memory.

Madame Chessy studied the collection. Among the drawings were Thaddeus playing cricket, Fall and Trip laughing at a shared joke, Captain Egan giving a VD lecture, Harold playing cards with Thorny, and Luther sharpening his tomahawk. 'They are family,' she stated.

'Yes, family,' he agreed.

'It would be an honour,' Madame Chessy placed a hand to her bosom, 'and you come back and collect? *Oui?*'

He nodded. One sketch remained: that of the mangy dog who wore Antoine Chessy's identity discs about his neck like a trophy. The ungainly animal was depicted sitting alone in the trench, the dead owner's discs clearly visible. Dave shut the book quickly, loath to distress his hostess.

Madame Chessy examined the drawings. At the bottom of the pile was a geometric sketch of lines and boxes. She tilted the drawing left and right, held it to the light and then rotated it. Finally the older woman placed it back in the pile and pointed to her recent portrait. '*Mieux*,' she said simply.

'Yes,' Dave agreed, 'it's better.' His interest in that particular style, borne out of his hallucinations last year, had waned with the increasing time spent at the front. He was looking at fractured lives and landscapes every day; there was little appeal left in disassembling objects when life was as disjointed as the pictures he once toyed with.

When a knock sounded on the door, the last person Dave expected to see was Captain Egan. 'Sir?'

'A word, Dave.'

Madame Chessy raised her chin. 'We will never forget *Australie*. You tell your mama, we never forget.'

'I'll tell her.'

'You've made a friend,' the captain noted once they were outside the farmhouse.

'She's a good woman, sir.'

They walked to the edge of the farmhouse clearing. Beyond the willow trees and stream the blaze from the bombardment haloed the horizon in green and yellow light. 'It will take much for the French to recover,' Captain Egan shared as the bomb flashes reflected off thickening clouds.

'Madame Chessy says it will rain, sir.'

'I hope not, Dave,' Captain Egan said stiffly. 'Unfortunately the topsoils in this part of France are quite shallow and the water table very close to the surface. Our advisers tell us that the rain percolates through the chalk bed and underneath that is gluey clay. Well, you're a farmer, Harrow, you can imagine what our artillery is doing to the countryside and what it will be like out there if we do get substantial rain.'

Dave was flummoxed. 'Sir, I've got no idea. I only know about sheep.'

The captain snorted. 'Sheep? I can't imagine you Harrow boys being content with sheep.'

'It's the land, sir, as wide and as red and as quiet a place as you could ever imagine, and the sheep dust the countryside like clouds.'

For a moment they both stared out at the trees blistered white by streaky jolts of light.

'Well, you remember that when you get to the front, son. That's what you're fighting for.'

Their conversation conjured visions of red ridges and the lanolin-smooth boards of the wool shed, fishing trips and the hint of green after rain. Dave yearned to be back at Sunset Ridge, cosseted by the great sweeping bulk of country that had always protected him in the past.

'Anyway, Harrow, I have a request and it's a simple one. In May this year Will Dyson was appointed the AIF's first official war artist. It's taken some time for agreement to be reached regarding the way in which the war should be documented but it seems General Birdwood is happy enough for a record of sorts to be made. Now, it's not in my power to give you some sort of special commission at the moment. However, you should be aware that I have sent word higher up with regards to your abilities. In the near future I hope you'll be documenting the war, not fighting in it.'

Surprise was quickly overtaken by anger. 'I suppose you talked to Thaddeus about this and he was keen for me to do it?'

'Of course,' Captain Egan agreed. 'Very keen.'

'Well, it certainly gets him and Luther out of a tight spot, sir.'

Captain Egan raised an eyebrow. 'I don't understand. You're extremely talented, Dave. I'd liked to see those talents made use of for the benefit of the war effort and the nation.'

Dave focused on the words that closed every letter they received from their mother.

Look after your young brother, Thaddeus and Luther. He is your responsibility now.

'If it's all the same to you, sir, I signed up as a soldier and I'd rather stay as that.'

Captain Egan turned to him. 'You'd still be in the thick of things, son. You can't document the war from the rear.'

Dave hesitated. He wanted to draw and the chance of being a commissioned war artist was more than he could have hoped for, yet the need to prove he was just as capable as his brothers was more important. 'It wouldn't be the same, sir.'

'It would be pretty close.'

Dave shook his head. 'No, sir. No, it wouldn't. They'd be charging across no-man's land and I'd be watching from the trench. It wouldn't be the same at all, sir.'

'You're a bloody stubborn lot, you lads from Banyan,' Captain Egan chastised.

'Yes, sir,' Dave agreed.

'Well, if that's how you feel. But I hope you change your mind.'

'Anyway, if it does rain like Madame Chessy says, there won't be much drawing going on.'

'We'll see. Roll call at six am in Tatinghem,' Captain Egan reminded him before walking away.

Dave watched him go, his knuckles clenched. He knew he'd made the right decision. He could still draw at the front even if his pictures were only for the benefit of the men he fought with. As for documenting the war, Dave wondered why anyone would want to remember it.

'You said n-no, didn't you?' Luther slunk out of the shadows, the tip of a cigarette glowing in the darkness.

'Of course I said no.' Luther seemed older than all of them now. Caution framed his movements, making him resemble a coiled spring. Dave was pleased he was on their side. He dared not imagine the horror of facing the tomahawk-wielding soldier that his brother had become.

Luther offered a cigarette and struck a match, cupping the flare of light with a palm. 'I told Th-thaddeus you would. Anyway, th-there are more drawings scattered about here than you can poke a stick at, and I've never gone m-much on this p-painting caper of yours.'

'I can look after myself, you know.'

'I know th-that,' Luther agreed, 'but Thad? Well, he's always had a m-misplaced sense of authority. It comes with b-being the eldest.'

Dave felt a little better. 'Can I ask you something?'

'Depends,' Luther answered, picking tobacco from between his teeth.

'Do you know what happened between Thaddeus and Harold? I've asked both of them but neither are talking and you always change the subject.'

'Corally Shaw happened,' Luther revealed. 'I didn't b-believe it at first but th-that's Harold's story.'

Dave was gobsmacked. 'So the fight –'

'Yep, all over a g-girl.'

'Bloody hell. That's just stupid.'

'Especially as women are such ch-changeable creatures,' Luther answered. 'Harold thinks he's engaged to Corally, and I guess Th-thaddeus reckons he has a chance with her. I don't reckon either of th-them have asked Corally what she wants.'

Dave took a long drag on the cigarette. 'But at the courthouse she helped *you.*'

Luther whispered conspiratorially. 'We shared a kiss, her and m-me, in the Banyan cemetery. And we write t-to each other.'

'Well, I'll be.'

'Don't b-breathe a word. The thing is, it's me she's keen on, but I th-think it's better if we don't tell the others, not with another p-push coming.'

Dave couldn't help but laugh. 'So, all this is because of Corally Shaw? The fight between Thaddeus and Harold at the show; you chopping off Snob Evans's finger, which led to all of us being locked up and eventually running away from Sunset Ridge? All of us ended up fighting someone else's war on the other side of the world because of a girl?'

Luther sat on the grass. 'I hadn't th-thought about it that w-way.'

'Bloody hell,' Dave repeated, joining his brother on the ground. 'Why?'

Luther gave this question considerable thought. 'B-buggered if I know.'

'This is too good,' Dave chuckled. 'You know, I never even liked marbles that much.'

A greenish light filtered the clouds. 'Th-hat girl's like a piece of candy to l-look at.'

'More like trouble,' Dave argued, thinking of the letter received from her.

'Well, if she is t-trouble, she's *my* trouble,' Luther replied confidently.

'I don't get it. Why Corally?'

'I just l-like her, Dave, I always have. She's different, I guess, really p-pretty, and Corally has something th-that no other girl I've met has: spunk. Now I'm over here she's even more important to me. Corally Shaw is w-what I'm fighting for.'

Dave thought back to the conversation with Captain Egan, about remembering what he cared about when they returned to the front. Dave knew he was fighting for a good cause and the constant hope of returning one day to Sunset Ridge. But it was different for his brothers and Harold. While they too were fighting for a future, fighting to protect each other and their comrades in order to put an end to the war so they could return home, it seemed they were also fighting with a woman in mind. The same woman.

'I'm going to g-get some shut-eye. Th-thaddeus tells me we're on work detail again.' Luther ruffled his hair. 'And you're wr-wrong, you know, Dave. This isn't someone else's war, it's ours too.'

Dave thought of Corally's letter as the ominous rumblings of the big guns filtered through the night. They were already in one war, he mused, and he didn't want to be part of another. Retrieving the envelope, he struck a match and held the flame inches from the girl's brief words. Dave wanted to burn it. He knew he should burn it. Instead he blew out the match and tucked the letter away.

≪ Chapter 34 ≫

Temporary field hospital, France
August 1917

Francois leaned heavily on the crutches and stepped out from under the portico of the chateau. The cobbled driveway was difficult to navigate and more than once the wooden tips of the walking aide became lodged in the rocky crevices. He headed towards a stone bench, his swinging stride gathering momentum on the soft grass. The weather was fine today and patients were strewn about the garden. Those who could walk strolled about the grounds as if on holiday; others lay on blankets reading and dozing in the sun. Convalescing soldiers lolled in deckchairs or sat in wheelchairs, their faces turned towards the sky like sunflowers. Stippled light filtered the stone bench as Francois leaned his crutches against the wide girth of a tree. Directly before him, the chateau rose proudly. The temporary field hospital had been his home for so long that the prospect of leaving it unnerved him.

Hopping on one leg, he landed heavily on the stone bench. He still had some way to go before his movements became more fluid, although Sister Valois continued to be pleased with his progress.

Roland ran through the trees bordering the edge of the chateau's grounds and came to a panting halt at Francois' foot.

'Where have you been?' Francois scratched the animal's nose. 'Chasing rabbits again, eh?'

Roland barked and whined in response and Francois could only imagine the tale that was being told. He patted the bench seat and Roland jumped, sprawling his body up across the cool stone so that his head lay in Francois' lap. He fingered the dog's leather collar, touching the smooth discs that had once hung around his brother's neck. It was a comfort to know that Roland had found Antoine; had perhaps laid a great paw on his chest and rested with him in the detritus of Verdun.

Francois wondered if he should have written sooner to his mother instead of relying on Sister Valois to do it. In her last letter she had sounded very sad, and he wondered if his letter explaining the improvement in the infection had not arrived. Francois wanted to be whole again, to return home the same man as the one who had left the chilly farmhouse last year. Putting pen to paper remained difficult. To try to explain everything that had happened, to write of the dark abyss he had crossed, the loss of his leg and of Antoine's death . . . Francois stroked Roland's back absently. It would have made everything too real, too final, and he wasn't ready for that. Francois had been in a dark place, a place part of him would never return from. He understood this was the way things had to be because his other half, his brother, lay in the muck and he had survived, and he would never understand why fate had chosen Antoine and not him.

Above, birds darted through the foliage. Roland followed the fluttering shapes with interest.

'Francois?'

A young aide was holding a long envelope. Francois accepted it and thanked the girl as an ambulance motored up the driveway towards the chateau. Roland sat up.

'And Sister Valois said to tell you –'

Francois waved her away. 'I know, I know.' By his side Roland barked.

The door to the American Field Ambulance opened and Captain Harrison emerged. Francois knew he should greet the doctor but instead he watched and waited as the American was directed to where he and Roland sat. The captain was no stranger to the chateau, having taken Sister Valois to tea on a number of occasions in a nearby village a week after his arrival with Roland before completing his leave at Amiens. Now, however, the man was clearly short for time. He crossed the lawn quickly, weaving between wheelchairs and more able-bodied soldiers.

'How are you feeling?' the captain asked, although his attention was diverted by Roland's enthusiastic greeting.

'Better,' Francois replied. Although the captain had a long way to go before he could speak French fluently, the American had benefited from his time spent with Sister Valois.

'So I see. You'll be going home in a matter of weeks, I hear.'

'And you to the front,' Francois answered. 'How was your leave?'

'Amiens is not as I remembered it. Parts of the city were shelled.' Captain Harrison petted Roland and joined Francois on the bench. 'Sometimes I think I should have stayed here and courted Sister Valois. I'm sure she's fond of me.'

It took Francois a few seconds to decipher what the captain spoke of, and then he laughed. 'Only a brave man would attempt such a thing.'

'Perhaps, but then we are surrounded by bravery these days, I'm hoping some may rub off on me.' Down the road leading to the chateau, two patients raced their wheelchairs. 'If there were Australians here they would be betting on that.' Two aides ran after the men, imploring them to stop before there was an accident.

Francois twitched Roland's ear. The dog nuzzled his way onto the bench until he had squeezed both men sideways and made a space for himself, his head level with theirs.

'He doesn't have to come back with me, you know.'

'I saw what he did at Verdun.' Francois' eyes shone. 'And you have told me of how he assists you with the wounded.'

Both men were petting Roland and the dog arched his neck under their joint attention.

Captain Harrison nodded. 'He's a remarkable animal. He seems to do naturally what other dogs take months to learn. But you of all people know how dangerous it is out there.'

Francois thought of his father and brother and all the others who had given their lives in defence of a land that now seemed unrecognisable.

'He doesn't have to die a hero,' Captain Harrison reminded Francois. 'And he is *your* dog. I think Roland has done enough.'

Francois cupped the dog's head and rubbed his forehead against the soft hair. 'I don't think the decision will be ours.'

Captain Harrison's pale eyebrows drew together. 'Well, unfortunately I must go.' He rose and took Francois' hand. 'It has been a privilege to meet you and Roland.'

'Thank you for bringing him back. It has meant a great deal to me.'

Captain Harrison patted Roland. 'It was something I felt strongly about. There are many stories about this dog and the two brothers he belonged to.'

Francois watched the American as he wound his way back to the ambulance, pausing to chat to two aides before greeting Sister Valois beneath the portico. They talked for long minutes and then Sister Valois held out her hand; the captain ignored this gesture and kissed her on the cheek, his hand lingering on her shoulder. Sister Valois touched her face as the captain walked away.

Roland's paw was heavy on Francois' thigh. 'You want me to give you my blessing,' Francois said softly, turning to look into the dog's dark eyes. Roland's breath was on his cheek. There was a smell of wet grass and freshly turned dirt. Francois' eyes blurred. 'You are not mine to own, but I hope you will come back to me.' Wrapping his arms around the animal, he hugged him fiercely. 'Go then,' he cried, 'go and do your duty.'

Roland leaped from the bench. Outside the chateau the ambulance chugged to life and reversed. Roland ran straight to the moving vehicle, which halted suddenly. The driver's door opened and the dog jumped inside the cabin. For a brief moment Captain Harrison stared at Francois and then he lifted an arm in salute. Standing unsteadily, with a single crutch propped beneath an armpit, Francois returned the salute.

'Don't let him go out into no-man's land!' Francois yelled. 'Promise me?'

Captain Harrison lifted his arm in goodbye. 'I promise.'

When the ambulance drove away, Roland's great shaggy head barked at him from the passenger window as Sister Valois walked a few steps after the departing vehicle.

In the ensuing silence Francois placed a palm on the warm stone where Roland had sat and wondered what would become of his life. Half his family were dead, he was maimed and virtually useless, and he doubted that he would ever see his beloved Roland again. As he drew his hand from the now cold stone, his fingers touched the envelope delivered earlier. He opened it quickly. There was a letter from his mother within, along with two sketches. He flattened them on the bench and stared at the finely drawn portrait of his mother and one of the farmhouse. The door was open at a right angle and beyond the figure of his mother the flagstone floor and wooden beams of the kitchen were visible. Tracing a finger across his mother's features, he was unaware of Sister Valois's approach until she stood opposite.

'You were deep in thought,' she interrupted. 'What were you thinking of, Francois?'

He looked at her, his cheeks wet with tears. 'Home.'

⋘ Chapter 35 ⋙

The chair on the veranda was empty. Placing the morning-tea tray on the side table, Lily noted the missing walking stick and the open gate. The postal rider had come and gone in her absence and the station mail was sitting on the foot stool along with the latest edition of *The Illustrated London News*, its pages fluttering in the breeze. Black-and-white photographs of the Western Front flickered back and forth. Lily stayed the moving pages, her hand coming to rest on a picture of a duckboard stretching endlessly through a decimated landscape of splintered trees, cratered earth and a cloud-tumbled sky. Beneath it was another photograph depicting great plumes of earth spiralling skywards; the caption beneath said one word, 'Messines.' For a moment Lily felt as if she were staring at a vision of hell. Never had she seen such a soulless place. If this was France, it scared her. The name Messines lingered like an unforgotten nightmare and she slowly realised where she had heard the word before. David, her youngest, had written of it. He had been there. All three of her boys had been there.

Lily lifted white knuckles to her lips. 'My boys,' she whispered. 'What have I done?' The pages of the magazine continued to flip in the breeze. It was not as if she was unaware of the danger, but seeing the images of the place her boys fought stunned Lily. Sitting heavily on the foot stool, she considered the months leading up to their desertion. In the end, agreeing with G.W.'s overzealous reaction to Luther's crime had not protected any of them from the war. In fact, it had had the opposite effect, and now the hell to which they had run was presented to her in gritty black and white. Where had her mind been these past months? What had she been thinking? If they wanted so desperately to go to war, surely it would have been better for them to leave with her blessing. Lily thought of the letters written to her beloved boys. In hindsight they were terse and not worthy of her. In fact, if anything happened to Thaddeus, Luther or Dave, Lily would be hard put not to blame herself or her husband.

'G.W.,' she called out. The words went unanswered. 'G.W.?' The open gate beckoned. Lifting her skirts, Lily ran down the gravel path.

'Are you all right, missus?' Cook stood on the veranda, angular elbows stuck out at right angles to her body. 'I saw Mr Harrow earlier in the library. I did ask him if he wanted a hand with that big book he had, it being so heavy, but he waved me away.'

'What book?' Lily asked impatiently.

Cook shunted narrow shoulders towards the sky. 'It was the bible, the one with the big silver latch on it. I put it away when he'd finished with it.'

At the gateway drag marks were visible. 'I will have to go and look for him. I can't understand why he's gone beyond the back gate.'

'I'll keep an eye on the time, missus. If you aren't back in an hour I'll come looking.'

'Very well,' Lily agreed.

She followed the trail made by her husband, cursing the thin house shoes she wore. The fine leather emphasised every pebble and hole in the uneven ground but she dared not waste time in changing them. Visions of her husband shuffling along and stumbling into a pothole pulled her onwards. Heaven forbid that he should fall and break a bone, or worse. She left the house paddock behind and walked swiftly, following the drag marks in the dirt. If she tried very hard Lily could almost forget the things G.W. had said to her the day he crossed the boys' names from the family bible, even if she knew that he had meant them.

The bush was quiet. Clumps of trees bordered the track G.W. had followed, the direction taking Lily away from the river and the homestead and into low scrubby bush and belts of trees that towered like guardians. The stables lay through the adjacent house-paddock fence, and beyond that the homestead roof glimmered in the distance. A knot of concern lodged in Lily's stomach as the vastness of the land bore down upon her. As far as she knew, all the men were out checking the livestock on the western boundary, which left three women and her missing husband the only people in a ten-mile radius. Lifting her skirts in annoyance, Lily swore that it was time to stop playing the lady of the manor. Voluminous skirts and pretty shoes belonged to another life and it was time she embraced her changed circumstances. Ahead lay the track that wound to the station cemetery. Lily pushed on, wondering what to do if she found her husband injured.

The track curled past a stand of spindly needlewood trees. At the next bend she spotted G.W. He was sitting on a log beneath a tree, staring at the rows of headstones through the wooden fence. He looked up on her approach.

'My dear, what are you doing out here?' she asked.

He turned back towards the cemetery as if seeking guidance from the relatives buried within.

'I could have driven you out in the dray if you had told me.' Lily sat down next to him and lifted a comforting hand, but he shifted away before she could touch him.

'Walk, needed to walk.' The words were halting, like a child unused to speech.

'It was the pictures, wasn't it? The ones of France? It looks just horrid.' Lily waited patiently for agreement. When it didn't come she watched a line of ants traverse the dirt track at her feet. 'I never would have agreed to your punishment, G.W., had I not thought it might keep them safe, keep them away from the war.' Kangaroos bounded through the grass. They reached the track and, seeing their path blocked, steered sharply away from the fallen log and its occupants. 'We made the wrong decision. We were too hard on them. We placed our need for control, our disappointments, above them.'

G.W. remained silent.

'If anything happens to them I'll never be able to forgive myself.'

'They would have gone anyway.' The words were spoken excruciatingly slowly. G.W. struggled upwards and shuffled to the cemetery fence. 'I would be there too if I could.'

'Are you telling me that you are more angry that they disobeyed you than the fact they enlisted? Heaven forbid, G.W., what kind of father are you?'

There were eight Harrows interred within the fence G.W. leaned upon. Men, women and children had lain together undisturbed since the last burial some twenty years ago. He pointed at the gravesite marking his own father's resting place. 'I am my father's son.'

A shiny black crow flew from a tree and settled on a crumbling headstone. Lily shivered. 'We should start back if you have rested enough.'

With him shaking off her offer of assistance, they began the long walk home. G.W. refused to rest, punishing his body into keeping up a steady pace and telling Lily to walk on ahead and leave him be. She was tempted to do just that.

371

'Manager?' G.W. puffed.

'Mr Taylor?' Lily reached for her husband as he stumbled and then regained his footing. He waved away her outstretched hands. 'He's doing a reasonable job, I think, but I wasn't sure if he was experienced enough. I couldn't find any references. I did mention that to you?' A blank stare suggested no memory of the event. 'I wrote care of the address in the ledger and I'm hoping I'll be able to find a previous employer who can vouch for Mr Taylor's suitability. If not, I think I will advertise for someone more suitable.'

G.W. struggled with a single word. 'Good.'

'Perhaps I should ask Mr Taylor to speak with you now you are feeling a little better? Certainly your strength has improved. It's quite a walk you led me on this morning, my dear.'

G.W. tapped a finger against his throat.

'Well, I quite understand if you want to wait until your speech improves, but it really is coming along extremely well.'

With the walking stick in one hand, G.W. persevered on the rutted track for ten more minutes before begrudgingly taking Lily's arm. They met Cook at the house-paddock gate, the whinging housemaid Henrietta by her side.

'We just went for a walk,' Lily said a little too brightly in response to their questioning stares.

'We aren't prepared for calamities, you know, missus, not when there aren't any menfolk about to help,' Cook stated.

G.W. grunted and briefly lifted the walking stick, waving it through the air in annoyance.

'Well, everything is fine,' Lily reassured. Cook and Henrietta were useless beyond their paid professions, and even their work attitude was questionable. Lily knew that if a tragedy did ever befall them it would be she who would have to saddle a horse and ride into the village for assistance. 'Let's not stand here talking,' Lily told them. 'You two go on ahead before we all expire in this heat. Mr Harrow and I will be fine.' The two women walked back towards the homestead, obviously pleased that nothing more was expected of them.

What a fool she was, Lily thought sadly, casting a glance at the man who now leaned so reluctantly on her arm. Her boys were at war and her marriage was deteriorating. Everything was far from fine.

≪ Chapter 36 ≫

Flanders, Belgium
August 1917

The Menin Road led out from the ruins of Ypres. Constant shelling by both sides had turned the area into a wilderness of decimated trees, craters, churned-up earth and piles of rubble where villages once were. The concussion was shocking. The screaming of shells, the banging and crashing of the big guns and the great spurts of flame were beyond imagining. Dave waited with the rest of the men for the order to be given to make the dash along Hellfire Corner. By the side of the road facing the Germans, great lengths of hessian had been erected in an effort to camouflage the movement of troops, supplies and munitions. It made little difference. The enemy's guns battered the road continually. Dave wet his lips. Ahead, horse-drawn artillery wagons raced towards them as shells spiralled overhead.

'Come on, come on.' Thaddeus willed the approaching wagon to safety. The low chant was taken up by the men around them.

The first empty wagon passed them at a gallop in a rattle of squeaking timber and leather. The driver urged the team onwards, his slouch hat pulled down over his brow, his body bent low over the reins. The horse's ears were flattened, the look of terror unmistakeable in the whites of the animal's eyes.

'Jesus,' Luther muttered.

Another wagon sped by.

Dave swallowed. The men were restless. Once the artillery wagons were through, they were next. His legs felt like jelly. 'I can't do it, Luther.'

'Sure you can. You just put your head down, Dave, and run. Run l-like the w-wind.'

'Besides,' Harold said laconically, 'there are thousands of blokes behind us who will run over you if you don't.'

It was true. Dave had seen hundreds of soldiers travelling towards Ypres. The surrounding area was awash with Allied troops as they were disgorged from trains, trucks, wagons and requisitioned village buses, while others arrived on foot en route to the front-line.

They watched as the third ammunition wagon traversed the road. Halfway along the long hessian wall, a shell made a direct hit. The wagon was speared up and onto its end by the force of the impact. There was no movement from man or animals once the dust settled.

Dave found himself caught up by the forward movement of the men. Soon they were running along the road, heads down, as shells buzzed around them. Spurts of dirt signalled how close they were to death. He tried to keep up with Luther and Thaddeus but instead found himself stationed between Harold and Thorny. Snatches of this new environment sped by; hessian, wrecked wagons, artillery shells, the bloated carcasses of horses and dead soldiers lined the road. A few fortunate men had their last resting place marked by a cross or an upturned rifle stuck into the ground, sometimes with a steel helmet on top.

By late morning they had left the plank road, which veered to the north-west, and were in a newly dug trench. The men were in good spirits. They had cheated death again and the relief showed itself in ribald jokes as they drank water and talked of the engineers and soldiers who had gone before them to cart timber, construct roads and dig trenches. Dave was beyond such idle banter and he noted that Harold too had distanced himself from everyone save Thorny.

'I don't like it,' Harold said. 'There are fortified farms out there with blockhouses, concrete pillboxes for machine gunners, underground bunkers and barbed wire.'

'We'll be right, mate,' Thorny placated. 'Besides, you promised me that you'd see me through this bunfight safe and sound, so how about I return the favour?' The two friends shook hands.

Dave squirrelled back against the trench wall and, tugging off his helmet, turned his skin to the sun. The Allies had been fighting around Ypres since 1915 and they still hadn't made much of a dent. This was it, he reckoned. Having survived Hellfire Corner, he doubted his luck could hold out forever. They had got in, but would they get out again? Putting pen to paper, he began to write.

I've done my best but I think my time is nearly up. Many fine men – mates – have gone before me, so I know that should I not make it home I will be in fine company. I wonder now if I should have accepted Captain Egan's commission and become a war artist. At least then I would have paid tribute to the gallantry I have been witness to. But then who but those who have seen what we have seen would understand the horrors we have witnessed? If I do make it home to Australia, I will never speak of the war again. No one should know of the hell we have seen.

It's strange, but I see death as a smudge on the horizon, like a storm hanging out to the west of Sunset Ridge. The smudge grows in size daily like a new world waiting to be discovered yet it remains at bay, waiting, marking time. I sense its presence but I find myself lost in the immensity of an event beyond comprehension. At this very moment I know that none of us sitting in this trench will ever be as strong and as fit and as brave as we are now, and we will never have this moment again. Our mortality makes us fearless yet it takes us to our death.

Dave scanned the words, signed his name and dated it. Now his thoughts were on paper he needed to be rid of them, but he also wanted to share them, to know that one person on earth knew his mind beyond the narrow trench he inhabited. It was not the type of letter a son sent to his mother. From his sketchpad he tore out the drawing of the war dog with the Frenchman's tags around his neck and, folding it carefully, included it with the letter. Then he addressed it to Corally Shaw.

Crawling on his belly, Dave scrambled like a dung beetle beneath a clouded moon. The last he had seen of Luther and Thaddeus was when they had attacked a German machine gunner in his pillbox minutes earlier. The two brothers had rushed forward under cover from Harold's Lewis gun, Luther managing to drop a number of grenades through the observation slit in the brick fortification. Dave manoeuvred his way over and between the dying, the dead and the decomposed. A German flare went up illuminating the wrecked landscape and he tumbled into the partially blown-up pillbox. Heart pounding, he listened for others who may also have sought refuge there, carefully slipping his knife free of its scabbard. He could hear ragged breathing. The blade of the knife glinted as the moon escaped the clouds overhead.

'He's dead.'

The muffled Australian voice startled him. 'Harold? Is that you?' He pulled away a sandbag. Harold squatted in the far corner, Thorny in his arms. Two dead Germans, one with a familiar slice to the neck, confirmed Luther's part in the action.

'Holy hell, Harold, I thought you were Fritz. Are you wounded?'

'My leg's gone to sleep.'

Dave peered over the shattered wall of the pillbox. 'We'll have to make a run for it. Come on, Harold.'

'I can't leave Thorny,' he replied.

'He's dead, isn't he?' Dave said gruffly. There was no time to waste.

'Of course he's dead. We're all dead.'

'Not yet we're not. Come on,' Dave implored.

'You just don't get it, cobber. It's just a matter of time. We're the decoy. Wipe out those bloody Australians, the Pommies are saying, make use of them first. We're just cannon fodder. Cannon fodder, and they're calling us murderers back home.' He held up a pistol, his hand shaking. Dave realised Harold's nerves had got the better of him.

'I've got this luger. I took it off Fritz, and I'll use it too, I will. I'll shoot you first and then Thaddeus and Luther and I'll do myself last. It'll save us all from being blown apart, put us back in charge of our own lives. Don't worry, I'm a good shot. You know I'm a good shot. That's why I'm a gunner and I've killed some men, haven't I?'

'Yes, Harold.' Dave felt his own guts churn as he slowly reached out his hand and gently placed it on the pistol and lowered it. 'You have.'

'It's the only way, Dave.' He hugged Thorny. 'He cried, you know. He said he was scared of dying. Can you imagine?' He smoothed the thumb thickness of Thorny's eyebrows with a patient finger. 'I told him he wouldn't be alone for long, that we'd be with him soon enough, and he smiled, he did. He smiled.'

Dave peered over the wall again. The artillery was still raging; whizz-bangs were skyrocketing overhead. Soldiers were rushing past them, *their* soldiers. He slid back beside Harold. 'Our boys are retreating. Like I said, mate, we'll have to make a run for it.'

Harold grabbed the front of Dave's tunic. 'You're a good shot. I've seen you. You could have been a sniper.'

Dave loosened Harold's grip. 'Can we talk about this back in the trench?'

'I want you to kill him. I want you to kill the German that did this to Thorny.'

'Harold, you'll never recognise him.'

'Sure I will. He was young and weedy looking with an egg-shaped skull. I would have got him only that he came from behind after Luther took this position and Thorny flung himself between him and me. He died instead of me and *I promised him that he wouldn't die.* You've gotta do it, Dave. I can't hold a pistol anymore. My nerves are shot. I can barely manage the Lewis gun.'

'Sure,' Dave agreed, 'I'll do it. Now let's get out of here.'

'I'm staying for just a bit longer.' Harold glanced briefly at Thorny before turning glazed eyes on Dave. 'Now piss off back to the trenches.' Very slowly he raised the Luger and pointed it at Dave's chest.

'Okay,' Dave agreed. 'Give me a minute.' As Harold tucked the pistol into his tunic, David punched him in the face, once, twice. 'Jeez.' He shook his hand in pain, Harold was out cold. He reefed Thorny's identification discs from around his neck and checked his pockets. There was a picture of a young woman, a baby tucked under each arm, and the sketch Dave had completed of him while they were on furlough. For a second he contemplated the drawing, then he pocketed the few possessions and tried to lift Harold's arm across his shoulder.

'Holy frost, not Harold?' Luther jumped down into the pillbox. His tunic and hands were covered in blood.

'He's only knocked out, but Thorny's gone.'

Thaddeus dived in beside them as machine-gun fire peppered the entrance. 'N-not the best place for a chinwag, fellas.' Assessing the situation, he heaved Thorny over his shoulder. Luther draped Harold across Dave's back and lifted the Lewis gun. 'Make a run for it. I'll c-cover you.'

Thaddeus hesitated.

'Don't pull rank on me now, brother.'

Luther opened up the Lewis gun on the enemy as his brothers scrambled over the shattered wall. Supporting fire came from his left and right flanks. He backed up carefully, lobbed a grenade for good measure, and then ran like a rabbit, zigzagging across the open field as he followed his brothers back to the trench.

'How is he?' Thaddeus squatted beside Luther and Dave. They were in an elbow of the trench with a makeshift piece of canvas slung overhead and empty munitions crates as seats. The rain bowed the canvas above them and Luther stuck a rifle butt against the sagging material, forcing the water to cascade over the sides.

'He's got a busted nose,' Luther said suspiciously. 'He's in the d-dug-out.'

Thaddeus took over from Dave, who had been using a hand-pump for the last hour. Their efforts made little dent in the continually accumulating water. 'Do you want to share anything with us, Dave?' Thaddeus asked. 'You don't really expect us to believe the story you told Captain Egan.'

'I had to punch him to save him. I couldn't leave him there.'

Thaddeus rubbed the stubble on his chin. 'Well, we all have our moments.'

'What if he remembers what happened?' Dave asked.

Luther drank down a ration of rum and wiped cracked lips. 'Duck,' he grinned.

Within an hour the rain stopped. Captain Egan appeared and delegated sentries to stand watch while work parties were formed to check damage and continue trying to hand-pump the water lying at the bottom of the trench. Harold reappeared with a swollen nose. He stood next to Dave who readied himself in case Harold decided to punch him in retaliation. Surprisingly, it seemed Harold had no memory of the night before, except for Thorny's death. Spreading his feet, Dave leaned into the sandbags cradling the small sniper hole, the butt of the rifle pushed squarely into his shoulder. The rifle sight scanned twisted barbed wire, the remains of a dray, a dislodged sandbag and the corpse of a German. Sweat dripped down his forehead, blurring his sight.

'That's him.' Harold stood nearby, his eyesight fixed on the mirrors attached to the end of a rod that served as a homemade periscope. 'See there,' he snorted through his bloody nose. 'Directly above stinking Fritz and to the right of that dislodged sandbag. Pale and weedy looking and egg-shaped, that's the one that killed Thorny.'

Dave directed the rifle sight on the young man's chest and followed the pale German's hands as they lit the stub of a cigarette. In the half-light he waited for the soldier to take a few puffs, to linger over the cloying smell of the tobacco, to draw some solace from the wafting smoke.

'Kill him, Dave.'

'I can't do it, Harold. Everyone's resting, for God's sake, them and us.'

'Look at me.' Harold's right hand was shaking so badly a cup of water would have been spilt in seconds. 'I can't, so you have to. Have you forgotten about what they are doing to our mates? If his sight was aimed squarely at your chest he wouldn't hesitate. Shoot him.'

The German was looking in their direction. He couldn't have been more than sixteen or seventeen. Dave felt he was looking at himself.

'Do it,' Harold urged.

A single shot echoed across the wasteland. The German soldier was flung back against the sandbags. The boy hung momentarily in a void of muted grey, his arms outstretched, head arched backwards. The unblemished whiteness of the enemy's throat slowly slid from view. Dave lowered the rifle.

'What the hell is going on?' Captain Egan's spittle covered his skin. 'Jesus, man, we've been fighting for days and the first sign of reprieve you fire off a stray round.'

An angry voice called out across no-man's land from the enemy trench. No translation was necessary.

'We'll be lucky if we don't get a whizz-bang on us in retaliation.' Captain Egan cupped his hands and called out the German word for sorry. 'Thaddeus, take your brother's place. Dave, you're on pre-dawn watch.'

Harold turned to the captain, his nose bulbous and bloody. 'He killed Thorny.'

'Jesus,' Captain Egan repeated before striding off.

Dave couldn't stop staring at the enemy trench. He could hear the Germanic mutterings of complaint as a shaft of light shone down from dark blue clouds. In that moment craters rose up, spewing forth decomposed and dismembered bodies, barbed wire scrambled after crawling featureless soldiers and the German trench rushed towards him with a violent lurch. Dave backed away.

'Are you all right, Dave?' Thaddeus asked, moving to the trench wall.

'Sure, I'm fine,' Dave replied, except he knew he wasn't. He'd had nightmares before, but never hallucinations.

'Well, you kept Harold happy,' Luther said, prodding at the contents of a can of bully beef with a knife. 'And I'm glad you got him.'

Dave sat on an upturned crate next to Harold, who had removed his boots and was massaging his toes.

'The fighting I can handle, but it's when we stop.' Luther chewed hungrily. 'I can't bear the waiting, the monotony of it all. I need things to keep happening so I don't think too much.'

'Did you hear that?' Thaddeus said in wonder. 'You just said a whole sentence, Luther, without stuttering.' He lifted his rifle and peered over the top of the trench.

Luther swallowed a mouthful of meat. 'Did I?'

'Yep. You've hardly been stuttering at all, and now,' Thaddeus grinned, 'you're cured.'

Harold examined the sole of his foot. 'Even my planter's wart has gone. Must have other things to worry about, eh?'

Luther jabbed at the meat in the tin. 'Well, something good had to come outta this blasted war.'

'Thorny had a premonition,' Harold said quietly. 'He told me he was going to get knocked and I ignored him. A man shouldn't ignore it when a mate needs to talk about it. You remember that, Dave. Anyway, you did a good thing, not that we'll know if that bastard you knocked was the culprit. But I feel better, don't you, Luther?'

'The only good Fritz is a dead Fritz.' Luther's knife stabbed the air.

'You said he killed Thorny!' Dave complained. 'You said you saw him up close, you said . . . Shit, we're not here to kill anyone that takes your fancy.'

Dave felt his eyes moisten and he bit his lip until the pain cleared his head. He wasn't like the others. He couldn't hate people just because they were Germans. Each side was following orders in a war orchestrated by generals who never came anywhere near the front-line. Dave went into battle because he was told to, like the young men on the other side of the barbed wire. He had nothing against the poor bloody Germans and he figured it was possible that Fritz felt the same. Where Dave stood there was no hate in war, only duty. 'Steady on, Dave. Now there's one less of the bastards to kill us,' Luther argued.

Unscrewing his canteen, Dave took a sip of water. He could sense the others waiting for him to agree, to say something that would make them all equal again, comfortable. 'No matter how we try to convince ourselves of the righteousness of our actions,' Dave began, 'causing a man's death is no easy thing; at least it isn't for me.'

'Holy Frost, Dave,' Luther said as he scraped the inside of the tin, 'you'll have me thinking I'm back in the schoolroom with Miss Waites if you keep this up.'

Overhead, dark twirling clouds mingled with a creamy whiteness. Dave closed his eyes and imagined the blue-green swirl of the river that ran through the heart of Sunset Ridge. He was riding towards the life force of the property, his mount eager for a gallop in the fresh morning air. There was a rise coming in the waterway, glistening bubbles on the surface signifying a coming flood. His hands gripped the reins and the horse flew over the whorls and curls within the bark of the fallen timber they jumped. Then a figure appeared through the trees. It was Corally Shaw.

'You better get some sleep, Dave.' Picking up his rifle, Thaddeus leaned against the sandbags. 'We don't want you nodding off before dawn.'

Dawn. Never again would Dave conjure up the wispy pink tendrils that stroked the sky without shuddering at what might appear out of the mist of no-man's land. Shoving his fingers into his pockets, he touched the last letter received from Corally. In it she spoke of life after the war. He squeezed the well-read letter. 'You were imagining home, weren't you?' Luther asked. 'I could tell. Tell us what you saw, Dave, and then draw it for us.'

'Yeah, go on, Dave. Draw us a picture of home,' Harold enthused.

Dave leaned back against the trench wall, pulling his hat low over his face. Although he tried, the image of Sunset Ridge melted away to be replaced by the many faces of the soldiers sketched since arriving in France. Their features were indistinct and yet they peopled his mind like a small town. Each portrait was attached to a body, a life connected to loved ones and friends and neigh-bours, and most of them were either dead or wounded. At night, when Dave closed his eyes, the drawings of the lost blew across the battlefield. The images papered a world on fire and just as quickly disintegrated.

≪ Chapter 37 ≫

Catherine passed the sketch of the dog to Corally. It was truly a remarkable drawing. No one could doubt the artist's talent. The animal's eyes appeared to follow Catherine about the room as if the dog could see inside her very soul. He was a large rangy-looking beast, with massive shoulders and a powerful jaw. Hardly well bred, he remained nonetheless an intriguing subject, particularly as Dave's depiction placed the animal in a trench with a soldier's identity discs around its neck. Catherine deciphered the name Antoine Chessy and assumed it was a friend, although the image disturbed her. Identity discs were never to leave a soldier's person, until death. Even then one was meant to remain with the body for identification.

'Well, what do ye think of it?' Catherine said to Corally. She was of a mind to ask the girl if she could keep the sketch.

The younger woman brushed a hand across the surface of the drawing. Corally sat stiffly erect in a sage skirt and cream blouse, both of which were spotless. Her long blonde hair was pinned back becomingly and her shoes had been patched and cleaned. Some weeks ago the girl had stopped dressing like a tomboy and was now a familiar sight walking the main street with one of Catherine's baskets draped over her arm as if she were like any other young woman in the district. Corally was also a regular Sunday worshipper at the Presbyterian Church, her choice of faith apparently decided by an aversion to confession.

'It's a dog,' Corally replied dispassionately. 'What does the letter mean?' Placing the sketch on Catherine's bed, she held the teacup to her lips, the saucer poised delicately in her other hand. 'Surely he can't be saying that death is a smudge in the sky.'

Catherine noticed the studied movements. Corally now possessed all the attributes of an educated young woman, and with this new knowledge had blossomed a shrewd mind and a propensity for astute observation. On more than one occasion Catherine's own gestures and opinions were mimicked by a girl who only a scant nine months ago could barely read or write.

'He is scared, Corally, and he needed to put his feelings down on paper.' Locating the sentence Corally referred to, Catherine read the section aloud for the second time.

'It's strange, but I see death as a smudge on the horizon, like a storm hanging out to the west of Sunset Ridge. The smudge grows in size daily like a new world waiting to be discovered yet it remains at bay, waiting, marking time. The words that he uses are really quite marvellous and yet it is so poignant the way he talks of mortality.'

Corally's brow creased. 'Thaddeus, Luther and Harold talk about other things. The farmhouse where they stayed, what the countryside is like. Really, their lives are very interesting. Don't you think it's strange? Dave didn't even start the letter with "Dear Corally". It's just a piece of paper signed and dated.'

Corally was not the regular visitor of old. Quite often she collected her mail from the post office on the day of delivery so that if Mrs Dempsey were present and assisting with the sorting

Catherine was not always aware of who wrote to her. Today, however, the young woman was at a loss as to the meaning of Dave's emotive lines; her appearance at the boarding house at eight in the morning was evidence of this. Catherine, although pleased to be of assistance, knew that Corally took some pleasure in speaking of the content of those letters not shared.

'He is young and far from home and he has the sensibilities of an artist.' Catherine could not imagine the girl before her ever appealing to David. Aesthetics were one thing, but there was more to a character than handsome looks and a basic education. Corally lacked understanding and life experience, something that Catherine imagined all the young men fighting abroad now had too much of.

'Well, apart from all that I think you're right. It sounds to me like he's just scared.' Corally sat the cup and saucer on the table. 'Anyway, it's not even a real letter, it could have been written to anyone.'

'Unlike the letters from Thaddeus and Luther?' Catherine purposely let the names linger in the cramped room. 'It's interesting that they still write to ye as if there was some form of shared attachment.'

Corally ran a finger along the rim of the teacup. 'They must be very lonely.'

Catherine felt an urge to slap the girl. 'I think we both know why they still write as if they were your beaus.'

'Really?' Corally held her gaze.

'Ye have been a quick learner, Corally. I hear that ye have applied for a position at the general store.'

'You're a good teacher.'

'Ye even style your hair in a similar manner to mine now.'

Corally narrowed her eyes. 'And once I have employment I shall eventually be moving into one of the rooms here in the boarding house. Does that bother you?'

'Should it? What will ye do if, as we all hope, the three Harrow boys and Harold Lawrence return home when the war finally ends?'

Gathering up the letters and the sketch, Corally sat the correspondence in her basket. 'I guess I will have to choose.'

'I didn't realise ye were quite so self-centred, Corally. If I had, I may not have chosen to help ye.'

The younger woman stiffened. 'And I think you're angry because you were their governess and all three boys write to me and not you.' She gave a little sniff and, rising to leave, adjusted the basket over her arm. 'You haven't spoken of your Rodger for some time now. Did you have a falling out? Perhaps he tired of you telling him what to do?'

Catherine blanched. She may have given Corally an education and unwittingly become the girl's role model in terms of social mores and dress, however it appeared that her tutelage did not extend to common decency. The worst of it was that the girl was right to some extent regarding Rodger. Although she had decided to cease sharing confidences with Corally, Catherine had not spoken of him recently because there was nothing to tell, at least not until a few days ago. Rodger's letters had stopped appearing over a month ago, and a few days prior she had received a letter from his platoon captain. The news was less than welcome. In fact, Catherine felt ill at the thought of the contents.

'I am grateful for your help, Miss Waites, however I am quite able to read and write now, so I won't be calling on you again. Besides,' Corally said a little more gently, 'you have your fiancé to worry about, so you needn't be concerning yourself with me.'

'Hearts are difficult things to mend, Corally, remember that,' Catherine advised. The door clicked shut. 'Please remember that.' The words swirled around the empty room.

Slumping back in the armchair, Catherine looked across at the bare timber wall. It was true. She was disappointed that the Harrow boys had not thought to write to her, especially David.

It was clear that she had inadvertently upset him. Why else would he have abandoned his sketches outside her room the night he ran away? And now her good intent regarding Corally had gone awry and three young men were being misled. It was too much, especially on top of the recent mail.

Her beloved Rodger was missing. Not missing in action, dead or wounded, but missing from duty; missing from the training camp on Salisbury Plain in England. That was why there had been no letters recently, which Catherine had stupidly imagined was due to Rodger having scant time to write because he was surely in the thick of battle. His captain wrote that Rodger had been absent without leave for a number of weeks, having not returned from a week's furlough in London. His whereabouts were yet to be determined. Quite simply, Catherine had been thwarted, for her fiancé had run away, not just from the army but from her.

It had been two days since the arrival of the captain's letter and Catherine's initial shock and sadness were slowly dissipating to be replaced by raw anger and embarrassment. Nothing was as it had once seemed, and as her anger festered and grew, her thoughts centred on the one thing she could put right.

Corally Shaw had manipulated her good intent so that Catherine was now party to a deceitful charade. Three young men, perhaps four if David had also been coerced into Corally's sticky web, believed they were the sweetheart of a young woman. Had Catherine not cautioned Corally that the boys were being misled? Had she not helped Corally construct the appropriate letters and, having witnessed the young girl write them, assumed that they had been mailed? Clearly Corally had written very different letters; letters that would be carried in uniforms in the heat of battle, letters that offered comfort and the possibility of a life beyond the war, letters that, God willing, the boys would carry home. Catherine could not be party to such pretence, not when sibling relationships could be harmed and friendships ruined by a young girl who clearly didn't know her place in society.

Selecting a sheet of writing paper, she pressed the nib of the pen against the creamy paper and began her letter to Harold Lawrence. Catherine would tell Harold who Corally really loved. Truth was the only acceptable path to take.

≪ Chapter 38 ≫

Sheila had kindly left her two paintings at Sunset Ridge for a few days so they could be photographed and studied. They were currently propped against the wall in the lounge room and it was here that George and Madeleine sat staring at the works. Natural light streamed in through the window, causing the gilt frames to shimmer.

'I'm glad you didn't leave yesterday, Maddy.' George took a sip of coffee.

They shared the plate of biscuits and cheese that Rachael had made for morning tea. With the property's financial problems now aired, her sister-in-law was gradually coming to terms with George's ultimatum, although more than once she had wondered aloud how she would ever manage to tend the garden *and* clean the house.

'Me too, George. Whoever would have thought these beauties would turn up?'

George's attention flicked from the paintings to the history book he was leafing through. Occasionally he would read aloud from the pages sharing details of the Allied battles during the First World War, the commanding officers and the astounding casualties.

'You know, it says here that *In Memoriam* notices first appeared in Australian newspapers during the Great War to try to help families and the nation come to terms with the terrible loss of life.'

Madeleine reached for a second cheese-and-biscuit. 'I can't imagine living through that time, can you?'

'No.' Closing the book, George pointed at the painting of their grandfather. 'Why did he paint himself in that great bloody coat? It totally dwarfs him and he looks almost haunted.'

'That's probably how he felt: engulfed by what he'd witnessed abroad and an alien in his old life once he returned home. The fact that there is a window between him and his governess suggests how isolated and lost he must have felt. The letter in Miss Waites's lap also interests me. Sheila believed she was engaged to be married at one stage. I wonder if her fiancé died in the war.'

'Possible,' George agreed, wiping crumbs from his mouth. 'And the torn bit? Any idea who the woman might be?'

Madeleine tilted her head to one side. 'Sheila mentioned that the governess also taught Corally Shaw. It may have been her.'

'So, why rip out her image?'

'Perhaps Catherine and Corally had a falling out,' Madeleine suggested.

'Over our grandfather?'

Madeleine turned to her brother. 'I hadn't thought of that. Do you think Corally and Grandfather had a thing for each other and Miss Waites didn't approve?'

George laughed. 'Now, that's something we'll never know. So, what happens now? Are you still driving to Brisbane in the morning?'

'Yes. I promised Jude I'd stay with her for a day or so and go through everything we've discovered in detail. Then I'll fly back to Sydney, write up all my notes properly and start approaching other galleries.'

'That's the spirit, sis.'

'What about you?' Madeleine asked.

'Actually, I'm not so stressed out now I've told Rachael what's going on.'

'You should have told her sooner,' Madeleine counselled. 'She *is* your wife.'

'I know. It's just that she has certain expectations.'

Madeleine nodded. 'Don't we all? The problem is that reality has a tendency to get in the way sometimes.'

They both looked at their grandfather's paintings.

'These are damn good, aren't they?' George declared.

'Yes,' Madeleine agreed, 'they are.'

Rachael appeared in the doorway, a washing basket in her arms. 'Maddy, Sonia's here.'

'Again?' George stood and helped Madeleine up from the floor. 'Does she have any more paintings with her?'

Rachael shook her head. 'I don't think so. She wants to take Maddy into Banyan.' She turned to Madeleine. 'Apparently there is someone in town Sonia wants to introduce you to. She seems a bit nervous.'

'Nervous?' George repeated. 'That would be a first.'

'Well, she's waiting outside,' Rachael replied.

'You better go,' George encouraged. 'You wouldn't know what the old girl's got up her sleeve.'

'You're right,' Madeleine agreed.

Sonia stopped the sedan outside a weatherboard house on the outskirts of Banyan. The square building was bordered by a gauzed-in veranda, with a partially dead lawn comprising the remainder of the half-acre block. A driveway led to an empty garage at the rear of the garden, while two potted geraniums added colour to the cracked cement steps at the front door. The house, although modest, was freshly painted and it enjoyed a pleasant aspect with the western side backing onto a ridge of dense trees. Madeleine, although impatient for the housekeeper to reveal their destination, was aware of the older woman's discomfort. The sedan's engine remained running and Sonia's grip on the steering wheel was turning her knotty knuckles white.

Madeleine sat quietly. The strange road trip appeared to have something to do with their conversation in her bedroom yesterday prior to Sheila Marchant's appearance. The housekeeper had referred to it twice during the drive into Banyan, as if Madeleine's passionate reasoning for wanting to hold a retrospective was the motivation for this particular journey.

Finally Sonia turned the key off in the ignition and wound down the driver's-side window. Clearly they were not going anywhere yet, so Madeleine did the same. The house was situated at the end of a side road and, although the distant roofs of village houses were visible, it was an isolated spot. Saltbush and clumpy burr stretched out across the paddock opposite the house while thick scrub encroached along the narrow road leading from the village. There was little breeze and the sedan soon warmed under the late-morning sun. Perspiration trickled down Madeleine's spine and she began to wonder if she was an unknowing accessory to a surveillance operation.

'Sonia, I –'

'You'll know soon enough. First, we must wait.'

Madeleine settled back in the burgundy upholstery, not altogether unhappy to be sitting in the hot car. It gave her time to process George's financial woes, which appeared to have been made worse by a lack of communication within his marriage. It was as if the past were playing out all over again with the property's salvation tied to her grandfather's legacy. This time, however, there wasn't a stack of masterpieces that could be sold. Commonsense and careful planning were the answers to the property's viability.

Five minutes later a utility drove down the lonely road and parked beside them. The man who emerged was instantly recognisable: Ross Evans. Madeleine said hello and received a nod in response; Sonia's presence was barely acknowledged before they were led down the dirt driveway to the rear of the house.

'Sue-Ellen will be back soon. In the meantime, can I ask you not to get Mum too upset?'

Sonia gave an offhand acknowledgement as the man swung the veranda door open and stepped inside, and then once again they were left waiting. There was little shade behind the house. A square cement slab was home to a foldable camping chair while a few feet away an empty hills hoist tilted alarmingly to the left in an otherwise bare backyard.

Madeleine slapped at the black flies that were keen to investigate her face and arms. 'Are you going to tell me why we're here?'

'Once we're inside you'll understand more.' The older woman walked down to the rear fence. Constructed of sheets of corrugated iron hammered onto wooden posts, it stood ten feet high, blocking any view. 'We used to come here as kids. Me and my cousins would sneak out of the house at night and throw stones at the windows. Whoever broke one got extra points.'

'Nice,' Madeleine said under her breath.

'I heard that.' Sonia turned towards her. 'There's one thing you should know about the bush, Madeleine, about small villages, especially out here where it's remote and folks only have each other to rely on: people always remember the past, and those who are wronged are the last to forget.'

The back door creaked open. 'She'll see you now, but I can't make any promises,' Ross Evans cautioned. 'Her memory is near gone. She should be in a home but, well, who can afford it?' He held the battered screen door open for them.

'Thank you,' Madeleine said softly.

Sonia muttered a comment about how the mighty had fallen.

Ross flicked a suspicious look at Sonia before nodding in response to Madeleine. 'As I said, Sue-Ellen will be home soon.' The man lingered on the cement slab. 'You'll do right by her?'

Sonia's lips were starting to curl inwards they were pressed together so hard. Bustling past Ross, she beckoned Madeleine to follow. 'I'm only doing this because of your grandfather,' the housekeeper whispered as they entered a dimly lit kitchen.

Timber shelving held old-fashioned screw-top jars and round biscuit tins, while a grimy window above the sink looked out onto a side veranda and the ridge of trees. The room was constructed of simple unlined timber boards with every available piece of wall space plastered with pictures. There were posters of saints and images of the Virgin Mary and Jesus as well as photographs of cathedrals and stained-glass windows. Strewn amid this obsessive devotion were numerous crosses and religious icons, while the linoleum floor and part of the kitchen table were covered in piles of old magazines and books. There was a fridge and gas stove along one wall, and an ancient creamy-yellow Aga was another spot for a collection of records.

'Look at this stuff.' Madeleine blew dust from a 1920s *Bulletin* magazine.

'Don't touch that.'

The croaky voice belonged to an old woman slumped in a cane chair in the corner of the kitchen. Madeleine was startled and embarrassed not to have noticed the woman among the clutter, and could only stare at the tiny birdlike creature. The woman's white hair was gathered into a wispy bun atop her head and she was dressed in a cream blouse and long dark skirt. Her feet were propped up on a low stool and within her reach a hospital trolley held water, bananas and a portable radio. Madeleine could not see the woman's face; her chin rested on a bony chest that rose up and down as if the next breath would be her last.

Clearing magazines and books from two plastic garden chairs, Sonia gestured for Madeleine to sit. The room was stiflingly hot, and the stink emanating from under the table suggested that a bull mouse had taken up residence and was making the most of the messy conditions. Sonia remained silent, her gaze drifting across the kitchen. It was as if she were weighing up the past in a room that was lost in it.

'It's been a long time,' Sonia said finally, loudly, leaning forward.

The woman didn't acknowledge either of her visitors.

'I've brought someone to visit.' The housekeeper paused and looked at Madeleine as if deciding whether she should proceed. 'It's Madeleine, David's granddaughter.'

The old woman lifted a hand to clutch a tissue to her chest.

Madeleine held her breath for a moment. 'Did you know my grandfather?' she asked.

The silence stretched through the suffocating room. Madeleine, thinking that either the woman had not heard or she had fallen asleep, turned to Sonia, who merely lifted a finger for patience. Very slowly the old woman raised her chin. Creased by soft lines, the aged face retained evidence of high cheekbones, a wide forehead and the symmetrical features of a great beauty. Yet it was the woman's eyes that struck Madeleine. Although the irises were filmy and ringed in grey, they were the most extraordinary coloured eyes she had ever seen.

'So, you're David's girl.'

'Granddaughter,' Madeleine corrected.

'And you brought her,' she said to Sonia. 'I'm astounded that you would put a foot inside my house.'

Sonia shrugged. 'So am I.'

The older woman gave a tired laugh. 'As visitors are a novelty, I had an excuse when it came to agreeing to your visit. What's yours?'

Sonia shifted her chair closer. 'Madeleine wants to hold an

exhibition of her grandfather's work. She's looking for anything that he drew or painted before the landscapes. Do you have anything?'

'Why would I?'

'I don't know. I'm just asking. Frankly, I didn't know who else to speak to.'

'Got a friendship going between the two of you, have you? Well, isn't that nice? Everyone needs friends.' The old woman peered at Madeleine. 'You look a little like your grandfather. The same nose, similar eyes. I suppose you have his Good Samaritan tendencies as well.'

'You make that sound as if it's a bad thing,' Madeleine answered.

'Depends,' the woman replied.

Sonia sighed impatiently. 'You don't owe David Harrow anything, I know that – what with your boy keeping an eye out over at Sunset Ridge all these years.'

The old woman laughed. 'Ross? I don't know what he's told you lot, but he didn't start poking around there on account of anything he thinks David Harrow did for me. No, sir,' she said, pointing at Madeleine. 'My boy saw your mother in Banyan in the 1940s, and he was smitten. Thought she was the bee's knees. He used to go out to Sunset Ridge and nose around in the hopes of running into her. He never did. Later she went away to a fancy school and when she did come back she was married.' She sniffed. 'She could have done a lot better for herself, your mother,' she said to Madeleine. 'Anyway, Ross has always been a bit of a loner.'

Madeleine opened her mouth to respond, but Sonia quickly interjected.

'Do you have any works belonging to David Harrow? Can you help us?'

'Help a Jackson?' The older woman sounded amused. 'Why should I? Your family blamed me for what happened all those years ago and you *kept* blaming me. And I did nothing.'

Sonia nodded. 'That's right, you did nothing. And you should have done *something*. You were her best friend.'

'Well, isn't it just like a Jackson to point the bone at the nearest target? If you have complaints, Sonia, bring them up with Cummins's descendants instead of picking on an old woman,' she puffed.

'The difference is,' Sonia snapped, 'you should have known better.'

'And your family should have stopped acting the martyrs decades ago. You never had any proof against Cummins, all you had was a second-hand story passed down from Julie Jackson, but you were all so damn furious you took your anger out on me.'

'And you spent the next few decades making derogatory remarks about my family to whoever would listen.'

The old woman sighed. 'No offence, Madeleine, but I can't see the point of dredging up the past, unlike some people.'

Considering the old woman's appearance and age, Madeleine was rather taken aback by her energy and clear-mindedness.

'Yes or no,' Sonia said brusquely. 'Do you have anything that could be of use to Madeleine?'

The old woman blew out a puff of air. 'Why should I help?'

'Because in the end this is for David Harrow, the artist.'

The older woman coughed. 'He *was* good with those drawings of his.'

Sonia leaned back in the plastic chair. 'So, you will help?'

Although the old woman turned her head slowly towards Madeleine, she spoke to Sonia. 'You better tell her, then. You better tell David's girl all of it.'

The room went silent. Madeleine heard Sonia swallow.

The old woman leaned forward. 'Tell it all and tell it true, and let it all be done.'

⫷ Chapter 39 ⫸

Flanders, Belgium
September 1917

The mail arrived and then a ration of rum was passed out to the men. Luther slid down over the trench parapet in the darkness, startling everyone.

'For God's sake, where have you been?' Dave asked. 'The sergeant has gone off his bean.'

Luther grinned, upending the contents of a sack onto a table made from two munitions crates. Two lugers, a loaf of bread and a round of cheese lay on the timber. 'Courtesy of Fritz who was having a nap when I stuck my head over. A little tap to the head with a length of timber and it was goodnight nurse.' He divvied up the food.

'You shouldn't go out there by yourself, Luther,' Dave cautioned.

Luther ignored him. 'Where's Harold?'

'Still lecturing his new number two, Piper,' Dave answered, his mouth now bulging with bread and cheese. 'Thaddeus is with Captain Egan.'

'Jeez, Piper will have a busted eardrum.' Luther broke off a piece of cheese, sniffing the pale round appreciatively. 'I see they've brought out the rum.' Chewing thoughtfully, he lowered his voice. 'You know, I've got this feeling, Dave, that by the morning –'

'Don't say it, don't you dare tell me that you've had a premonition.' Dave watched his brother light a cigarette, making sure he used the third lit match for luck. Each of them had a talisman or ritual prior to an engagement. For some it was the sight of a photograph of loved ones, for others a few lines penned from home. Many prayed, their belief weighed against reality. Others turned inwards, silently withdrawing but always remembering what they had left behind.

Luther gave a crooked smile as if placating a child. 'Draw us a picture, Dave, take me home.' The cigarette dangled from his fingers as he squatted in the dirt of the trench.

'I can't. I just can't do that anymore.' Overhead the sky gave off a phosphorescent glow.

Luther sighed. 'You shouldn't have left your drawings at the farmhouse. Fat lot of good they are there.'

Dave tried to recall Sunset Ridge, the scent of the pre-dawn dew, the whirl of red dust in the house paddock and the smell of rain after drought. Yet all this and more he had forgotten. All the pure memories distilled and mixed within his artist's palette were now distorted, cracked like an aged oil painting. He knew that beauty still existed, but it lay hidden in another world, an old world, out of reach. Dave wanted that world back, yearned for it, but in his heart he knew the impossibility of it ever being the same, even if he did return home.

'I think about Sunset Ridge, you know,' Luther began. 'Probably not the way you do, Dave, because to be honest I was never that attached to the place. At least not the way you are. I know you love it. I see that in your sketches.' He smiled his crooked smile. 'Not that I'll ever think sketching is a good thing for a man, but you see something in the property that I never have: beauty. That's a gift, Dave. The ability to create something out of nothing, well, to me that's a gift. As for Thaddeus, he's always known Sunset Ridge will be his one day, so he can't imagine any other life, and I understand that too. But it's different for me.' Luther paused as if trying to find the right words. 'I never really felt I belonged there, and it's not the homestead or the land itself or even Mother and Father that I think about when I say that. It's just that in comparison to what I can do here . . . Well, I'm *needed* here, I fit in here, my life means something here. I guess I'd like to be remembered for that, which is why I would like you to sketch me.'

Luther's request scared Dave more than his premonition. 'Don't ask me that.'

'I know what's coming, little brother.'

'You can't be sure. Plenty of men have premonitions and nothing comes of it.' Even as he spoke, the words sounded false. Surely Luther didn't really want to assign him this dreaded task. Surely he couldn't be that selfish. Dave thought of the numerous likenesses crafted over the previous months and the few soldiers he had drawn who still survived. 'Don't ask me, Luther, please.'

Luther sat on one of the upturned munitions crates, his slouch hat at a rakish angle. 'I don't think I've ever asked you for anything.'

'No,' Dave agreed, 'you haven't.'

'Then now isn't the time for arguments.'

Dave didn't move.

'Come on, Dave,' Luther coaxed, 'we both know you'll draw me eventually, and I sure would like it done before this next push. Besides, I need something to remind Corally of how handsome I am.' Cracking his knuckles, Luther settled back on the munitions crate.

Slowly something dwindled away inside Dave. It was as if the essence of him were being chipped at the edges by an unseen force. He needed to be strong, he needed to fulfil Luther's wish, but doing it would probably kill both of them, one physically, the other spiritually, if what Dave thought would happen did in fact come to pass.

'Dave?'

Luther was waiting.

An image came to him of Miss Waites leaning over his shoulder. How long ago was it that a childish crush led Dave to run away from home? Sometimes it felt like days, at others years. That night outside the governess quarters he had felt so desperately abandoned and it had taken months for his sadness to ease. With time he had come to understand why he had been so enamoured with his old governess. Catherine Waites had filled a void untouched by his family. She had made him whole, she had believed in him and in his craft. It didn't matter that his father had burned the art magazines she had ordered and he had never read, or that a few coloured plates in school learners and a basic introduction to drawing were the limits of his formal training. If Luther was made for war, then Dave was born to capture it.

'Dave, come on.'

Reaching for the sketchpad, Dave began to draw. The charcoal flowed effortlessly across the page, contouring a young face grown old by savage experience.

The artillery barrage began as the last few crinkle lines appeared at the edges of Luther's eyes. Dave wiped at the drops of moisture on the page as the great noise of the Allied bombardment began. Initialling the sketch, he inspected it critically, wanting it to be perfect. Luther's legs were outstretched, his uniform awry and in one hand a pannikin held his rum ration. Luther stared out from the page, defiant yet happy, and Dave knew he had succeeded in capturing the very essence of his brother. He saw in Luther's expression the reason for this relaxed state: the war had become Luther's life's work, he was damn good at it and, most staggeringly, he was unafraid.

On examining the work, Luther handed it back to Dave for safekeeping. 'Thanks, little brother.' They shook hands, and then embraced. 'If it happens, if my time comes, live a good life for both of us.' Luther freed himself from Dave's grasp and together they hunkered down by the trench wall.

Dave closed his mind to a world gone mad, swearing never to draw another person. Luther was the last. His brave brother was now immortalised and the honour of having rendered such a man in charcoal would remain with him for the rest of his life. From beneath the rim of his helmet Dave's restricted vision centred on the opposite trench wall as dirt ran down it. The vibrations stung both mind and body and his ears began to ring. In an hour or so Captain Egan would give the order to stand-to and then they would hop the bags and walk behind the creeping artillery barrage to some forward objective measured in men's lives.

As the earth crumbled above and around them, Harold and Thaddeus appeared. They sat close together talking, their faces becoming increasingly animated as the conversation progressed. Eventually Harold retrieved a letter from his uniform and, with great hesitancy, handed it to Thaddeus. Dave watched as his older brother read the contents and then re-read it. Very slowly Thaddeus folded the letter and handed it back to Harold, then both men turned their attention to Dave.

'What?' Dave yelled. The noise of the guns carried the word away. Thaddeus shook his head disbelievingly and slumped back against the trench wall. Harold merely continued to stare at Dave.

'What's going on?' Dave yelled in Luther's ear.

'Looks like a reconciliation,' he shouted back. 'About bloody time. Corally must have written and told Harold the engagement's off.' Luther punched Dave in the arm. 'You make sure she gets that sketch, won't you?' He didn't wait for a reply. 'If the worst happens, if I don't make it, those two will be arguing about Corally all over again. Although if Thaddeus makes lieutenant, Mother will make sure he marries a grazier's daughter.' Luther threw a clod of dirt at Harold and Thaddeus. 'Friends at last?' he yelled at them.

Thaddeus didn't answer. Harold moved on further down the line.

⊰◈⊱

'Fix bayonets.' Captain Egan blew the whistle.

The men clambered over the sandbags rimming the trench and ran out into no-man's land. The pre-dawn sky was alight with the glow of shells and flares as the guns crept steadily forwards, the men following in the wake of the barrage. Although the natural tendency was to group together, the men spread out as they advanced, their pace steady, reliable. Great chunks of earth were shot high up into the air, the dirt falling down upon them as they forged ahead. Dave smelled the tang of smoke and the acrid scent of cordite, and then the putrid stench of the dead assaulted his nostrils. He walked between his two brothers, comforted by their presence, knowing that Harold and Piper were close by. Ahead, splinters of light illuminated a land pitted with craters and depressions as the guns repeatedly decimated and then reformed an ancient countryside. A stretch of barbed wire came into view. At the partially destroyed fence the men crossed where they could, others snipped at the wire, making holes through which their companions could move. Dave shook free the entangling wire, as men fell around him and once on the other side increased his pace in time with his brothers.

Another whistle sounded and Luther charged ahead; more were drawn into his wake. The barrage had ceased and wild yells sounded along the line as the men swarmed forward towards the heavily shelled enemy trench. The remaining Germans were quick to regroup in the wake of the attack and they trained a machine gun on the Australians. Luther dived forward, avoiding the deadly spray of bullets, and lobbed a grenade into their midst. Then he was on his feet again, sprinting towards the machine-gun nest, a rifle in one hand, the tomahawk in the other. Within seconds he shot the gunner, threw his tomahawk, hitting a German in the neck, and then turned the German machine gun back on the enemy trench.

'Luther!' Thaddeus yelled at his brother.

Some of the enemy scattered like rats into the bowels of the earth or over the top of their trench; others turned and fired. Thaddeus and Luther jumped down into the enemy trench and fought back-to-back, stabbing and slashing with bayonet and tomahawk. Above them Harold had seized another machine-gun nest and was training the Lewis gun on attacking Germans approaching from the support trench. His body shook under the vibrations as machine and man became one, the barrel growing red-hot. A German bullet hit Piper between the eyes, another struck Harold's shoulder. He gritted against the pain and roared.

Firing off a bullet that found its mark in a German's stomach, Dave yelled to Luther, 'Harold needs help!' Behind him another German rushed the bend in the trench. Luther knocked Dave sideways and, wrestling the soldier, decapitated the assailant with a saw-bayonet. Then he was running again, shooting oncoming Germans with a captured pistol.

'Can we hold them?' Captain Egan shouted to Thaddeus.

Before he could reply, a bullet hit the captain in the chest. Thaddeus dropped to his side as a thin spray of dark arterial blood pumped out from a small hole in his uniform.

Luther grabbed Thaddeus on passing and together they reached the section of the trench that speared off to the place where Harold was surrounded.

'Cover me, Thaddeus.'

'You know I will, Lu.'

Thaddeus threw two grenades and followed up with rifle-fire as Luther flung himself out of the trench. He ran along the top of the trench wall, firing downwards, and then jumped into the machine-gun nest. Harold had been shot in the arm in three places, yet he jammed another cartridge in the Lewis gun and kept up a constant stream of fire.

'Good day for it,' Luther joked as he began to fire at the attacking Germans. Behind him Piper lay dead, as a weak dawn sky straddled the horizon. Harold's eyes were glassy. Thaddeus and Dave jumped into the hole and joined in the defence.

'Reinforcements?' Luther yelled across the noise of the gun-fire.

Thaddeus chanced a look over his shoulder. 'None yet.' There were skirmishes breaking out all along their section. 'Hell, we'll be out of ammo soon.'

The Lewis gun choked and jammed. 'Shit!' Harold bashed the burning-hot barrel with his hand. 'We're sitting ducks.'

The enemy were targeting them. Whizz-bangs were landing only feet away. The four of them hunkered down in the nest and divvied up the remaining ammo. There were all-too-few rounds left.

'That's my last round for the Lewis.' Harold grimaced as Thaddeus tried to bandage his shoulder and arm wounds.

'Well, we either make a stand or die in this shit-hole,' Luther told them.

Harold grabbed Dave's arm. 'Promise me you'll look after her, for all of us.'

They ducked as rifle-fire whizzed across the tops of the sandbags. 'What are you talking about?' Dave asked.

'Corally,' Thaddeus answered. 'She loves you.'

For a moment Luther appeared winded. He fell back against the wall, and then very slowly he gave the slightest of nods as if understanding had finally been granted.

Dave shook his head. 'That's not true, Luther, it isn't true.'

'I'll be damned,' Thaddeus said to Luther. 'You too, eh? She *has* been busy.' Thaddeus turned back to Dave. 'You've got letters from her too, I suppose?'

Dave didn't answer. He thought back to Madame Chessy's farmhouse when he had almost burned the first of Corally's letters.

Harold clutched at his bloodied arm. 'Miss Waites wrote to me. It seems she wanted to put things straight.'

Dave wanted to say that they were wrong, that he didn't want Corally Shaw at all – yet one look at their faces and he clamped his mouth shut. If he said anything negative they wouldn't understand. It would be akin to throwing away a precious gift.

For a few seconds the four men sat amid the carnage, then Luther peered across the top of the sandbags. 'Nothing like having half the German army in front of us,' he stated laconically. 'I reckon we should make a run for it and try and join up with our lot and wait for support. Are we ready?' Luther looked meaningfully at Thaddeus and Harold, gesturing towards Dave.

For a second Dave was lost in the incredible scene, the whorls of smoke above, the rush of artillery and the great noise of the fighting around them. A dawn sun was angling through the battle haze, falling like a shaft of hope on those below, and he closed his eyes and offered up a brief prayer.

Standing as one, the four of them jumped the lip of the nest. Dave tried to move apart from his brothers and Harold as they had been trained but instead found himself shoved into the centre of their tight group. And then they all ran into the light.

❧ Chapter 40 ❧

Banyan, south-west Queensland, Australia
September 1917

The bell on the general store's door tinkled as Corally walked happily outside onto the street. She was to commence her new role in the morning and Mr Whittaker was only too pleased to oblige the owner of the boarding house with a letter of employment ensuring that Miss Corally Shaw would earn sufficient funds for accommodation. Studying her reflection in the shop's window, she fixed her mind on a new straw hat and a jar of Stearn's Peroxide cream as soon as her monies allowed. Having noticed at church last Sunday that the daughters of the landed were pale-skinned and soft looking, while in comparison she was deeply tanned with hands belonging to a field worker, it was vital she make every attempt to blend in. Across the street the Jackson family caught her attention and waved. Corally pretended not to notice the enthusiastic greeting and made a point of studying the display in the butcher's window.

'Corally, hi.' A bubble of enthusiasm coated Julie's greeting.

The Jackson girl was reflected in the glass. To Corally, she looked such a child with her dark hair tied back over one shoulder, although she was appropriately attired in an ankle-length dress, the bodice of which had a row of good-quality pearl buttons.

'I didn't recognise you. You look all grown up,' Julie stated, her voice instantly cautious when Corally was slow to respond. Julie had lost weight, revealing enviable womanly curves.

'That's because I am.'

'You sound different too,' Julie replied, the initial expression of expectation on her face dwindling away.

'Really? How quaint of you to say so.' Corally moved the basket from one arm to the other as two older women, members of the Presbyterian Church congregation, passed. They nodded a greeting to Corally and then mumbled something about foreigners. Corally was instantly alarmed. She knew better than to mix with the Jacksons. 'Nice to see you, Julie. My regards to your family.'

Julie's mouth puckered. 'Please wait, we haven't talked for ages.'

'That's hardly my fault, Julie, what with you rarely coming to the village anymore and me getting on with my own life. Anyway, I'm a little busy right now. I am employed at the general store and I'll be moving into the boarding house tonight. So, as you can imagine, I have quite a few errands to run.'

Her old friend gaped. 'But last year you couldn't even –'

'Read or write?' Corally lifted an eyebrow. 'Well, I can now and I really must go.'

Julie held her back with a restraining hand. 'Mother was wondering, if we gave you some money if you would buy us a few things from the store. The thing is, no one will serve us and even though that's against the law the coppers won't do anything to help us.'

Corally stared at the girl's fingers until she was released. 'That's not really my problem.'

'Corally, please. Things have got so bad that no one will work on the property for us. Mr Cummins has suggested we move on and has offered to buy the farm, but at a very unfair price. You know he's been trying to buy it for ages and Father thinks he's the one who has been causing trouble for us here in town.'

There was a kerfuffle outside the ironmonger's shop, and a small crowd was gathering. Corally eyed the spectacle greedily. 'Well, maybe you should be sensible about things and sell the property, Julie. After all, when we win the war things will only get worse for you Germans.'

'But we're best friends.' Julie's eyes filled with tears.

A part of Corally wanted to relent and help Julie, for they had been friends, but best friends? No, Corally decided, they weren't best friends. Quite often in the past it had seemed like Julie was just tagging along.

'Please,' Julie pleaded.

Corally stared at the smoky-eyed girl and began to wonder if the Jacksons had a Harrow boy in mind for their eldest daughter. She thought of her own mother's words, of how jealousy could ruin the best-laid plans and, lifting her chin, she bustled past Julie in the direction of the commotion, glad of the distraction. She couldn't stand to be shunned the way the Jacksons were, not when she was trying so hard to better her place in the world.

Really, she thought, how on earth could she be friends with someone like that, when all her boys were fighting the enemy abroad? What on earth would they think on their return if she was friendly with a German?

The crowd was attracting more people by the minute and had now spread from outside the ironmonger's to the middle of the street. Corally wanted desperately to lift her skirts and run to see what was going on but instead she moved sedately, her eyes on the shop windows although her ears were finely tuned to the ruckus ahead.

'I said no and I meant no, and it's my right as a store-keeper to decide who I serve and who I don't.' Mr Lawrence was joined by a number of other men, including a bear of a man who had just stepped out of the barber's shop. He was clean-shaven and broad-shouldered and was watching the altercation with obvious enjoyment. Corally caught his eye and was rather pleased when he winked at her.

Julie Jackson's father was red in the face. 'For pity's sake, man, I have a family to care for. It's bad enough that this town's bigotry has cost me my stockmen, but you're refusing me service on groundless accusations.'

One of the men in the gathering crowd stepped forward. 'Groundless accusations? My boy is dead thanks to your kin. Died in France of shrapnel wounds a month ago.'

'My boy's dead too.' Corally recognised Mrs Marchant, a neighbour of the Jacksons. 'I'm sorry for you, Mr Jackson, but if there is no cause for concern, why do the constabulary require you to report in weekly?'

'Stupidity,' he retorted. Mr Jackson turned on his heel and pleaded to the encircling crowd. 'My mother was German, it's true, but she married an Englishman and she's been in this country for thirty years. I was born and raised here and so were my children.'

'Having you here is just a bit too hard for some of us, Jackson. Right or wrong, you've been offered fair money for your farm. Take it and move on,' Snob Evans called from outside the funeral parlour.

Corally thought Snob quite handsome, although how he could touch dead bodies was beyond her.

'You know who's at the bottom of this? Cummins!' Mr Jackson told the assembled crowd. 'He's always had an eye to buying my place and isn't he making a show of ensuring he gets it? I listen to the rumours too. I know he's been spear-heading the lies about me.'

There were murmurs of *rubbish* and *liar*. Mrs Dempsey and Miss Waites walked from the post office to join a huddle of matrons with their backs to the timber building. They were like a gaggle of geese with their pale, puffy-sleeved blouses and full skirts, and represented a mishmash of villagers and the visiting land-owners. Corally took her place somewhere in the middle of the group, sneaking a glance at the post-office building and thinking of the metal money box within, wondering if maybe the postmistress had only pulled the door shut. *Really, Corally,* she chastised, *it's not worth the risk.*

The postmistress raised her voice. 'My boy has half of his face blown off. That's him that these good people can hear at night when the land is quiet and the good and the kind should be safely asleep in their beds. That's him moaning and groaning in pain and despair. He sounds like some ghoulish intruder.' Mrs Dempsey wrung her hands together. 'And that's how he looks.'

The noise of the crowd rose and fell like a rumbling storm as Corally thought of the number of times Miss Waites had complained of an eerie noise and sleepless nights. Now they all knew why.

'But it's not my family's fault,' Mr Jackson protested.

One by one the gathered crowd lost interest and walked away, until eventually Mr Jackson was left alone to face the freshly shaved stranger.

'And what are *you* looking at?' Mr Jackson queried. 'You're not even from around here. You're probably some cold-footer who has wangled himself out of active service.'

The stranger took two paces forward and punched Mr Jackson fair in the nose. The force spun him backwards and he landed with a thud in the dirt of the street. Julie, her mother and four younger siblings rushed to his side.

'Corally!' Julie called from where she knelt in the dirt at her father's side. 'Please help us!'

Corally turned her back.

'Is this what the war has done to us?' Miss Waites complained to the women gathered near her. 'Can ye not see it? We are fighting ourselves.'

The women hesitated. Two matrons took tentative steps towards the Jacksons.

Corally shaded her face against the warming sun. 'He,' she said loudly, pointing at Julie's prone father, 'is not one of us. But we don't expect you to understand, Miss Waites. After all, you're not from here either.'

The two matrons thought better of offering assistance and walked away.

Across the street the stranger who had thrown the punch doffed his hat to the baker's wife, Mrs Evans.

'Now, there's a man who doesn't waste words,' one of the older women in the group commented.

'That would be Mr Nathanial Taylor,' Miss Waites said tartly. 'Ye know, the reprobate from Sunset Ridge who your husbands believed would fail in his role as manager? Ye are all very quick to not only pass judgement, but also change your minds.'

Corally tried to think of a clever retort but Miss Waites was making her way towards the beleaguered Jacksons. Seeing her approach, Julie gave the governess a grateful smile.

Cook's announcement that Nathanial Taylor was waiting to see her took Lily by surprise. The manager was early. Tidying the sheet music, she set it atop the piano.

'Send him in here, Cook.'

The older woman looked askance.

'I did send for him, remember? Just give me a few minutes to collect myself.' Lily patted her hair and licked dry lips as Cook left the room. The day had dragged. G.W. seemed unable to relax since his unannounced walk some weeks ago and had become increasingly silent, to the extent that Lily sensed he did not even notice her presence at times. And now she had the unenviable task of confronting Mr Taylor and giving the man notice. The letter written to the address noted in the ledger had been answered; it seemed that Mr Taylor was not Mr Taylor. In fact, Lily had no idea who Sunset Ridge's manager actually was.

'Good evening, Mrs Harrow. You wanted to see me?'

He sat in the wing-backed chair as directed and Lily did her best not to stare. Her first impression was that a stranger had arrived in her home. Sunset Ridge's manager was freshly shaved; no traces of the thick beard or unsavoury neck hair remained and his hair was closely cropped. 'Mr Taylor,' Lily tried unsuccessfully not to appear stunned, 'truly, I did not recognise you.' His altered appearance encompassed his dress, for he wore a clean white shirt and a new jacket, although his trousers and boots had seen better days.

Lily waved the recently received letter in the air. 'It would appear that you are not who you say you are, sir.'

'Well, clearly it doesn't bother you, otherwise I would not be in this room.'

Lily faltered. The truth was that she was not alarmed by his presence. There was little reason to be, for no harm had come to person or property since his arrival. In fact, Sunset Ridge was enjoying a healthy profit and her days had been buoyed by his strong male presence. But she was intrigued. 'You are here under false pretences. If you are not the man whom my husband employed last year, who are you?' The last three words were emphasised by the pointing of the letter she held.

Taylor rose and took a step towards her. 'Anyone you want me to be.' His voice was low.

'I will scream,' Lily warned.

'And I could bar the door with a chair,' he retaliated. 'But,' he continued smoothly, calmly, 'I don't think you will scream. You've been alone in this big house for too long.' He held out his hands in a conciliatory gesture. 'Besides, have I not done a good job in your employ?'

'Reasonable,' Lily replied. 'And I remind you, sir, that I am *not* alone.'

'Yes, yes.' He waved away her words as if they were unwanted flies. 'A wily cook, a young housemaid and an invalid.'

'I want to know who you are.'

Taylor sat in the wing-backed chair and crossed his legs. 'Well, I'm not the man your husband employed,' he admitted, flicking a piece of lint from his trousers. 'Now, *he* was a shrewd character – long grey hair, a shaggy beard to his chest, missing teeth – but he knew his cattle, oh yes, he knew livestock. You know he was shacked up out there on the western boundary with scant supplies and wasn't fussed either way if the supplies arrived on time or not?'

'Go on,' Lily replied.

'Well, he was a canny old fellow, talkative too. He told me all about Sunset Ridge and the wayward sons who ran away to join the great adventure, the fools.' Lily's face hardened. 'Having said that, I would have gone too had I the opportunity.'

'And why didn't you?'

He met her gaze. 'I was on the run from a disgruntled husband and I ended up in that shack with that old, wizened man who told me that the only person who had laid eyes on him was the boss, Mr Harrow, who was now beyond recognising anyone.'

'Did you –' Lily couldn't finish the sentence.

'Kill him?' Taylor burst out laughing. 'My, how your imagination runs, Mrs Harrow.' Uncrossing his legs, he laughed again when she flinched at the movement. 'I might be many things, but a man's life is sacrosanct. The old man died of natural causes and I gave him a proper burial. Of course, you will have to take my word for that.'

Lily couldn't believe it. 'So, you took his name and job.' She was frightened by his story and amazed at the man's audacity. She gripped the letter between her fingers to still their trembling. 'Well, my sources place the real Mr Taylor at seventy years of age, so that confirms part of your story.'

'The rest is simple. I needed a new job and a new life, and I found both here at Sunset Ridge.' He walked towards her.

Lily moved away, her hands clanging the keys of the piano as she backed into it. 'I want you to leave. I have already advertised for a new manager.' He was close enough for his breath to waft across her skin.

'Why do I have to leave?' His voice was low. 'I was falsely accused of forcing myself on a woman, when in fact the attraction was quite mutual. I've spent two years on the run because of it.' His fingers traced the length of her arm. 'I've done a good job here for you, Mrs Harrow.'

'Go,' she pleaded. His eyes were a cool grey with flecks of blue. How could she have entertained even the slightest thought regarding this man?

'You're a spirited woman, Mrs Harrow. I can be discreet, at least until your husband is mentally beyond caring.'

When he leaned towards Lily, her scream was loud and shrill. In the distance, yells and the sound of hasty footsteps were heard in response. A door slammed. Lily pushed against the strength of the man and slapped at the hard, determined face. Behind them the music room door was flung open and G.W. charged towards them. The man known as Nathanial Taylor was jolted sideways. With a mighty roar, her husband lifted the mahogany walking stick and brought it down hard upon him. Again and again he bashed the manager like a madman.

It was Cook who stopped the thrashing. The woman yelled until G.W.'s arm stilled and the bloody walking stick lay next to the senseless body, next to the bloodied face.

'My Lily, my darling Lily.' G.W.'s arms encircled her.

Burying her face in his shoulder, Lily wept.

The maid was sent to find a mirror and on her return Cook placed the glass above the manager's mouth, waiting for the mist of condensation that would prove he lived. Cook inspected the result and turned to the Harrows, who were consoling each other.

'Is he alive?' G.W. asked.

'Mr Harrow,' Cook swallowed noisily, 'you've done murder.'

≪ Chapter 41 ≫

The soldier was ensnared in the barbed wire. Roland flattened his body on the ground as rifle-fire struck the earth only feet away. He tugged relentlessly at the young soldier, yet something held him fast. Whimpering, Roland continued to pull at the weight, straining against the pain until finally the wire gave way and Roland fell back, losing his grip on the man's shoulder. He sniffed cautiously at his leg, licking at the bloody wound, and then turned his attention back to his task.

Snuffling at the inert body, Roland opened his jaw and clamped it hard near the collar bone. His hind legs gained purchase in the dirt and very slowly he began to drag the man towards safety. Their progress was laborious. There were bodies to detour and the pitted ground yawned at him, revealing cavernous holes. At the edge of a crater he dragged the soldier to the lip and over the edge, watching him tumble down the walls. Roland whined at the tangle of arms and legs, at the sound of men groaning, then he put his head down and raced back towards his master.

Captain Harrison was attending to a neck wound when he felt the dog's wet nose on his cheek. They were in the reserve trench behind the front-line from where the Australians had attacked. Only God knew if the brass's objectives had been reached; even if they had, once again it came at too great a cost. Captain Harrison called for stretcher-bearers and then patted Roland. The dog panted heavily. The sides of his muzzle were torn and bleeding and there was a great ragged tear down his flank and barbed wire caught around a front leg.

'Roland, what have you done?' Captain Harrison called for wire snippers, and one of the walking wounded came to assist.

'It looks like he's been out past the barbed wire to the other side.' Roland sat patiently as the Australian soldier carefully cut the wire from around his hairy leg and then pulled the embedded spikes clear of his flesh. 'Jeez, Captain, I think I got it all but I really can't be sure; it's too dark.'

Captain Harrison examined the cut on Roland's flank. 'You silly mutt. You're not meant to go into no-man's land – we promised Francois.' He wound a length of bandage around the damaged leg as Roland licked the captain's hand. 'I suppose you've got wounded out there?' The dog barked. Captain Harrison scratched his head. Not once since their temporary partnership began had he let Roland near no-man's land. It was dangerous enough working in the forward positions. 'Can you round up a few men for a rescue party?' he asked the soldier.

'There are men out looking already, sir. We haven't any officers left and we're missing a whole platoon, including the captain.'

Roland nudged Captain Harrison in the leg and then limped away, urging him to follow.

'Best you wait here, Captain,' the soldier suggested. 'Fritz has something on the boil.'

Captain Harrison hesitated. While his responsibilities did not include risking his life out in no-man's land, neither did they allow him to shirk his duty if he knew wounded men were in need of his care. The dog placed his paw on the captain's boot. If the stories about this great ungainly dog were true, Roland would lead them to the wounded, and it appeared that that was what they were both here for. 'Well, we better be quick, then.'

With his injury Roland couldn't clamber up the trench wall, so the captain helped him up the ladder and out of the trench and together they walked carefully to the front-line. The diggers were talking in muted voices, sentries had been posted, and although it was quiet these men stood with their rifles at the ready. Sliding down into the trench, Captain Harrison held out his arms for Roland. The dog slithered down the wall into his arms and the man nearly buckled under the weight.

'You're a bit far from the casualty clearing station, aren't you, mate?' an Australian sentry whispered.

The captain peered over the trench wall. 'They afford me a bit of flexibility. Any sign of the rescue party?'

'Nothing. They could be pinned down. The worst of it is that the wounded have been out there in the sun all day and half of the night. Fritz hasn't been very cooperative today,' the sentry explained, petting Roland. 'We saw your dog out there. One of the men reckoned they saw him dragging a body across the battlefield, but we figured he had the willies.'

Captain Harrison crouched on the ground and examined Roland's leg. 'Do you think you can take me out there, Roland? Just one more time?'

Roland placed a paw on the captain's boot.

'Good boy.'

'But, sir, you can't go out there,' the digger complained, 'not with a dog. Fritz might be quiet at the moment but they've re-taken their trenches.'

Roland stood up on his hind legs and rested his paws on the earthen trench wall.

'Will you cover us, Private? Cover me and my dog?'

The sentry scratched at cheek stubble. 'That dog isn't –'

Captain Harrison nodded. 'Yes, it is. It's the French war dog, Roland.'

The sentry appeared mesmerised. Reaching out a hand, he tentatively patted Roland between the ears. 'Is it true what they say about him?'

The captain looked at the dog by his side and then out across no-man's land. 'I hope so. So what do you say, Private?'

'I reckon we can give you a hand.' Introducing himself as Walker, the sentry ordered the resting men to stand-to. Within seconds thirty rifles were positioned over the sandbags.

Captain Harrison lifted Roland over the top of the trench as a rush of nerves cramped his stomach. He'd never been out in no-man's land. He climbed up the ladder. The private followed, rifle at the ready.

Roland sniffed the wind and then limped out across no-man's land. Once out in the open they kept low to the ground. Although the occasional burst of rifle-fire echoed over the damaged land it was eerily quiet. The squeak of leather and the gentle whack of the medical kit slapping his back sounded inordinately loud to the captain, as did the private keeping pace beside him. The man's breath came in ragged gasps that told of damaged lungs. The ground rose and fell in a patchwork of lumps and holes and they stumbled frequently under the cover of a cloudy night. When a flare went up they fell to the ground and waited, Roland crouched beside them, the men's breath catching in their throats until the land became dark again.

Roland veered left and then straightened, heading deeper into no-man's land. For a moment Captain Harrison believed that the dog intended to continue towards the barbed wire but instead the animal veered left again and stopped at the edge of a shell crater. The captain and private crawled on their stomachs to the edge and looked inside as a flare went up. In the ghoulish green light they made out the bodies of at least twenty Australian soldiers. They lay scattered like rag dolls, their arms and legs intertwined.

The private's eyes rounded like organ stops. 'Christ Almighty,' he whispered, looking at the men in the hole. 'How the hell did they all get in there?' Very slowly he turned to the mongrel dog at his side.

Captain Harrison thought of all the stories he'd heard regarding the dog and he swallowed noisily as he patted Roland and then skidded down into the pit. Most of the men appeared to be alive. 'They're nearly all here,' the private muttered, joining him. 'Look, there are two of the Harrow boys and . . . Jeez, I thought they'd all bought it for sure. The last time I saw them they were making a run for it. Fritz had them cornered in one of their machine-gun nests and they let off a whizz-bang directly overhead.'

The captain looked up to where Roland crouched at the rim of the crater. The dog had breached the wire somehow, managing to rescue these men from the German lines. 'I need you to go back and form another rescue party,' he told the private. 'Then get back out here.'

'Yes, sir.'

As the private climbed from the crater Captain Harrison began to examine the wounded, doing what he could to ease their suffering. Some would not make it; others had a chance. Above, Roland gave a soft whine, his flinty-eyed stare penetrating the dark. Then he disappeared. A few minutes later a series of blasts echoed across the battlefield.

≪ Chapter 42 ≫

Banyan, south-west Queensland, Australia
September 1917

W allace 'Snob' Evans did not consider himself to be a merce-
nary man. The altercation with Luther Harrow the previous
year may have turned him sour against the world for a short time,
but since then, under his father's guidance, he had prospered
despite inclination. The compensation due him for the loss suffered
to his finger allowed certain renovations to be done to the family
home and in return his father supported him when he decided to
go into business. It wasn't a hard decision when it came to choosing
a career. With the opportunity to fight for his country denied by his
maiming, Snob understood that he was one of the fortunate few
to be granted a reprieve from the carnage. Business suited him,
especially the type that required little manual labour.

There were negative aspects to his choice of profession. However,
he was adamant when he purchased a quarter-share in the funeral
home that the ancient undertaker, Mr Mortimer, would not take
advantage of him. He was prepared to receive and discharge
bodies from the home and handle all necessary arrangements with

relatives, especially when it came to the sale of caskets and linings and the choice of stationery for funeral cards. The addition of a biblical verse was an added service that he saw to personally and was proving to be popular. Other than that, Snob drew the line at going to the cemetery. The place gave him the creeps.

This afternoon he was awaiting the arrival of the constabulary. He knew through experience they would probably be delayed, which meant an internment tomorrow and a smelly one at that for the gravediggers. He could, of course, have called in Mr Mortimer; after all, the deceased he was waiting on had been murdered – despite Constable Roberts' report – and the old undertaker was particularly fond of the more gruesome type of injuries. Today, however, Snob wanted to witness what the Harrows had done this time.

Initially Snob had not been inclined to accept the man into the funeral home. There were two vital criteria that every prospective client must meet before entry was granted through the rear of his establishment. First, the person in question was required to be confirmed dead by the doctor – Snob refused to entertain another deceased person miraculously awaking as the body was being washed down – and second, they had to be moneyed. There were no free rides in this world, whether it be to heaven or hell.

This case, however, deserved attention. With the incident having occurred two days ago the village was agape at the news. It appeared that the manager of Sunset Ridge had attacked Mrs Harrow in her own home, the music room to be precise, which instantly awoke suspicion as to how the man managed to be in the homestead. Furthermore, with reports of G.W. Harrow having suffered a turn the previous year and the doctor confirming the man's invalid status, the locals were astonished to discover that old G.W. had killed the manager in defence of his wife. It also appeared that Mr Nathanial Taylor, who wasn't really Mr Nathanial Taylor, may or may not have killed another Sunset Ridge employee last year and assumed his identity. The whole event was far better than any work of fiction and would make Snob Evans quite the man of the hour for many weeks to come.

Snob opened the rear door to the funeral home as the dray halted in a squeal of gravel. He stood back as two men carried the cloth-covered body inside and arranged it on the table.

'He's all yours now, Mr Evans.' Constable Roberts gave a nod towards the victim and handed Snob a copy of the death certificate. 'All signed and sealed, and Mrs Harrow said that they would pay for a coffin.'

'So, we have no name?' Snob queried, checking the details of the death certificate. He could sense the constable's discomfort. Mr Mortimer kept his rooms spotlessly clean yet there was always the faint sickly whiff of embalming fluid and his tools of trade for embalming, cleaning and suturing injuries sat next to the row of compounds that restored a more human appearance to the recently dead.

'No, only the good word of the Harrows.'

'Such as it is,' Snob replied. 'And the rumours of the murdered employee last year?'

'If there is another body out there, no one would ever find it.'

'And the verdict. Murder?' he asked hopefully.

The constable pressed his shoulders back. 'Self-defence. Mr Harrow was protecting his wife and his own person.'

Snob thanked the police constable and closed the door behind the men. *Typical*, he thought, lifting the cloth covering the body. The Harrows were beyond reproach once again. The deceased's face was badly disfigured. Snob gave a grunt of distaste and gave the man's pockets a cursory search, knowing that the constable would have pocketed anything valuable. The man's coat appeared new and unstained, however, and Snob struggled to remove it from the stiffened corpse. A few days in the sun's heat and the stink would be out of the material and it would fetch a pretty penny on the second-hand rack at the general store. Unlike Mr Mortimer, Snob drew the line at the extraction of gold fillings.

Snob was readying to close up and go in search of a village child to track down one of the gravediggers when he noticed the man's boots. They were past their prime and the soles were holey. But his attention was caught by what appeared to be a piece of paper sticking out a scant inch from the side of a boot. With difficulty he tugged one boot free and then the other. Deciding against placing his hand inside, he took scissors and cut down the leather sides. There was paper at the bottom of each one. Wadding, no doubt, yet when he pulled the stuffing free and unfolded it he found himself looking at what appeared to be sketches. Those packed in the middle were the most recognisable, while the ones that lay closest to either the man's foot or the leather sole were ruined. Snob flattened two of the works on the counter between the dead man's feet and, noticing the initials written in charcoal, gave a satisfied grin.

It really was turning out to be an extraordinary week in the district, reflected Snob. First Mr Jackson was found near beaten to death outside the blacksmith's, and now there had been murder at Sunset Ridge. Snob unlocked the cupboard that was home to his personal effects while at work and sat the sketches inside along with two silver fob watches, a locket and a pearl brooch. Although it would be some time before the items could be sold without arousing suspicion, he was content knowing that his nest egg was growing each year.

⋘ Chapter 43 ⋙

Temporary field hospital, France
October 1917

Sister Valois closed the soldier's eyes and covered his face with the sheet. It was raining again, raining so hard that the battle known as Passchendaele was becoming a byword for horror. There were stories of maps rotting as they were held, of boots being sucked off by the ooze that infected every wound, and both men and animals sinking into the mud never to be seen again. With a sigh she called for an orderly to remove the body. The bombardier was a non-commissioned officer and was one of four soldiers to die under her care in the past seven hours. Today she had played myriad roles, from mother and lover to the delirious, to inadequate nurse and confessor, the weather having cancelled the priest's visit.

She thought wistfully of Captain Harrison. In spite of the handful of moments they had spent together and the single chaste kiss he had given her at their last parting, she hoped for more and yet doubted his interest. The American was a kind man and generous of spirit, so it was possible he simply felt friendship for her, yet in the minutes before sleep overtook her at night intuition told her that theirs was a relationship that had every possibility of extending beyond a shared profession and a dog named Roland.

The wind changed direction and a spray of cool air and rain splattered the rich parquet flooring of the dining room. She tugged at the heavy window, careful not to slip on the floor. For a moment Sister Valois pressed her brow against the cold glass. Outside, the hospital grounds were empty, the sky a roll of grey cloud. A burial party crossed the patchy grass, their shovels slung across shoulders, faces downcast. The field hospital was full to capacity, food was short thanks to the boggy roads, and winter was coming again. How would they survive, she wondered, as two orderlies stretchered out the dead soldier. On passing she tucked the dead man's hand under the sheet before reminding the orderlies not to tarry.

She almost resented the young bombardier leaving. There would be a place made for him in the hospital cemetery. Beneath and surrounded by French soil, he would lie in the bosom of her beloved country, forever loved, forever safe. Age should have made her wiser, yet it was experience that tempered Sister Valois's attitude. What little optimism she once had was now gone, eroded by the years of suffering and the awful, endless waste of human life.

In the salon overlooking the front garden of the chateau she went about her rounds. The floor-to-ceiling windows barely let in any light such was the thickness of the rain, yet in the dim room men were sponge-bathed, dressings changed and charts checked. Part of the aisle now held cots, and moving from one end of the ward to the other was an obstacle course demanding patience. At the foot of a cot beneath a window she stopped. The young man propped up with pillows was the recipient of a shrapnel wound to the head, and she knew that he hated her twice-weekly administrations as much as she detested performing the task. Saliva gathered in her mouth as she waited patiently for a volunteer to appear with the requested forceps.

'Please, Sister, don't do it again,' the soldier pleaded almost inaudibly.

Soothing him to quietness, Sister Valois prodded at the thick scab that ran from his hairline above the brow to the middle of his skull. Most of the hair had been shaved and the wound, although deep, was healing well. With a scalpel she flicked up the end of the scab and then, taking a firm hold of the crusty flap with the forceps, she pulled the entire scab off in one movement.

'Oh, but you are fierce, Sister,' he complained through gritted teeth.

She dropped the forceps and scab in a ceramic bowl. 'Not as fierce as you.' She pressed a bandage to the bleeding wound. 'It will heal faster this way.' She looked through the window and saw an ambulance approaching along the gravel drive. It halted at the entrance to the chateau, the American Field Ambulance service insignia visible through the curtain of rain. Leaving the soldier in a nurse's care, Sister Valois went to greet the new arrivals, prepared to tell them that there was no possibility of accommodating more patients unless they put more in the aisles, and then she would be faced with the worsening problem of short supplies.

At the entrance to the chateau Sister Valois was met by Captain Harrison. For a split second she imagined herself running across the parquet floor into his arms. Instead she cautioned herself against an emotion of which she remained unsure. He smiled at her, his gait hampered by a substantial limp, the shadows beneath his eyes speaking of more than exhaustion.

'I didn't know where else to go, but I thought you might help.' His eyes grew moist as he spoke to her in her native language. 'Please help.'

Taking his arm, she led the captain to a small settee pushed against the wall.

'I operated, but the wound will not heal and not all the injuries were attended to. If I had not been hit it may have been different, but when we got to the casualty clearing station they would not let us stay together.'

Kneeling, Sister Valois pulled up the leg of the captain's uniform: blood and white matter oozed from an untended wound, while a bandage covered a suppurating injury with thirty or more stitches. 'Speak English,' she advised.

'They say he saved at least twenty men before the blast got him, Sister.' An orderly appeared, carrying a stretcher with another man. 'The captain here begged us to bring him to you. I don't know if the brass will take kindly to us commandeering an ambulance, but when we heard who it was for . . .'

Level with the stretcher, Sister Valois turned slowly. Roland the dog stared back, his eyes filmy. For a moment the sense of hopelessness seemed too great for her to contend with. Was everyone and everything to be ruined by this bloody campaign? The captain's hand was on hers, his gaze willing her to action. Sister Valois gripped it back.

She called for a senior nurse and orderlies, her clear, firm voice echoing about the aged walls of the chateau. The staff came running at the urgency in her tone and set about following her brusque instructions. The captain was placed on a cot in the kitchen, Roland on a thick blanket on a table only feet away. In minutes the captain's trouser leg had been cut away and two nurses washed the wound. Sister Valois set up plasma and offered him opiates for the pain.

Captain Harrison grabbed her wrist. 'No. No opiate.' He pointed at the table. 'Roland. You know what he did, what he has done. You must save him.'

Sister Valois turned her attention to the injured dog. The lower part of a hind leg was missing and although the suturing appeared strong the wound wept. She set about cutting away the matted hair and then sopped disinfectant on the injury with a rag boiled in water. Roland twitched at the sting.

'You're safe now, Roland,' she said in answer to his whining. The wound to the flank was long but neatly stitched. This she covered with a cloth soaked in disinfectant.

'His leg.' Captain Harrison pointed from where he lay.

Beneath the dirty bandage on the front leg the wound was bloody and raw. Sister Valois prised apart the hair and flesh, checking for shrapnel. Instead she found barbed wire. 'There is wire wrapped around his leg,' she told her assistants. 'I need tin snips, anything.'

An orderly rushed out to the salon ward.

'If he loses that leg as well –' Captain Harrison warned.

'Do not tell me what I already know,' she snapped.

The orderly reappeared with wire snippers, and shadowing him was a French soldier.

'*Sacré bleu!*' Louie Pascal crossed himself. 'It's the Chessy boys' dog, it's Roland.'

Roland wagged his tail and then stilled.

'Light, I need more light,' Sister Valois demanded as the orderly and French soldier came to her assistance.

Candles were brought and more water boiled. 'You should be in bed,' she said on seeing the Frenchman standing at her side. The boy had lost an arm and was also recovering from a near-crippling case of trench foot.

'This dog, this dog was at Verdun.'

Sister Valois paused in her ministrations. 'So was I,' she replied to Louie Pascal. 'Roland and I have already met.'

It took an hour to cut the wire free and then unwind the barb embedded in Roland's flesh. It had reached the bone, effectively cutting off the circulation to his paw. It was possible that the dog would only have two legs, that he would never walk again – if that happened he would have to be put down. Visions of such a tragedy befalling this intelligent creature caused the bile to rise in her throat. Sister Valois washed the wound tenderly, noticing the red raw paws, and then dressed it. 'Go back to bed now, Louie, there is nothing more that can be done.'

'Will he live, Sister?'

'I don't know,' she admitted. 'He needs at least three legs. All we can do is pray.'

When the kitchen finally emptied, the captain spoke. 'Will he survive?'

'You should be asleep,' she admonished, checking the captain's wound and temperature. 'You were stupid not to get that attended to sooner.' The chateau was quiet. Night had come. The captain sipped at a cup of water while she supported his shoulders.

'I could hardly put myself before Roland,' he explained. 'Besides, he doesn't belong to me.'

They both turned in the dog's direction. He slept, exhausted.

'You are right,' she agreed. 'He belongs to God.'

The captain took her hand. Sister Valois settled in a chair between the American and the French war dog, not daring to hope beyond the moment.

'I carried him from the field. I don't know how. Look at him. He is so large and such an ungainly mutt.'

'Shush, you must rest.'

Captain Harrison squeezed her fingers. 'With or without Roland, I still would have come back to you eventually.'

She met his eyes. 'I wasn't sure . . . I didn't know . . .'

'I wasn't sure either, at least about how you felt,' he replied, smiling tiredly. 'I thought you may think I was rushing you, but I hoped.'

'I'm glad,' she said shyly.

Near dawn Sister Valois awoke in the chair. A mottled daylight seeped through the single window, giving the kitchen shape and shadows. The candles had burned out, leaving a pool of wax on the end of the table alongside a plate of untouched food left by a kind soul. She checked on her patients. Both man and dog breathed steadily. Reaching for the cross about her neck, she prayed aloud to the Saints and the Virgin. Captain Harrison would survive, but Roland? What of Roland's injury?

There was a noise at the entrance to the kitchen and she turned, expecting to be confronted by an emergency or a death or a disgruntled staff member. She did not think she could be party to such problems today.

Before her, a dozen wounded French soldiers sat on the cold flagstone floor. Behind them were a number of men in wheelchairs and two orderlies. Sister Valois touched the cross around her neck as the features of those gathered grew clearer as the sun rose. They bowed their heads, their skin awash with the morning light and then they began to pray.

⋘ Chapter 44 ⋙

Banyan, south-west Queensland, Australia
February 2000

Madeleine turned to Sonia. 'So, your aunt, Julie Jackson, and Corally Shaw were best friends?'

The kitchen in the weatherboard house was growing hotter by the minute. Sonia's story of Julie's father being left lying in the main street after being abused by the townsfolk was startling.

'Yes. Although not even Corally would help the Jacksons. Of everyone in that town, only Miss Waites gave the family a hand.'

'You forget, Sonia, that the entire Jackson family was under suspicion by the local authorities. No one wanted to risk associating with them, not the way people felt about the Germans back then,' the old woman stated irritably from where she sat in the corner of the room. 'As for that Miss Waites – well, she wasn't from here anyway, so she had nothing to lose.'

'And Corally did?' Madeleine questioned.

The old woman and Sonia exchanged a hard look.

'But surely you can't stop someone from buying goods in the village?' Madeleine exclaimed.

436

The older woman pointed at Sonia with a crooked finger. 'She wasn't there but I was. Thousands of our boys were blown to bits in the war and never came home and those that did were ruined just the same.'

'It got worse,' Sonia interjected. 'Cummins took advantage of the ill feeling directed towards my great-uncle and pursued him relentlessly. He'd wanted to buy the Jackson farm for years and he thought he finally had his chance. Of course as the hatred for the Jacksons intensified, Cummins' offer became lower and lower. It was late 1917 when my great-uncle was left for dead outside the blacksmith's. They say it was only because of concern for his family that he lived out the week following the attack – the doctor said his injuries were shocking. Cummins made another offer for the Jackson farm and this time he had no choice but to accept. It was all rather convenient for Cummins.'

'Wait.' Madeleine touched Sonia's arm. 'This sounds as if you believe that Cummins had your great-uncle attacked in order to get his hands on your family property.'

'One of the boundaries on the Cummins property adjoined the Jackson farm and Cummins was desperate to increase his holding and his sheep flock,' Sonia explained. 'Cummins was getting quite a name in the industry for his wool at the time. He wanted that land.'

'And he got it?' Madeleine asked. 'Through foul play?'

'Whether directly or indirectly, yes, he got it,' Sonia replied, 'but we lost far more than that. The Jacksons were ruined. You have to understand, Madeleine, that before the Great War the family had prospects. We owned good acreage and were of respectable, hard-working stock. And Julie was educated and attractive and it was hoped she would marry well – there were few eligible girls in the district at that time.' Sonia lifted her palms to the ceiling. 'There was even talk of her marrying one of the Harrow boys.'

'Really?' Madeleine replied. She looked at the housekeeper, they could have been related if not for the events that had occurred.

437

'I knew it!' the old woman spat.

Sonia ignored her. 'Well, no one wanted anything to do with the family after that. I guess people were looking for something to direct their anger and grief at, and the Jacksons, with their German heritage, fitted the bill. Aunt Julie moved with her mother and younger siblings – including Nancy, your previous housekeeper, and my father – to a shack in the village after my great-uncle was buried in an unmarked pauper's grave. The owner of the funeral parlour, Snob Evans,' she glared at the old woman, 'your dead husband,' she said sarcastically, 'refused my great-aunt's request to pay for a decent Christian burial by instalment. In fact, he wouldn't even allow the body in the funeral home.'

Madeleine glanced at the old woman. No wonder the Jacksons felt badly done by.

'And that was the beginning of the end of the Jackson family. Until David Harrow returned from the war.'

≪ Chapter 45 ≫

Sunset Ridge, south-west Queensland, Australia
June 1918

Lily trotted across the paddock from the sheep yards to the homestead, the winter sun warming her flushed cheeks. The new mare was proving to be a solid purchase and the two of them were now a familiar sight roaming Sunset Ridge. The coming spring looked promising. With the sale of the two thousand ewes last year and G.W.'s original mob of cattle culled to retain only the younger cows for breeding, the native grasses were in good condition. If the normal spring rains graced the property, the grass should come away quickly. With a click of her tongue Lily urged the mare onwards. There was still paperwork to attend to and she was yet to make a choice regarding the cloth required for her new riding pants. True to her word, Lily's dresses and skirts had been relegated to evening and house wear only. Every time she walked outdoors now she dressed in riding pants. Cook would mumble something about standards and G.W. appeared outwardly disapproving, though he could not always hide his smile. At the back gate Lily dismounted and, wrapping the reins around the fence railing, walked up the path and collapsed into the chair next to G.W.

'Well?' he asked, peering over the top of a newspaper.

Shearing was into its second week and, although there were the usual disgruntled employees, the arguments had lessened once the overseer insisted on a dry camp. 'No problems, my dear, and Mr Cambridge is very pleased with the fleece yields to date and has even given tacit agreement to the slight change in the breeding program that I hope to implement.' She tugged at the leather gloves, freeing her hands.

'I've been thinking about Taylor, or whoever he was.' Although G.W.'s speech was much improved, he still spoke slowly and deliberately.

Dropping the tan gloves on her lap, Lily turned to her husband. They rarely spoke of the man called Nathanial Taylor. The incident had brought them together again and Lily was so grateful to have the G.W. of old back that she had not pursued her initial concerns after the shocking event, hoping instead that one day her husband would choose to talk of the incident of his own free will. For her part Lily would never forget the fierceness of her husband's attack. G.W. had bashed a man to death, a man who had proved indispensable in the management of Sunset Ridge, despite his lies and threatening actions in the music room. On the other hand, her husband's appalling temper had all but abated since his part in Mr Taylor's death. It was as if all the anger and bitterness and remorse and guilt that had accumulated within G.W. during his lifetime had been expelled from his body with the savagery of the assault. Confusingly, good had come from the man's death.

'What of Mr Taylor, G.W.?' Lily asked.

Her husband barely lifted his eyes from the paper. 'If we knew his real name I would make efforts to trace his family, perhaps make some sort of monetary gift, anonymously of course.'

'An excellent idea, my dear.' This was the first time G.W. had voiced regret for his actions. His acknowledgement loosened something tight within her. 'Unfortunately I fear that his identity will never be known.'

'Quite,' he agreed. 'Even now I can't quite fathom what happened that day.'

'Nor I,' Lily replied. 'Mr Taylor was a good man at heart.'

Her husband cleared his throat. 'My only thought was of you. The thought of losing you after all we'd been through, after what I'd put you through . . .'

He reached out and briefly took her hand. It was a long time since she had felt such joy.

'It's done now,' Lily soothed. 'Let's put it behind us.'

G.W. gave her a grateful smile.

At the time, Mr Taylor's demise appeared to be an insurmountable scandal. In the days following the man's death, the distress Lily felt at his murder was gradually replaced by other concerns. She worried not only about G.W.'s brutality but also the damage that could be done to the Harrow family name. She need not have been so concerned. They repaid the investigating constable's discretion with a monetary gift as well as a number of sketches found in the dead man's possessions. The works were instantly recognisable as Miss Waites and although they bore David's signature and were remarkably life-like, Lily did not hesitate to give them away. The drawings were of little consequence in the scheme of things.

At the time Lily did not know how true that thought was, for they were yet to receive the news from France.

'Hmm, I best be on my feet come spring, lest I become redundant and that new manager takes over.'

'Never.' Mr Cambridge was proving to be well worth the money. Married with young children, his only concern was one of education. 'You know that our former governess is employed at the

Banyan Post Office? I was thinking of contacting her and asking Miss Waites if she would consider taking up her old position.'

Folding the newspaper, G.W. rested it on his lap. 'You never liked her.'

'I never liked her modernist ideas towards education, nor her loose morals.'

'Did they ever find Rodger?' G.W. asked.

'No, he seems to have disappeared, into the English countryside, no doubt.'

'He didn't seem like the type to shirk his duty, not having gone all the way over there.'

'Well, you may be right.' Lily poured water from the glass pitcher on the table and took a sip. 'It's only a rumour. But they *were* engaged, so if he is eventually declared legally dead it's possible that Miss Waites could apply to the courts to be a beneficiary of his estate. It appears Rodger's mother was not without funds, and his only brother was killed in 1916.'

'I doubt she would do such a thing. Still, a moneyed governess.' G.W. raised an eyebrow.

Lily giggled. 'Heaven forbid, society is changing.' It was good to laugh again. After the shocking end to last year she had truly believed that they would never recover from it. If it were possible to die from grief then surely she had come close to being a candidate. The most miraculous thing about the terrible year of 1917, however, was that G.W. saved her. Despite Mr Taylor's death and the extent of their marital problems, both had paled into insignificance with the earth-shattering telegram that had arrived from the War Department. That single typed line, *we regret to inform you*, would haunt Lily for all the days of her life.

And yet they had endured; mainly because G.W. constantly reminded her of what they still had, of what they could have in the future. Above all she would never forget that moment on Christmas Day when she had sat beside G.W. as he had re-written their

442

sons' names in the Harrow bible. Forgiveness did exist, but at what cost? Beside her, G.W.'s gaze was directed to the line of trees frilling the horizon. 'Let's have a pot of tea, shall we, and a slice of Cook's treacle cake?' Lily suggested.

G.W. inhaled sharply and reached for his walking stick. The newspaper slipped to the ground.

'My dear, whatever is the matter?' She followed her husband's gaze out across the paddock. The sky was cloudless, the air so crisp that Lily imagined she could almost count the white cockatoos nestling in a tree down near the stables.

G.W. limped to the edge of the veranda and then stumbled down the wooden stairs, dragging his useless left foot.

'Wait, G.W., where are you going?' Lily uncrossed her legs. She had been in the saddle on and off for three hours already and was not in the mood for one of her husband's impromptu walks about the house paddock. With a distinct lack of enthusiasm she pushed herself out of the chair and leaned against the timber pillar. She looked to the horizon and saw a thin plume of dust silhouetted against the sky. It grew in size until a wagon appeared through the tree line. Bouncing over the rutted track, it barely slowed on entering the house paddock. Lily could hear the creak of the wagon's wheels and, as it rushed towards them, she lifted a trembling hand to her mouth as the cockatoos near the stable took flight. Then, finally, the unmistakable shape of the driver came into focus.

G.W. clutched at the back gate. 'It's my boys come home to us, Lily. It's them riding in from the scrub.'

The wagon came to a screeching halt at the homestead gate, and Lily watched as Dave threw down the reins and jumped to the ground. Her youngest was tanned and fit, tall and older, much older, but he was alive as his letter had promised. G.W. dropped the walking stick and reached for him.

'My boy, my boy, my boy,' G.W. sobbed as they embraced.

Overcome, Lily lifted a hand to her youngest son's cheek. It was then she noticed it. There was no light in his eyes.

'Mother. Father.' He walked to the rear of the dray and tugged at the canvas cover. 'I've brought Luther home.'

Lily grasped her husband's arm. After everything the family had endured over the preceding years, she doubted she could face another calamity. By her side G.W. stiffened. This was the moment they had both lived and breathed for, the return of their sons. 'What's wrong with him, Dave?'

Her youngest rolled his lips together and gave a self-conscious smile. 'He's drunk.'

≪ Chapter 46 ≫

Banyan, south-west Queensland, Australia
February 2000

For a moment Madeleine didn't believe the two women. Yet here they were corroborating each other. 'Are you telling me Luther survived the war?'

The old woman nodded.

'It's not possible,' she argued. 'My mother said Thaddeus was killed on the battlefield on the Western Front and Luther died a few months later in an English hospital from wounds he received in the same attack.'

The old woman raised a muscle where an eyebrow once would have been. 'That's right about Thaddeus. But as for Luther – well, the first bit's true enough, eh, Sonia?'

'And how would you know?' Madeleine asked, her voice tight.

The old woman gave a cackle. 'Because I married him and cared for him until his death from those same wounds in 1921. My girl, I'm your great-aunt, Corally Shaw.'

In the heat of the kitchen, with the stench of the bull mouse that could be heard rustling in the papers at her feet, Madeleine could only think of one phrase, the phrase Sonia had used: *white trash*. She picked up a dusty magazine and fanned her face as she stared blankly at the birdlike creature opposite her. In the background the screen door screeched and the weather-beaten woman from the museum walked in.

'This is Sue-Ellen Evans, Corally's granddaughter,' Sonia introduced tersely.

'Didn't you give us a right shock showing up like you did the other day at the museum? I should have seen the similarities, but I've only ever seen pictures of the Harrows, and with you lot never coming into the village, well, how's a woman to be sure?' Sue-Ellen shut the kitchen door and switched on the refrigerated airconditioning unit built into the wall. 'Gran doesn't like the cool, she ain't used to it.'

The refreshing breeze wafted around the room. 'You were married to my great-uncle?' Madeleine asked Corally, looking to Sonia for clarification.

'It's as she says,' replied Sonia.

Corally pointed irritably to a plastic container near the Aga. 'Well, go on, Sue-Ellen, go fetch it for the girl.'

Sue-Ellen did as she was told, sitting the thick scrapbook from the container on the kitchen table.

'Go on, girl, have a look.'

Wiping the perspiration from her face, Madeleine opened the book. There, on the inside page, was a charcoal sketch of Luther Harrow.

'Handsome man, wasn't he? That was the last sketch Dave ever did of a soldier,' Corally explained. 'Luther said he drew hundreds during the war. The men wanted them to send home to their loved ones, but of course every time he drew a soldier they were usually killed. Dave took it real hard, as if the drawings were bad luck. Luther said he begged to have his portrait done because he didn't expect to survive the war.' Corally sounded wistful. 'In a way he didn't.'

446

'Why didn't my mother tell me about any of this?' Madeleine asked.

Corally lifted her birdlike hands. 'Jude probably doesn't know the truth. Luther and me, well, we were an embarrassment to the Harrows – individually and together. Me because I wasn't good enough and Luther because he wasn't the returning hero that the family expected. They'd already lost Thaddeus and they couldn't understand why Luther couldn't get his act together and live a normal life on his return from the war. Old G.W. never got over how changed Luther was. He died a few years after Luther passed and that proved too much for Lily. They say she only stayed on for your grandfather's sake. Dave was a changed man as well and he had his own share of problems after the war ended, but they ran the place together until her health got the better of her and she moved to Brisbane.' Corally blew her nose, then tucked the tissue up the sleeve of her blouse. 'I think that after so much tragedy your grandfather chose the best bits to pass on to your mother. The Harrows were a real proud family back then – stuck-up you'd call them nowadays. It was pretty obvious that Luther wasn't right in the head when he came back from the war and when he left Sunset Ridge for good and then took up with me.'

The old woman rolled her eyes. 'Well, how shocking,' she said dramatically. 'Lily visited Luther a few months before he died, but G.W. stayed away. He was mightily embarrassed by the whole thing. Your grandfather,' the woman cleared her throat, 'probably thought it best if everyone thought Luther died over in France.' She looked blankly at Madeleine. 'In a way, he did.'

Madeleine digested this. 'But what happened to Luther?'

Corally nestled her hands in her lap. 'It's difficult to explain. It's like Luther left part of his mind over there. Everyone said he drank too much and that was what killed him but I knew it was his nerves – that and the shrapnel they couldn't remove from his spine. He drank to numb the pain. Except the real pain was in his head. Shell-shock. Every so often Luther would go walkabout and I would find him naked under a tree trying to wash himself clean with dirt. He told me in the weeks before he died that Thaddeus and his mate Harold Lawrence were blown to bits in front of him. They were trying to protect Dave by huddling around him, but in doing so they made themselves a bigger target for the Germans. When they were hit Thaddeus and Harold were splattered all over Luther and Dave.'

Madeleine felt as if she'd been winded. Sue-Ellen sat cross-legged in front of her grandmother.

'I never knew that.' Sonia was white.

'Me neither,' Sue-Ellen said.

Corally tapped the hospital trolley impatiently. 'Luther knew he was different when he returned home. It didn't matter what Dave said, there wasn't any way he was going to stay out at Sunset Ridge. It was too quiet, he reckoned, and his parents' attempts to act as if everything was normal only increased his anxiety. He used to imagine the Germans were approaching across a red ridge, readying to clamber over the homestead fence at dawn. During those hallucinations he'd lie in wait on the homestead veranda with a loaded rifle. Eventually Dave realised that his brother would end up shooting someone, so he convinced their parents that Luther needed to leave the property for a while until he settled down. That's when he moved to the boarding house where I was living. And that's how Dave got friendly again with Miss Waites.'

≪ Chapter 47 ≫

Banyan, south-west Queensland, Australia
July 1918

Dave sat on the bed, waiting for the shaking to stop. Some-times he wished he had agreed with Luther's improbable suggestion of staying in France. The long, languid summer days at Madame Chessy's farmhouse returned regularly to remind him of how the world could have been were it not for those who chose to ruin it. Often he would picture those heady days amid the bloody fighting: his oldest brother playing cricket, the lush green of the willows framing Thaddeus as he whacked the cloth ball skywards, Trip and Fall stumbling in pursuit or Luther and Harold bartering goods for the sketches he drew. Most of all he thought of the young French girl, Lisette, and the kiss he had so desperately yearned for and never received.

In the end Dave did not sketch her, nor had they returned to the farmhouse. He would have liked to visit Madame Chessy once more, to talk with someone older and wiser who understood the magnitude of loss. At the time Dave thought such a conversation, fragmented by Lisette's translation, may have helped his transition back to his former life. He realised now how simplistic this thought had been. It was only when they were on the troop ship during the long sea voyage home to Australia that Dave was clear-headed enough to understand the enormity of the change within him. The sense of loss he felt at the death of his brother, of his friends, of his innocence, of his very perception of the world weighed on him heavily. To survive he would have to bury his feelings, disguise his night horrors and never talk of what he had witnessed. What sane person would believe what he had seen?

What Dave hadn't been able to hide were his fanatical tendencies. In his old room at Sunset Ridge he slept under his bed, his great coat hanging in clear view on the knob of his bedroom door. He would not stand with his back towards a window, nor go near the music room. In the mornings he was compelled to rake the ground circumnavigating the homestead fence. Left undisturbed he would gather the dirt and leaves, sweeping until an arc of tidiness surrounded his home or his father stilled him with a firm hand.

'Throw me a smoke, will you, Dave?'

Luther was sitting in a chair in the corner of the room, his shirtless torso lathered in sweat. Dave tossed his brother a blanket, concerned he would get a chill now the fit had passed, and then lit two cigarettes and passed one to Luther. 'I don't like leaving you here, Luther. I know you've made your decision but it just doesn't seem right.'

Luther took a drag of the cigarette as the last tremors subsided from his body. When they were in hospital together his brother had not seemed so distressed, in fact Luther had joked and laughed once the operations were finally over and even made a habit of making passes at some of the better-looking English nurses. He had not been considered a model patient, a label that most of the other convalescing Australian soldiers had aspired to.

'I'll be right. A few months to clear my head is all I need.'

'Sure, Luther, sure,' Dave agreed. It seemed to Dave that during his recovery Luther managed to contain the demons within, his body focusing on healing the flesh while the horrors witnessed began to erode his mind. If anything, the hallucinations were getting worse. Dave never shared his. In the pit of his stomach Dave doubted if Luther would ever see Sunset Ridge again. It was as his brother explained that fateful night in the trench before they had gone into battle that last time. He didn't belong at Sunset Ridge and he never would, especially now they knew what lay in store. The doctors advised against further operations. The shrapnel lodged in Luther's back could not be removed safely and there was every possibility it would gradually make its way into his spine. The outlook was dim.

'There is some advantage to slowly losing your mind, Dave. If I end up not being able to walk I won't know about it.' His hand snaked down to rub at the imaginary tomahawk lost in the filth of Flanders.

'That won't happen,' Dave said adamantly.

Luther stubbed the cigarette out on the timber floor. 'Losing my mind or not being able to walk? Actually, mate, I think they're both a done deal.' He ground the cigarette stub with the heel of his boot until the gritty remains were scattered across the boards. 'I blame that damn dog for saving me. How a mutt could drag a man from the German lines,' Luther lit another cigarette, 'it beggars belief.'

Dave rubbed subconsciously at his shoulder. 'I remember looking up into those dark eyes and thanking God.' The war dog had found them at night. Dave recalled reaching for the animal as it snuffled among the remains of Thaddeus and Harold. 'Take Luther,' he had whispered as if the dog could understand. 'Take my brother first,' he had pleaded. The dog had given him a cautious lick and then, with his great bony head beneath his stomach, had turned Dave onto his back. The pain alone nearly killed him. Then there was only the sound of his body being dragged through dirt, past men who watched their steady progress with unseeing eyes, the great animal's pants coming heavily with each dogged step. 'Go back!' Dave had cried once they reached the lip of the crater, the pain keeping him lucid. 'Go back for Luther.' The dog had pushed him into the shell-hole and Dave had tumbled into the dark.

'What will you do, Dave?'

He shook away the images in his head. 'Me? I'm going to stay at Sunset Ridge. Father's past running it.'

'I always knew you'd go back,' Luther responded.

'I thought of doing other things.'

Luther nodded. They both knew that Dave would not leave Sunset Ridge again. 'It will be left to you when the time comes.'

'You could come back and help me,' Dave suggested. 'Father's already asking my opinion, although Mother has some strong ideas regarding livestock improvement. Hell, I'm still getting over how much she's changed: riding astride in pants, commenting on blood-lines and telling the manager what to do.'

Luther gave a short laugh. 'I don't think she'll forgive me for what I did to her piano.'

Dave agreed. Luther had taken to the German-made piano with an axe on the third night back at Sunset Ridge.

'You'll handle it, Dave.'

'Yeah, sure.' Dave lit another cigarette. 'What are you thinking about?'

'She's here, you know. I saw her,' Luther said softly.

'Who?' Dave asked his brother.

'Corally.'

Dave knew that it was true. The girl was ensconced at the far end of the hallway. Dave had been aware of someone peering at them from behind a partially open door when he had helped Luther move in yesterday and it took little time to discover who the other occupants of the boarding house were.

'Miss Waites is here too,' Luther told him.

'I know.' Although Dave would have preferred to blend into the blue haze of the scrub he missed so much in France, the Harrow boys were treated as returning heroes and it mattered little whether they were interested in the local goings on within the village or not, there was always a kind soul willing to share every skirret of information.

'You know that letter Miss Waites wrote, Luther? She could have been mistaken.'

'Go and see her, Dave. It's you she wants.'

Dave thought back to the machine-gun nest and the revelation that Corally, having written to them all, was actually in love with him. There was no reason not to believe Miss Waites and yet he felt ambivalent where Corally Shaw was concerned. In the pit of his stomach he harboured a kernel of anger towards both her and his former governess – he couldn't help but wonder how that last day in Flanders may have panned out had it not been for Miss Waites' admission. Would Thaddeus and Harold have survived, and Luther escaped unscathed, were it not for that moment when those three soldiers, his brothers-in-arms, his blood, had decided to protect him, protect him not only because he was the youngest, but because they all loved Corally Shaw and she loved him?

'I'll wash up, then.' Luther dragged his body upright with a wince, and poured water into the ceramic bowl on the washstand. 'The three of us could have a meal together. What do you think?' He slopped water on his face and neck, the liquid dribbling over the scars on his back.

'Sure thing.' Captain Egan's words rang in Dave's ears – they all needed something to fight for in an effort to understand the carnage they were a part of. Thaddeus, Luther and Harold had found that something. They had all gone to war and ended up fighting for love – a love that went beyond a spirited young woman on the other side of the world. There was no other way to explain the fierce loyalty to be with one's battalion, with one's platoon, with one's mates, no matter the consequences. Love for fellow man led many to their deaths, yet it could also save.

It was with Luther's salvation in mind that Dave walked down the narrow hall and knocked on Corally Shaw's door while his brother dressed in anticipation. When the door opened Dave caught a glimpse of a well-dressed, beautiful young woman and then Corally was in his arms, sobbing and calling his name. He inhaled the scent of lavender and powder and the cheek against his was plump and soft. With difficulty he untangled her arms. The girl blushed but didn't move.

'You came home,' she said, reaching for his hand.

Dave allowed the soft fingers to rest within his. 'Luther's here.'

'I know.'

'You should see him,' Dave suggested, wondering how anything so fresh and clean and beautiful could cause such turmoil among men.

'I can't. It's not right. None of it's right.'

Dave led her to the narrow bed where they sat, their fingers entwined. 'I don't know why you wrote to everyone while we were at war, Corally.' She hung her head as if ashamed and the anger he harboured shifted a little within him. Dave lifted her chin with a cupped hand. 'But I want to say thank you. It gave us something to hang onto, something to believe in.'

'Really?'

'Yes.' For a moment he faltered. Dave recalled the night at Madame Chessy's farmhouse when Corally's letter nearly went up in flames, yet Dave had kept it, dirty and bloodstained though it was. 'They all cared for you, Harold and Thaddeus and Luther.'

'And you, Dave? Do you care?'

Dave couldn't answer. In truth he didn't know how he felt. 'Luther's here now and he's in love with you.' The warmth of her hand slipped away as Corally moved to stare out the window. 'It's him you should be with. Hell's bells, Corally, it was you he was thinking of when he chopped off Snob Evans's finger.'

'That time is like a distant memory, Dave.' Placing a hand on the window, she looked down into the street below. 'I watched you ride in yesterday. I've been waiting so long to see you that I thought I would burst with anticipation when I heard you'd returned to Sunset Ridge.'

'You've grown up,' Dave said with appreciation. He knew what it was like to be with a woman. He had accompanied Luther to a brothel in London after they had been released from hospital and although he had not been a willing participant initially, the girl was caring and careful and Dave had gone back a number of times.

'And you,' Corally replied. 'Dave –'

'Don't say it, Corally. Please don't say anything.' Maybe it was because Dave knew that she loved him or perhaps he realised what it meant to have such a beauty waiting on the other side of the world, but while Luther dressed at the end of the long hallway Dave drew Corally to his side.

Corally's long hair was twisted about his wrist. Dave tugged at it playfully, flicking the strands against her cheek as her slight body melded with his. He traced the whorl of her ear as the late-afternoon sun slanted through the partially drawn curtains onto the end of the bed. It was too late to ride back to Sunset Ridge and he was beyond explaining to Luther why the morning had drifted into the afternoon and he was yet to return, although he figured his brother would guess. There was only the present and the sense of wholeness that seeped through his body. The war had barely entered Dave's mind since stepping into Corally's room and he was aware of a sense of freedom, of having moved beyond the chaos of the battlefield to a place where peace reigned. This, he told himself, was what it felt like to be back among people who knew what it was to be human, who knew how to treat each other with respect and love. This was what it meant to be home. He thought of Luther down the hallway and his own good intent. He wanted Luther to have Corally. She should be his, yet he couldn't move from her side.

Corally leaned on her elbow, her finger forming a pattern on his sweaty chest. 'I must tell you what happened while you were away, Dave.'

He touched the tip of her nose and then stretched and yawned. 'What?'

'The most scandalous thing. It turned out that Julie Jackson's grandmother was German. Of course the authorities were onto them straightaway.'

Dave sat up. 'They weren't accused of anything, were they?'

'Well no, not that we ever heard.' Corally squirmed upwards in the bed, clutching the sheet against her body. 'But everyone was shocked that they hid their ancestry and then, once it was out, they complained about the way they were being treated.'

'And how were they treated?' Dave asked, not knowing if he really wanted to hear the answer.

Corally twisted a corner of the sheet. 'As you can imagine, no one wanted them around. Here you boys were, fighting the Germans over the seas and we have the likes of them here behaving as if they should be treated like everybody else.'

Dave took a cigarette from the table and lit it, he didn't like the direction this conversation was going. 'Why wouldn't they be treated like everybody else?'

'Because they were Germans. Anyway, Mr Jackson began disturbing the peace and blaming Mr Cummins for inflaming the situation and then Mr Jackson was found beaten up one afternoon.'

Dave couldn't believe what he was hearing. 'Bloody hell, that's awful. How's Julie?'

'Julie? I don't speak to her.'

Dave exhaled cigarette smoke. 'Why not?'

'Because her grandmother was a German.'

For a moment Dave didn't think he had heard Corally properly. Stubbing out his cigarette he turned to her. 'What did you say?'

'Anyway,' Corally continued, 'she isn't anything to anyone anymore. After her father died, Mr Cummins bought their property and the family moved to a shack on the edge of town.'

'But, Corally, you and Julie were best friends.'

'No we weren't, well, not really. I don't talk about her anymore,' Corally replied uncomfortably. 'No one does. They're just an embarrassment and, quite frankly, I don't know why they don't move on. It's just like Mrs Dempsey's son – they've got no consideration for people's sensibilities. You know, Dave, that poor boy lost half his face – blown off, it was – but he's still howling in pain every night, disturbing the village and keeping most of us awake for all hours. Wouldn't you think Mrs Dempsey would pack him off to a home like everyone says? That's the best place for him. And then there's that Miss Waites, busybody that she is. Mrs Dempsey and I are quite surprised that she decided to stay in Banyan after turning down your mother's offer of that nice governess job at Sunset Ridge. It got me to thinking that her fiancé Rodger probably went AWOL because Miss Waites can't help but stick her nose into everybody's business. You know, she practically complained to me that none of you boys wrote to her while you were at the war. Well, now I understand why none of you did. Heavens, she even made a fool of herself helping the Jacksons in the main street last year just before Julie's father was bashed to death. You know, hardly anyone talked to her for a good six months, well apart from Mrs Marchant, but then everyone thought she had gone a bit funny as well having lost her son in the war. Dave, what are you doing? Why are you dressing?'

Dave pulled on his trousers. 'What do you think we were all doing over there? What the hell do you think we were fighting for, Corally?' he yelled. 'Heaven forbid, you can't be that narrow-minded.' Sitting on the end of the bed, he tugged his socks on and laced his shoes. 'Men died. Men were blown apart in front of me.' He stood and tucked in his shirt. 'We were helping people protect their homes and their country; we were helping women and children, farmers and bank clerks, people just like us, from being invaded. And why did we do that? Because we were told it was the right thing to do. Just as those German boys were told that what they doing, what they were fighting for, was right. We were fighting for the right for people to live their lives, for hope and common decency and freedom. Most of all I believe we were fighting to ensure future goodwill towards men.' Dave's anger threatened to engulf him. It radiated out through his arms and legs so that his toes and fingers tingled. With a roar of anger, he walked out of the room.

⋘ Chapter 48 ⋙

Banyan, south-west Queensland, Australia
February 2000

'That's a pretty fiction,' Sonia said sharply. 'You and David Harrow lying together.'

Corally took a sip of water through a long straw. 'Think what you like, but Dave was never warm to me again. Luther said he was upset because he believed the Germans were just like the Australian soldiers, poor silly bastards who were sent to kill men on foreign soil. Dave didn't hate the Germans, although Luther told me he didn't feel too kindly towards them.' Corally shrugged. 'Men are queer beasts sometimes.' Leaning back, she took a deep breath. 'However, Luther agreed with Dave regarding your family, Sonia. He thought they were badly treated. The difference was, he didn't harp on about it. Maybe Luther and Dave were right, but it didn't seem like that to the residents of Banyan all those years ago. Anyway, in the end I didn't measure up to Dave's expectations. It's as simple as that. I belonged to a world he was beyond comprehending. He wanted to come home and have things unchanged, he wanted the old days back. How he expected everything to be the same on his return, I'll never know. What I do know is that for all your grandfather's sense of righteousness regarding the Jackson family, his sense of common decency didn't figure when it came to his treatment of me. He knew I cared for him, but he was quite happy to lie with me and then pass me on to his brother and make a new life on Sunset Ridge.

'Six months later Luther and I married quietly and moved into this house.'

'Did Luther know,' Madeleine enquired softly, 'about you and my grandfather?'

Corally chuckled. 'Of course he knew. Your grandfather told him. That was one thing about Dave and Luther – they were real tight when they came back from the war.'

'And he didn't mind?' Madeleine asked. 'I mean, from everything you've told us, Luther cared for you.'

The old woman pondered Madeleine's question. 'Luther asked me if I loved your grandfather more than him. I did once . . .' Her voice trailed off. 'Anyway, I said it was a mistake, said it would never happen again. Luther believed me, if only because he knew that his brother would never forgive me for the treatment of the Jacksons.'

She tapped her finger on the hospital trolley. 'If you ask me, your grandfather was just plain angry at the world, after the war. He needed someone to blame, someone he could direct his anger at. I was that person.'

'So you married Luther?' Sonia prompted.

Corally smiled and nodded. 'He kept his illness from me initially, although I still would have had him, dying or not. A single woman has to consider her position in life, and Luther was a catch. Once a week Dave would ride in from the property, and Luther and he would sit out on the flat, talking and drinking long into the night. It was Luther who told me that Dave purchased a house for the Jacksons. Old G.W. and Lily were probably so pleased to have one son on the property who was not a family disgrace that they agreed with Dave's decision. Well, if that wasn't enough to rile the towns-folk, he then offered Julie employment at Sunset Ridge, starting a tradition that's continued ever since. For years no one said anything but what he did festered like a sore. He should have let bygones be bygones, instead your grandfather made a lot of people feel guilty and he was vocal in his complaint of the Cummins family, telling anyone who would listen that Mr Cummins took advantage of the Jacksons. And of course Luther and I were tarred with the same brush.'

'So, Horatio Cummins's grudge extends back that far?' Madeleine muttered.

'Yes.' Corally coughed and blew her nose again on the soggy tissue.

'Gran's getting tired,' her granddaughter announced.

'Shush up, girl.' The old woman waved a finger at Sue-Ellen. 'What you don't know is that Dave's brothers and Harold asked him to look after me. At least that's what your grandfather told me. I'll never know if that was the truth or not. Personally I reckon with Luther's health problems Dave wanted to make sure his brother was well taken care of. Luther couldn't work and his army pension wasn't much and by the end of the first year of our marriage I spent more time caring for him than I did working at the general store.'

Corally fiddled with a stray thread on her blouse. 'After Luther died your grandfather continued to help me financially until I remarried in 1930. I figure it was his way of thanking me for looking after his brother.'

'Only you could aspire to being an undertaker's wife,' Sonia said flatly.

'As opposed to being a bitter old maid? Snob was real good to me.'

Madeleine waved her hands in the air. 'Please, please, this is my grandfather you're talking about.' She scratched her head. 'Well, at least I know that George and I were right about the expenses in the station ledgers. Two households, staff . . . no nder the

461

property went broke and Mum sold his paintings. Is there anything else I should know?'

Corally snuffled into the tissue. 'My Snob wasn't known for his godly ways. He went out to Sunset Ridge and collected your grand-father's body and took a few things, sort of like keepsakes.'

'Keepsakes, my foot,' Sonia replied tightly.

'Don't go judging him. Besides, when Snob told me what he'd done I didn't let him pawn everything. They're in that container.' Corally pointed to the box on the table. 'There's a watch and sketches and a miniature painting of Dave's wife's favourite horse, among other things. Now, wasn't that one for the books, when your grandfather upped and married Meredith Bantam's younger sister, Corinne?'

Lifting the lid on the box, Madeleine selected a plastic sleeve. The painting appeared to have been torn from a larger work. It was of a young woman and her shoes were missing from the composi-tion. 'Did you tear this from a bigger painting?' Madeleine passed the old woman the plastic sleeve. She examined it carefully and then handed it back.

'He never drew a picture of me for me. All I ever got was a drawing of a mangy-looking dog he'd sketched in France. So, when I heard he was painting Miss Waites in her room at the boarding house I wasn't best pleased. I couldn't help it. So, I went into her room one day when she wasn't there and I ripped myself out of the picture. Fair enough, I thought. Your grandfather never asked if he could put me in it and considering he knew that Miss Waites and I didn't see eye-to-eye, well he had some hide.'

'So they were good friends then?' Madeleine said. 'Grandfather and Miss Waites?'

'Very good friends,' the old lady conceded. 'Luther reckoned that Dave took a real liking to Catherine on his return. She asked for those two paintings to be done and offered to pay, but Dave ended up giving them to her as a present. Then, at the end of 1918,

462

Catherine upped and moved to Sydney, leaving behind the two paintings your grandfather did. Actually, she gave them to a friend of hers, a Mrs Marchant.'

Corally looked knowingly at Madeleine. 'Catherine wrote to your grandfather once or twice after she left. Dave passed on her news to Luther and he would tell me. Personally I think Catherine left because of your grandfather. She was a good five years or so older than him and I think she found his attentions embarrassing.' Corally snorted. 'Can you believe it? Like she had anything better on offer, at least that's what we thought. Anyway, she fell on her feet, she did – married a widower with a swish house in the northern suburbs. She had a fiancé who went to the war but he did a runner. I don't know if she ever heard from him again.'

Madeleine knitted her fingers together. She could feel everyone in the room looking at her, waiting for her to speak. She cleared her throat. 'I need to ask one more thing of you, Mrs Evans.' Madeleine hesitated over the formality of the word Mrs, however she wasn't comfortable calling her anything else. 'Apart from the paintings of you and Miss Waites that were done in 1918, do you know why my grandfather stopped painting for so long after that?'

'Lily and G.W. didn't go much on it,' Corally stated. 'And he had to run that property of yours.'

'Surely they would have let him paint if he really wanted to,' Madeleine argued.

The old woman sighed. 'Your grandfather was sad after Catherine left. He had painted her likeness and then, much like the soldiers he'd sketched in France, she too was dead to him.' Corally opened her mouth as if to say more, and hesitated.

Madeleine leaned forward. 'What were you going to say?'

Corally directed her sea-green eyes at the young woman. 'A few months before my Luther died, your grandfather told him that there wasn't any beauty left in the world and that he would never paint again.'

'And?' Madeleine persevered.

'Luther said that one day Dave would wake up on Sunset Ridge and walk to the back gate. He would watch a rising sun and realise that there were still some things left to be grateful for. On that day he would take up his brush and paint once again.'

Madeleine's eyes filled with tears.

'Sunset Ridge saved your grandfather,' the old woman said simply. 'He was one of the lucky ones. That land meant so much to him. Out there, he belonged.'

When she'd composed herself, Madeleine thanked Corally for her time and asked if she could take the box of keepsakes and sketches with her on leaving. 'I'll return them to you, I promise.'

Corally waved Madeleine away. 'Yes, take it all. I've had him for long enough. It's time you took your grandfather home.'

'Can I come again and talk to you if I think of anything else?' Madeleine asked.

Corally considered the question and the young woman standing in front of her. 'No. No, you can't. Take the box and don't come back.'

They left the house abruptly. Sonia barely gave Madeleine time to set the container on the back seat and retrieve the scrapbook before the sedan accelerated and headed down the rarely travelled road to Banyan. Madeleine sat quietly, the sketchbook secure in her hands. There was almost too much information to absorb. Her head reeled with the stories shared and the old woman they'd left sitting inside the house. In spite of everything Madeleine had just heard, she felt sorry for her.

'Well, aren't you going to have a look inside?' Sonia asked.

Madeleine opened the sketchbook, knowing that her grandfather's work would now be tinged with a new sense of intimacy and sadness.

'Do you have enough to entice someone to stage an exhibition?' Madeleine was glad Sonia was with her. The housekeeper's voice was calming. She turned the pages. A very creased picture of an abstract chicken was followed by an elongated woman. Her mouth went dry as she continued to flick through the other pages. 'I think so. There are another five sketches. This is fantastic, absolutely brilliant. Even if the exhibition doesn't go ahead we have these, Sonia. I have part of my grandfather's artistic legacy back. At least something positive has come from the mess of the past.'

The sedan turned a corner and they drove into the main street of Banyan. 'You may not agree with your grandfather not wanting to discuss Luther and Corally's relationship,' Sonia said carefully, 'or his keeping your mother in the dark about how, when and where Luther died, however I think it was all too painful for him and we will never know what anxieties Dave suffered thanks to his time at the front.'

Sonia drove out of Banyan in the direction of Sunset Ridge. 'In the end, I firmly believe that your grandfather wanted to remember Luther the way he was before the war.'

'I'm trying to understand, Sonia. It's just difficult to believe the social hierarchy that was in play all those years ago.'

'Yes, well, it's certainly true that the wealthier families expected their offspring to marry well. After all, a good marriage could increase a family's social standing and wealth. But Luther's fall from grace went beyond moving into Banyan and marrying beneath himself. Back then there was a real stigma attached to victims of shell-shock. People couldn't understand a wounding of the mind. It was beyond them.'

'A little like my own father,' Madeleine replied.

The housekeeper reached across and patted her hand. 'What else have you got in that book?'

'Heavens, look at this.' Excited by her find, Madeleine thrust the scrapbook in front of Sonia, who promptly slammed the brakes.

The car skidded off the road to stop unceremoniously in the dirt.

'Good God, girl, you'll have us up a tree if you're not careful.' Sonia looked at the mangy animal before her. 'That's one grungy-looking dog.'

'That's not just any dog,' Madeleine said breathless. 'Look at the identity discs around his neck.'

'What is he, then?' Sonia asked. 'A war dog?'

Madeleine nodded, too emotional to speak. 'He could be, Sonia. He very well could be.'

❊ Chapter 49 ❊

Chessy farmhouse, ten miles from Saint-Omer, northern France
June 2000

Kate Chessy draped a leg over the arm of the ancient chair and flipped the pages of the old newspaper. Through the open door a blank canvas stood empty on an easel in the middle of the grassy clearing. Beyond it the stream beckoned with its clear water and cloistered willow trees. Such an aspect should have been enough for any artist, but with her craft in its infancy even a languid week exploring her great-gran-mama's home had done little for Kate's creativity. It was some time since her last trip to the farmhouse. Although the family only used it during the long summer months when Paris became cloaked in a muggy heat that threatened to strangle her inhabitants, Great-Gran-mama Lisette's death two years ago had kept the family away from the farm.

Kate found it difficult to reconcile the passing of the family matriarch. Lisette Chessy was mother to five children and grand-mother to twelve, and although she had lived in Paris for the last twenty years of her life, her great love was for this plot of land, although such affection was secondary to that she felt for her husband, Francois. Kate, intrigued that the frail woman had been a spy for the French resistance during the Second World War, had often sat long into the night in their Paris apartment listening to her stories. Although Lisette had risked her life during the second German invasion, it was to the Great War that her thoughts always returned. She would speak of soldiers and food shortages and of the great halo of light that blazed across the horizon as the war raged in nearby Flanders.

Kate had grown used to Lisette's peculiarities. Although her great-gran-mama was an excellent knitter she also liked to play with balls of wool and there had always been a basket of wool by her chair that she would roll and unroll as deftly as any spinner as she shared her knowledge. Kate had learned how to make a rabbit casserole and cook the plainer dish of steamed courgette with pasta while listening to Lisette, and from an early age her fondness for wine was encouraged by her great-gran-mama whose own palate had been cultivated by Francois' mother. Of particular interest to Kate was the story of Roland the dog. Named after an ancient French ballad, the animal was said to have saved the lives of many men during the Great War and mention of him was made in French military records of the period.

Roland had belonged to Francois and his twin brother Antoine, and his story was part of Chessy family lore. The one disappointment was the lack of any photo or drawing of the animal. Lisette and Kate had often discussed the unfortunate timing of having a young Australian soldier billeted at the farmhouse. They both knew he would have been more than capable of sketching the dog, as David Harrow's drawings of Madame Chessy and the farmhouse hung in the family apartment in Paris. There were other drawings as well – drawings that it was said were left with Madame Chessy by the Australian soldier for safekeeping. Lisette had safe-guarded the drawings for many years in the cupboard of the farmhouse, honouring her mother-in-law's conviction that the young artist would one day return. He never did and so they too were stored in Paris.

Kate continued to flip through the newspaper. She was here to paint willows and water, to soak up the ambiance of this beautiful place. However, she couldn't concentrate. Selecting another newspaper from the stack on the table, she considered inspecting the cellar. There were some dusty bottles of wine below and the cheese and fresh bread purchased this morning in Saint-Omer. It was not quite time for lunch but food was a tasty diversion. Flicking the paper's pages, Kate stopped at the classified section. There, in the middle of a bordered square, was an advertisement asking for information concerning the Australian artist David Harrow. Reference was also made to the sketch of a dog that had been authenticated by the Australian War Memorial and was said to have been drawn on the Western Front during the First World War. The dog wore a set of identity discs around its neck and the name the discs bore belonged to Antoine Chessy.

Kate sat the paper carefully on the wooden table and looked around the tired farmhouse with its twin bunks in the alcove and the wood-burning stove. There were wooden crosses above the doorways and on the cupboard stood a faded picture of the Chessy brothers. Beside the picture was a cloth ball ragged and aged and in that instant she imagined Roland bounding across the grassy clearing to the farmhouse. There were telephone calls to make and time zones to wait for and, amid the buzz of excitement, Kate knew that Roland was finally coming home.

≪ Chapter 50 ≫

Chessy farmhouse, ten miles from Saint-Omer, northern France
July 1919

Francois sat on the grass beyond the farmhouse. Inside Lisette and his mother were cooking and laughing. Having promised eggs and chips for lunch, they were busy frying the perch Francois had caught that morning, glad of the change in their post-war diet that spring brought. Francois planned on a busy year. They needed to replenish their stocks of wheat and potatoes and try to barter for a pig to fatten for the coming winter. Having managed to hang onto the milking cow, they only needed a few more hens to add to his mother's best layer and the scraggly rooster and then, he hoped, the farm would slowly return to normal. Francois needed to concentrate on these simple tasks. There were two women dependent on him now and although his mama and Lisette appeared capable of managing without him, Francois needed to prove that he could not only cope with his new life but assume the mantle of responsibility easily.

So, Francois kept a ready smile on his lips and the images of Verdun locked away in his mind. At times the memories would escape to wander beyond his carefully constructed wall, and during those moments he would hobble through the fields crying in remembered pain. He loved his homeland, he loved France, but in the end he had only kept going over the top of the sandbags for the men beside him, for his brother, and now all of them were gone. When he was on his knees, gagging in the dirt, it was then that Antoine would come to him, easing his thoughts away from the dead and the ravaged, enticing him back into the light and life.

Francois ran a finger between the leather strapping of the wooden leg and his thigh. The device bit into the flesh above his knee and he remained positive that the wooden length did not match his good leg, although both his mother and Lisette had measured it more than twice. The crutch remained Francois' preferred method of getting about the farm, particularly because he could move freely with it and was not haunted by the other device becoming unattached. Walking down the aisle of a church was a different matter, however. Francois did not want to be on crutches when he took Lisette's hand, and so he persevered with both the wooden leg and his fear of it.

Across the wheat field, beyond the stream, two figures approached. Francois didn't recognise them and he hoped it was not more men looking for work. Some became quite pushy when they saw his injury, convinced he was not capable of running the farm, and Francois needed to be adamant to send such strangers away. On one occasion his mama came to his aid, adding her voice to his and together, mother and son, they had forced the three men on their way. Francois looked across the field, remembering another time when he and Antoine made a pact to go to war. The figures grew closer, and then a third.

Balancing on his hands, Francois rose, reaching for his crutch. He could feel him. He could feel the great heart of the animal close by. 'Mama,' he cried. 'Mama!'

Madame Chessy and Lisette rushed from the farmhouse as the two people jumped the stream.

Francois watched as the couple laughed and waved, their hands linked together. There was an animal with them, a big mongrel-looking dog, wolf-like in appearance.

'It's Roland,' Madame Chessy cried. 'Roland has come home!'

The great animal lumbered forward on three legs and then, with a bark, jumped into Francois' outstretched arms.

'My Roland, my Roland!' Francois wept. 'Thank you, Captain. Thank you, Sister.'

Captain Harrison and Sister Valois took Madame Chessy's warm hands in theirs, then the older woman knelt on the ground. Drawing Roland close, she noticed the identity discs around the great animal's neck and read the name.

'Thank you, Roland,' Madame Chessy whispered. 'You have brought my other son home.'

If you enjoyed *Sunset Ridge*, look out for Nicole's stunning new novel

The Great Plains

It is Dallas, 1886, and the Wade Family is going from strength to strength: from a thriving newspaper and retail business in Texas to a sprawling sheep station half a world away in Queensland.

Yet money and power cannot compensate for the tragedy that struck twenty-three years ago, when Joseph Wade was slaughtered and his seven-year-old daughter, Philomena, was abducted by Apache Indians.

Only her uncle, Aloysius, remains convinced that one day Philomena will return. So when news reaches him that the legendary Geronimo has been captured, and a beautiful white woman discovered with him, he believes his prayers have been answered.

Little does he know that the seeds of disaster have just been sown.

Over the coming years three generations of Wade men will succumb to an obsession with three generations of mixed-blood Wade women: the courageous Philomena, her hot-headed granddaughter Serena, and her gutsy great-granddaughter Abelena – a young woman destined for freedom in a distant red land. But at what price . . . ?

From the American Wild West to the wilds of outback Queensland, from the Civil War to the Depression of the 1930s, *The Great Plains* is an epic story about two conflicting cultures and one divided family.

Read on for a taster . . .

≼ Prologue ≽

May, 1925 – Condamine Station, Southern Queensland

Wes Kirkland found the manager of Condamine Station sitting in the dirt under a tree. The bullet had punctured the fifty-four-year-old in the shoulder. Not a fatal wound, unless he'd been tethered to the tree's wide trunk with rope and left there for four days without water. Wes kicked the man's leg. Meat-ants had found a welcome food source and were clambering over the body.

'I'm still alive, you bastard!' Hugh Hocking gasped. His skin was burnt red from the sun, his lips a line of blisters.

Wes squatted by the man, leaning across to flick an ant from Hocking's thigh. 'Tough old bugger, aren't you?'

Hocking gave a raspy cough. 'Not as tough as you,' he replied sarcastically. Overhead, the sun shone hard and hot. A grassy plain extended out from the shade of the tree; air and sky merged in a haze of heat. A few miles behind them lay the Condamine River, water and shade out of the wounded man's reach.

'The thing I don't understand, *mate*' – Wes's American accent had a harder edge to it compared to Hocking's – 'is why you'd keep stealing Mr Wade's livestock when you knew I was about to arrive?'

474

'Does it matter?'

'Yes, it does.' At forty years of age, Wes was large framed with red hair and freckles and a temper easily roused. He retrieved a water bottle from his horse and returned to dribble the warm liquid into Hocking's mouth. 'You've made yourself a tidy pile in his absence all these years, so why let yourself get caught? You were a month away from heading home.'

Hocking licked his ruined lips. 'Because I don't care anymore, about the money or the Wades.'

'And by my reckoning you've no family left in Oklahoma,' Wes added.

'I thought the bastard would show himself one of these days, but I guess he's too busy chasing those Injun relatives of his.' Hocking tried to raise enough saliva to spit in the dirt.

'He's not as soft-hearted as his father, Aloysius, was and you seem to be forgetting that this property forms only a fraction of Edmund's combined business interests.'

'Rubbish, that's why he hasn't come to look at this great pile of land he purchased,' Hocking puffed. 'You forget, Kirkland, I was the one Edmund Wade came to for advice when he decided to purchase a property here in Australia. And why did he buy down here? So he could run away with that Indian squaw of his.' Hocking's head fell back against the tree, his chest heaved. 'Edmund may not be as soft as his father but the Wade men were obsessed with that woman.'

Wes took a sip of the water and offered more to Hocking. The suffering man choked and spluttered.

'Mr Wade's not coming but his son Tobias will eventually,' said Wes.

'And how do you know that?' Hocking asked breathlessly.

Wes screwed the lid on the canteen. 'He and I used to ride together back in Oklahoma.'

'So you think you're his friend?' The question lingered. 'My father thought that. Aloysius Wade offered my father silver shares, and they sent him broke. He killed himself.' Hocking coughed, his head drooped on his chest.

For a moment Wes thought the man was really dead this time.

'Over forty years of service with the high and mighty Wades and look what he got for his troubles.' Hocking was barely audible.

'What's this then? An accountant's revenge?' Wes laughed but the man had passed out.

Across the flat country came the familiar pounding of hoofs. Two Aboriginal stockmen and a scraggly white man eased their mounts into a walk. Wes noted the unease on the men's faces. He'd arrived only months ago from America, and the Australians, regardless of whether they were black, white or brindle, were reluctant to talk to him. They were a suspicious lot, wary of strangers and no doubt expecting him to fail in his role as the new station manager. The only stockman with any noticeable confidence was the straggly bearded white who stared down at him from the saddle. Evan Crawley was leading hand on the property, what Australians called an overseer. The man knew livestock, had the ear of the men and so far had done everything he'd been told. This situation, however, would test him. Evan had been friends with Hocking.

'Mr Kirkland.' Evan gave a nod and dismounted. 'You've been busy.'

It was difficult to see the stockman's eyes under the wide-brimmed hat he wore but his voice was steady, a reasonable sign that the man had the stomach for work such as this. 'Evan. Nice of you to join me.'

'I'm guessing you wanted some time for Mr Hocking to become acquainted with your management style otherwise you wouldn't have sent us ten mile in the opposite direction.'

'This is bad business,' one of the Aboriginals commented.

'Then pack your belongings and leave,' Wes replied calmly.

'Take off, Chalk,' Evan told the elder of the two Aboriginals.

476

'Take your boy and head back to the bunkhouse. We'll be along soon.'

The Aboriginals turned their horses and left.

'Can they be trusted?' Wes asked.

'They'll be right,' Evan assured him. 'They know what side their bread's buttered on.'

Wes put pressure on Hocking's shoulder wound with his hand. The man awoke with a groan.

'We usually get the coppers when stealing's involved,' Evan said sociably.

'Well, I've ridden with the law and the best kind of justice is the quick kind.' Wes took a rifle from his horse and, lifting it, fired into Hocking's thigh. There was a splat of bullet and bone. Hocking screamed, Evan winced.

'For the love of God, Evan, do something!' Hocking pleaded, as blood seeped from his leg. 'This isn't the wild west. We've got laws in this country.' Evan lit a pre-rolled cigarette and wedged the smoke between the dying man's lips.

'Australia isn't my country.' Wes cut the ropes binding Hocking with a pocket knife and coiled the two lengths up. 'At least drag yourself away from those blasted meat-ants.' He turned to Evan. 'It seems Hocking had a difference of opinion with Mr Wade's father, something about silver shares, which isn't much of an excuse when it comes to stealing livestock and siphoning funds from the books. I never did like accountants.'

Evan sniffed. 'Don't have much of a need for them myself.'

They caught their horses and mounted up. Both men gave Hocking a fleeting glance before riding off, as the former station manager attempted to drag himself away from the ants.

The two Aboriginals hid in the scrub until the white men disappeared across the plains, then they rode back to where Hocking lay, face down in the dirt. They picked him up and carried him deep into the trees, where they gave him water and a strip of salted mutton to chew.

'You be right, Mr Hocking.' Chalk, the older of the Aboriginals, cut away the bloodied shirt and prodded the wound. 'Gone straight through, Mr Hocking.' He left the maggots wriggling in the dead flesh surrounding the festering injury and pulled a mix of dried herbs from a leather pouch, then added water. As he mixed the concoction, his son Jim checked the bullet hole in Hocking's thigh.

'The bullet's still in there.'

'My leg's broken,' Hocking told the boy tersely. 'Best shoot me and get it over with. I'll not survive.'

Chalk divided the poultice between both wounds and bound the injuries tightly with strips of Hocking's shirt as the land grew dark. The man fell unconscious.

'This is a bad business to be tangled in, Father.'

Chalk gestured for his son to assist him and they lifted Hocking onto a horse. 'Kirkland cannot take the law into his own hands.' Once the unconscious man was tied securely to the saddle, they led the animal towards the river.

'Are all Americans like Mr Kirkland?'

Chalk glanced at the lifeless man slumped on the horse. 'I've only known two. Hocking talked many times of America,' he told his fourteen-year-old son as the branches overhead grew thick and daylight dwindled. 'Hocking talked about the red peoples called Injuns, abducted relatives and black men kept as slaves. These Americans are no different to the white man here. Their greed makes them want to conquer all others, but most of all they want to conquer the land.'

'Is that why they came here, Father?'

Chalk sucked in the dry scent of the bush. 'Not initially. Hocking said a woman was involved, but it's not her we need to worry about, or Kirkland. I have waited for the All-father to show me what lies ahead. In my Dreamings I sense another all-powerful one and I worry for what may come across the great waters in the years ahead. You must remember our people, our teachings, Jim, and remain committed to our beliefs.'

The trees grew wide and old. The thick girths of the ancient plants lined the steep bank of the waterway. The men navigated ancient roots eroded by bygone floods and finally, on the sandy banks of the river, they lay Hocking on the ground. It was dark and shadowy between the water and the trees. Overhead the night sky was bright with stars.

'Will he live?' Jim placed a rolled blanket under the man's head.

Chalk looked upwards at the Emu in the Sky. The great bird's body lay across what the whites called the Milky Way, its head a dark smudge near the bottom of the Southern Cross, its murky body stretching across myriad stars. 'Bring my medicine.' Chalk selected some quartz crystals and shells from the saddle bag, and placed them in a line on the man's chest. 'I cannot judge whether he should or should not die. I only know that he was our friend.' He mixed wild tobacco weed with ash from an acacia bush and placed the drug behind Hocking's ears and on his bare chest.

Jim looked on. 'I don't know this place, but it feels different.' On the far bank a number of the trees showed scarring, the waterhole in the river was still and wide.

'My father found me as a child in his dreams and sent me to his wife, but I came too early and was born here at this sacred site, where the rainbow serpent rises for a breath.' Chalk removed his shirt and sat cross-legged next to Hocking. His lean chest showed three deep scars, thick black welts against blacker skin. 'You will leave me, son. Return in five days and bring food.'

'Evan will wonder where you are, Father.'

'Tell him what we have done. Tell him that Hocking was his friend and ours and that we have done what he could not. Tell Evan I will return.' He chewed on a wad of tobacco weed. 'Go.'

Chalk watched as his young son gathered the reins to their horses and began to ascend the riverbank. When the boy finally disappeared through the trees, he took a knife from his belt and cut a fourth, deep line in his chest.

Through the pain the world grew still. Chalk focused on the great waters that bordered the land. On the land beyond the waters, and the people known as Wade. Then a shadow appeared and wings grew from the shadow. Overhead the Emu in the Sky stayed constant, but from afar another great bird called.

≪ Chapter 1 ≫

Thirty-nine years earlier
September, 1886 — Dallas, Texas

Aloysius Wade looked down at the main street of Dallas from the second-storey window of Wade Newspapers. Timber shops and business houses lined the wide dirt road. Men on horseback fought for space with covered wagons, drays and sulkies as full-skirted women lifted their hems above rain puddles. At the far end of the street a wagon laden with buffalo bones was halted outside the hotel. The pieces of skeleton glinted in the late morning sun as a black child in cut-off pants and bare feet stood guard, perched on a wagon wheel.

Dallas had once been the world centre for the trade of leather and buffalo hide but with the animal practically wiped out, the desperate were gathering the sun-whitened bones of the slaughtered beasts and selling them to fill the demand for fertiliser back east. Aloysius had briefly considered entering the market, but his head had been filled with images of bedraggled men, women and children scouring the carcass-strewn plains. Collecting the bones of the dead was not a legacy he fancied even if there was substantial coin to be made.

He still couldn't help but marvel at the growth the city had undergone over the past three decades. His father had first sent him and his older brother, Joseph, west to Dallas in 1857 with a view to making men out of them under the guise of expanding the family business. At that time Aloysius had held little hope of a successful venture. The brothers expected to be killed en route either by Indians, accident or some other wily character. As it was, one of their wagons was lost crossing the Red River.

There had been less than six hundred inhabitants on arrival, which Joseph considered to be an impressive population considering a few years earlier a trading post had been the only feature. The streets were orientated to a bend in the Trinity River at the site of a limestone ledge, which was meant to be the head of navigation. In fact the river was unnavigable but it was the best crossing for miles and Aloysius and Joseph grew used to seeing the billowing clouds of dust that signified hundreds of head of cattle being driven along the Shawnee Trail. Dallas had grown on the back of farming and ranching, but it was only with the arrival of the railroads that the city had prospered.

'Mr Wade, sir.'

Aloysius greeted his assistant brusquely. Fifteen-year-old Hugh Hocking was the son of his closest friend, Clarence, who was also his accountant and advisor.

Hugh placed the day's mail on Aloysius's desk. 'My father called regarding the State Fair.'

'And?'

A single rifle shot echoed in the distance. Aloysius reached automatically for the colt holstered at his hip.

Hugh flinched. 'He's on his way, sir.'

Aloysius turned to resume his perusal of the street as Hugh exited the room. The heady days of shoot-outs in the main street were almost as rare as feathered frogs, but there were still scrapes between liberated slaves and whites. And there was invariably the odd drunken cowboy or old Indian who came into town to pick a fight. Only last week a black had been lynched on the outskirts of East Dallas for insulting a white woman. The Civil War had changed much and Aloysius knew many southerners wished Dallas had perhaps not been so prosperous at the end of the war compared to other southern cities, although the influx of blacks meant there was rarely a shortage of domestics or fieldworkers, even if they did have to be paid.

The war. Aloysius couldn't think or speak the phrase without remembering his older brother, Joseph. On impulse, he opened the top drawer of his desk and reached for the letter Gregory Harrison had written in 1863 from Fort Sumner. Gregory, an old friend from their Charlestown days, had been killed a few months later, shot through the heart by a Kiowa Brave. Aloysius re-read the letter, as he had every week for the past twenty-three years. It was the last time his niece's name had been written in ink. Philomena was presumed dead.

We are now facing renewed hostility from the Apache and assume from previous engagements that retribution will be fierce. On that front I was most sorry to hear of your grievous news. In answer to your investigations my advices suggest that it was indeed Geronimo or one of his band who captured your niece, Philomena. The girl's abduction following the murder of her brother and father is now well-documented in these parts and, although missives have been sent in an effort to broker her return, there is no news.

Aloysius had spent a lifetime revisiting the events that had led to his brother's death. At the outbreak of war he'd argued with Joseph for the right to join the Confederate Army. Their father had forbidden them to both enlist in an effort to protect the family line. Joseph eventually grew tired of quarrelling with his younger brother and they agreed to toss a coin to see which of them would go to war. Joseph won.

A sharp knock on the door broke Aloysius's reflections and he replaced the letter in the drawer. Straight-backed, of medium height and brown hair, in middle age Clarence Hocking veered towards being overweight. In comparison, Aloysius in his forty-ninth year remained slim and fit. He rode to work every day and took a constitutional along the banks of the Trinity River after lunch when time permitted. After pleasantries were exchanged, Clarence came straight to the point and handed Aloysius a copy of the financials for Dallas's inaugural State Fair. Due to open next month, Aloysius was part of the private corporation behind the venture. He and his partners were hoping for crowds that would edge the 100,000 mark, thereby ensuring a healthy profit. Aloysius checked the figures.

'I have no doubt that we will exceed our projections, Aloysius,' Clarence explained. 'We certainly have the necessary transportation in place to bring the masses to our fair city.'

'Yes, well we are all agreed on that. The railroad has made this town. Believe me, there was a time when I had my doubts as to my father's sanity when he sent Joseph and I out here.'

Clarence Hocking shuffled papers and slid another document across Aloysius's desk. 'And in all deference to your father, I too was a little perturbed when he asked me to join you.'

'Well, it certainly worked out well, for both of us.'

Hocking's mouth twitched. It was the closest he ever came to a smile. Five years older than Aloysius, he'd been a widower on arrival, but he'd quickly remarried and fathered seven children, all of whom had survived and most of whom were law-abiding. The hopes of the family lay with Hugh, who'd shown himself to be intelligent and hardworking. Hocking pointed to the document sitting on the desk. 'I have copies of the profit and loss statements for Wade Mercantile and Wade Grocers & Provisions. Did you want me to run through them?'

'Are my sons making a profit?' Aloysius enquired, checking the rows of figures.

'Joe is overseeing the mercantile end of things very well but, of course, like most businesses everything is on credit. As long as the farmers are productive he'll be paid in due course. And he seems to be managing the plantation well.'

'The costs of shipping to the coast are too high,' Aloysius commented. 'If the cotton prices ever dropped significantly . . .'

Hocking agreed. 'Exactly, which is why Dallas must continue on its path to becoming a self-sustaining industrial city.'

Aloysius had been one of the earlier owners to see the benefit of sharecropping following the changes wrought by the Civil War. Both free black farmers and landless white farmers worked on the Wade plantation in return for a share of the profits, and the arrangement was proving lucrative for the family, although many a time it would have been far simpler to revert to the old ways and simply flog the Negroes who got uppity. Diversification remained the signature reason for the Wade family's success. It was Aloysius who convinced his father to extend their interests beyond newspapers and into farming and retail a few years after their arrival at Dallas, while Joseph had travelled to New Mexico to investigate the tin and silver mines. Their early business ventures had also been significantly buoyed by two prudent marriages. 'What about Edmund? Has my youngest lad reached the agreed sales figures?'

Clarence gave a sigh that assumed a father's disappointment. 'Frankly the store should be doing a lot better. Settlers are passing through Dallas and heading north into Indian Territory in greater numbers every year. The trade for goods and provisions should be rising accordingly.'

Aloysius selected some newspapers from a side table and spread them across the desk. 'The Civil War and subsequent restructuring of the South continues to affect many.' Aloysius pointed at the newspapers, the *Cherokee Advocate*, the *Indian Journal*, the *Indian Citizen*. 'All of these tribal newspapers talk of the influx of white and black farmers into Indian Territory. The Indians are making a fortune leasing their lands or sharecropping them. Why, the Cherokee lease their six-million-acre Outlet to the Cherokee Strip Live Stock Association of Kansas for 100,000 dollars annually. We're talking 300,000 head of cattle on Cherokee rangelands.'

Clarence shook his head. 'I'm not moving to Indian Territory, if that's what you're suggesting.'

'I'm simply saying that there are many inflationary and deflationary pressures affecting people since the war. People are looking for a new start. Edmund should be taking advantage of the situation. You mark my words, the civilising of the West has just begun.'

Clarence couldn't fault his old friend's argument. The massacre of buffalo by the military, who knew that the extinction of the animal might well result in the destruction of the Indians by depriving them of a significant part of their culture, had led to an increase in cattle. And while Clarence still owned a ranch, the days of open-land ranching with corrals and cowboys had swiftly changed with the arrival of barbed wire. Cropping farms were increasing and overseas capitalists were making substantial investments in the cattle industry.

'The government won't let the tribes keep their land when there are good honest folk willing to make a living.' Aloysius thumped the table with his fist for emphasis. 'Why, those savages shouldn't

485

have any rights at all. If there is money to be made, we're the ones who should be making it. I still think back to the June of 1876 when we heard of General Custer's slaughter at the Battle of Little Big Horn and, to this day, I can see no good reason for any Indian to be accorded land or rights.'

Clarence waited as his old friend calmed. 'And how will the Indians make a living? I seem to recall them being here first.' Purple was not quite the word for the colour Aloysius's face had turned but it was close. Clarence was aware he shouldn't taunt his friend, not when he knew first hand of Aloysius's obsession with his abducted niece. He was, however, one for giving his word and keeping it. The Indians had been assigned lands by the government of the day, lands where they could hopefully make a living and live quietly. Clarence considered this a fair result. After all, they may well be savages but one could hardly act like they didn't exist. 'My apologies, Aloysius, we have differing views on this subject.'

'A place for everyone, eh, Clarence? Yes, yes, but as far as I'm concerned the only good Indian is a dead Indian.'

'Well, in the meantime we have the problem of your son to address. Might I suggest we promote the Harbison lad to store manager and perhaps Edmund should join the newspaper? He's not been the same since Jenny's death.'

Aloysius was not immune to Clarence's placating tone. Gathering up the newspapers, he sat back at the desk, his gaze wandering absently over the framed headlines from the earliest editions of the newspaper. Edmund, Aloysius's youngest son, had been slow to mature and even slower to marry. With his wife dying in childbirth along with their hoped-for first child a year earlier, it was time the lad selected a new bride and got down to the business of successful breeding. 'He needs a wife. There's nothing like children to keep a man at the office. God knows, Annie and I managed three girls and two sons, which was enough to keep my nose to the mill.'

'So you'll speak to him?' Clarence confirmed.

'I daren't send him out to the plantation or the farm. He'd be just as likely to give half the cotton and wheat we produce away.' Aloysius poured two whiskeys from the cut-glass decanter on his desk and slid a tumbler across to his old friend. 'What? You've got that look in your eye, Clarence, like you're intending on a lecture.' Aloysius took a sip of the strong spirit.

'I was thinking about the past, specifically your family's,' Clarence swallowed the whiskey in a single gulp. 'I know how much you hate the Indians.'

'Apaches, I hate the god-damn Apaches, and I've every right. Twenty-three years, Clarence, and not a single word,' he replied, clutching the glass.

'Until today.'

Aloysius sat forward in his chair, a lock of greying hair fell across his brow. 'What are you talking about?'

Clarence withdrew an envelope from his coat and held it across the desk. 'The letter came to my office,' he stated by way of explanation. 'Geronimo has surrendered.'

Aloysius stared at his old friend as if the contents could be discerned from the intelligent eyes opposite him.

Clarence sat the letter on the desk. 'A Captain Henry Lawton and First Lieutenant Charles B. Gatewood have led an expedition that has brought Geronimo and his followers back to the reservation.'

Aloysius reached for the envelope, flicked open the broken seal and unfolded the paper. 'Why didn't you tell me of this immediately?'

'Because wanting something doesn't mean it will happen,' Clarence replied. 'There was a white woman with the Apaches.'

Aloysius stood, his chair falling backwards to land with a loud thud on the timber floor. He scanned the contents of the letter.

'The similarities are strong,' Clarence said evenly, 'but obviously we cannot be assured that the woman mentioned is –'

Aloysius tapped at the letter. 'They say she is blonde-haired, striking in appearance,' his eyes grew misty, 'and aged in her thirties.'

'The details are compelling, I admit, but I urge you, my friend, not to get your hopes up,' Clarence replied carefully.

'It's her. It's Philomena.' Aloysius's voice grew tight with emotion.

'I know how long you have prayed for this moment, Aloysius, but the probability that this woman is indeed your niece remains slight.'

The single sheet of paper trembled between Aloysius's fingers. 'They have found my dead brother's daughter.' He looked to the ceiling. 'God be praised.'

'If it *is* her,' Clarence cautioned, 'if it is indeed your niece, as your friend I can only advise you to temper your happiness until you learn the true nature of her state.'

Aloysius frowned. 'What rubbish are you speaking of, Clarence?'

'It is over twenty years since her abduction.'

'And I have never stopped thinking of the child. She is my brother's blood.'

'She has been raised by savages,' Clarence countered. 'Please, dear friend, I share your joy if indeed the woman is Philomena, but I also urge you to prepare yourself.'

Aloysius folded the letter, returned it to the envelope and tucked it inside his suit coat. 'I have been preparing for this moment for twenty-three years, Clarence. My niece was born a Wade and no Indian, Geronimo or not, can ever take that away from her.'

No, Clarence thought, they can't take a name but they can take other things.